RAGGEI

N J ED

ISBN 978-1-0685936-3-5

Editor: Bridget Scrannage

Published by SouthToll, May 2025

SouthToll

RAGGED ISLAND

N J EDMUNDS

BETRAYAL – MURDER – VENGEANCE

Dedication

For the true inhabitants of Ragged Island

All characters and events in this story are fictional, but Ragged Island is real.

One of a string of Caribbean islands in the Bahamas, Ragged Island lies some 150 miles from the coast of Cuba.

Most of the already sparse population was evacuated in 2017 after the devastation of Hurricane Irma. Gradual rebuilding continues.

A Note from the Author

The idea for Ragged Island grew in me in the aftermath of the storming of the Capitol in Washington DC in 2021. Many times over the course of the next four years I considered scrapping the project altogether, believing it to be too unbelievable, even for a work of fiction.

However, as events in the last few months unfolded, I began to think some of what happens in Ragged Island might be less inconceivable.

Nick Edmunds
April 2025

INTRODUCTION: When it Finally Happened

The end of the US took Quinn Tarrant by surprise. It was the first of many shocks.

It had seemed like it happened overnight, but earthquakes of that kind never do. Great powers move like tectonic plates, but once in an eon a single event sets off a chain reaction, fault lines merging and worlds colliding. When serious turmoil gets going, it happens by chance. Doesn't it?

Looking back now from his new country, another marriage and another child later, Quinn thought it must have been about 2029 when things around him began hotting up. The changes had been taking place before that, of course. Without anyone noticing, at least not anyone like him. Just like always, nothing improved, and life was hard.

The seesawing dominance of the right, left, then right again felt like business as usual. Even when one US state after another started formal secession proceedings it was widely accepted that the courts would deliberate for years before rejecting the applications. The States would remain united.

Quinn viewed from afar the concurrent tumult in Europe and South America with the detached interest his university course required.

The first big domino to topple – that phrase would later resonate with him – was the United Kingdom in the late-20s. Quinn had thought UK's sudden decline was a one-off. But when the London Stock Exchange imploded, Wall Street soon followed. Public services degenerated, overnight it seemed.

Long-festering grievances on both sides of every polarised argument burst like abscesses, poisoning politics and feeding civil strife until armed conflict within and between states led to civil wars. Wars that were still going on, eight years later.

It all happened so quickly that sometimes Quinn wondered if perhaps the stranger who entered his life was right; chance had nothing to do with it. Someone had planned all this.

PART ONE

THE REFUGEE

Chapter One

New Orleans, Mid-January 2030

Quinn's first thought was that his father was choking on his burger. His lips were still mouthing the chant that echoed all around, U-S-A ... Number 1! ... U-S-A..." Then blood, welling out between teeth and through torn cheeks. Wide eyes fixed on Quinn as his body crumpled, sliding down to lie beneath a store window, its shutters dented by the bullet that had ripped through him.

There had been sporadic firing into the air throughout the march, rewarded with hollers and good-natured cheering from the raucous stream of plaid, camouflage and beards. Smiles from National Guardsmen had confirmed tacit approval. The lines of guards had done a good job of keeping the USNo.1 marchers well apart from counter demonstrators. Groups of liberal opponents of the outgoing president could only barrack from behind cordons of riot shields.

It wasn't until the clamouring throng approached the Superdome that Quinn noticed a new tribe coalescing. A subgroup of tattooed, mainly white men in black singlets and yellow bandanas gathered in military-style ranks, and the good-natured jeering took on a threatening tone. He didn't know which side they were on.

Horror and confusion now fixed Quinn's eyes on his bloodied dad. When more shots rang out he threw himself to the ground, an image of Mannie's gurgling white face and matted red hair framed against asphalt. Shouts of alarm and anger replaced the thronging crowd's coordinated chanting. He risked raising his head and chest to look around. The wide and forceful flow of bodies now split like a river delta, streams parting around islands of looting, gunfire, and chaos. Still in shock and struck dumb by the sight of his father's last spluttering convulsions, he forced himself to his feet as the crowd built around him. Guardsmen had formed a corral around Mannie's body. When Quinn tried to break through, all he could say was, "My dad."

As a rifle butt pushed him back, he heard, "Later, Buddy, you can visit at the morgue."

The surging crowd carried him away. Three blocks on, an alleyway let Quinn extract himself from the throng and run to a wide road. Hundreds of trucks had used the dirt median strip as a makeshift parking lot.

He stumbled onwards, sirens passing him like banshees. Few cars moved, and shutters or nailed boards covered the windows of shops and cafés. Over the rat-tat-tat of gunfire, he heard louder explosions. Helicopters thumped the air above, heading towards downtown.

He saw others scurrying to escape the strife. In twos and threes, they ducked and weaved as they retreated from the sounds, carrying their red and white caps in their hands, their flags discarded. Quinn's head was also now bare, the sun already burning his pale scalp.

At last, he recognised the vacant lot where he'd parked the truck. Thankful he had held on to the keys when they arrived, he clutched them in his pocket, scanning the vast ranks of vehicles. After trudging up and down the lines of cars and trucks his legs felt heavy when he finally heaved himself into the cab. The air inside smelled of Mannie's sweat. Through the dusty windscreen he could see an access ramp leading up to the I-10. The same road they had driven on, excited, just an hour-long lifetime ago.

It was meant to be a celebration. They were in high spirits, sporting latest edition USNo.1 caps when they drove to New Orleans that fateful Saturday in January. It was good to see his father so buoyed up. The election seemed to have boosted Mannie Tarrant. His firm belief in the president's good old white American values had made him smile again.

Before Quinn and his dad had set off, Leonie had taken his arm and looked serious. "Will you be OK, though, Q-T? The TV says there'll be Liberals there to block the way. Don't take a gun."

With a reassuring grin, he kissed her and patted Riona's head. The toddler was hugging his thigh, shining blue eyes appealing up to him. "It's all copacetic, Mrs Tarrant. Just me and the ol' man taking a trip. No need for guns." He smiled and put his cap on. Leonie still looked worried when he waved back as he crossed the front yard.

Quinn drove his father's work pickup on the road from Rayville, crossing the state line near Natchez and then heading South and back into Louisiana. The traffic was heavy by the time they approached New Orleans. They stopped at a roadside diner for meatballs and mushrooms, streams of cars and trucks passing by with horns blaring and banners flying.

The rally was Quinn's first opportunity to visit New Orleans. When he had started college he had thought Monroe was big, but it had nothing on this. As they edged through slow traffic, passing vast industrial complexes and residential areas, he smiled as he remembered the first eye-opening weeks of his three years at the University of Louisiana.

Quinn was a small-town boy on a scholarship. His housemates in the accommodation block at ULM were from bigger schools and seemed to have limitless resources. At first, he had been seduced by their largesse and their apparent tolerance of a backwoods boy, but by the end of his first year, he'd grown to despise them.

Leonie had been a janitor at ULM, and Quinn's gentle courtesy marked him out as different from the boorish students she was used to. They fell in together and were soon a couple, much to the sneering amusement of his housemates. He couldn't pay for an apartment of his own, and it seemed Quinn might have to leave college until Leonie persuaded him to move in with her.

In his final year at ULM, Riona Tarrant-Dugas was born, and Leonie's Cajun parents hosted a wedding in Monroe. Graduation and the end of his course meant he had to return to Rayville with Leonie and the baby.

As they searched for a parking space nearer downtown New Orleans, Quinn had looked across at Mannie, wondering whether his dad thought all his sacrifices had been worth it. With his background Quinn was always going to find it hard to move on, even with a Bachelor of Arts in Mass Communication. He'd spent the last year working as a car park attendant. It hadn't quite been the journalism career he had set his sights on, but it would pay the bills until an opportunity came along, he'd thought.

###

Now, leaving New Orleans and his father's body behind him, Quinn drove more slowly. It was two hours later when he pulled off the highway at a quiet roadside cafe just past Baton Rouge, the sound of the gunshots still echoing between his ears. He had to find a payphone to call Leonie. His new cell phone was still back in his dad's jacket pocket, wherever they had taken him. Mannie had forgotten to charge his own and borrowed Quinn's to film the march.

"Thank God!" Leonie screamed as she picked up. "I left a thousand messages on your cell. Where in hell are you?"

Quinn had told himself he wouldn't break down or tell her about his father until he got home, but hearing Leonie's voice almost breached his resolve. She talked on fast, though, and he couldn't have interrupted if he'd had words.

"Was your cell on silent again? Oh, Quinn! Quinn! Oh god! Are you OK? I mean..." When she did pause, Quinn couldn't speak. "Get home, Q-T. I think it's happening here. I can see smoke from downtown. Two trucks just drove by with dudes in the back. They were firing shotguns out at folks' cars and houses. Just local boys, but real scary."

The news that unrest had already spread to Rayville shook some of Quinn's stupor away.

"Is Riona safe?"

"She's fine, Babe, but she cries at the guns. Get home, Quinn, please!"

Back on the road, he switched on the radio. Every channel carried the news. Riots and looting, police cars on fire. As he had passed Baton Rouge, he had passed convoys of trucks heading

South, horns blaring and the ends of yellow bandanas trailing behind the shaven heads of men wielding automatic weapons. Now it was getting dark and the traffic was lighter, but it would still be two hours before he was home in Rayville.

When he approached Natchez, he could see bright lights on the road ahead and he slowed down a little. A car was on fire at the roadside and as he approached, he could see three trucks parked side-on, blocking the way.

More men in black singlets and the same yellow headgear manned the roadblock. Still unsure if they were for or against Marcus Finch, he pushed his red and white USNo.1 cap under the seat. A man directed him to pull up on the road shoulder, and when an automatic rifle muzzle rapped the window, he slid it down.

"Where you headed?" When the man leaned forward to peer into the cab, a smell of tooth decay and stale tobacco wafted in. There was a wavy swastika tattoo on his neck.

"Rayville."

"Where you bin?"

"Baton Rouge. See my sick mother."

"Who won the election?"

Quinn knew he had to gamble. Both sides claimed to have won, and he had to choose the right one. "The President!" He tried to sound enthused, and followed up with, "USA Number 1! Finch! Finch! Finch!" The words almost stuck in his throat, but the face grinned back at him and Quinn followed up with his most convincing fist bump. The man waved him onwards, and he drove up the turf banking to skirt the roadblock. He could still feel the man's bony knuckles.

A nagging feeling of unease tempered Quinn's relief that he had guessed correctly. The men in bandanas were on the side he'd marched for, in support of the outgoing president. He agreed that the election's official result was fake, but surely the President would never condone the use of armed force to overturn it.

A little after 9 pm, Quinn drove along Main St. in Rayville. Passing his workplace he saw his Saints coffee flask lying on the sidewalk amongst broken glass and ash. Someone had smashed the grimy windows of the parking lot's grey metal booth. Beyond it, all eight cars and trucks his customers had parked for the weekend had been torched.

He turned at the next intersection to head home, the town growing even quieter the further he drove. No lights showed in windows. Other than the burned-out cars and some upturned trashcans, though, he saw no signs of ongoing trouble. A police patrol car standing guard outside the Post Office was the only vehicle he saw until another one drew out to follow him. Turning into his driveway, Quinn waved at the officer who nodded recognition and drove on.

Leonie pulled him in and hugged him. By the light of the streetlamp, he saw tear stains on her cheeks before she closed the door.

"Don't!" She grabbed his hand before he could flick the lights on.

"Huh?"

"There's a curfew. Police have been going round with a loudspeaker. The mayor's ordered no lights after 9 o'clock."

Quinn kissed sleeping Riona in her cot, smoothing her curly locks away from her forehead. He had given her auburn hair, but behind her flickering, sleeping eyelids her eyes matched her mother's azure. Leonie had brought boudin and crackers when he returned to the living room. She told him what she had seen on TV when all the local stations had cut to the rally, with aerial footage of rioting and burning vehicles. She had started phoning him when lines of ambulances were shown arriving at hospitals.

"My Dad." It was all Quinn could say, as the memory of Mannie's torn face and quivering body retook his mind.

"Is he at home? You drop him there on the way here?"

Quinn turned to look into Leonie's eyes, and his own overflowed. "He's dead. At least I think he is."

He saw Leonie's face drain of colour and her hands going up to cover her mouth, her head shaking in disbelief. Other than an initial gasp, she remained silent as Quinn burbled through chokes and sobs, recounting what had happened. It was when he tried to describe his father's bloody, frothing face that Leonie gave in to convulsive weeping. Quinn clasped her to him, shushing, but her howls set Riona crying in her cot.

When she came back from settling Riona, Leonie put her arm round Quinn's shoulder. He could only stare in front of him. She told him about the explosions she'd heard from Rayville centre, and the wailing sirens that followed. Police patrols soon appeared, quelling trouble and scaring off the excited, gun-toting youths in their trucks.

The President had spoken. Quinn pictured him tall and thin, gripping the lectern as he addressed his people. Leonie repeated his words: "Return to your homes. We have done our job. We have won this election. We have done tremendous work."

It heartened Quinn a little to hear that President Finch was in control. His supporters, the men in the yellow bandanas, would no longer be blocking roads and threatening fellow citizens with automatic rifles. Thanks to the President, the trouble would be all over by now, and tomorrow he would drive back to New Orleans to find his father's body.

Chapter Two

Rayville, LA

Quinn woke with more visions of his father's Irish red hair and exploded face. In the background, a distant loudspeaker was getting louder, more distinct.

"Stay in your homes. I repeat. Stay in your homes. By order of the mayor. Stay in your homes. Stay in..."

Light was filtering into the room through the screen door, and he realised Leonie was sitting in the armchair with Riona on her knee.

"What time is it?"

"Dada!" Riona beamed at him.

"A quarter past eight. I left you sleeping."

He pushed himself up on one elbow, yawning, and waved to Riona. "I'd better get going. I want to go back. Find out where they took my dad."

Leonie walked across to sit on the edge of the bed, and Riona jumped from her arms onto his stomach. "Ooft! Baby, you're heavy."

"Riona big girl. Riona big girl!"

Leonie spoke over their daughter. "Q-T, you can't go to New Orleans."

"No, I need to. There's no one else. I'm sorry."

"I mean they won't let you. They've put roadblocks all around the city. Same with Baton Rouge."

Quinn looked out of the window. A police patrol was rounding the corner and disappearing out of sight, its loudspeaker still repeating the mayor's orders. He hadn't been dreaming.

The TV was on in the little kitchen. Riona tugged at his ear as he carried her through the doorway to watch and listen. The cable news channels all showed their versions of the same carnage. Interviews with grave politicians and police chiefs played between clipped footage of looted stores, burning cars and teargas clouds.

Flicking channels, twice in two minutes he saw President Finch with his slick, jet-black hair addressing the rally. Quinn heard "We won!" and "Unite, America!" and "Take Back Control" over and over. The same slogans were scrolling across the bottom of the screen.

One reporter described the apparent onset of violence. "Good-natured protesting turned nasty when hundreds of men arrived wearing black vests and yellow headscarves." The memory of his father's destroyed face flashed at Quinn again, and he sat down. As salty tears overflowed, he held Riona out to Leonie.

The 24-hour curfew in Rayville worked well to suppress any further unrest. On Sunday afternoon a patrol car toured the streets, announcing by loudhailer that the mayor was easing restrictions. Lights could stay on after 9 p.m.

Quinn had no workplace left to go to, but on Monday morning he still walked to the parking lot. It had been closed off from the sidewalk, and he had to duck under Police tape to retrieve his coffee flask.

Rayville was a sleepy place at the best of times. As he walked on into the town, shops and diners were open but traffic was even lighter than usual. He reached Crannock's Cars, Mannie's long-time employer, an idea forming. He walked over the forecourt, between rows of trucks and cars bearing this month's sale stickers.

Joe Crannock was at his desk as usual, but today he carried a shotgun as he bounded to the door to greet a potential customer. Instead of his trademark wide grin, he had a look of suspicious aggression. It didn't suit Joe's round face.

"We're closed for a stock-take, sir, ... oh ... Q-T, it's you. C'mon in. Shut the door, will you?" he said, returning to his desk.

Quinn owed Joe Crannock. When his mother died, it was Joe who paid for the funeral. He had taken an interest in his mechanic's son, allowing Quinn to polish cars after school. For two years there had been a 'Q-T's Special' on the forecourt with extra-low finance and mats thrown in.

"Mannie's late. I hope he's on his way. He sick?"

"He's dead. At least, I think he is." Quinn shocked himself that he could say it.

Joe dropped his pen and looked up. Shaded by the shining black Toyota SUV that had pride of place by the window, his face was blue in the reflected light from the login screen on the desktop PC. "Man! What happened? Sit down."

Quinn leant against the Toyota. "Shot. At the rally."

"Jeezus!" Joe's eyes flicked to the SUV and Quinn pushed himself away from the paintwork. "Who in hell's gonna fix my cars? I knew that rally was a bad idea."

Mannie had told Quinn that Joe had been encouraging the whole town to go to the rally to support Marcus Finch. He would be there, he'd said, with the mayor. Everyone should go. He even let his trusted mechanic borrow the work truck for the weekend, once he'd checked the odometer reading. But on the day, Joe needed to meet a potential customer and was in his office as usual.

"Listen, Joe. I need another job. You have anything?"

"I heard they torched the parking lot. Pity about that." The hint of a smile raised the corners of Joe's mouth, betraying his schadenfreude. For the first time, it occurred to Quinn that the only business targeted in Rayville had been Joe's rival. He shook the notion away.

"I really need a job, Joe. Anything."

"Not a good time, Q-T. Sales are bad, and if we don't get justice for the President the Dems are gonna stick us with taxes and rights for workers, n' that kind a shit. You can't fix motors, can you?"

"Sonofabitch! "It was unlike Leonie to cuss, and Quinn put his arm round her shoulders.

"Joe's all right. I'd never have met you if not for him. We'll sort somethin', Honey."

He tried not to let his despair show, but was biting his cheek and had a sick heaviness in his midriff. He had no work and no idea where to turn. Not only had Joe been unwilling to give him a job, he had also demanded his truck back. As Quinn had set off for home, dejected, he'd only trudged halfway across the road when Joe called from the forecourt, "You walked? You lose my truck?" He was scanning around, looking for his battered old pickup.

"No, it's back at my place." Quinn answered. All the way home he regretted his honesty. The night before he and Leonie had been discussing their situation. She wanted him to tell Joe that rioters had destroyed his precious truck at the rally. They could respray it and change the plates. He'd been surprised at her guile for coming up with the idea, but couldn't help grinning and as he shook his head. Now he thought it would have served Joe right.

But Quinn knew that underneath his brash persona, Joe was good. Mannie's loyalty to his boss had been absolute, and Quinn remembered a few hundred dollars always turning up when things were desperate for the mechanic and his son. Mannie had mentioned in passing that his son's teachers had said it was a shame a good brain was going to waste, and Joe had used his contacts to help secure Quinn a scholarship to ULM.

The lack of a car was a problem. They had no income, and he had little prospect of finding more work in Rayville. The only realistic hope was back in Monroe, over 20 miles away. Since they had moved to Rayville two years before Leonie had found a few temporary shop and cleaning jobs, but nothing since last summer.

The TV news was getting hard to believe and social media was flooded with juddering phone videos of explosions and bodies, in one a helicopter gunship firing rockets at what looked like civic buildings; that was fake, Quinn told himself. For the next two days, the relative calm of Rayville felt a world away from the riots and evacuations that filled screens. They watched more and more reports of gangs in yellow bandanas, now referred to as the PBC. Grave but smug journalists in Washington smirked that perhaps this stood for the Po'Boys Club, or the Pecker-wood Boys Club.

There was a spectrum of opinions.

Liberal commentators theorised that years of bad government had facilitated loose associations of 'redneck gangs' from rural areas in the South to come together, fighting for the outgoing president and what they believed was justice for America.

Broadsheet columnists speculated that the organisation of such disparate rabbles into a coordinated force must have required planning and strategic input. The Washington Post went as far as hinting that in its last months the Finch administration had prepared the ground, 'expecting but not accepting defeat.'

Seven states had already started secession proceedings, releasing polished statements condemning the insurrection.

Right wing cable channels claimed what they termed 'Democrat rebel states' had stoked the fires of division in their attempts to break up the Union.

Army generals described the PBC as just a few undisciplined fanatics posing no threat to the security of the USA.

Whatever was the truth, the PBC Quinn had faced at roadblocks had been organised and firmly behind Finch.

Soon enough, the PBC showed up even in Rayville. Three pickup trucks rumbled along Main Street on Thursday morning, each with two bandana wearers in the cargo bed. They stopped all traffic by circling round and round the Main Street intersection for five minutes firing assault rifles into the air.

Leaving smoking tyre trails on the tarmac, they then roared off before stopping outside the First Baptist Church. In seconds they had shot out its windows and polka-dotted the white doors with bullet holes.

By that evening, shop owners and businesses had shuttered or boarded up their premises, and police patrols were continuous. The Mayor's curfew was back in force but superfluous. The population was in hiding.

By Saturday, Quinn's last car lot wage packet was almost spent. He and Leonie discussed their options. He still hoped to go to Monroe to seek work.

"But nothin's open, Q-T, there's no work, no business, no nothin'. We've gotta get out." Leonie pointed at the TV. Lines of cars headed north towing trailers.

"But where? Rayville's our home, Honey."

Quinn knew, though, that some Rayville townsfolk had already decided to leave. The PBC incursion had succeeded, and the choked freeways meant panic was spreading nationwide. It was only a week on from the New Orleans rally and insurrection had spread across the Southern states.

For every National Guard patrol that had shown its presence on Main Street, there had been three PBC trucks in Rayville's residential areas, firing in the air and intimidating residents. President Finch understood his people's frustrations and appealed for calm from his golf course. He was mobilising the military, he said, and would soon restore order. The incoming White House administration claimed it was them who had control of the US Army.

Quinn picked up today's Advocate, the one luxury purchase he still allowed himself. Detroit and Chicago were full to bursting, reports said, and predictions of food shortages had prompted panic buying. The front pages of tabloids, he knew, carried colour images under headlines describing 'floods of frenzied refugees fleeing strife.' Quinn, still clutching journalism aspirations, wondered if press hyperbole was stirring the melting pot. He threw The Advocate down.

"We should head east," he said, clenching and unclenching his hands.

"Or west. California? Mexico?" Leonie was clutching Riona tight. "I wish we still had that truck."

"No, east. North's jammed, and we can't go west through Texas." News reports appeared to show organised PBC units in control of Houston, Dallas and most of the state. Quinn was starting to believe the suggestions that this was part of a long-planned campaign.

"My mom had a sister in Florida," he said, standing up. "Always said it was civilised there. Quiet."

"Where are you going? Quinn!"

"Gonna see Joe." He smiled and ruffled Riona's hair as he headed towards the door. She continued playing, babbling to herself, "Dada," and "east."

He'd expected Crannocks Cars to be closed and shuttered, but Joe was busy putting fresh signs on all the vehicles on his forecourt. Quinn was confused by a handmade banner which read 'Closing Sale.' Joe welcomed him with an eager wave.

"Q-T, come here, I need your help," he called, wiping sweat from his huge face.

"I came to ask you if I could rent—"

But Joe waved him to be quiet. "I'll give you a hundred bucks if you'll drive around the neighbourhood and pass these out." He thrust a pile of papers to Quinn. They read 'Come Get A Car For FREE' written in clumsy black marker below the Crannocks Cars logo.

Before he could ask, Joe continued. "Goddam PBC phoned me, said they're coming to take all my vehicles at noon. Threatened to kill me and my wife if I didn't have them all fuelled up and ready to go."

"But? What?"

"I'm finished, Q-T, but they're getting nothin! I'm giving them away to folks who want to leave town. Take your pick, but help me spread the word, it's past 9.30, we gotta hurry!"

The world was changing fast, thought Quinn as he passed out Joe's flyers. Fathers sent their children to tell friends and neighbours, and word spread quickly. By the time Quinn had completed one circuit of the neighbourhood in his dad's old work truck, a huddle of grateful men and women surrounded Joe as he handed out keys. Used pickups, sedans, and SUVs were being manoeuvred out of the forecourt.

"But what are you gonna do, Joe?"

His grin still in place, Joe said, "Me 'n' Selina's gonna stay indoors till this all calms down. I'm done with business. Gettin' too old for this shit, anyways."

"But the PBC? They're gonna be back."

"I'm gone from here by then. They don't know where I live, and anyways, I cain't help it if I'm a smart salesman! They shoulda got here quicker!"

###

"He just gave you a car? Joe?" Leonie's disbelief matched his own, but Joe's newfound generosity and determination to thwart the PBC meant Mannie's old work truck was Quinn's now. They spent the rest of the day loading it up with what they thought they could take.

Quinn risked a quick trip to his father's deserted home and took three jerry cans from his basement. He reflected on the widower's sparse life, wishing he had spent more time with his dad. The picture of his parents on their wedding day looked down on him from the wall above their bed. His mother's dark, Creole skin contrasted with the fair Irish look of his father.

Quinn ran his hand through his reddish hair and made himself dismiss the brief temptation to head to New Orleans in case his dad was still alive. He lifted the tin cashbox from under the bed. His mother's necklace and over two thousand dollars. Mannie Tarrant had called it his funeral fund.

Chapter Three

"Huh? Why have we stopped?"

They had left Rayville at midnight. Quinn saw three other loaded cars leaving town, heading north under cover of darkness. The Tarrants went east, skirting around towns where they could and passing few other vehicles. Now, five hours later, Quinn had pulled up at the roadside.

"I think there's a roadblock up ahead."

Leonie stretched and looked behind her. "Oh, Q-T, look at Riona! Didn't you check on her?"

"I couldn't see her in the rear-view mirror."

Quinn turned and couldn't stop himself from smiling. Riona was fast asleep, slumped to one side with her neck at right angles. Her little hands had let go of the seat belt, and the strap had ridden up across her face. When Leonie stretched back to free her there was a deep crease over her cheek, but still she wore an angelic smile.

"Where are we?" said Leonie through a yawn, as she turned to look at the road ahead.

"Just coming near Mobile."

Ahead, the straight road sloped upwards, appearing to melt into a barrier of flames. Sparks shot up like fireflies into a dark smudge on the faint orange glow of the city beyond. As their eyes adjusted, vague blobs wavering in the firelight became trucks, and they saw men shining torches. Fumes of burnt gasoline were reaching Quinn's nose and throat.

"They must be PBC. There's no police lights. We'll have to go back, find another way."

While they sat looking at the roadmap on Leonie's phone, headlights approached from behind to pass them by. Anxious faces peering out and packing cases on the roof rack suggested it was another family on the move.

"Let's see if they get through," said Leonie. "We'd have to go right back to Hattiesburg to find another route."

Five minutes later, the car had turned round. As it passed them, a woman in the front appeared to be crying.

Leonie spoke first. "The worst they can do is turn us back. I've got an idea."

Quinn watched as his wife pushed a pillow up under her sweatshirt and laid both hands on the bump. Her pained expression confused Quinn for a second, until he roared off towards the roadblock, grinning. A row of oil drums stretched across the road, flames reaching up from each and highlighting pale faces and yellow bandanas against the darkness. There was room enough for one car to pass, and Quinn braked hard as he approached men with rifles. The braziers warmed his cheek as he slid the window down.

"Hospital! My wife! Let us through!" He pointed at Leonie, who was moaning and gripping her pregnant belly.

"Oh Quinn! Quicker! It's coming!"

The worried guy in the bandana waved them through. Quinn slowed a little once they were out of sight of the roadblock, and their relieved laughing and whooping woke Riona.

"We're not gonna risk trying that again, Q-T. We've gotta stick to back roads now, right?"

Soon Quinn only had the steady diesel rattle to distract him from what he thought he had seen at the roadblock. A few miles on it was Leonie who broke the heavy silence between them. He could see out of the corner of his eye that she had turned towards him, and was shaking her head. "Did you see what one of them was wearing?"

He nodded, staring at the road.

"US Army uniform," Leonie whispered, loud enough to rouse Riona again.

"At least two of them," said Quinn.

"What in hell is happening, QT?"

When Quinn saw the lights of Mobile ahead, the night sky beyond just beginning to pale, he drew to a stop on the road shoulder. "We'll skirt round the city," he said. "Look for a left exit."

With Leonie giving directions from her cell phone satnav, Quinn took the next left turn, heading north. Keeping the city to his right, they weaved a disordered route until it felt safe to turn south towards the sea and the coast road. Progress was slow, but they didn't meet another roadblock.

Leonie took over driving, and Quinn took the chance to sleep when Riona let him. Every few miles she would ask, "Where goin', Dada?"

Chapter Four

Florida

Quinn thought he was still dreaming. Riona was splashing in shallow water on a white beach a few yards away from him. Leonie was clapping her hands each time their daughter tried a little jump. With sun streaming in through the open car window, he stretched, trying to understand. A roaring above his head made him cower down, shouting a warning. When the sound receded, he raised his head. Leonie appeared unconcerned and Riona continued playing, both of them laughing.

The beach was real. Leonie explained she had grown too tired to continue, and drawn off down a dirt slip road before she reached the next town, Destin. Quinn realised he had slept all the while Leonie had taken them round Pensacola and another fifty miles into Florida.

"I just tucked the pickup in under the bridge and went to sleep."

Above them, the highway crossed a narrow inlet. The roaring Quinn had heard was a passing truck. Across the water and about a mile away he could see the town spread along the shore.

"You should have woke me up, Hon," he said.

Leonie rolled her eyes. With an ironic grin she said, "The air force jet that damn near took the roof off the truck couldn't wake you."

Quinn looked at his watch. It was approaching midday, and he'd slept for over five hours. Though only a few miles from Destin, the hideaway Leonie had chanced upon felt safe. The highway above them seemed quiet, but to satisfy himself they couldn't be seen, Quinn crept a short way back up the slip road. The track had presumably been made when the bridge was constructed, and theirs were the only tyre tracks.

Riona was lining up shells in the sand when he returned to the beach, and Leonie lay watching over her in the shade of the truck.

"We should get going," Quinn said. She jumped, and he realised she had been half asleep.

"I need a rest, QT, and Riona's been stuck in the car all night. We've got food and water."

Leonie wanted them to stay that day and overnight. Heading for Florida had been a good choice, she said. "I feel safe. We can move on tomorrow."

Partly swayed by the joy of seeing his toddler playing on her first beach, Quinn was persuaded. The PBC had been conspicuous in Mississippi and Alabama, but they had seen no bandanaed armed patrols since before Mobile. They could leave early next morning.

As the sky lightened above Destin, Quinn topped up the gas tank from the jerry cans. But when he turned the key, his dad's old work pickup gave out, the battery dead. They had left the cab lights on to comfort Riona before going to sleep themselves.

Rested and relaxed after their stopover, they were able to laugh off this setback as part of their family adventure. With no choice but to walk, they crossed the bridge hand in hand, swinging Riona off her feet. Leonie had rolled her eyes when Quinn said that Destin must have been their destiny.

The sleepy, small town of Destin appeared untouched by the strife elsewhere. In a shaded café, after coffee, pancakes, and a popsicle for Riona, they asked the server for directions to a garage. A regular customer overheard Quinn explain the battery problem, and soon they were crossing back over the inlet, this time in the man's truck. When he had jump-started the pickup, the Tarrant family followed their new friend to the Miracle Strip RV Resort.

Chapter Five

Todd was a short, smiling man who was missing the third and fourth fingers of his left hand. He owned the Miracle Strip, and offered to let them park there and use one of his units. It was the quiet season, he said, and they could stay a few days while they decided where to go next. Instead of payment, they agreed to clean all his cabins to make them ready for Spring.

Todd's wife, Tina, managed the Miracle Strip. Matching Todd in height but at double his weight and with arthritis, Tina was struggling. After ten days the Tarrants were still planning to move on when Tina and Todd came to their cabin one evening to ask them to stay on. As well as the campground Todd owned four boats that fished out of Destin, and he offered Quinn work as a deckhand.

Leonie soon became indispensable. She would spend mornings cleaning and ordering, and afternoons managing arrivals and departures. Even when it became clear the US was descending into protracted internal conflict regulars still came to the resort, mostly from nearby Pensacola. Their news suggested Florida had so far been spared from the worst, but they wouldn't dare go outside the state.

Todd paid them both the minimum wage, deducting rent for one of his older cabins.

At 14 months old, Riona was still an unsteady toddler when they arrived in Destin. Soon she was running. Her vocabulary expanded almost daily and Leonie would update Quinn on her progress each time he returned from work. Though always busy, Leonie was happy and laid back. To match most of his crewmates

Quinn grew a wispy red beard. He told Leonie it was to help shade his pale skin against the sun, but she still insisted he shave it off.

The Tarrants agreed to stay on for the summer season, and move on in the fall when the campground closed for the cooler, quieter months. Their new life suited them, though, and in September 2030 they sold the pickup to pay rent to Todd over the winter. They had hardly been able to use the truck since gas prices had skyrocketed, and Quinn would still have the use of Todd's truck to shift nets, fish boxes and ice.

Quinn was glad they'd left Louisiana when they did, and began to wonder if they might settle in Destin for good rather than going further south. The north of Florida was still being spared most of the violence and strife. They rarely saw attack helicopters, jet fighters, or PBC patrols, and the warships that had patrolled the Gulf in the early months of the war were now few and far between.

Quinn's crewmates told him the US Navy had remained loyal to the new government in Washington DC. It was said most naval firepower was concentrated further west, and on still nights a distant roaring that wasn't thunder sometimes disturbed Quinn's sleep. With no reliable news sources, he could only imagine the horrors unfolding in parts of his homeland.

A traditional white Republican area, Florida was a PBC recruiting ground. Quinn's crewmates told him of sons leaving Destin to join the fighting, some with encouragement from their parents. At one time, joining up to fight might have tempted Quinn, but not since his father's death. At work he spoke little in the fishermen's debates. The rally in New Orleans had rocked his faith in the truth and wisdom of former president Finch.

The few available TV reports suggested many of the cities in the South were lawless no-go areas. Politicians on both sides continued to avoid talking openly about civil war, and Army generals were presented for interview by both sides of the conflict to profess the army's undivided loyalty to the government of the United States.

Quinn reflected that it was no longer clear who was in control. Even respected mainstream media outlets described the armed forces as being fractured into opposing factions. Tabloid news editors were less coy, and splashed wilder claims that troops on both sides had been brainwashed.

From what Quinn could gather it seemed that fluid frontiers of sorts had formed. Forces loyal to Marcus Finch were concentrated in the south and the midwest, still maintaining that the election was fraudulent, the courts unlawful, and his cause just. The northeastern and western states had formed a new government and considered Finch a rebel.

Reliable information was hard to find. Just days after the New Orleans rally that killed Quinn's father, Finch's last act before leaving office had been to close down non-government TV news stations and national newspapers. It had astonished Quinn when the incoming administration, 'for reasons of National security,' decided against reversing the decision. It felt like the last nail in the coffin of his journalism aspirations.

After that opposing propaganda outfits produced the only available bulletins. At 6 pm each day, Whitehouse TV, the news channel under control of the new administration, broadcast an hour-long news programme. Florida-based Magavision simultaneously put out contradictions. Both claimed to be the only official media. For a time, Quinn and Leonie had played a game, flicking between the only two channels to compare the opposite viewpoints being expressed. Each of the opposing forces, it seemed, was advancing triumphantly and predicted an early end of the conflict as soon as the other side was 'crushed like cockroaches' or 'successfully forced into submission.'

Both sides claimed near-zero casualty figures. At the same time, Quinn saw ever more wheelchair-bound amputees and disfigured burn victims returning from the conflict, discarded, broken and fending for themselves.

In April 2030 bitter social media debates were ended overnight when the White House took emergency measures to close Facebook, X, Instagram and Google. The attention of the public soon switched to new platforms, and public access to the internet was closed down completely.

Communication became even harder as one by one the major mobile phone networks were closed down, and both sides destroyed all mobile phone masts. Landline phones were unreliable after decades of underinvestment and little maintenance. Satnav was gone, and road signs obscured to confuse potential invaders.

The opposing forces were said to communicate via satellite. Back in the mid-2020s, in the second of his three presidential terms, Marcus Finch had authorised the sale of NASA to private interests controlled by his billionaire backers. Sometimes, sleepless in the narrow Miracle Strip bed, Quinn wondered if speculations he had dismissed as conspiracy theories might have had some validity. Perhaps super-rich playboys funded their billion-dollar space toys with an eye to the future.

Other than propaganda, the only news of the outside world came by word of mouth and rumour. It was said some had escaped abroad to a safe haven. The northern border was closed, but Canada was said to be accepting refugees. Quinn remained sceptical, smirking at the irony when he heard Cuba mentioned as a favoured destination..

The Tarrants were still at the Miracle Strip a year and a half later. For much of that time they lived in resigned contentment. Over the summer of 2031, though, something changed.

.

Chapter Six

September 2031

The slam of the cabin door behind him sent starlings flying. Through the open kitchen window, he heard Riona whine. Then Leonie's calming voice. He could picture her strained expression as she spoke. "It's OK, Baby, Mom's got a headache and Daddy's gone to work. You want Cheerios?"

Quinn punched the steering wheel as he reversed away from their cabin. Through clouds of tyre-spinning dust, between the slats of the kitchen blind he could see Leonie watching him. He felt small for his part in the latest petty squabble. Heading to work in Destin, the argument receding behind him, he wondered again what was going wrong between them. It had all been so good when they settled in Destin, but now there seemed to be fights every day.

His pulse slowed, his grip on the wheel loosening as he made his way into Destin heading for the dock. It had been getting like this for months, he thought. Their arguing had worsened over the summer, but even before that Leonie had been short with him. And cold in their bed. The last time he remembered her being her old self was before the 4th of July. Now in September he was doing extra work days to escape, wondering all the time what he would go home to.

Tonight he was going to ask her straight out what the hell was wrong.

After another day brooding at sea, he drove to the campground ready for the confrontation. But when he got home, Leonie was in tears and packing their bags. She sat down on the end of their bed to tell him they were leaving.

"But why, Honey? I mean—"

"We just are." With a flick of her red-rimmed eyes, she showed him that Riona had wandered in behind him. He felt her little arms tighten around his thigh.

"Dada, we're moving on. Moving on. We're moving on." Riona was singing to herself, her Minions11 backpack stuffed with soft toys.

"But–?"

Leonie shushed him and pointed at the little office shack opposite. Todd was locking up to go home. As he headed to his car Leonie watched him with disgust in her eyes.

"Todd? But what..?" Suspicion rose in him. Todd had spent less time at the dock in recent months. "You mean? I'll–"

"No! Q-T, stop." Leonie caught him and put her arms on his shoulders before he could open the door. She turned him round, and it felt good to feel her touch again. Pulling him to her she gripped him tight, putting her wet face under his neck. "We're just gonna go."

Todd had driven off in his car by the time Leonie relaxed her sobbing embrace. Quinn snatched at the truck key and started to follow him. His hand was on the cabin door handle when her shocking yell stopped him.

"Stop! If you go out that door, I'm taking Riona and leaving without you." He choked a silent roar and leant his forehead on the door jamb. The key threatened to pierce his palm, and it felt good. He gripped it tighter until the pain seared through the surface of his fury. Tears were stinging his eyes when he turned to face Leonie. Riona started her merry song again.

"But what..?"

"I'll tell you later. When we've gone from here." The look on her face told Quinn to ask no more.

She went back to packing their things, her focus only diverted by Riona. Leonie's smiling patience with their daughter warmed Quinn a little. As the evening passed, he noticed her smile linger when she turned away from Riona, and just once she caught his eye before her stony mask was back in place.

Her quick, prepared answers swatted aside his occasional 'but hows?' When Quinn reminded her they had no car, Leonie nodded towards the truck he'd brought back from Todd's boatyard. "That bastard can afford it."

Whatever her boss had done to her, Leonie wasn't going to tell Quinn until they had left the Miracle Strip. When he had made his wife and child safe, though, he could return to tackle Todd.

Quinn wanted to set off in darkness, but Leonie persuaded him to wait until morning. If they started the truck in the middle of the night one of the regulars on the campground might get suspicious, she said, pointing to the old RV nearest the campground gate. Its occupant, Joe, was a light sleeper and had become an unofficial night watchman.

She had thought this through, he realised. Planned and prepared to leave. He was relieved when he saw she had packed a bag for him.

It was after 7 o'clock the next morning when Leonie strapped sleepy Riona safely into Todd's truck. She was small enough not to be visible through the windows, but Leonie had to slide down to hide in the passenger side footwell. Quinn, keen to get going but sticking to the plan, climbed in behind the wheel. He was wearing his work clothes and his best false nonchalance. As they passed out of the campground, he made himself roll down the window a little and call out to a man walking his dog, "Mornin', Sam. I gotta go in early today, I left a helluva mess last evening." He pointed over his shoulder at the bed of the truck, where he'd piled nets and boxes to conceal their suitcases.

Once at the dock, they'd filled up with gas from Todd's shed and topped up his dad's old jerry cans. Quinn left a note on the door for when his workmates arrived. "Sorry guys gotta go get stores for Todd will be back soon."

Stealing Todd's pickup truck gave Quinn a brief rush of satisfaction, and Leonie had thrown him a scrap of a smile when he whooped as they left Destin. For the next few hours, though, as they drove east with the bright sea to their right and the shade of tall trees opposite, only Riona's singing and questions broke the silence.

A little after midday Quinn saw in the rearview mirror that Riona was asleep. The quiet made him fidget until Leonie spoke. They were just passing the entrance to a sawmill, a sign reading 'Tate's Hell Forest Logging Company.'

"I didn't let him, Quinn, but he came damn near to forcin' me."

Quinn pulled to a stop on the shoulder between red and white safety bollards. He turned but looked past her at the cobalt blue. "You should've let me go after him." Now that Leonie had spoken to him at last, Quinn wondered if he wanted to hear what she had to say.

When he killed the engine the sudden stillness was oppressive. Leonie spoke first.

"Look at that, it's beautiful," she had turned to the sea and he couldn't see her face.

She pressed the buttons to open all the windows before getting out. Quinn made sure Riona was in the shade and followed her.

Standing between scrubby trees Leonie took his hand. It felt good, her fingers warm despite the breeze. He had to strain to catch her words when she spoke again after a few minutes, still looking out over the sea.

"He started by taking Riona for a walk. It let me get on. Then sometimes he would leave her with Tina and check if I needed help with anything. He was kind, and Riona enjoyed playing with Tina." Quinn turned to watch her face, but she kept her gaze on the distance, her bright blue eyes wide despite the strong sun.

"Then it got creepy."

Quinn bristled. He wanted to hold Leonie close, kiss her chocolate brown hair. Anything to stop her from talking.

"He was brushing past me too close, freaking me out. When it got too much I asked him to let me get on. I said he was getting in the way, but he just sort of grinned at me."

Quinn had to say something. "When was this? I mean how long..?" She glanced at him but went on as if she hadn't heard.

"One time I was cleaning a cabin toilet he tried to come in with me. I told him no, and he got angry then and pressed against me in the doorway. I could feel it through his shorts. I shouted and he put his hand over my face."

Quinn's mouth was dry. He remembered a little scratch on her cheek. She'd told him she'd been clumsy with her comb.

"I put my knee where it hurt him. He said he'd sack you and throw us out if I said anything."

At last, she turned to Quinn and looked up at him. He felt his jaw clench and his scalp squeeze tight, and now it was his turn to avert his eyes.

"When?"

"July 3rd. He made me go hang bunting after, like nothin' had happened."

Quinn continued to stare at the horizon.

"He didn't touch me again, Quinn. And he didn't touch Riona, I know it." A new fear shivered over Quinn, and Leonie squeezed his hand before going on.

"But every time you went to work I got scared. We were fighting all the time, and I wanted to get out."

Quinn's shoulders slumped. He felt his hand pull away from hers, but she gripped it back. "All of us, I mean. Yesterday morning when you stormed out again I started to pack our–"

She turned and rushed to the truck, where Riona was trying to climb out of the window. "Oh, Rio-baby! Careful!"

With Riona rescued, they set off again. Riona's giggling about her adventure was infectious. While Quinn and Leonie said little to each other, they laughed along and exchanged genial smiles. When Leonie stretched across to hold his hand he had to blink away a tear.

Half an hour further on the road veered south down Florida's west coast. Months before, before the ice had begun to form between them, they'd discussed where they would have gone if they hadn't found such a welcome at the Miracle Strip. Leonie had also heard the stories of peaceful normality in Cuba, A cabin guest had told her that the right money could buy safe passage there, but like Quinn, she'd laughed at the idea. From the tattered road atlas they had found in the door pocket of Todd's truck they knew they were some 400 miles from Miami. That was far enough away. They nodded to each other and Quinn drove on south.

Chapter Seven

Miami seemed the obvious destination. Quinn would find work there, and Riona would be hundreds of miles from the civil war's major battlegrounds. But the farther they drove in the stolen truck, the less appealing southern Florida became. While they encountered no roadblocks, they saw dozens of armed patrols on the move. It was after dark before they neared the city and they decided to spend the night in a highway rest area.

Riona was asleep between them in the reclined truck seats when Leonie told him where she wanted to go. "We've gotta leave the US. I don't want to live like this, Q-T."

"We'll be OK in Miami, Honey. War's not gonna come here. I'll get a job–"

"Cuba. It's not so far. Della at the mothers' group back in Destin told me folk can get a boat from Miami."

Quinn pushed himself up to look at Leonie. "But–"

"Five thousand dollars, Della said. We can sell the truck for that."

It had been months since either of them had mentioned the crazy rumours about Cuba. Leonie had been thinking about it, though, Quinn could tell.

By the time he went to sleep Quinn had agreed to sell the truck, but the idea of passage to Cuba was too much for him. They would use the money to live on until they found jobs and settled in Miami.

Their night at the rest area was disturbed twice by partying PBC fighters who screeched their truck round the lot, whooping and shooting in the air. Miami was just as threatening, armed men in yellow bandanas seeming to outnumber civilians. Quinn saw an old woman on the sidewalk waving her stick at the driver of a flatbed truck as it roared past. Its bandanaed passenger hollered at the old woman, firing into the air. Riona cried.

Selling Todd's truck raised less than half of what they'd hoped. The round-eyed dealer with a five o'clock shadow and dirty shoes wouldn't budge past $3500. Times were uncertain in the motor trade, he'd said, from under his USNo.1 cap. Their truck bore a $9000 price ticket when they had walked past an hour later. Quinn swore.

It was in a diner that day that a couple from Richmond, Virginia approached them. In the toilets, the man had whispered to Quinn without looking up from the urinal.

"Are you bound for the Keys?"

Quinn was on edge about having left Leonie and Riona alone in the café. He said nothing and made to leave, but the man went on. White, taller than Quinn, he said quietly, "It's OK. When we saw you walk in with your bags, we guessed you were like us."

Turning to leave, he held out a piece of folded paper. When Quinn didn't take it, the man placed it on the window ledge and left. He had smooth hands.

Quinn looked at the note for a moment before picking it up. It could be a trap. The man didn't look like he was PBC but the Destin fishermen had spoken of spies being everywhere. When he read, 'Do you want to travel in our car? It is safer in larger numbers,' he was still uncertain.

He returned to the table and whispered to Leonie, telling her what the man had said and slipping the note into her hand. She unfolded it under the table edge. The man was sitting with a woman at the other end of the diner. She was stick-thin, tapping her fingers and jumpy. She didn't look like a spy.

A PBC truck was rattling past the window behind Leonie when she looked up from her lap. Quinn murmured, "Maybe they think the Florida Keys is safer?" flicking his eyes towards the couple.

"It's nearer Cuba," whispered Leonie, glancing over. The woman caught her eye, and with her foot she pushed a chair out in invitation.

By the time they had finished their churros, the Tarrants had decided they could risk hearing what the couple had to say. They moved to join them. In quiet tones, the man explained he had been a teacher in Richmond, Virginia. His wife had been a lawyer. They wanted to escape to Cuba, but were becoming wary of travelling alone. The woman had bitten nails and didn't say a word. She sat clutching a framed picture of a little boy on a bicycle. He was never spoken of.

The couple had heard the Keys was the likeliest place to buy a boat crossing, but that getting there could be difficult. It was clear they assumed the Tarrants were also intent on reaching Cuba.

The teacher explained that south Florida had been firmly in the hands of rebel forces since early in the conflict. He shared Quinn's suspicion that the civil war had been predicted if not planned. He went further, explaining that the outgoing president had consolidated a base in Miami, which was also a training ground and R&R resort for the PBC. It was relatively peaceful, he said, the gunfire mostly the fighters' fun, letting off steam and shooting into the air. He had, though, heard of blacks or Cubans used as target practice. With no enemy to engage with, recently trained PBC fighters filled the time before they were posted to real action by intimidating civilians and testing their loyalty. Catching a traitor meant kudos, a badge of honour.

The reality of the danger they were in had hit home for Quinn when, deadpan, the man from Richmond explained that a large family on the road would be messier to dispose of.

Before the couple left the diner, the man pointed out their SUV. Quinn and Leonie watched them cross the road towards it and climb in.

"Big car. Big red car," said Riona, pointing and smiling. "We goin' in big red car." Leonie shushed her and put a finger to her lips, and Riona stifled a giggle.

"What d'you think?" whispered Quinn.

"I don't like it here."

He looked across the road, and the man cast a glance back at the diner. As what sounded like popping gunfire started up outside, Quinn drummed his fingers on the white tabletop. Looking at Leonie, then back at the red car, he whispered, "He seemed to be saying you've got to go down the Keys if you're gonna get to Cuba."

Leonie put one hand on top of Quinn's to stop his tapping, grasping the handle of her suitcase with the other. "Let's just go, Q-T. I want to get out of here."

###

The Chevy Suburban left Miami on the I-1. Quinn noticed road signs were still displayed, and the teacher said Finch was confident his Florida base would never be threatened.

They soon came on the first roadblock.

"Where you goin' and why?" a man barked after rapping the car window with his gun.

The two families had agreed on their story, and only the teacher spoke.

"Key Largo. My father's funeral."

A tail of the man's bandana was blowing in the breeze. He looked in the car and gestured at Quinn and Leonie in the back, with Riona between them.

"Who are they?"

"My cousin and his family."

"Nice car. Virginia plate?" The man spat on the ground.

"We moved down to Miami last year. Nearer my Dad."

The second roadblock was just a few miles on. They told the funeral story again, but the questioning went on longer. When one of the PBC men thrust his rifle through the open window, Riona screamed and wet herself. Her shrieking didn't stop until the men backed off without searching the car. As they drew away, the teacher's wife put her head in her hands and started mewing like an injured cat. Leonie was holding Quinn's hand so tight her nails drew blood.

When they were out of sight of the roadblock, the teacher drew into the side and all four adults sat numb. The only sounds were the woman's sobbing and Riona sniffing back tears.

Quinn mumbled, "We can't go on. I can't...we can't..."

The teacher pulled his wife close to him. "We're not going through another roadblock. We've got to get off the I-1."

No one objected when a moment later he started the motor and drove on. He turned left off the Interstate, and soon an overhead sign told Quinn they were now on the Ronald Reagan Turnpike.

There were no more roadblocks, and a few miles farther south the teacher broke the silence.

"I'm not going back on the interstate," he said. His wife was staring ahead of her, both hands still fidgeting with the picture of the boy.

"There's no other way to the Keys." Quinn could think of nothing to suggest.

"Look." It was Leonie. She was pointing at a road junction coming up. They were just entering Florida City, and a sign pointed right to The Everglades National Park. The teacher looked over his right shoulder at Quinn, who nodded assent.

"There's got to be another way of crossing to The Keys."

They followed the road through the Everglades National Park until it ended. At the southernmost point of Florida, excepting the Keys, they found the Manatee Visitor Centre. The teacher had heard of it, and said before the war it had been a popular destination for tourists and naturalists. Now its buildings were locked, windows boarded and storm damage unrepaired.

A shanty town of ramshackle shelters occupied one of the car parks. A boy and a girl who looked to be about eight or nine started approaching the SUV until shouts called them back to the huts. Quinn and the teacher got out.

"No guns or flags," Quinn said, looking around.

The teacher walked towards the shanties and a man and woman came to meet him. Quinn saw the woman looking across at the SUV while the teacher spoke with the man. When he came back to the car he said, "It seems there's a few families settled here and there's been no PBC for months."

All five slept in the teacher's SUV at first, until scavenged boat parts from the centre's marina provided enough for them to build leaky shelters.

Unlike most of the refugees, Quinn built his shack under the cover of trees in a shady RV park, well away from the main car park area. None of the seven families living there objected. Their fancy RVs may have had LPG stoves and solar panels, but from brief interactions with some of them Quinn knew they were just as desperate as the rest of the few dozen other timid families who had gravitated to the Everglades like sediment. Like the Tarrants and the couple from Virginia, most of those at the Manatee centre had come there in the hope of finding a quick route onwards to Cuba. All had so far been disappointed. Reaching Cuba from the Everglades would have meant a long sea passage around the Keys. The people-traffickers were only interested, it was said, in the shortest crossing possible.

Over the next few months, though, one by one most of the RVs left. One woman had told Quinn her fuel supply was low and she was leaving with her kids before they were marooned at the Manatee centre for good. When the last RV occupants had pulled away from the campground, Quinn and Riona raked through their trash.

One deserted RV remained, that had belonged to an old hippy. It was on its rims, the ripped door hanging off and all windows removed. It was only a respectful few weeks after they'd buried the man before nocturnal raids on his van started. Several of the shanties in the main area soon sported plexiglass windows, some still with ban-the-bomb blinds. Quinn always felt guilty when he looked at the fuel tank that was now the Tarrants' water store. It took months for the gasoline taste of their boiled creek water to wear away.

They were closer to Cuba than they had been, but it seemed farther away than ever. With no direct sea route from the Everglades, their only option was to try again to reach the Keys via Miami. The teacher and his wife had made it clear they would never risk that, and without transport of their own Leonie and Quinn faced a hungry life in the swamp, unless something changed. For now it seemed a price worth paying to remain relatively sheltered from the worst of the civil war.

The Tarrants kept largely to themselves. Life for the refugees was mostly peaceful, but there were occasional disagreements between families. Quinn saw one man tending to wounds by the creek. He looked to have been severely beaten.

Some children appeared to Quinn to have been sent out to steal from other families. A plastic water carrier he had salvaged from the hippy's RV disappeared one day. A little girl a few years older than Riona had turned up to play with her. Leonie had watched over them, and had to intervene when the visitor started screaming at Riona for no apparent reason. Sending the girl away, Leonie watched her walk off between the trees. She met up with an older boy, from the look of him a brother. The pair whooped and laughed, running off together. The water carrier was gone when Leonie next went to use it.

Leonie and Quinn didn't fight often. When they did, it tended to be when one of them had become too frustrated by their lot. "We should never have come here." "We'll never get away from here." "You brought us to this hell!" It didn't matter which one started it. They would bitch and snipe at each other for minutes or hours, until one of them burst into tears or Riona's crying silenced them.

Much of their diet was fish. Rods and lines were in plentiful supply; the refugees had found a well-stocked hut at the small Visitor Centre dock. Leonie and Quinn took turns to fish. They had caught garfish, the occasional snapper, and once even a snook. The old hippy in the RV had grown corn, and after he died some families in the main area kept this going, trading their crops for seafood. There was no traffic on the road into the Centre and it had been a long time since they had tasted roadkill.

In late 2032, someone managed to connect a scavenged radio to a truck battery and a solar panel. It meant occasional snippets of news could whisper around the settlement. Quinn was almost relieved to have it confirmed that the civil war was continuing. At times he had lain awake thinking of marooned Japanese soldiers in the jungle waiting decades for World War Two to end.

Reports indicated Finch's rebels and forces loyal to the White House were mired in bloody conflict along a front stretching from the Delta to Ohio. Localised battles also raged within and around some of the states that Quinn remembered had been trying to secede from the United States when war started. Las Vegas was said to be under perpetual siege, but it was unclear who by. Quinn found it ironic that all involved claimed they were fighting for American unity.

What shocked Quinn most was news that Mexico was at war with Brazil, the latter having invaded and taken over much of Central America. At one time, Quinn had wondered if Mexico might have been an alternative escape route if the battlegrounds of the southern US could somehow be crossed.

From the seaward side of the Manatee Marina, the tantalising lights of The Keys hung on the horizon like sparkling necklaces strung between the offshore islands. The tenuous radio connection to the outside world revived in the Tarrants the unlikely hope of escape to Cuba. They weren't alone. For the shanty town's residents who hadn't resigned themselves to staying until the war ended the Florida Keys and onward passage to Cuba remained the dream. For a time rumours spread that new routes would open up soon.

The PBC roadblocks on the Interstate meant no one considered reaching The Keys by car. With dense mangroves and sawgrass for miles around, trekking on foot was impossible. Crossing the Whipray Basin would require a decent boat, but marauding PBC patrols had destroyed all the marina's cruisers and sailboats in the early days of the war.

A few families, desperate to the point of recklessness, had built rafts. Strong currents and erratic winds meant most broke up not far from shore, and those who could swim or paddle made it back to safety in the swamp. On one of his frequent forays into the swamp to fish for gar, Quinn had found the part-eaten body of a little boy wedged under a mangrove root. His Atlanta Braves sweatshirt showed Quinn he was from a family that had paddled away a few weeks before. It took Quinn an hour to bury the child in the slime, trying not to look at the little boy's empty eye sockets. He didn't tell Leonie.

Chapter Eight

Autumn 2034

Quinn's boot caught on one of a thousand tufts of sawgrass that had begun to erode the edges of the visitor centre compound. Small mounds erupted like mini volcanoes, greenery shooting up, cracks radiating out over the concrete like lava streams. He picked his way between more of them as he approached the blurring edge of the deserted car park, looking for the path his boots had worn into the brush.

Despite hopes having been raised for a few months by scraps of contact with the outside world, three years after the Tarrants first arrived at the Manatee there was still no realistic prospect of escape. They had adjusted to their new life in their makeshift shack near the edge of a mangrove creek. Leonie had even grown used to Quinn's ginger beard, now long enough for Riona to pleat. A razor was a thing of history. It was years since any murderous PBC patrols had visited, but Quinn still preferred the relative seclusion of the RV park, well away from the Miami road.

Then hopes of escape rose again. One summer morning in 2034 Quinn noticed an empty shack. Outside an arrangement of usable possessions, with a note scratched into a plastic panel inviting others to help themselves. The pair from Virginia had disappeared into the night.

Quinn had never learned the names of the teacher and the sad lawyer they had arrived with in the fall of 2031. Despite their seclusion and relative security, contact between the refugees in the campground was scant. Few were willing to share their identity, even though no one still believed PBC infiltrators could be amongst them after all this time.

Rumours spread round the shanty town that the Richmond couple had paid to cross the Basin to Layton. Traffickers had opened up a new route, they said. Across to the Keys and onward to Cuba. Quinn had always assumed the lawyer had money, and that night counted out the dollars he and Leonie had pooled.

Others began to disappear. Cars would be heard to slip into the old centre's reception area in darkness. Days later a shanty would be vacated overnight.

Now, three months since the first departure, every night Quinn ventured as far as he dared outside the campground area to conceal himself. He waited there until morning, hoping for a chance to approach a people-trafficker.

On his way to his hiding place tonight, Quinn was sweating. The weather had been hot for months, and he guessed it must be about September or October. The last couple of years had told him the nights would soon cool a little, and sleep would be easier. His hopes were high, though. Another family had spirited themselves away last week.

Quinn's chosen spot was a hundred yards north of the main area, by the roadside ditch. He was intent on being the first to meet any approaching traffickers. Having left the relative safety of the campground area, it was always a relief to reach the cover of thick vegetation. He settled himself for another ten hours of the smells and sounds of the mangroves. It was risky. PBC patrols were unlikely, but alligators were never far away.

As he settled himself Quinn tried as usual to remain positive, while not getting his hopes too high. He knew that in all likelihood, in the morning he would return to the shelter disappointed. Leonie's ever-hopeful expression would morph into resignation, before she would go back to chopping wood or playing with their daughter. Riona's smile would cheer him.

Lying in darkness on the cool dirt by the dried-up ditch, Quinn passed the time by picturing his daughter. Now nearly six, Riona Tarrant-Dugas was a wiry kid, and cleaner than some in the campground. The Tarrants washed in the creek daily. Quinn had sat watching her the day before, playing and chatting to herself as she arranged her fish skeleton and beetle collections. He wondered sometimes if she could remember what a TV was or if she would ever see one again. Or a cell phone.

Although mostly content whether alone or with kids from the main camp area, Riona often asked them about her grandparents. They had explained that Grandpa Mannie had gone to heaven. She didn't really remember Leonie's family in Monroe, but it was very unlikely they would ever meet again.

Quinn was brought back to the present. Something was different. The nylon money belt was digging into his skinny waist, but as he shifted position he knew it wasn't that. Silence. Something had hushed the amphibian chorus.

His other senses sharpened, and he blinked sweat beads from his eyelids to peer along the dark roadway. He tried to filter out the noise of his breathing and the pulsing in his neck, but whatever the bullfrogs had sensed, he couldn't. He heard a scruffling behind him, then a splash. An alligator had sensed it too.

A misty pallor appeared in the inky distance, lightening to a yellow glow. He stared into its centre as a sound emerged ahead of it. A dull thrumming. A vehicle, its dim lights barely penetrating the brush. Did he imagine the gasoline smell? He scrambled across the ditch and up onto the road.

Half an hour later, a black car pulled away. Quinn's plan had worked. He didn't think any residents of the main area had even been aware a trafficker had come to the Centre. Flushed with pride and his money belt $500 lighter, he hurried back to his hut.

Lying on their mattress of scavenged RV cushions, Leonie had her arms round Riona. He couldn't bring himself to wake them. As the sky lightened, he watched their beautiful faces and listened to their breathing, desperate to share his news.

Leonie's reaction surprised Quinn.

"But a thousand dollars just to get to the Keys?" He could tell from her furious face that she would have liked to shout rather than hiss her words. "And we don't even know if we can get to Cuba from there, Q-T."

His excitement drained away. He started to regret paying the deposit on the strength of such a vague promise. He'd been a fool, tricked into wasting $500. He stashed the money belt and went outside, away from Leonie's glare.

The pails felt heavier than usual as he trudged back from the creek with water for the day. He was ready for more silent fury, but Leonie wanted to hear the plan again. Wanted to stretch out his shame, he thought, get her 500 dollars' worth. He put down the pails and went over the arrangement he'd entered into.

The man in the car had told him the PBC still had an effective stranglehold on the Florida Keys. There were roadblocks as far as Key Largo, and for several miles beyond that gunboats patrolled the waters to the north and south. Anyone caught attempting to leave the US was shot, the trafficker said. He promised to transport them across the bay to Layton, much further west.

Leonie listened, letting Quinn finish this time.

"We'd just be stuck on The Keys, Quinn. We'd be better stickin' it out here."

"But I told you, the guy I paid said he knows a guy on The Keys who pays the PBC to let his boats through." Quinn heard the pleading in his voice.

Leonie bit on her lower lip, frowning. Not saying no.

"He said loads of folks had made it," Quinn went on, "and we've got enough to pay the guy at Layton. Six thousand dollars. Just think, we'll be in Cuba, Honey."

"I don't like it."

Chapter Nine

Leonie came round to the idea that if they didn't take this chance they might never escape the Everglades, let alone reach Cuba.

Three nights later they crept in darkness along the trail from the campground to the beach, small suitcases in hand and Riona sworn to an excited silence. To Quinn's relief, there was an inflatable boat waiting for them. They paid the remaining $500 to the boatman, and he rowed them out onto the black water. When he judged they were out of earshot he risked starting the outboard, and they chugged away into the night.

By dawn they were on another beach. It was just outside Layton, the boatman assured them. Leonie didn't trust the man, and Quinn was relieved when they crept up onto the road opposite a sign on the lawn of the Layton Community Baptist Church.

Their instructions were to walk south out of Layton for a mile and take a left turn down a track into Long Key State Park, then wait there all day. Quinn had memorised the trafficker's words: "Hide in the brush between a parking lot and the beach. Stay out of sight. A boat will come at night. $6000."

It was a long day. Well after nightfall there was still no sign of a boat. Their water supplies were low, and a stiff breeze off the sea made the air much less humid than they'd grown used to in the Everglades. Riona was cold and fractious. Leonie was quiet but suspicious.

Quinn's anxiety was growing when at last, the sidelights of a dark sedan car slid past them on the track. It stopped facing the sea, and the headlights flicked on and off three times. A moment later, Quinn made out the sound of an engine. Soon a black shape formed on the sea. Leonie squeezed Quinn's arm, her other hand gripping Riona tight against her. The amorphous outline became a boat.

"Walk to the beach now."

Quinn tensed at the sudden instruction, and felt Leonie do the same. He turned and saw the car door had opened. Its driver emerged and walked past them towards the sea. From another bush nearby, two more shapes stood up. Then one more. As the Tarrants made their way onto the open beach, more shivering people revealed themselves. Quinn realised they had been far from alone as they waited in silent concealment.

Quinn had an arm around Leonie's waist as they stood watching the approaching boat. He could now see it was towing two smaller wooden dinghies. Lit by a clouded first quarter moon they looked tiny and exposed. Riona sat on the suitcase between Leonie's knees looking up at her mother, the dim lights of the sedan reflecting from her dilated pupils. Leonie gripped her little bony shoulders. "It's all right, Rio-baby."

Soon, a small crowd came together around the people-trafficker. He directed them to stand in line near the dinghies. Most of the hopeful passengers were on their own, and carried small bags of possessions. Clutching Riona into her side Leonie stayed back when Quinn joined the queue. Before it was his turn to approach the man and empty his money belt, he saw five rolls of banknotes being handed over.

Then the trafficker dropped the bombshell. The $6,000 boat fare was now per refugee. Quinn felt sick. He pleaded with the man, who smirked and held his hand out for more. Times were bad, he said, real dangerous. Prices were going up everywhere. Dressed all in black, his pasty face was stark in the car light.

With what they had left from their savings, the sale of the truck, and Mannie Tarrant's funeral fund, Quinn and Leonie had 9,400 dollars. Enough for only one of them to board the boat. Quinn stood, speechless and stupid, and the man soon turned his attention to the next in line.

Leonie's questioning look drew Quinn back over to where she stood. When he whispered the news her face showed wide-eyed horror, then the furrowed brow of deep thought. Seconds later, grim and determined, she said, "Right."

With rising alarm, Quinn watched her grasp Riona's wrist and stride the few paces across the sand, her chin thrust out. Pushing into the queue ahead of an enormous man, she grabbed the trafficker's attention. After a whispered exchange, Quinn saw her nod and pat the man's arm in a gesture of apparent gratitude. She then ran back to Quinn with moonlight catching her determined smile, pulling a confused Riona beside her.

"Give me the money, now." Leonie held her hand out, panting.

Quinn shuffled their bundle of notes, trying to understand what was happening. "What did you say to him?"

"I appealed to him as a mother. C'mon, Quinn. If we give him all the money, he says Riona can go in the boat. We've got to get her safe, Q-T!"

"We can all go?" Quinn asked. A rumbling noise was building in the background. Leonie was shaking her head, looking back and forth between Quinn and the boat, holding Riona tight. The trafficker had dealt with his last customer, and now stood impassive, eyebrows raised, the hand outstretched again.

"No. Hurry, Quinn!" she said, grabbing the money. "He's gonna let Riona go for half price, but it's only one adult, Either Riona goes with one of us in the boat, or I take her to Miami with the man. He'll find us work to make more dough." She started back towards the trafficker, leaving a hurried kiss on Quinn's cheek. Riona was looking back at him.

The rumbling was now a roar, and the ground was trembling. Quinn never knew if his next words had been heard. "You and Riona can go in the boat. I'll stay here and follow–" The smiling trafficker was beckoning Leonie and Riona towards the black sedan. Looking behind him, he saw the boat that had towed the dinghies ashore disappearing back into the dimness. He made to turn and follow Leonie, against a tide of refugees streaming around him towards the flimsy craft.

What happened then would stay with Quinn forever. The car was lit by the sweeping beams of vehicles veering off the highway. The trafficker's eyes narrowed. He moved towards the sedan, now pulling Leonie by the wrist. Quinn saw her tense, pallid and wide-eyed, resisting the man as her head turned from Riona to Quinn and back towards the sedan.

Two trucks thundered onto the beach. Horns blared, searchlights swept the sand, and rapid gunfire filled the air. Puffs of sand erupted ever closer to the refugees. The panicking huddle around him fought to clamber into the boats, outboard motors coughing and spitting. Pulled by a desperate man, Quinn fell headlong into a dinghy, more bodies piling on top of him. The automatic gunfire drowned his shouts to Leonie as he tried to escape the tangled bodies. As he felt the boat float out into the waves, he forced his head above the gunwale. His last sight of Leonie and Riona was them being dragged into the black car, silhouetted against the night and lit by the strobe lighting of gun flashes. Riona wore her scream face.

Terror and shame choked Quinn as he cowered down in the flimsy craft, covering his ears and peering through smoke and sea spray. The dark sedan pulled onto the road above the beach, disappearing into the night with his wife and daughter.

Chapter Ten

2034 Ragged Island – Day One

He hoped he would be dead soon. There was sand in his mouth and now even his legs were burning, no longer cooled by the sloshing saline in the dinghy. His blistered body lay on a beach, but in his mind, the world was still floating.

Thoughts of his wife and daughter sparked hope in Quinn, until his next thought snuffed it out. Days earlier, he had watched from the dinghy he'd been dragged into, helpless to stop Leonie and Riona being led away into the night. The gangmaster hadn't glanced back, but Quinn's mind saw his face lit with lascivious glee.

The smoking, choking outboard had pushed the little craft just yards from the Florida shore when two militia trucks that had been spraying the strand with gunfire began strafing the sea. Minutes later the other dinghy was sinking, bloody bodies floating nearby.

Quinn owed his sorry survival to a huge stranger. It was the same man Leonie had pushed in front of minutes before, when she went in appeal to the trafficker who had cheated Quinn. As the fragile boat rocked out from the shore, the colossus had stood defiant at the stern, sacrificing himself to shield companions he had only just met. Soon after, holed and bleeding, he crumpled into the water. Quinn was one of three refugees left cowering between the boat's flimsy wooden sides.

Quinn's two companions were brothers. One of them had a compass on a lanyard, and steered until the outboard gave out when they were still within sight of the shore. After a couple of days of drifting Quinn roused from seasick stupor to find one of the brothers had died. As Quinn helped to heave his body into the sea he saw a bloody crater in the man's back. When the food ran out the other man despaired, gave Quinn his useless compass and followed his sibling over the side.

Weak, alone and with only rain to drink, Quinn drifted in the dinghy. When the sea roused itself he would cling to the gunwale for minutes or hours until the waves died down and he could let the bliss of coma swamp back over him.

Now, behind him he could hear waves breaking on sand. A singeing, salty breeze rubbed grit into blisters on his desiccated body. He let his eyes crack open, and once the searing blindness of the bright sun receded, he made out a bumpy horizon below a cornflower sky. He must have been been tipped out of the dinghy, thrown onto a beach.

A sudden gunshot terrified him. A single shriek echoed. Had he drifted back to the mainland and the raging civil war? Had it all been for nothing? Just let me die.

Over the panicked pulsing in his ears, he made out voices, coming from nearby. An innate desire to survive paralysed him. Death would have to wait.

As he held his breath, there were shouts, then laughter, another gunshot, cheering and talking. Exhaling at last, his thoughts focused. This couldn't be a routine militia patrol, they were too relaxed. The talking went on, still from the same direction, not any louder. These soldiers weren't on the move. If they were officers on leave, that could be even more dangerous. They might be drugged or drunk, trigger-happy.

Something else was wrong. The voices Quinn heard spoke English, but not the English of the Southern US. Had the PBC started bringing in foreign mercenaries?

Continuing to listen to the men's chatter and laughter, Quinn felt less threatened. They weren't coming for him. He doubted they were aware of his presence. Even if they were, he was too weak to move. He might as well lie where he was, let whatever happen. The voices melted into the background and his mind returned to his lost family, and pain.

When Quinn next woke his eyes were gritty. The sloping sand he lay on had taken an orange hue, his back cooling. He must have slept for some hours. The sun must be speeding down, he thought, unable to turn to look. The voices continued, but less animated.

His burnt body was cold and overwhelmed by pain. His neck screamed at him when he lifted his head. Stretching his fingers he felt sand, blown against him, half burying his right side. Thirst and hunger forced his limbs to move him. As he began to drag himself up the gentle slope, sand rasped his pale Irish skin.

The tops of trees appeared above his horizon. Quinn paused to listen. The strange accents. In the background, running water.

"More champagne, Isaac?" The words were slurred. Another shot rang out.

"I've had enough for today, thank you. Perhaps another line, though. Lay two lines out for me, would you?"

The other voice spoke again, coarser than 'Isaac'. "Where's bloody Horace gone anyway? Wasted, I suppose. Christ, he can't party like he used to."

"Saul's seeing to him. Needed topping up."

Quinn was alert enough to work out that there must be at least four men. Isaac was one of the two he could hear, and they seemed to be drunk, or drugged. Horace and Saul must be elsewhere.

Quinn crawled like a chilled lizard, edging up the beach, pausing when lights showed beyond tangled trees. Nearer, sparks were rising from a fire. Inching his head up more slowly than the sun was descending, he saw two men by the edge of a gleaming blue swimming pool, lights shimmering beneath its surface. One was long-limbed, skinny, with neat white hair. He was leaning on a cane, looking down on the other man who was seated at a glass table, his shiny scalp catching the light.

"Come on, Derek. Big day tomorrow," he said. The words were clearer now.

'Derek' stood up, pinching his nose. He was stouter and shorter than the man Quinn now knew must be Isaac. The two men weaved away into the jungle, guided by dim ground lights that edged a winding path. Night was falling fast, and as Quinn waited more and more lights flickered on. Vague shapes in the mirk became buildings among the palm trees. The men appeared to be heading towards huts on stilts, each with steps to a wooden terrace. This is like nowhere in Florida I know, he thought. Did I reach Cuba after all?

These strange men would be no immediate danger. In casual clothes and lounging beside a blue pool, they didn't appear to have guns. But Quinn hadn't forgotten the danger he was in. There were buildings. He'd heard gunshots. The men must have guards. He might be captured at any minute. Scared to move further, he surveyed the scene before him.

After years in privation trying to keep his family alive, the luxury on display was transfixing. The pool was fed by a stream, and Quinn's eyes followed it up a gentle slope through a grove of palms. As darkness deepened above, twinkling lights in and around the pool seemed to brighten, highlighting manicured gardens. An outflow stream tinkled as it channelled towards the sea, making his dry throat ache.

Thirst overcame Quinn's fear and pain. He slithered between trees, ignoring the possibility of a bullet in his back as he picked his way through a security cordon of spiky cacti and jagged rocks.

Exposed, he threw himself down to gulp water from the cool, fast stream. Its freshness shocked him but it was tasteless, unsatisfying after the brackish creek water of the Everglades.

Remembering himself, he slipped behind a bush. Guards would arrive any minute. All he heard, though, was flowing water and the jungle rousing itself for the night. His nostrils sensed food.

It was days since Quinn had eaten. In a futile gesture of sympathy he'd shared his little knapsack of dried fish with the bereaved brother in the dinghy. The poor man had drowned himself just hours later.

He risked venturing forward between the rocks, towards the pool. Scattered chairs and low tables cast long, shivering shadows and lights shimmered under blue water. He heard no shouts or advancing jackboots. His mouth watering for the first time in weeks and with an emptiness yawning deep in his midriff, hunger overpowered Quinn.

Glasses and plates were scattered on the tables, and he scooped congealing black fish eggs from a bowl. It didn't taste as good as the Florida gar roe, but it was the first thing he had eaten in days. His hunger intensified.

Fear evaporated as he moved from plate to plate, stuffing himself with crumbling sweet biscuit and delicate white fish. The men had barely touched their food.

He burped after draining warm, fizzy wine. A screech answered him, silencing the jungle's frogs and insects. Cursing himself for his recklessness, he ducked and crawled behind scratchy bushes bordering the path.

His gut was objecting to the combined assault by food and drink, cold sweat beading on his brow and colic crushing him. He fought against gravity as collapse drew him to the ground, the night's discordant sounds screaming in his ears.

When he came to, he couldn't tell how long he'd lain on the cold earth. He'd been fishing in his grandpa's pirogue in the Delta, but at the same time floating on a warm, sunlit Everglades creek. Now he was shivering in frightening darkness.

The pool's lights were off. Fleeting shimmers peeked from beyond trees, reflecting from the inky water. He brushed a large insect from his neck and stretched up to sit. As his senses sharpened, vague shadowy outlines clarified, and the calls of the jungle became distinct.

The sounds and smells were unfamiliar, though. This wasn't like Florida or Louisiana, and the sheer luxury of the pool in its landscaped setting were nothing like he'd imagined of Cuba.

The nocturnal chorus was hushing itself, and he knew daylight was coming. He crawled away towards the sea, following the efferent stream from the pool. He found a home beneath a leaning palm tree by the beach. Behind the hanging fringe of its exposed roots, he was as certain as he could be that patrolling guards wouldn't see him.

Shivering, and with sore, burned legs, he lay looking out over the sea. One by one the stars were switched off, and the sky began to lighten.

Chapter Eleven

Day Two

The sun was up above the trees when Quinn dared to emerge from his cocoon. His belly was aching. Last night's poolside titbits had only strengthened his hunger.

Still seeing no sign of any guards he crept into the trees, drawn towards the pool and the prospect of more scraps. Crouching in dense foliage he looked and listened. There was no one there, and all signs of last night's activity had been swept away.

Three tables had been laid with white tablecloths and shining silver, two chairs at each. Bamboo loungers were arranged in line, with neat pillows and folded white towels. The men he had seen must have staff, Quinn thought. Servants to pamper them and prepare breakfast. Still, there were no guns or soldiers.

The stream that fed the pool babbled, taunting his dusty mouth. He crept forwards, vicious branches jagging his bare torso. Between the screeches of birds, he heard dull, rhythmic thudding.

The noise seemed to be coming from beyond some trees. He could make out the huts he'd seen the previous night, but still no people. Dashing over a path he crouched to lap at cool water until he could swallow no more. Back under cover he lay down, a deep chill in his belly and a drum beating in his chest. He had to have been spotted.

But no guards came. When his heart slowed he thought he could hear voices, also from the direction of the huts. His nose prickled with hints of an aroma. Thirst quenched, his sense of smell took over. Bacon. He hadn't tasted it for years. For a moment he was back in Louisiana before he had ever heard of the PBC.

The men he had seen and heard the night before were nothing like the brutish PBC. With clipped English and no tattoos, he wondered if they were from the East coast. Somewhere cultured, maybe Connecticut or New England.

Lured by the smell he crawled on towards danger. The thudding continued, and as the outlines of the huts became visible through the jungle he heard chattering, one voice a woman's.

Concealed, he peeked out between waxy leaves. Lit by the sun, the shapeless buildings he'd seen last night were substantial dwellings. There were four cabins, suspended on dull steel posts. Three of them had wide wooden verandas facing out onto sloping sand. The stream Quinn had drunk from appeared to have been diverted to feed the swimming pool. Where it should have flowed onwards, instead Quinn saw a pristine, white beach. The cabins looked west over the azure sea, and for a moment he forgot his hunger and pictured idyllic sunsets.

The fourth building was drab and shaded, facing inland. The sounds and the alluring smell came from behind it. Servants' quarters, he guessed. He crawled on past the luxury dwellings, picking his wary way between rocks and shrubs.

The voices grew clearer and the aroma was torture. In an open area between the cabin and the enclosing jungle, a rope hung between two posts. As Quinn crept forward the thudding noise was explained.

A patterned rug in red and ochre hung over the line. It was being beaten by a young, dark girl swinging a wooden beater. Each thwacking impact ejected a little dust from the rug. He watched her, distracted by her regular, rhythmic movement.

The girl paused, turning to laugh over her shoulder. Above hissing and sizzling sounds Quinn heard a deeper voice. He edged forward until the broad back of a middle-aged black man was in view, standing at a bank of grills and hotplates arranged on a trestle.

Their words were easy for Quinn to translate. His Creole mother had spoken Spanish as well as French, and until she died when he was twelve Quinn had spoken both.

"Alita, stop that while I am cooking. You're spreading dust all over the ham!"

"Tell the fools it is pepper! Special island herbs. Here's some more for their eggs!" She laughed, beating the rug again.

He was right, Quinn thought, these people were servants. They didn't look threatening.

Shots had been fired last night, though. He looked all around him again, remembering his alarm. Bright flashes caught his eye. Beams of white sunlight shot between trees like lasers, reflecting from the serene sapphire pool. But still no guards or security.

Turning to the three larger cabins he saw each had a rear stairway down to a smooth path that appeared to lead into the jungle. The guards must be based along that path, he thought. They were bound to have sophisticated monitoring systems. He scanned around him for cameras. They were probably watching him now.

All he could do was wait for capture. He watched the girl take the rugs from the rope and disappear into the back cabin. She reappeared shortly afterwards with three trays which she laid out on a counter beside the man. He deftly transferred bacon and eggs to plates, and she added a jug of orange juice from a low refrigerator. The cook took a basket of bread rolls from an oven. They had a well-equipped outside kitchen.

Salivating, Quinn watched the girl as she walked swiftly towards the luxury cabins, sashaying back a short time later to collect another tray. His thoughts turned to Leonie and his daughter Riona.

The smell from the hotplates drew him on round the perimeter of the clearing. Even capture would be worth it to taste that bacon. Concealed just a yard from the cookers, he listened to an array of meats sizzling amongst tomatoes and mushrooms. For a moment the sight of king boletes transported him back five years to a New Orleans café, the day he and his father had gone to the rally. Just before the civil war had started.

The cook began piling up his pots and utensils, and Quinn's hopes rose when the man took them away into the back cabin. He left two breakfast plates on a warmer, but before Quinn could break cover to steal them, the girl returned. As she lifted the plates and turned away, Quinn slumped down into the vegetation, all tantalising aromas replaced by smells of moist earth and pungent leaves.

Soon the girl was making repeated trips to and fro bringing dirty plates back from the luxury cabins. She scraped food scraps into a bin, and Quinn took his chance when she went into the servants' cabin with some of the crockery.

Two pieces of fried bread were poking out from a pile of plates. He slithered down a slight slope to snake a hand up and pull the greasy bread free. A silver fork slipped from the top of the pile, reflected sunlight flashing at Quinn as it appeared to fall in slow motion towards the hotplate. A metallic clatter made birds screech in alarm, the sound echoing between his ears as he darted back under cover. Cramming his mouth, he resigned himself to capture. The last meal of a condemned man.

Back for her next dishwashing pile, the girl hesitated, looking down at the fork lying in the dirt underneath the trestle. Quinn watched as she leaned down for it. She paused again, looking puzzled, scanning left and right into the overhanging trees. She murmured to herself, leaning forwards to check the ground on the other side of the worktop. Gathering up the dirty dishes she turned to go, but stopped stock still, staring directly in Quinn's direction. Survival reflexes stopped him chewing. From behind his leafy veil, he stared back at her for a lifetime.

Eventually, she shook her head and turned to head back to the cabin. He heard her mutter, "Mi imaginación! Los pájaros."

Chapter Twelve

When the girl tripped away with the remaining crockery, Quinn stayed paralysed by fear, struggling to believe she hadn't seen him. When he finally decided it was safe to escape back to his beach shelter, the cook came out of the cabin. He was carrying garden tools and started trimming shrubs near the pool.

His escape route now blocked, Quinn could only crawl up an incline through a dense, untended tangle that merged with the jungle. He might reach the beach by skirting round the other side of the compound, he thought. Before he'd gone far, he came across a wild pig, which appeared to have been incinerated by an electric fence. If it hadn't been for the smell of charred meat, he would have stumbled into the fence and electrocuted himself.

His mouth watering, he retreated and moved more directly towards the sea. He would have to pass close by the cabins, but he had no choice if he was to avoid capture. Pausing, he heard the same voices and accents from the previous night. Creeping onwards, soon he could see three men lounging on a raked beach, shaded by thatched umbrellas. He recognised one of them, Derek who he'd seen the previous evening. Going any further meant being seen immediately. With the electric fence behind him and the cook cum gardener blocking his only other route to the sea, Quinn was trapped.

His hunger had only been made worse by the puny morsel of fried bread he had stolen, and his spirits were already sinking fast when a gunshot sent birds screeching.

"Some fizz, Saul?"

When his heart slowed, Quinn smiled to himself at the irony. The gunshots had been corks popping. The men on loungers were drinking champagne.

Despite the mid-morning heat, one of them wore long sleeves and trousers, topped with a USNo.1 baseball cap. Distinctive in its bright red and white quarters, it brought hairs on Quinn's neck to attention even before its wearer turned and the logo came into view. But this man had no gun or bullet belt, and his face bore no tattoos. He was not PBC.

"It's too early for me, Horace," the cap wearer said. "Derek, take that bottle from him. He's had enough already."

A podgy, sallow man in the shade of a thatched umbrella swigged furiously from a bottle. Horace, Quinn thought. He watched Derek get up and wrestle the champagne from him.

"Fucking, fucking, fuck! Dombey you fucking spoilsport!" The fat one, Horace, slumped back into his chair, his limp right arm hanging down and his head to one side. He was either very drunk or drugged. Quinn remembered talk of 'bloody Horace' needing 'topping up.'

Weak as Quinn was, he felt no direct threat. These weren't fighting men, and behaved more like civilians on vacation than soldiers on leave. From their accents, he now suspected they might be British.

He had more to fear from the men's servants. There had to be more of them, and probably armed guards. He looked back towards the cabins where the gardener was still busy pruning and sweeping.

Isaac, the tall man he had seen before, now came striding along a slatted wood pathway towards the beach. Again carrying his cane, with his other hand he held a cell phone to his ear. Upright and precise, he wasn't wobbling now.

"Good morning, Derek; Saul; Horace. Oh...Horace! Not already, old chap!"

With no opportunity to move on, Quinn lay listening, trying to follow the men's conversation. The one in the USNo.1 cap responded to 'Saul.' Horace had cursed him as 'Dombey.' Saul Dombey, thought Quinn. Have I heard that name before?

Derek stood up and swung a chair into place. "There you go, Isaac."

Back beyond the cabins the gardener was still working his way around the compound. With no option but to stay put, Quinn tried to make himself as comfortable as he could in his shaded concealment.

Twice while Quinn watched and listened, the servant girl came from between the cabins. Each time she approached, the men paused their conversation. Isaac thanked her and Derek helped her serve tea, coffee and cake. At one point, Fat Horace roused and leered at her, raising an arm in her direction.

"Come here, girl, I want you," he slobbered as she walked round picking up glasses and cups, keeping her distance.

"Oh Horace, give it a rest." Derek smiled apologetically towards the maid. "Don't pay any attention to him, Alita. He couldn't hurt you nowadays." From his hiding place in the undergrowth, Quinn watched her walking by. The serrated edges of leaves in front of his eyes broke her lithe movement like an ancient movie film. She passed within five yards of him, muttering to herself, and he thought he could smell her fragrance.

"Let me have more fizz!" Horace was shouting. "I'm phoning Marcus. Where is he, anyway?"

Isaac sighed. "Oh dear, poor Horace is back in 2020 again. Plus ça change, if you'll excuse my French."

Saul Dombey was looking daggers at Horace. "Cretin! When will you fucking learn? You may have had Marcus Finch's ear in the past, but he isn't the fucking president now. There's no US at all, for fuck's sake."

These men are friends of the President? Until he heard Finch's name, Quinn's mind had been wandering.

Dombey went on, spitting his words now. "And those stupid Yanks sold everything they had to the highest bidder! Refineries, pipelines, Christ, even the fucking satellites for fuck's sake! All of it! Chinese, Russian whoever the fuck–"

"Calm down, Saul, calm down. Here, smoke this."

Dombey threw his USNo.1 cap on the sand, reaching out to accept the fat cigarette Derek was holding. Before it reached his lips, Horace mumbled something Quinn couldn't hear, and Dombey, who had turned away, now rounded on him again, his left eyebrow raised.

"What did you say? We should have stayed in Europe? We shouldn't have left? Don't you fucking dare start that again. You were all for it."

The United Kingdom leaving Europe was something Quinn had been made to study at college.

Dombey went on. "And that's what kicked off the whole fucking shambles we're in now. Started the States off on their fucking race to the bottom."

Isaac stepped forward, ushering Saul Dombey towards a lounger. "Oh, Saul, calm down," he was saying. "You still have your Saudis. And we're arming both sides everywhere we can. I made several millions last week alone. Civil wars mean money, and South America is even more lucrative than the States have been. I've always said..."

"I know! I know... 'The arms trade is our real banker.'" Dombey, now more truculent than aggressive, sat on the lounger with his red and white cap in his hands.

"Look, Saul old boy, we have more riches than we could have dreamt of if we were still trading in the markets." Isaac sat down, picking up an iPad. They have internet, thought Quinn.

Dombey was back on his feet. Pacing on the white sand, in a raised voice he said, "The fucking foreigners have taken back control of Europe. And everything fucking else that was ours!" Quinn noticed the eyebrow again.

Derek, the small man with the shaved head, now took a turn at calming Dombey. He walked across the sand with a glass in his hand.

"Here, Saul, come and sit down. I asked Alita to make you a Jack Daniels."

Dombey took the drink. Guided back to sit under a straw umbrella, he sat down looking like a dejected schoolboy.

Quinn was close enough to hear every word. Other than the snippets from the radio in the Everglades he had heard no news for years. In the next few minutes he heard talk of the wars in the US and all over South America. And if he understood, these men on Ragged Island were profiting from the conflict. Selling arms to both sides.

"You shouldn't get so angry, Saul," Isaac said. "Bad for your heart."

Saul sat back, pointing over his shoulder with a thumb. "That slob Witte sets me off. Always back in past. The UK's fucking history!" The eyebrow had risen again.

"Now, now, Saul," Isaac said, "Horace bought us the island, remember?" He waved around him at the cabins, the pristine beach.

As if on cue, Horace roused. "It should be called Sevenquean Island."

Dombey looked across at Isaac. "I know, I know, Horace Witte owns a fucking bank!" Through gritted teeth, he said, "But RI7 was all my idea."

So Horace's surname is Witte, thought Quinn. He looked at Witte. *That* owns a bank?

Isaac went on. "The RI7 was very clever of you. With everything you've done for The Table, I should be not in the least bit surprised if they offer you a seat."

Derek spoke. "Let me fetch you another drink, Saul. Isaac's right, you'll soon be..."

"Oh, fuck off, Vernon, you low-life grammar-school imbecile! You don't understand any of it."

Quinn had the impression Derek, whose surname he now knew to be Vernon, was very much the subordinate member of the group. Isaac had spoken of his wealth in billions. Horace Witte bragged of having bought Ragged Island, and he owned a bank. Dombey, though, seemed to think himself superior even to them. He was wondering what 'The Table' might be when their next topic revolted him.

Isaac got up to pour more tea. "Now, boys, let's calm down, shall we?" He was looking at Dombey. "The special flight should land soon and you know what that means, Saul. We can all blow off steam."

Saul Dombey's angry, disaffected expression softened. His eyes narrowed, a suggestive curl at the corners of his mouth. "Yes, and they promised some even younger girls this time." The men's sudden leeriness made Quinn squirm. Isaac's next words deepened his discomfort. "At least last time around they finally brought me a couple of boys."

Quinn shrank back into his foliage, disgusted. One minute these awful men talked of arms dealing and profit, the next about girls and boys being delivered for them.

Isaac sprang up from his deckchair, like a spring-loaded stick insect.

"Hark! I think I can hear Max's jet. I'm going for a long soak to prepare. Alita! Draw me a bath, will you?"

Chapter Thirteen

The surreal drama playing out in front of Quinn had kept his attention while he waited for an opportunity to escape. He was becoming distracted now. Having drunk his fill of water last night and this morning, for the first time in days he felt a pressing need to empty his bladder.

Saul Dombey followed Isaac back to the cabins, as did Derek Vernon once he had spread sun cream over bloated Horace's folds. With only snoring Horace Witte left on the beach, Quinn waited for a chance to escape. Every now and then Witte would stir and mumble something, and once he sat up, grunting "Sevenquean" before slumping back to unconsciousness. It was what he'd said Ragged Island should now be called.

After the joy of a long pee in the dirt under a bush, Quinn crept along near the electric fence. The vegetation thinned as he neared the sea, the pool's outflow stream channelling across the strand between him and his hiding place. He was tempted to scoop a few mouthfuls of water but scurried on, waiting for a bullet. Back in the shelter of his tree root nest, he lay motionless until the pulsing in his neck lessened and his breathing slowed.

Quinn hid in stifling shade throughout the afternoon, the fried bread of that morning a haunting memory on his palate.

He wondered what sort of place he had washed up in. The men at the pool had a relaxed air of security. Surely they must have protection, but still no guards had come.

It made no sense. A group of Englishmen, very wealthy, living on this remote tropical beach. After the first time he had seen and heard them Quinn had wondered if starvation and dehydration could have made him hallucinate. Now he had seen them again, and what he had overheard was hard to process.

He was disgusted that the men were expecting a delivery of young people, presumably for them to defile. That was bad enough, but they also claimed to have influenced, or even caused, some of the tumult of the last decades. They'd spoken of making fortunes from the Covid pandemic, and the arms trade.

The odd man named Isaac had said, "Civil wars mean money as long as you're arming both sides." He'd gone on to say it had been the standard practice of the British 'for centuries,' adding, "Our transatlantic cousins picked up that trick from us, I'm proud to say."

Saul Dombey had shocked him most, though, when he said the collapse of the United Kingdom had been the spark that lit a fire under the US.

Quinn's exhausted mind wandered back and forth between this present unreal situation and his dream-like life before the war, passing through the nightmare years in between. He lay looking up at the splaying roots that formed the roof of his shelter like nature's basketwork. Rayville and the smells of Louisiana taunted him from his past. He thought of his father. This time he could picture his dad's high forehead, widely-spaced eyes and red hair. For years it had been Mannie's bloody, torn face that starred in his nightmares.

Before a hungry sleep overtook him, Quinn's thoughts were of his life back in Louisiana before the war.

###

Some of the men from the cabins had appeared in Quinn's sleep. Stick-like Isaac had strolled by swinging his walking cane. Horace Witte's grotesque body had Derek Vernon's face one minute, Saul Dombey's the next. Quinn marched with them all on a rally in London. Mannie was there.

When he woke, his mouth was dry and his teeth gritty. He looked through a gap in his protective curtain of tangled roots and saw the sun descending. It seemed to move ever faster and grew into a huge orange as it approached the sea. It wouldn't be long before nightfall, and a safe drink from the stream.

While he waited, Quinn's mind drifted back to something he had heard that afternoon that resonated with him. Dombey's fury about the UK's relationship with Europe reminded Quinn of his third year at college, before the civil war.

Professor Jill Carson, head of the International Affairs module had been obsessed with Europe. She directed Quinn to produce a paper on the United Kingdom's exit from the European Union a decade earlier. With only a vague idea of the make-up of the UK, Quinn had used *Cuubl:-)* to check exactly where it was. He remembered commentators having opposing points of view. To some the UK's departure would cause weakening and eventual collapse of Europe. Others predicted European prosperity borne of a renewed cohesiveness between the remaining states. Quinn was bored by the subject.

Professor Carson's ideas were fanciful, but they allowed Quinn to practice writing and publishing. By then in his third year at college he saw a career ahead as an investigative journalist. He produced a series of blog posts under the banner "Power Beneath." It examined another of the professor's hypotheses, that a cabal of self-interested billionaires based in London had brought about the UK's exit from Europe.

Professor Carson believed this English group was a mere cog in a much larger mechanism – a secretive worldwide power brokerage, more powerful than any of the traditional superpowers. As well as influencing governments everywhere, it manipulated public opinion using global social media algorithms. It was Carson's view that this organisation – she didn't have a name for it – had ordered the UK's exit from Europe.

Quinn had humoured her. At that time he considered the rest of the world unimportant. The IA module was a box he had to tick.

In the five years since, his country had descended into a protracted civil war that showed no signs of ending. Now he'd heard weird Englishmen on a remote desert island claim the USA no longer even existed. Worse, they had appeared to take responsibility for that. He remembered Dombey saying the UK had 'started the States off on their fucking race to the bottom.'

I've had too much sun he thought, shaking away his college professor's outlandish beliefs and the dream-like unreality of his present situation. He sat up, and the woody canopy of his shelter scratched his inflamed forehead. He decided it was dark enough to emerge from cover and find some water. If he didn't he would lose his mind altogether.

After slaking his thirst at the stream, the prospect of more scraps of food drew him onwards. In the evening darkness, he made his careful way towards the blue iridescence of the pool. From concealment in foliage, he could see that the poolside was deserted. Blue light wavered over plates, books, and glasses left on low tables. The loungers now lay at random angles, some pulled together into pairs. Brighter lights shone from beyond the palm trees where he knew the cabins were, and he thought he could hear music and girls laughing.

Quinn watched the path but could see no one. He guessed some kind of social gathering had moved indoors when nightfall approached. He tried not to think about who had been served up to the men.

Creeping out of cover he crawled towards the tables, salivating. He crammed three crackers into his mouth. They were spread with a dark brown paste, and a spicy, meaty flavour caught the back of his throat. On another table across the pool, he could see a neat pile of sandwiches. Caution now overcome, he sped round to grab as many of the crustless triangles as he could, devouring two before he returned to the shadows of the shrubs. For a moment all he heard was his noisy chomping.

Plates clanked nearby and he locked his jaw, scared to chew or swallow. The servant girl from the cabins had arrived to clear up. She had to have seen him as she came along the path. While she gathered detritus from the tables and loungers she sang to herself. She didn't look once in his direction, even though he knew in his rush he hadn't fully concealed himself.

The girl piled dishes onto a tray and placed it on the table nearest the path. She moved between the loungers shaking crumbs from towels and draping them over her arm. As she neared Quinn's hiding place, light reflected from the olive skin of her bare calves.

Something appeared to catch her eye, making her pause and stop humming. She sighed, before edging around a lounger and dropping the pile of towels on it. Quinn was sure she could hear his heart thumping as she moved straight towards him. Her legs were within three feet of him when with horror he noticed he had dropped a sandwich. She crouched to retrieve it from the crazy paving, muttering impatiently to herself.

When the girl stood up and turned to move on, Quinn allowed himself a silent breath. But she stopped, turned back to face the bushes, and crouched down. Her loose tan shorts rode up over smooth tanned thighs and Quinn averted his gaze upward. He looked straight into her big, smiling eyes.

Chapter Fourteen

Day Three

Quinn spent a restless night in his beach sanctuary, waiting for inevitable capture. In fitful dozes, he saw Leonie serving tea to the men on the loungers and heard yet again guns on a Florida beach. Now awake, he slowly untangled his dreams from reality. The white sun was high, and he faced a long, hot day with no water.

He knew the girl had seen him. Why had she looked away and carried on? Why hadn't she sent the guards? Perhaps she hadn't noticed him after all? She hadn't been real. He had hallucinated, after the rush the food had given him.

The men had called her Alita. Her eyes had fixed on his. They'd been smiling eyes. The pool lights had formed a halo around the dark silhouette of her pretty face, and when he closed his eyes, her image remained.

He tried to think of Leonie instead. Leonie and Riona, who could have been taken anywhere by the man who took all their money. When he'd seen them spirited into the dusk, he'd been cowering in the dinghy with his doomed companions. The roar of the approaching trucks and the onset of gunfire had focused his instincts on his own guilty survival. In his days drifting in the dinghy, when there had been periods of lucid thought, he'd wept his eyes dry. Since then, he had tried hard not to think of them. Now he forced himself to.

It was hard to banish visions of the girl in her shorts.

By late evening, he had still not been discovered. His thirst fought with the risk of meeting the girl again. Water won. He had to break cover.

He made himself wait until the sky was as dark as stars would allow, then longer until he thought she would have finished her work. The only sound was the jungle night. First, he supped at the stream. Creeping on, a dim haze between trees ahead grew paler until the brightly lit pool emerged. The tinkling stream that fed it ruffled the surface, a blue canvas splodged with blobs of quivering white.

He risked stretching up out of concealment, looking for more discarded scraps. The tables were bare and the crazy paving swept. His empty stomach groaned at the thought of another night of hunger. But as he turned away, the light reflected from something white. A little parcel, resting on a rock. He regarded it for some minutes, suspicious but intrigued.

It was proof the girl had seen him. Placed exactly where he had been when their eyes met, the parcel was wrapped in folded cloth. It had to be a trap. A trap for him, that only she could have set.

He hated her. Devious, scheming witch. She'd smiled at him, showing no alarm. Twenty-four hours had elapsed since they saw each other, and no sirens had screamed. No search party had sought him out. She had tortured him, while she planned to set this trap.

The parcel looked at him from its rock. He could smell food.

Quinn accepted defeat. Temptation pulled him forward through shrubs to grasp the package. Clutching it under his arm, he hurried into the night waiting for floodlights and sirens.

Back under cover, he lay until his palpitations slowed. He looked at the parcel. Its linen wrapping was decorated by milky strips of moonlight filtered by his palm root curtain. A tantalising aroma mingled with the fragrance of fresh laundry. His mouth watered.

After one last anxious peer along the dark beach he untied a towelling strap, unwrapping the parcel onto the dry, cooling sand. Seconds later he had torn through folded foil and devoured the first of three rotis, swallowing it without tasting the filling. He slowed himself to savour the other two. Still warm, the flatbreads enclosed a spiced mix of chicken and potato. He lay back on the sand, wishing the taste in his mouth would last forever.

A welcome warmth in his belly and the gentle lapping of the calm sea soporated and soothed Quinn into careless sleep.

Chapter Fifteen

Day Four

Quinn was startled awake by sirens. The sound filled his head, frantic, rising and falling, then becoming less harsh; the lazy wauls of seabirds. His right ear was gritty with sand, folded against his head, and the taste of last night's feast had dried on his lips. It had been another cold night, but now the bright sunlight had warmed his shelter. He became aware of his bladder, and rolled over to push himself up. Stretching, once again he scraped his head on the rough roots above.

Grabbing at the empty foil wrapping he licked it clean before burying it in the sand. The napkin that had held last night's meal was still partially folded. For the first time, he noticed the present he had been left was double-wrapped. An edge of pale, fawn cloth showed between two squares of stiff, white linen. He pulled the napkins apart to find a folded pair of light cotton shorts. An image of the girl's thighs in the same shorts flashed in front of him. He looked down at his own pair, rags now encrusted with sand, salt, and fish scales.

After relieving himself in a shaded hollow in the forest, he buried his waste and his ragged shorts. Returning naked towards his cage, he paused to scan the beach north and south. Breaking cover, he scuttled to the sea. Lying flat in the shallows he rinsed himself clean, refreshed by the cool shock of the water.

The sun's heat dried him by the time he had darted the few yards back to his tree root home. Pulling out the new shorts he stepped into them before slipping back into the shelter. The softness of the fresh fabric against his washed body brought to his mind a brief waft of his mother's clean washing.

Swatting away that memory as his father had taught him to, his thoughts returned to the gift. It couldn't have been a trap, or he'd have been captured by now, or worse. Why had the girl been kind to him? Were her employers altruists? Had they encouraged her to help him? He dismissed that thought. They were callous arms dealers, and probably paedophiles.

No, the girl's gesture of kindness had been her own. He looked at his new shorts. Sitting on a napkin to keep them clean, he ran his hands over the smooth fabric and felt something in the right-side pocket. Unbuttoning it, he pulled out a rectangle of stiff card. It was like one of the business cards Joe Crannock handed out. By moving into the light by the edge of his shaded canopy he could see neat handwriting.

'Estas a salvo'

Spanish. You are safe. He repeated the words to himself. "You are safe." Had the girl written them? On the other side of the card, 'RI7' was printed in bold capitals, royal blue against the matt white card. The same was embroidered on the linen napkins. And on the breast pocket of the girl's polo shirt.

When evening finally came Quinn dared to leave cover, a little earlier than the previous night. Although some of him still thought 'Estas a salvo' was a cruel lure to tempt him into a trap, he was impatient to know if he would find another gift. He paused only briefly to drink at the stream.

When he approached the poolside, his shoulders drooped. He cursed himself for not waiting. The low tables between the loungers still bore the strewn detritus of the day's luxuries, but the rock where he'd found the gift was bare. The girl, Alita he allowed himself to call her, hadn't been yet.

She might come any minute to start her chores. Despite her apparent kindness Quinn didn't want to be seen. She might not be alone. He put the folded napkins on the rock where he'd found them, before turning to creep back the way he had come. Weaving between rocks and shrubs he passed the disordered array of loungers. A smell drew his eyes towards a plate balanced precariously on the edge of a side table. More of the same crackers he had sampled two evenings ago.

A couple of reckless minutes later he lay back in the shrubs with his tongue cemented to the roof of his mouth by the sticky meat spread. The intense flavour and the dry biscuit demanded water, and as if he no longer cared he returned to the tables to drain the dregs of water, beer and what he thought might be milky tea. A movement caught his attention and drew him back to his senses. Someone had crossed in front of the lights by the path from the cabins. He was in full view.

For an instant, his mind played a film of his life, backwards. Leonie in the Everglades, his tiny daughter in her cot, his father in tears, his mother's shining funeral casket. He was beaten. They had discovered him.

It was the girl. She stopped at the edge of the pool, and though he was certain he'd been spotted Quinn dived under the cover of the bushes. He lay panting, waiting. Glasses clinked and plates clattered. The girl continued with her duties, swishing her brush on the paving and humming, louder as she made her way round the pool towards him.

The splayed, finger-like leaflets of the bush he had chosen provided scant cover, and when she stopped just a yard away, he knew she could see him, even if she couldn't hear his heart's drumming.

"Estas a salvo," she whispered. The words echoed louder and louder around his head, drowning the beating in his ears. Her brush started moving and her sandals turned away. He watched her gather crockery and glasses, and she looked over her shoulder at him as she bent to lift a tray. Her muscled calves headed away, and he watched her walk back up the path and out of view. Quinn felt a nervous laugh shake his diaphragm, then vomited a mouthful of warm liquid. It just missed his new shorts.

When his thoughts had reordered, the only sounds were the bubbling of the pool pump and screeches from the jungle. About to start his crawl back towards the beach, he stopped and took a last look at the tables for scraps the girl might have missed. She had left him another gift.

Chapter Sixteen

Day Five

After sleeping all night with a full stomach Quinn felt secure enough to wash in the sea as the sun broke over the hills above the beach. The previous evening he had snatched the parcel before returning to his hideaway as furtively as his hunger would allow. This time the gift contained the same delicious rotis, three sweet cookies and two plastic bottles of water. Like the linen and the clothes, each bottle bore the RI7 logo. I heard the men on the beach talking about 'RI7,' he thought.

In between the napkins, this time he'd found a polo shirt to match the shorts. It was when he'd pulled on the shirt he found the note in its breast pocket.

Quinn read the note yet again. Each time he had woken overnight, he had unfolded the paper to make sure he hadn't dreamt the words.

"DOMINGO. 8.00 pm. Alita y Robert."

It was an invitation. Or a trap. But the girl had now seen him twice and brought him food and clothes. If she had been going to raise the alarm he would have already been captured. Alita, as he had heard her masters address her. *'Alita! draw me a bath, will you?'* The note confirmed her name. Now she had told him herself. He guessed Robert was the cook, the man who also tended the gardens.

They wanted to meet him on Sunday. Since he'd left his job on the fishing boat in Destin, Quinn knew he and his family had spent three dry seasons in the Everglades. So the year was now 2034. He knew from the trafficker it was in October that he'd left the Keys, and he guessed he had spent at least a week in the dinghy and a few days on this beach. But he had no way of knowing what day of the week it was.

To accept the invitation would mean going to the poolside after sundown every evening until the girl and the cook turned up.

When darkness fell that day, he started out for the poolside. Hearing laughter and music from the direction of the beach area, he moved slowly. Bright lights flashed at him from between the palm trees as he edged forward. Nearing the poolside he saw tables and a wheeled barbecue.

The man who must be Robert was preparing food, and while Quinn watched from the shadows he saw four figures come down the path from the direction of the cabins. Holding hands with a girl and a boy, he recognised Isaac and Derek. More young party guests and their older hosts soon followed them, and Robert began serving food and drink.

Quinn watched with a mixture of disappointment and revulsion. Long after he was sure eight o'clock had come and gone, he gave up for the night and took his hunger back to his hideout.

Chapter Seventeen

Day Six

Quinn spent the next day cursing himself for finishing all the food Alita had left him. Two furtive forays to the stream to fill his water bottles did little to break the day. Both times he heard shrieks, laughter, and music, and could tell that last night's party was still going on. He hoped that meant there would be some leftover food.

Still with no idea if this was Sunday, Quinn was under his customary bush by the pool not long after sundown. Chattering, chairs scraping, and occasional girlish squeals had continued to reach him through the trees until well into the afternoon, but now the poolside was silent. He had watched a jet plane climb away, trying not to think about those on board.

On a trolley, he could see a large pile of crockery, scrunched napkins and used cutlery. The tables were bare, but crumbs and smears of trodden food soiled the floor tiles. A martini glass lay on its side at the edge of the pool.

He toyed with the idea of sneaking over to scavenge for scraps, but decided to wait. If the two servants had invited him here, then surely they would bring him food? Please let this be Sunday. Domingo. 8.00 pm. Alita y Robert.

Despite the invitation, Quinn's fear surged when the man he knew must be Robert came down the path with a pail and mop. The girl, Alita, was with him, just ahead and looking straight through the leafy curtain Quinn cowered behind. Her smiling face glistered in the reflected light, and he thought her eyes flashed excitement. She was whispering to Robert as they approached the poolside.

Robert stopped at the end of the path and set about scrubbing the tiles, throwing frequent, pointed glances in Quinn's direction. He looked anxious, but Alita strode confidently to a table two yards from Quinn and wiped it clean before setting on it a large linen parcel. As she turned away, she flicked her brown eyes between the gift and Quinn's hiding place before setting about wiping chairs. Was she inviting or taunting him?

As the man mopped his way around the pool towards him Quinn's pulse sped up and his crouching limbs stiffened. Abruptly, the man leant his mop against a chair. He stood with his back to Quinn, not a yard away. Drawing cigarettes from his shorts pocket he shuffled his feet as he scrabbled to light one. Then with his free hand, he pointed at the parcel on the table in front of him and hissed, "It's for you."

Quinn's breathing stopped and his head whirled. He still feared a trap. It surprised him that the man had used English. Alita had also stopped work and moved to stand next to Robert. They were waiting, and Quinn's dry mouth croaked when he tried to whisper, "Thank you. Gracias."

Alita spoke. "It is OK. You can come out. They will not be coming here tonight." Her English was perfect. When he didn't move Robert turned round and reached forward to part the vegetation. Pool lights shone on Quinn's face like a searchlight, and he shrank back.

"Come. It is safe. I am Robert Moncur. Do as my daughter says." The man beckoned to him, and Quinn stood up, his eyes fixed on the path from the cabins. Robert held out his cigarettes and smiled.

"Alita is right, they will not come." He kept his voice low. "But we must be careful, they mustn't know you are here." He grinned and held an imaginary glass to his lips. "But they will know nothing tonight after their party. They drink all day and snort cocaine when they have girls to play with. We will have peace until they have recovered."

"They are filthy pigs." Alita pretended to spit. "Those girls are babies; they don't know what they are doing."

Quinn was now leaning forward from the bushes. "Girls to play with? D'you mean...?" He didn't want to say it out loud.

"Yes. They fly them in, use them and send them back." Robert paused and turned to Alita. "Did you see the new whoremaster? The ginger one?"

"I heard them say the other one is dead. An accident. Good!" She spat on the ground for real this time.

Quinn stepped over a low wall bordering the crazy paving, and stood between them. "Thank you. For the food, and my clothes." All three of them were now dressed in the same tan cotton shorts and matching polos. The silk embroidery of the RI7 logo reflected light when they faced the pool.

"What is your name?"

"Q-T." He wasn't sure why he used the abbreviation.

She smiled. "Well, Cutie, you are hungry. Sit and eat. We will keep you safe."

"Q – T. My name is Quinn Tarrant. He shook Robert's hand, then Alita's, and sat down to unwrap the linen parcel they had brought him. There was another set of clothes and a towel. He relaxed as he ate more rotis, and enjoyed watching Alita continue her chores while Robert finished sweeping. It was the first time he had sat at a table to eat for three years.

Robert's voice drew his attention. "Alita, look away."

"Oh, Papa! You must not." She smiled at Quinn and shook her head. Robert stood at the end of the pool and emptied his bladder into the water, a large white smile on his face. "He does that every night."

"I hate them. I think of them swimming in my piss when I spit in their food," Robert said as he returned and sat at the table next to Quinn, who glanced towards the pool's outflow, his water supply. Cleaner than creek water at least, he thought.

After wiping his mouth on a napkin Quinn sat back, exhaled, and smiled in satisfaction. "Thank you. For all this. I thought the guards would find me and kill me."

"There are no guards. They don't need guards. There is no way in or out of here except the tunnel, and they have fingerprint codes to lock and unlock the steel gates. It was a miracle you dodged between the beach fences. If you hadn't washed up at night in the middle of a storm you'd have been seen right away."

"What tunnel?"

Alita put down a tray of dishes on another table and joined Quinn and Robert. "You have seen the cabins, I think? I saw you at the breakfast bar."

"You knew I was there?"

Ignoring his surprise Alita continued, "At the back of the cabins there is a path to the tunnel. It is the only way in or out of here. There are steel security doors. With the electric fence, we are in a prison."

Quinn didn't understand. "What do you mean? Are you – captives? Slaves?"

Robert continued. "Supplies come in through the tunnel. The outer gates have to be opened by triple-lock security. I can't open them. It's only when they've locked them again that I can open the inner doors to carry their precious English food in." He spoke through gritted teeth.

"And that is how Cleeter brings their girls and boys in." Alita spat again.

"Cleeter?"

Alita and her father looked at each other, and Robert took Alita's hand. "My daughter was one of Cleeter's girls. When I found out what she was being made to do for him I went to him with money. To try to make it stop. He is so powerful." Robert had tears in his eyes.

Quinn didn't know what to say. He looked at Alita. She glared at Robert.

"This Cleeter, he's a pimp?" whispered Quinn, still looking at Alita.

Robert snorted. "Hmph. Cleeter's no low-life street pimp. He's a billionaire, supplies girls to powerful people. A huge international operation. He's untouchable." He turned away and before he went on Quinn heard what might have been a sob. "One of his women tricked Alita in Nassau."

Quinn was shaking his head in confusion and looking in horror at Alita. She was staring at nothing, motionless with a hard expression. After a pause, she swallowed before beginning to speak in a monotone. "She came to my school and asked me and my friend to help her with childminding. She paid us, gave us gifts. She was nice. Like a mother." Now Quinn saw tears in the corners of Alita's eyes. "But then it started."

Robert broke in. "He doesn't need to know more, Litl-A." He looked at Quinn. "Will you help us?"

"Help you? Me? How? I mean..." Quinn put his hands out in a gesture of helplessness.

"I found your boat. We can escape."

Chapter Eighteen

Back in his shelter after two bottles of Kalik and a feast of Alita's rotis, Quinn lay with a stretched, painful stomach. He hadn't had beer for years, but his head was clear as he retold himself his new friends' story.

Robert Moncur had agreed to work on Ragged Island to prevent the onward sale of his daughter. As he spoke Quinn wondered if describing his daughter as a commodity, part of a transaction, helped Robert deflect himself from thinking about what she had been used for. By then twenty years old she had outgrown her usefulness to Cleeter. She would have been passed on to a different market had Robert not sold his taxi to buy her back. There was an additional price to pay for Alita's freedom, however. Father and daughter were now both enslaved, forced to work where Cleeter's fixer commanded.

"'Buy One, Get One Free.'" Repeating the fixer's treacherous words had silenced Robert for a moment, and Quinn had looked away, embarrassed for him. There were tears on Alita's cheeks.

More than a year on Robert and Alita were still trapped, forced to work for the men on Ragged Island. Quinn had never heard of the island. He now knew that by the time he had been shipwrecked, currents had swept the drifting dinghy way past its target. Ragged Island was some 150 miles north and east of Cuba.

Robert had found the battered craft upturned on the beach one morning. He had dragged it into the forest, already thinking of ways he and Alita might escape. When he noticed what he thought was a drowned corpse on the strand he decided not to tell his masters in case they discovered the dinghy. Intending to bury the body he returned to the beach in darkness, only to find it had gone. Robert had worried all night, not sure whether to tell Alita, but the following morning she had sensed someone near the cabins. That evening her eyes had met Quinn's.

"I was excited, and when I told Papa he told me about the body on the beach. We knew someone was here."

Quinn now lay thinking of Alita's lilt. She and her father had talked on, safe in the knowledge their masters were sleeping off their partying. Alita had told him how nervous they had been about trying to contact him, and Robert had gone on to describe the island and the men they worked for.

Ragged Island had been deserted after a devastating hurricane some years before, and despite the Bahamian authorities' intentions, had remained cut off from the world. Almost every dwelling had been destroyed, and the small airport soon fell into decay. The few brave islanders who refused evacuation lived in the only settlement, Duncan Town.

Robert knew before he came to work on the island that it had been bought by lawyers in Singapore. "It was in the Freeport News. They refused to let the rest of the islanders back. They're still in huts near Nassau."

From what he'd then overheard from his masters, it was actually the RI7 that had bought the island. Robert had pointed to the logo on his shirt.

Quinn said, "I heard one of them say the fat one paid for it. He owns a bank." He was glad to tell his new friends something they hadn't heard. "So the 'RI7' is what those men call themselves?" He'd pointed towards the cabins.

Robert and Alita nodded. "It must mean Ragged Island Seven," she said. "They look harmless, but they are evil."

A workforce had been brought in to open the airstrip and build the luxury compound. The Moncurs said the RI7 men spent months at a time on the island, and when they did leave they allowed Max Cleeter to bring in other groups of men to be entertained.

"The Russians were bad," Robert had said, looking at his daughter, "but the Koreans were worse. It was almost a relief when that lot came back after visiting their families." He gestured over his shoulder with his thumb, a sneer of distaste on his face.

"I thought they were on holiday until I heard them say they owned the island," Quinn had said.

"They think they own the world, the way they talk!" Robert spat. "But they are owned and controlled, just like us."

Quinn smiled as he recalled Alita's teasing of her father when he'd explained his wilder theories. "I tell you," Robert had said, "I've heard the crazy one, Dombey. He's always threatening the others, says something like, 'if we don't do what we're told it'll all be over.' I tell you, there's someone, some people controlling them. They're scared of something. I tell you."

"Don't go on about that again, Papa! There's no one more powerful than these men. Stop it, you'll make Sñr Tarrant think you are a fool."

But a few days back, as he lay hidden and trapped near the beach, Quinn had heard the men talking about 'The Table.' They'd been arguing about Russia, China, and other world powers. He'd more or less dismissed what he'd heard as fevered imaginings of his starved and exhausted brain, but Robert's words now made him wonder. Was Jill Carson onto something?

"Does the name RI7 mean there are seven of them?" Quinn had asked.

Alita said, "There must be. Sometimes other ones come. Always men."

Quinn counted off to himself the four men he'd seen.

"I've only ever seen six, said Robert. "They were always fighting and arguing at first. It got calmer after Dombey strangled the famous one." Quinn was shocked, but Alita had spoken before he could say anything.

"Papa! You don't know that. They said it was his heart."

"I saw them fighting. And it was me. Me!" Robert had stabbed at his breastbone with a thick forefinger as he went on, "It was me who had to bury the body. I saw the marks on his neck."

"One of them died? Here?" Quinn asked.

"Eliot Myal," said Robert.

"Jesus! You're joking. *The* Eliot Myal?" Quinn hadn't thought about Myal for years. In the early 2020s, the outspoken Englishman was a controversial figure, never out of the news in the US as well as in Europe. Expressing extreme views on race, he became a spokesperson for right-wing groups on both sides of the Atlantic.

"Yes. They all seemed to argue when he was here." Robert explained that until Myal had appeared on the island he thought the other men were rich businesspeople from the Bahamas. Myal had started flying in for a week or two at a time, and it was his presence that made Robert start paying attention to the men's conversations.

"And he's dead? Died here, I mean?"

Even now, back in his shelter going over everything the Moncurs had told him, Quinn found it hard to believe. Not only were those pathetic men luxuriating here while they waited for deliveries of young flesh to abuse, they had killed one of their friends. If the RI7 had murdered one of their own they might do anything.

Robert said he had seen Saul Dombey and Eliot Myal fighting, the others braying encouragement from their loungers. When Robert had next returned to the poolside he was told Myal had collapsed and died. Derek Vernon was finishing a call on his mobile phone. He said the Attorney General in London had advised them to have Myal buried. His history of severe heart disease was well known.

Quinn and the Moncurs had then moved on to discuss escape plans. At one point, Alita had looked up at Quinn.

"Sñr Tarrant, can I ask you? Your wife and daughter are still in Florida?"

"I hope they've made it to Cuba." He'd had a lump in his throat. The possibility of escaping made reuniting with his family suddenly seem more real. He had then asked, "Why don't we leave now? If they're all drunk or drugged, I mean?" He'd pointed towards the cabins.

"No." Robert spoke firmly. "It is the best time to go, but we haven't planned. Or even prepared the boat. We need to leave after their next party."

"But what if there isn't another party? I mean–"

"There will be one, they happen every two weeks at least." Alita was nodding as Robert went on. "They fly their little girls in on a Friday, and the real action happens on the Saturday. Right through the night. They are always wasted on Sundays. That will be the time to go."

Alita and Robert were involved in the planning of parties, ordering extra supplies and collecting them when they had been delivered into the secure tunnel. There would be opportunities to set aside provisions. It was obvious to Quinn that Robert had given the escape plan a lot of thought.

Deciding on the destination was easy. "My wife, Alita's mother, is dead. Litl-A was just seven years old." Quinn had noticed Robert used his pet-name for Alita when he was being protective, or referring to events in their past. "There is nothing for us in Nassau now, and to get there we'd have to take the boat round the North of Ragged Island."

Staring at the sea, he continued, "No. We head south west to Cuba."

"And Mr Tarrant will find his family."

Alita's words had given Quinn hope. Now lying concealed by the beach his thoughts went back to his lost family. He pictured Leonie and Riona being led away by the trafficker, wondering where they were now. If they were alive.

After he and Alita had finished work the following evening, Robert led Quinn along the beach to show him the boat. He had concealed it in undergrowth near the perimeter of the compound. As they approached it Quinn could see the electrified fence by the light of Robert's torch. He had been correct to assume it enclosed the whole compound. The fence even extended out of the jungle edge into the sea, on a low, concrete pier that stretched at least 100 yards.

Quinn looked behind them and along the beach to where the other end of the fence completed a horseshoe-shaped enclosure. Robert was right. The dinghy being washed through the gap and onto this little stretch of shore was a miracle. Robert saw him looking and seemed to read his thoughts. "If the sea had thrown your boat into the fence the fire would have lit the sky. And you'd be dead by now if you'd landed anyplace else. Nothin' else on this side of island but the airstrip, and it's too far through the jungle." He shrugged. "No flights anyway, except Cleeter's."

Robert's big smile was reflected in the moonlight as he pulled the palm leaves away to expose the upturned dinghy. Preparing it for sea was to be Quinn's job.

"I found it when I was checking the perimeter after the storm." Speaking quietly, he pointed along the strand. "I saw your body lying along there. My mind was full of escape, using the boat. Me and Alita. But I knew I had to bury your body. Then when it was gone the next night, I got scared. And confused. I knew if one of the scum – the masters – had found you, they would have made me deal with it." There was a fizzle when he spat towards the electrified fence.

He shone a torch on the boat. "The outboard is underneath. I took it off."

Quinn's heart sank. "I forgot. There is no gas. Those motherfucking traffickers gave us about a pint. I'm sorry, we–"

"I have gas." Robert was smiling in the torchlight, his forehead shining with sweat. "We had to make the place beautiful before those pigs arrived," he said, gesturing over his shoulder, "and when we came there were power tools. Trimmers, chainsaws, all brand new, in boxes. And fuel. I use only hand clippers. There is plenty gas!"

Chapter Nineteen

Quinn tried to allow himself some hope that he might soon be reunited with his wife and daughter. It was too hard, though, for him to banish guilt altogether. He didn't deserve them. A part of him would always believe he had betrayed Leonie and Riona, that he should have resisted being dragged into the dinghy instead of abandoning them to save himself. After they had been through so much together.

There was a chance, though, that the devious trafficker on the Layton beach would do as he promised. Leonie and Riona might already be en route to Cuba via Miami. Quinn had to hold on to that.

Every morning after Robert had shown him the dinghy, Quinn made his way along the beach. Robert had assured him the men would never see him that far round the bay, but he still crept under the cover of the jungle.

The sheer weight of the tiny craft surprised him. The sea had tossed it about like a feather, but turning it upright was difficult. He still had no memory of his stranding, but Robert had said there had been a storm. He expected the boat to be badly damaged, but its hull was intact. The dead refugee's compass hung from the locker handle where Quinn had tied it. Once he had lugged the old dented motor back into position, it looked just as it had when it had spluttered and died not far from the beach at Layton. While he tightened the fixings, he smiled to himself, remembering his burning hatred of the outboard while he'd lain for days and nights, drifting and helpless.

When he first started preparing the dinghy Quinn discarded the empty, rusting gas can. Robert had new ones. It was now almost two weeks later and despite having scrubbed the small bow locker every day, when he opened it gasoline fumes still stung his nostrils. Their provisions and clothes would smell.

He had built up a stockpile with supplies pilfered by Robert and Alita. Robert had said the RI7 men never left the immediate area of their luxury compound and that it would be safe to store them in the boat. Instead, Quinn had decided to secrete the supplies in deep jungle shadow, close to the electric fence. Now, for the last time, he took out all of the packages from under layers of banana leaves and laid them beside the dinghy. Wrapped in strong plastic and gaffer tape, only one of them had been nibbled by a rodent. Quinn smiled as he imagined the hungry animal's disappointment at finding only tins inside.

Robert had insisted on having two tin openers in case one was to fall overboard on the sea crossing. As he packed the locker ready for the next day's departure, Quinn reflected on the Bahamian's meticulous planning and attention to detail. Robert would do everything in his power to secure his daughter's safety. At one of their nightly meetings, he had estimated it would take at least two days to reach Cuba. They had built up enough food, water, and fuel supplies for a week. Robert had made use of the power tools at last and had fashioned oars using rake handles and marine plywood.

On the Sunday morning of the planned escape, Quinn made his last preparatory trip to the boat. Heading along the beach, from the direction of the pool he could hear shrieks and splashes. The party he and the Moncurs had been waiting for was still swinging. The thought of the young girls and boys he had glimpsed the day before made him shudder. He'd seen two of them, barely teenagers and looking intoxicated, being led away from the poolside towards the cabins. He and his new friends were powerless to help the children. Now, looking out over the sapphire sea, he tried to concentrate on escape.

They set out after the Moncurs had finished work. Robert had the homespun oars strapped to his back as he walked towards the boat, a large gasoline can in one hand. Moonlight reflected from Alita's hair as she strode beside him, smiling and whispering in her excitement. Quinn followed with the backup gas can.

Looking back once at the tree root home he had spent three weeks in, his thoughts returned to how he had ended up on this tiny island, separated from his wife and daughter. Memories played like a surreal fantasy film, telling the story of the four years since he and his dad had gone to the rally in New Orleans.

N J EDMUNDS

PART TWO

CUBA

Chapter Twenty

October 2034

"Wake up Sñr Tarrant! Look!"

"Leonie..? What..? You're safe..? Where..?" Quinn shrank himself below the gunwale of the dinghy, confused. The voice wasn't Leonie's, and the sun was blinding him. Seconds earlier he had been in pitch blackness, the noise of automatic gunfire battering his ears.

"You've slept for three hours, Quinn. Wake up now, we're nearly there." A man's voice from behind him, and not one of the brothers he'd shared the dinghy with. The sea smell was tainted with gasoline, and when his eyes accommodated to the light, the smiling face of Alita Moncur looked back at him from the prow. She turned away, pointing ahead.

"Look!"

"Sorry, I must have been..." He sat up and let his eyes follow Alita's outstretched arm. A coastline was visible, a narrow strip of white separating turquoise sea from darker green land beyond. Rising above the horizon a blurred outline of hills merged with a few light grey clouds.

"We should hit the coast in about two hours I guess," said Robert.

Quinn was desperate to reach land. The little outboard meant progress was slow. For nearly two days they'd chugged over the endless swell, Robert steering, the tattered lanyard of the compass tucked under the collar of his polo shirt.

A few weeks ago, alone in this dinghy, helpless and starving, Quinn had been oblivious to sunrises and nightfalls. This time

137

with company, food and water the minutes had dragged. With Cuba now in sight, two hours seemed like a lifetime. He continually searched the horizon, a hand shading his eyes as if he might see Leonie and Riona.

The sun was high, and if Robert was correct they would beach the dinghy in the afternoon. Despite his impatience, Quinn knew they had made better time than expected, presumably assisted by the wind or the tides.

As details of the land became distinguishable, the reality seemed to dawn on them all that they were arriving as refugees in Cuba.

"Are you sure we shouldn't hold back and go ashore in darkness?"

Robert held the tiller steady and continued to look straight ahead. "Face it, Quinn, we will be at the mercy of the Cuban government. We'll have to take what comes."

They had discussed the likelihood of being confined to a detention centre for weeks or even months while the Cuban authorities decided their fate. None of them had heard of refugees being refused entry or returned to their country of origin, but nor did they know if anyone escaping the US really had made it as far as Cuba.

Rumours of peaceful sanctuary there had kept Quinn and Leonie going in the years they'd spent in the Everglades. But that's all they were: rumours. He tried not to think that his wife and daughter, even if they had reached Cuba, might have been sent straight back to the US.

More than once on the trip Quinn had concluded that even if Robert and Alita Moncur were welcomed in Cuba, for him as an American, a period of detention was likely. For decades the

US had imposed harsh sanctions on Cuba, and he knew how his country had treated economic migrants from impoverished countries. He was now ashamed that at one time he had sided with those who called for the US to strengthen its borders against migrants from Central America. His opinion had softened after Riona was born and he'd seen CNN reports of children jailed like animals in cages. It would be understandable if Cuba treated refugees from the US the same.

He looked at Alita, sitting in the bow of the boat with excitement lighting her face. She was little more than a child herself, despite the experiences he knew she had endured. As if he could read Quinn's thoughts from behind him, Robert continued.

"One thing is certain. They will not separate me from Alita."

Robert's resolve to protect his daughter was unshakeable. Care and respect for her seemed to be his driving forces. Twice during the crossing he had ordered Quinn to face away while he held up a blanket to allow Alita some toilet privacy over the stern. Quinn could understand why he had given up his life to become a slave to the men on Ragged Island if it meant he could shelter her from more horror. Quinn would do the same for Riona.

"Have you considered the Cubans might just force men to be separated from women? When they jail them, I mean."

Robert shifted his focus from the shoreline ahead and trained his gaze on Alita, who was still at the prow. "I will not allow it."

139

As they approached the shore, their view of Cuba became confined to a stretch of white sand expanding before them. Tall palm trees beyond became distinguishable, and the breaking waves crashed. The buildings they had seen from further out had disappeared beyond a headland to their left. The curved bay appeared deserted.

Quinn jumped from the prow and into the shallows. As he pulled the dinghy onto the sand Alita joined him to help, and Robert tilted the outboard to lift its propellor out of the clear water.

Robert and Alita each had a small knapsack with some belongings. Quinn had nothing but his shorts and polo shirt. They stood for a few moments. After shaking each other's hands and congratulating themselves on reaching their destination, they stood looking around them.

"Look out! Police!"

The sight of a uniformed man approaching made all three of them shrink back to stand behind the little wooden dinghy, as if it would conceal them. Robert was clinging to Alita's arm. The man wore a tan uniform with red epaulettes and a badge on his breast pocket. As he neared them he reached into a satchel attached to his belt. Quinn flinched and Robert moved to stand in front of Alita. But instead of a gun, the man pulled out a small notebook and opened it. He stopped walking and glanced into the dinghy before jotting something with a pen he took from his breast pocket. A broad smile of big, straight teeth lit his face and he pointed, first at himself, then at the three by the boat, then back at himself. He laughed.

"Somos lo mismo!"

Alita let out a nervous chuckle. "We are the same." In their matching tan shorts and tops the three refugees wore the same colours as the official with the notebook.

The man walked forward, his right arm outstretched. "Welcome to Cuba, my friends."

Chapter Twenty-One

After taking their names and dates of birth, the man took photos of their faces on a cell phone. He spoke into it while making notes about the dinghy, outboard and gasoline cans, before leading them from the beach to a path through dry, flat scrubland. Alita chatted in Spanish to the man as they walked, and Robert told Quinn they were being taken to a reception centre in a town called Nuevitas. Rounding a headland, beyond a stretch of water they could see a collection of small, neat houses hugging a curved shore. A short boat ride took them across to a small café where they awaited onward transport.

They drank bottled water while the welcoming official, Sandro, took more notes about them. Quinn felt humbled when the Moncurs stated their origin as Florida, USA. They hadn't discussed it with him, but were willing to risk harsher treatment to keep the three of them together. Their knowing smiles to him as they spoke confirmed their gesture of solidarity. None of them mentioned Ragged Island. Sandro explained that after coastguards spotted their dinghy approaching he had been sent to escort them to the refugee centre.

A minibus picked them up from the café, and twenty minutes later they were in Nuevitas, a bustling town with a busy harbour. The bus stopped outside a single-story, white building, and Sandro escorted them in. Quinn read a green sign above the door – CENTRO de SOPORTE. He had read the same on Sandro's breast pocket badge.

Sandro shook their hands and left once he had shown them into an empty waiting area. A short time later a woman in the same tan uniform and insignia appeared. She gave each of them a printed sheet with their names, photos and dates of birth, the information they had given to Sandro. She left saying she would return in a few minutes.

"Look at that! They've already got our photographs and details," said Quinn.

"I noticed Sandro was sending emails from his phone all the time we were in the minibus," said Alita.

"I thought Cuba was supposed to be stuck in the last century," said Quinn looking around him. "They must have a network the guy Sandro could upload details to. From his phone. Slick."

The official came back in with a tray of bread, fruit, and cups of strong black coffee.

"Can you tell me who owns the dinghy and motor? I need to assign it to the correct owner. Then the Soporte will reimburse you once we have re-purposed it."

###

Once the Soporte staff knew that Alita was Robert's daughter, far from being separated they were assured they would be found accommodation in a family unit. All three were each given subsistence vouchers, before being taken to temporary accommodation rooms at the rear of the Soporte building. Arrangement were made for assessments of their health and employment histories. It was already clear that the Cuban authorities had well-established systems in place for the care of arriving refugees.

They were told they were free to explore Nuevitas that evening but to be in their accommodation by 9 pm. They wandered along the harbour front and exchanged some of their vouchers for hot meals in a small café.

Having expected to be treated with suspicion and probably imprisoned, they each expressed surprise at the warm welcome.

Alita was excited. "Sandro told me they had so many refugees arriving since the wars started that the government set up a special team. He said we'll be expected to work. They will find us jobs."

"As long as Alita and me can be together I don't care what they want me to do," Robert said.

Alita smiled at Quinn. "Sñr Tarrant, this means you will soon be able to meet up with your wife and daughter. The Soporte will know where they are."

Quinn tried to smile in agreement, but inside he was hearing the gunfire on the beach at Layton, and seeing the look on the face of the double-crossing trafficker as he'd led Leonie and Riona away into the night.

Chapter Twenty-Two

The Centro de Soporte had no trace of Leonie or Riona Tarrant having entered Cuba. The sympathetic staff at the Soporte office in Nuevitas could only advise Quinn to keep checking back for news. His health assessment told him only that he was malnourished. He would be given extra food vouchers until he reached a healthy weight.

After details of his education and work history had been recorded, Quinn joined Robert and Alita in the café near the harbour.

"We are to be taken to another town tomorrow," Robert told him. "There are more jobs there for us."

The next day, together with two other new refugees they boarded an ancient and overcrowded bus. There was a rolling destination reel above the windscreen. Quinn watched the driver wind it round with a brass lever. When he had removed the handle and stored it behind a metal flap on the dashboard, the sign on the front of his bus read Camagüey. Not all technology has to be updated for a society to function, Quinn thought.

On a lacquered bench seat Quinn sat among two quarrelling families, whose clamouring exchanges varied from minute to minute between heated argument and shared laughter. He decided the two women in charge were sisters. The little boy next to Quinn eyed him with apparent wonder, picking at the embroidered RI7 logo on the pocket of his shorts. When a sister slapped his hand away he turned his attention across the bus, staring at Alita.

Two stifling hours later they passed a sign reading 'Bienvenido a Camagüey', and it seemed to take an age for the bus to steer its way into a bustling town centre. They were dropped outside another Soporte office. The two other refugees, a man and his wife from Knoxville, Tennessee, remained on the bus. They had spoken little on the journey but had said they were being sent to Havana. The man had a thick bandage on his left leg, and his wife said they thought he was being sent for a skin graft.

As Quinn and the Moncurs walked into the Soporte, sliding doors closed behind them. Air-conditioned calm replaced the hubbub of the street and its honking traffic. They presented their appointment cards to another uniformed man at a small reception desk. After checking a computer screen he smiled at them and stood up.

"Señor Moncur, Señorita Moncur, y Señor Tarrant? Bienvenidos!"

The official escorted them through double doors into a department called the Refugee Reception Office. The process of accepting them into Cuba continued, and by late afternoon they had been taken to their allocated workplaces and introduced to their new employers, before being delivered to their accommodation.

Robert and Alita were given a two-roomed apartment on the first floor of an accommodation block near a busy bus station. Quinn had a room in a building a few blocks away. The accommodation was basic and clean, but had running water. A razor was another luxury he hadn't known for three years. Thinking of Leonie, he removed his long, dirty red beard.

###

The three met later to use some of their food vouchers. Robert had been allowed to accompany Alita when she was driven to see her appointed place of work. She was to grow vegetables on an urban farm, and described her surprise that there were rows and rows of neat, productive allotments within the walls of an old factory. The roof had been removed, allowing tomatoes, corn and potatoes to flourish in sheltered sunshine.

Robert's experience as a chauffeur in Nassau meant he was to work behind the wheel of a taxi. The old Hudson Commodore didn't impress him. He had looked under the hood. "It's got a Russian engine!" was his verdict.

Quinn cursed himself for stating his previous occupation had been a car park attendant. His limited Spanish meant his journalism degree was of no use. He would be bused daily to a nearby airport to clean and prepare hire cars.

He was delighted, though, that the Cubans had made them so welcome. Security and sustenance was what they had hoped for. To be given paid employment, menial work or not, was more than than Quinn could have dreamt of.

Their food and clothing vouchers would remain valid until each received their first wage tokens from their respective jobs. In addition, they were each apportioned an equal share of tokens to the officially-assessed value of the dinghy, outboard and gasoline.

Chapter Twenty-Three

Late November 2034

Quinn met Robert and Alita Moncur most evenings, a little envious of Robert's travels and Alita's obvious joy at helping produce fresh food. He realised how fond he had become of both of them when Robert announced he and Alita would be leaving. It was a Thursday some three weeks after they had arrived in Camagüey, and the evening in their habitual café had progressed as usual. When they had ordered food there had been enough left over from their pooled vouchers to provide each with a bottle of beer. Quinn had already noticed Alita had been a little quiet, but knew something was wrong when Robert had to clear his throat before speaking.

"We have some news, Sñr Tarrant." Robert spoke with a pained expression, looking at Quinn over the top of his glasses. Alita turned to face out over the paved square.

"Alita and me, we are leaving, Quinn. Havana."

A business providing luxury chauffeured tours had offered Robert a position. He would be based near the airport in Havana, where Alita was to be the company's receptionist and bookings clerk.

"It means we will both be paid in real money instead of tokens. We can save for the future."

After the Moncurs left, Quinn's life in Camagüey dragged. Without the prospect of hearing Robert and Alita's news each evening, the cars he cleaned all day seemed dirtier. The lack of opportunity to improve his Spanish compounded his lonely drudgery. His few social interactions were with fellow travellers on the bus to and from the airport. They were friendly to him, but he couldn't keep up with their rapid chatter to each other.

He was trapped at the airport car lot from early morning until after office hours, and no longer had Robert or Alita to call in at the Soporte for him to ask if there was news of his family. Daily disappointment was better than wondering if Leonie and Riona had arrived in Cuba and were trying to find him.

On Sunday, his day off, he would linger near the Refugee Reception in case its door was opened for an arriving asylum seeker. He was lucky just once, but when he made his enquiry the officer's checks of the Soporte system resulted only in more sympathy.

At least his isolation didn't last long. Two weeks after the Moncurs left Camagüey a typed letter addressed to Sñr Quinn Tarrant was waiting for him when he arrived at his hostel after work. He left it on the end of his bed, stealing looks at it while he washed and ate.

It would be some official notice from the immigration authority, he tried to tell himself. His mouth was dry and his stomach churning as he peeled the envelope open. Somehow news might have reached him about Leonie and Riona. He pictured lifeless, bloodstained bodies on the Layton beach, and the trafficker still smiling.

Instead, relief and excitement filled him when he dared to read it. In Robert's careful, formal English, he was invited to travel to Havana to start a new job as delivering for a fast-food company. Robert had sought work for him and recommended him highly.

Quinn read the letter again and again. He recognised the handwriting from the note on Ragged Island, on the night he'd first met his friends. 'DOMINGO. 8.00 pm. Alita y Robert,' it had read.

His spirits rose even more when he read Alita's handwritten addition to the end of the letter – Please come to join us Sñr Tarrant, we miss you. And I like you better without your beard.

The Soporte staff helped Quinn prepare to join his friends, giving him a list of addresses for Centros de Soporte in Havana. Robert had put a train ticket in the envelope and Quinn replied with a promise to repay the fare once he earned some money.

Since he'd arrived in Camagüey, he'd been surprised almost daily by something new that showed how wrong his preconceptions about Cuba had been. Quinn had expected a brutal, militaristic state and poor, miserable people. Instead, the warm welcome and benevolence refugees received from the authorities was matched by the friendliness of the locals. There were crumbling buildings, and most of the vehicles were relics kept running by resourceful mechanics, but everywhere there were signs of the 21st century. Many people carried cell phones, and a swift and efficient rail system ran through Camagüey, even if some of the rolling stock was dated. Food was in plentiful supply, and life seemed to make the people of Camagüey content.

When Quinn emerged from Havana's modern railway station with his small backpack he soon realised the capital city was something else again. A real revelation.

In December sunshine, the wide avenue in front of him was busy with cars and taxis, many of them modern and of European make. Opposite the station were colourful old buildings. Narrow side streets thronged with people shopping and enjoying bars and cafés. Men and women in smart business suits talked into cell phones, carrying coffee flasks as they hurried on by. In every direction he could see building work in progress, huge cranes towering over men and women in hard hats calling to each other as they worked. Mirrored monoliths were rising to compete for sky.

Robert had told him to wait for his lift outside the small public park near the railway station. He sat on a low wall surrounding manicured lawns. A shiny electric Mercedes pulled up. Quinn thought it must be dropping off a dignitary, but as he prepared to move a respectful distance away from the park gates Robert stepped from the driver's seat. He was dressed in a crisp, teal uniform. Quinn guessed the white gloves he wore were to prevent smudges on the car, and on the patent black peak of his cap.

"Sir," Robert said with a sweeping flourish, as he held the rear door wide for Quinn to enter.

Quinn walked forward and pulled at the front passenger door. "I'll ride up front with you."

"Very good, Sir." Robert's wide grin split his big round face as he took Quinn's backpack and closed the rear door.

Relaxed behind blackened glass Robert turned to his right and took his cap off. "Man! It's good to see you, friend!" They shook hands and hugged before Robert drove off. Quinn settled back into cool leather to enjoy the air conditioning.

"Jeez, it's some city! I had no idea it would be so busy."

Robert kept his eyes on the road as he spoke, guiding the big car through heavy, slow traffic. "Cuba has expanded. I hear a lot of business clients talking on their phones. All the international banks are building new headquarters here, and everyone I pick up is looking for office space."

"What happened? Cuba used to be almost cut off. Y'know, no-go. Off-limits."

"Things have changed all over. Since the pandemic and the wars – you know. The USA is finished." He glanced briefly in Quinn's direction and continued. "And South America – lawless. Did you know the Panama Canal was destroyed?"

Quinn was staring at new buildings everywhere. A hospital, itself vast and with lines of ambulances parked outside, looked insignificant beside its neighbour. A futuristic cone of glass towered above all, reflecting bright sunlight and demanding attention.

"What's that? It's fantastic!" Quinn pointed, wide-eyed like a child at Christmas.

"The BC. La Bourse Cubaine. It's the stock exchange. The new Wall Street, but Cuban."

"It's French?"

Before they reached the Moncurs' modest apartment near the airport Robert had outlined Cuba's rise since the collapse of the Americas. Although Bahamian himself, he sounded proud of Cuba's new place as a global trading centre.

"The BC has taken the place of Wall Street and the City of London. Even the Cayman Islands, and Panama." Robert had learned that the major world powers were now China, India, Europe and Greater Arabia. Cuba, he said like a proud civic guide, was now the dominant financial centre in the West, and seen by the rest of the world as a hub of commerce. Governments and venture capitalists vied with each other for the opportunities Cuba presented to exploit the Americas when peace returned.

"The Communists of Cuba have been very, very smart." He went on to explain that every peso the banks spent on building, running and staffing their headquarters had to be matched by investment in infrastructure, health and social services for the indigenous population. "Have you noticed the fields and plant nurseries all over the city? Every new building has to have an urban farm attached."

They were now leaving the centre of the city and traffic was thinning a little. Quinn saw planes approaching from over the glossy sea and wondered if he would ever be on one. One of them might bring Leonie and Riona to join him. He dismissed that thought. He was over-excited by his new surroundings; his family would arrive by boat as he had. Unless a miracle intervened.

If Havana was now such a major centre, though, who knew what might happen in future? He was feeling almost optimistic as Robert drew the limousine up outside an ochre-painted building.

Alita was waiting for them. She had prepared her special rotis.

Chapter Twenty-Four

For his first few weeks in Havana Quinn lived with Robert and Alita, sleeping on a couch in their two bedroom apartment near the airport.

He soon learned that as a fast-food delivery agent, the early morning rush of coffees and French toast was when he could earn most. Office workers needed their fix. His employer, ComerAquí, was the biggest fast food chain in Cuba and its large number of delivery riders all competed for business. It took Quinn over an hour to bicycle from the airport to the busy financial district, and he was often late for the lucrative morning rush. Most nights by the time he was home Robert and Alita had gone to their beds.

Towards the end of December Quinn learned that one of the ComerAquí bakers was moving to become manager of a new branch, 100km away in Matanzas. Quinn borrowed money from Robert and took over the rental of the baker's hostel room.

Starting the day in the heart of the old town meant he could earn enough to live on by early evening. He could allow himself some leisure time, and every week or so would meet up with the Moncurs. With a routine, good food and most of his day spent cycling, he recovered his strength and stamina. His medical examination in Nuevitas had been the first time he'd noticed what a toll the years of near-starvation in the Everglades had taken. The food vouchers had helped him, but weeks later when he'd first arrived in Havana, his gaunt reflection in a shop window had still shocked him. Now he had muscles and shape.

ComerAquí paid him the statutory minimum wage and he earned commission on any orders he secured himself. Tips were rare, but conditions were good and his room in the state-subsidised residence was clean. An ancient woman kept the shared toilets and washrooms spotless. She was said to have refused the help of the Soporte, and Quinn suspected she slept in her store cupboard. Residents would give her a peso when they could afford it.

It had been one of his regular customers, Yannick, who had advised him to apply for the mailroom job at La Bourse Cubaine. Quinn had always always waiting with hot coffee and croissants when the suited executive stepped from his polished taxi at 7.30 am. Quinn's punctuality and reliable presence must have impressed him. A reference from Yannick opened doors and lowered barriers. Even Quinn's lack of a passport proved immaterial in securing the position. He was still on the minimum wage but saw the move as a step up.

He soon became a popular fixture on the 7th and 8th floors of the Bourse. A Cajun mother meant the French language was familiar from his early childhood, and Quinn found much of his basic French had stayed with him. It was now the adopted international language of finance, he learned.

Despite the European influences on the state-of-the-art, high-tech international stock exchange, Quinn's lapel badge read 'Mailman.' Even if it seemed quaint he realised the job title was still appropriate. Not all internal communications were electronic, and he soon discovered that the hundreds of international businesses with offices in La Bourse Cubaine still valued the exchange of discreet and deniable paper notes.

Quinn kept an 'unread' pocket and a 'shred' pocket in his uniform cargo shorts and soon knew which of the traders would be likely to require his unofficial, discreet services. A nod or a wink from one of them would tell him there an under-the-radar memo to collect. As he delivered the official mail around the BC he would often make an extra pass through a particular section of the open-plan office spaces.

###

A week into his Mailman post Quinn had asked one of the traders he regularly delivered to if she would let him see the main Trading Floor. A tall, thick-set trader with brown hair and red-rimmed eyes, Uliana was from Gdov in Western Russia. She laughed and said, "You are on the trading floor. The entire building is about trading." Until then Quinn had thought the hushed, busy workers at their keyboards on the 7th and 8th floors performed a back room function, away from the major action.

"But, I thought – I mean..."

"There's no need for all that buzzing around like bees in a hive, shouting and waving. And there's nothing here like that stupid Wall Street bell."

Uliana went on to say that the BC was a novel entity, created after the collapses of the Wall Street and London exchanges. Fearing a domino effect, the remaining major trading countries moved quickly. While observing the growing political instability in the US and UK they had already been looking for a neutral location to host a new, worldwide trading hub. They chose Havana. Protected under international law, it was conceived to provide stability and allow the new superpowers to safeguard each other's interests.

"But how did they agree? All those governments? I mean…"

Quinn could tell Uliana's laughing over his words wasn't unkind, but to him, the idea of competing powers reaching such an agreement was hard to believe.

"It wasn't climate change or world poverty they were trying to cooperate on. It was money. The people at the top – the people who hold power – people like that always work in their own interests. No one else's," she said. "They don't care about governments or countries."

"But why Cuba? I mean…?"

"For a 'neutral' base, Europe wanted Switzerland, obviously." She rolled her eyes, and Quinn must have looked puzzled because he knew from his ULM days that the Swiss never joined the European Union.

"You are a smart man, for an American, Mister Tarrant," she went on. "The world powers have been doing their illegal business in Zurich and Geneva for centuries. Even the most corrupt of all – the City of London. The Europeans thought Switzerland was an obvious choice and would let them carry on their criminality."

Quinn could tell Uliana's convictions ran deep.

"But India, China and Greater Arabia, the newer superpowers, chose Cuba. For decades the Cubans had been politically and financially isolated. Irrelevant, but essentially neutral." She had confirmed Robert's view that Cuba was well placed to exploit what remained of the Americas when the wars ended.

"And," she had said with a wry grin of satisfaction, "choosing Cuba was a kick in the teeth for the English and Americans." The Russian's account had intrigued Quinn, even if she'd hurt his remaining pride in the former USA. He noticed, though, that she hadn't included her own country when listing the superpowers.

As he made his rounds over the next days, he paused to listen in to the chatter between traders. He questioned some of them he had come to know. One sunny day in early February, a tall, black man called Stringer had confirmed to Quinn that the BC was indeed the overarching world financial centre. Its function was to monitor trading in every other stock market, worldwide.

Stringer always wore a yellow sports shirt with a green collar and 'AUSTRALIA' emblazoned across the chest. He'd leant back in his chair with his hands behind his head and said, "When it's money that matters, decisions get made. Wars and nuclear weapons are all secondary, mate. Christ, the FGA means there's even been peace in the Middle-East for three years." Quinn realised he had forgotten about the Federation of Greater Arabia that had been trying to establish itself when he'd been at ULM in the 20s.

Stringer had gone on to explain that all trading worldwide was now exclusively online. With secure, encrypted access to every stock exchange the BC could police every trade in real-time. Permanent cloud-based records were backed up and made only accessible through Havana.

Far from being backroom boys, the traders Quinn watched and joked with were the elite. Sent from all over the world, their function was not to make the trades but to monitor all financial activity on behalf of their home governments.

A man from Athens who always smelled of coffee and sweat had been listening to Stringer and Quinn. Without irony, he said, "We all spy on each other, all the time. And everyone knows everyone else is a spy."

"At least we don't have to worry about the Russkies now, though," said Stringer with a wry smile, "now that they're a busted flush like the USA." Perhaps that explained why Uliana had been quiet about Russia.

What Stringer and the Greek man had spoken of saddened Quinn. He'd long accepted that the USA would never be the same again, but it bothered him that despite living through the early years of the civil war he new very little about it. He wanted to know how things got so bad so quickly. At his next break, he logged onto *Cuubl:-)* on the computer in his storeroom, typing 'US civil war'. The first pages of search results were mostly about the nineteenth century conflict, and he modified the search to add '2030.'

Scrolling past results in arabic, russian and chinese, at first he was surprised there were no american articles, until he remembered news outlets and the internet had been closed down in the US. The main English language sources were European. To his journalisitc eye, he found *FRANCE V-q* to be balanced and neutral, if a little haughty.

Before his break was over, Quinn knew that in the opening months of the war each faction had sabotaged the other's refineries, oil depots and lithium battery stockpiles. The resulting fuel shortage meant all commercial aircraft were permanently grounded. Both sides then set about destroying all opposing military aircraft. In his time in Destin, Quinn had noticed the decline in aircraft activity; he had put down to their deployment in areas where action was concentrated.

Reports described the fighting from then on to be low-tech, even hand to hand. "Twentieth century" was how one correspondent described it, kinder than the "mediaeval savagery" used in other reports.

Quinn couldn't bring himself to read more about his country's descent. As he made his collections and deliveries, he now concentrated on learning about the traders' work. A few weeks later a woman with 'Floor Manager' on her lapel took him aside. He thought he was going to be in trouble for distracting the traders, but she offered him a job.

She needed a relief trader who could take over for brief periods of absence, and had noticed Quinn's growing interest in the BC and his intelligent questions. His position was to be different in that he was to be employed by the BC itself. As an American, he would not be seen as a threat by any country. He barely noted this latest reminder of his homeland's new insignificance in the world, excited as he was at being chosen.

He jumped at the chance. Cuba was turning out to be a land of opportunity. In only five months he'd had four jobs, each a step up from the last.

Chapter Twenty-Five

March 2035

"No, Robert, I'll get this."

Since Quinn had moved from Robert and Alita's apartment to central Havana they had met every second Thursday evening in one of the cafés in the old town. Robert smiled and shook his head, reaching for his wallet and waving the bill towards the waiter.

"Save your money, Quinn. You can pay me back when you are a millionaire."

Quinn reached out and took Robert's wallet from his hand. He put it on the table between them, looking between Robert and Alita and grinning. "No, I mean it. I've got a new job." With a flourish, he took a fold of notes from his pocket and dealt a pile of them on top of the bill.

"Oh, Quinn. Well done. A proper job, more money?" Alita's brown eyes were as wide as her smile.

All evening Quinn had been itching to tell Alita and her father his news. He had joined the varied conversations and listened to Alita babbling in her endearing mix of Spanish and English. Now he sat back with his hands behind his head.

"I'm no longer a gofer at the BC. I got made a trader two weeks ago. Well, not quite a trader, but I'm training to be one."

Robert rose from the table and walked round to shake his hand. "Man! That's just wonderful!" Alita shuffled along the banquette and leant in close to him. A gentle, innocent kiss on his cheek sent a guilty tingle through him.

"Sam!" Robert was calling the waiter. "Three margaritas, please!"

When they had finished celebrating his new job, the three friends parted on worn flagstones outside. Music was still ringing in Quinn's ears when Alita stretched up on tiptoe with another light peck on his cheek. The Moncurs took a taxi and Quinn weaved his way along noisy streets to find his tiny apartment. He lay on his narrow bed regretting the last margarita, but it was the aftertaste of the other highlight of his evening that filled him with self-reproach as he drifted off to a restless sleep.

###

Quinn was surprised to feel fresh the next morning. His night had been disturbed by dark and tangled dreams laced with guilt, but his subconscious mind had shown him the obvious. It wasn't Alita's fault she always made him happy, but he couldn't let himself give in to distraction. If his wife and daughter hadn't been able to reach Cuba, he had to find out where they were and go back to fetch them.

It was spring 2035 already, and his new, busy work routine had meant checks at Soporte for word of Leonie and Riona had become less convenient. In his lunch break that day, wearing his his dress shorts and BC polo shirt, he called in at Soporte.

"Hola, Señor Tarrant! Looking good, my friend!"

"Hola, Felipe!" Quinn smiled and fist-bumped the slim man in the tan uniform. Quinn had grown to like Felipe, who had the perfect teeth most Cubans seemed to. There were numerous

Centros de Soporte around Havana, but whenever he could Quinn chose the one he'd visited when he first arrived in the city. Robert had taken him there on the day he picked up his ComerAquí uniform and bicycle. Felipe had clicked open Quinn's records and supplied more vouchers to tide him over until he earned some pesos. He had promised to alert Quinn the minute Leonie and Riona appeared on the Soporte system.

"What can I do, my friend? Spent all your wages on fast cars and women again?"

It had been several weeks since he had enquired for news, and Quinn bantered as patiently as he could. Felipe congratulated him on his new job, but it was clear from the clerk's expression that there was no news.

"Can I ask you something?"

"Of course. I think you must have woman trouble! Did you make the latest one pregnant?" Quinn knew Felipe well enough not to be offended. His age- and sex-tailored quips were a façade that would make way for sincere concern when his subject was seated in private.

Quinn motioned to the crowds of other staff and clients babbling and laughing.

Felipe nodded and waved him to follow. They walked to the end of a row of baize-lined interview alcoves that provided some privacy.

"There's no one else here today, Señor Tarrant. You can say what you like." The genial smile was gone, and he continued in a sombre tone. "I am sorry, Sñr Tarrant. Still, I have heard nothing. I check every week the lists of all new arrivals in Cuba, including refugees. I promise I will contact you as soon as I know anything."

"I've got to do something, Felipe. Do you know how I can contact the traffickers? The people I paid to escape from Florida?" Quinn kept his voice low and his eyes fixed on the Cuban's. Felipe stayed silent, looking back at Quinn for a moment before he splayed his hands out palm upwards, smiling in mock surprise.

"Don't tell me you want to go back, Sńr Tarrant!"

Quinn told Felipe with his eyes he was serious, and in a loud whisper said, "Look Felipe, it's been six months now. You've got to help me. I've got to know where my wife and daughter are." He was aware his voice was becoming louder, his words more urgent. "I need to trace the trafficker who took them. If he won't bring them here I'm going back for them myself."

Felipe looked uncomfortable, shrugging his shoulders, sympathy in his eyes but saying nothing.

"I left in a dinghy from near Layton. With some other men, but they died. I was supposed to come straight here, to Cuba I mean, but I was blown off course, and ended up on Ragged Island."

He thought he heard a creaking sound coming from the direction of the next booth along. Though Felipe had said they were alone,

Quinn had an irrational feeling that someone was listening. He lowered his voice and went on, hissing through gritted teeth.

"I want to find the trafficker. I need to know where my wife and daughter are. Where they took them." He outlined to Felipe how they had eventually managed to make the crossing from the Everglades to Layton. "But then trying to leave the Keys, the bastard cheated us. The trafficker, I mean. We got separated and he took Leonie and Riona. To Miami, I think." He could see the pity in the clerk's eyes. And hopelessness.

"I will try, Señor Tarrant, but..." Again, the splayed hands of powerlessness.

Quinn heard another sound from across the partition. It was a cough. Someone was there. Felipe stood up, and as he reached to shake Quinn's hand he looked over his shoulder and said, "Oh, hello Señor Edge. I didn't know you were here." As they made for the door he went on, hushed and flustered. "Señor Tarrant, I am so sorry! I thought we were alone. Señor Edge has been here helping us with the IT system."

As Quinn left, he glanced back and caught the eye of a man whose red hair was more fiery than his own. The man looked away and rose from the workstation, taking a cell phone from his suit pocket.

Quinn had started his day filled with optimism, but now he returned to the BC feeling like a burst balloon. As he had left the Soporte, Felipe had promised him he would make discreet enquiries, but offered little hope. He had no way, he said, of tracing people-traffickers.

For the first time, Quinn allowed himself to consider the unthinkable: he would probably never see his wife and daughter again. He tried to hope the challenges of his new job would deflect him from his loss.

Chapter Twenty-Six

That evening Quinn logged out of his workstation to allow the night shift to take over, watching his four monitors fade out to the Bourse Cubaine screensaver. He'd had the busy afternoon he'd hoped for. Watching the trades whizz across his screen left little time to think of anything else.

As he checked in his security pass on the way through the cooled marble and glass foyer, the guard on the desk said, "Oh, Señor Quinn, someone is waiting for you. He's outside in the café. A man with a sailor hat."

Even without the guard's message, Quinn had a strong feeling that someone was watching him as he crossed the forecourt of the BC, which doubled as an informal café and breakout area. Waiters weaved between tables under the shade of lush palm trees and cream umbrellas.

A man rose from one of the tables and approached Quinn, his right hand outstretched. In a pale linen suit and a Breton cap, he looked cool and fresh despite the intense heat of the late afternoon.

"Trevor Edge, Mr Quinn. We met earlier today, at the Centro de Soporte. I think I can help you. I've ordered you a beer – I hope that's OK?"

Confused, Quinn let the man take his hand in a vigorous handshake. It was the IT technician, the man who had been in the next booth when he'd asked for Felipe's help. Before he could think of what to say, or wonder how this man could help him, he was seated at Trevor Edge's table as a waiter set down two glistening schooners and a plate of olives.

"I'm sorry, Mr Quinn, I couldn't help overhearing you earlier. Talking with Felipe, I mean. He's a pleasant chap, isn't he?" He spoke in the same accent the men on Ragged Island had.

"I – sorry – yes he is."

"Awful business, back in the US, isn't it? Shocking how quickly it all happened. Still, we've got to move on, haven't we?" Quinn noticed Edge tended to finish with a question.

"I'm sorry, Mr Edge, I'm not sure how you can help me. I think you might have the wrong person."

"Relax, Q-T, relax. It's OK if I call you Q-T, isn't it?"

Other than the embarrassing time Alita called him "Cutie" when they had just met on Ragged Island, no one had called him Q-T since he left Florida. Leonie and Riona now filled his mind, and the man in the linen suit seemed able to read it.

"Please, let me explain. I might be able to help you trace your wife and daughter, Q-T. Part of my work for Centro de Soporte is to supervise the keeping of records of all refugees arriving on the Island. Researching and recording their origins. I know a lot of the traffickers' methods and routes. You said you left from Layton, I think?"

Felipe had suggested no one knew anything about the traffickers, Quinn thought.

"Err – yes, a beach just outside of Layton. But how...?" The man called Edge unsettled him, but still, he felt compelled to answer the flow of searching questions.

"And when was this? You arrived in Cuba on the 8th of November. Not far from Nuevitas – that means 'new life', did you know that?" Edge smiled before probing deeper. "But I think you said you had been somewhere on the way? Ragged Island, I think?"

Quinn outlined the journey from the Everglades to the Keys, and his best guess of the approximate date he had last seen Leonie and Riona. "I'm sorry, it's just until I got to Cuba I had no idea of what day it was, let alone the date. I can only work backwards from when we arrived in Nuevitas."

Trevor Edge was making notes on his phone as Quinn spoke. "This is good, Q-T, good. I can work with this. I have a lot of contacts. If you can give me a couple of days, I'll be able to help you. So – goodness me – you must have been in the Everglades for getting on three years after you left Destin! Tell me about Ragged Island – what was it like?"

Chapter Twenty-Seven

April 2035

Quinn's trial period as a relief trader was short. After little over a week he was called into the floor manager's office, emerging soon after with a rota of shifts to cover over the next two weeks. He also had a brand new smartphone, preloaded with BC software to allow him 24-hour access to the markets. It felt strange to hold a phone again, and it was heavy in his pocket. The first call he made, from the privacy of a toilet cubicle, was to the Soporte.

"Is that you, Sñr Tarrant?" Felipe congratulated him again on his rising status. "Your very own cell phone! The address book is full already with all those girls' numbers?"

"Can I ask you something different, Felipe? Do you have a number for Trevor Edge?"

"Sñr Edge? You have an IT problem at BC? I thought they had–"

Quinn explained he had met Trevor Edge by chance but had lost his phone number. "I said I would find out something for him." He wasn't sure why he felt the need to lie.

"I have his business card. 'Edge IT Services.'" Felipe read out the number and made Quinn repeat it back to him. "Don't forget us here at Soporte when you are a billionaire, Sñr Tarrant!"

For the rest of that day, Quinn tried dialling the number at every opportunity. Edge IT Services needed to hire a new receptionist, he thought, as he hung up yet again having wasted all of his coffee break pressing the redial button.

He had arranged to meet Robert and Alita that evening. Before he left his apartment, he couldn't resist trying one more call to Edge. It surprised him when this time the line went to voicemail. Trevor Edge's brief message was an instruction, rather than an invitation. "Edge IT. Leave a message." Compelled by the authority in Edge's voice Quinn spoke after the beep.

"Er – hello, Mr Edge, it's Quinn Tarrant speaking. You remember we met and you – I hoped – can you let me know if you have found out – my wife and daughter – can you phone me please on this number, anytime." About to hang up, he checked himself, "Well – not tonight, please, I will be at La Neptuna – with Robert and Alita, the people who came with me from Ragged Island. Phone me tomorrow, please."

He ended the call, feeling embarrassed at his hesitant, pleading tone. Almost immediately the siren sound of his new phone's ringtone made him jump, his pulse quickening when he saw the Edge IT number displayed on the screen.

"Mr, Tarrant? Trevor Edge here," the voice said as soon as Quinn answered. "I have just received a message from a contact of mine, Q-T. I thought I'd read it to you. 'Positive re LT and RT. Will call.'"

Quinn interrupted, "When? When will you hear?" He could feel his pulse beating in his neck.

"Tomorrow, I think, Q-T, that's good isn't–"

"Can't you call him now?"

Edge said no, his colleague was travelling, but promised to let Quinn know as soon as he heard anything. Before Quinn could ask again Edge changed the subject. In a light, conversational tone, he asked how Quinn's job was going. They chatted for a moment before Edge said, "Must go, duty always calls, doesn't it?" before hanging up.

Quinn was buoyed up as he weaved through the evening crowds on his way to meet Alita and Robert. Excited to tell them his news that tomorrow he would be hearing about Leonie and Riona, he headed for the small café that was becoming their favourite meeting place. He hoped Alita would be there this time.

Alita hadn't been at their last evening out, and again Robert sat alone at a corner table. After a few minutes of chatting about work while they looked over the menus, Quinn looked towards the door and said, "I hope Alita's coming?"

Robert sat back, smiling. "She's out tonight, Quinn. Lance is taking her to dinner."

Quinn was surprised by his reaction. Robert explained Lance was one of the chauffeurs from Tres Reyes Transfers, the company he and Alita worked for. As he went on Quinn drew a mental picture of the man Alita was out with. For no rational reason he disliked this Lance. Distrusted him. He said nothing, but his face burned and he was glad of the low lighting.

Robert read his reaction nonetheless. "It is good Lance took my encouragement to ask her out." He continued, wagging an admonishing finger. "We like you a lot Sñr Tarrant and want to keep you as our friend, but you are a married man. Your wife may soon be joining you here, right?"

Quinn looked at the floorboards between his feet, feeling Robert's eyes burning into him.

"I have seen the way you and Alita look at each other, Quinn. I can't let you hurt my Litl-A."

Quinn was ashamed of himself. And guilty. Though her light pecks on his cheek had been the full extent of their physical interaction, that he could be jealous of another man was a serious betrayal of Leonie.

Even with the prospect of hearing about Leonie and Riona the next day, Quinn's appetite soured. He could only pick at his shredded beef, trying to smile and keep the conversation going. He didn't mention Edge. He had barely admitted to himself the connection he had developed to Alita, but Robert had sensed it. If he knew Quinn had let his feelings show at the very time he should have been thrilled about news of his wife and daughter, Robert would think him a monster.

He was gauging how early he could excuse himself when it happened.

A sudden voice spoke from behind, startling him out of his self-absorption. Robert looked up and Quinn turned, craning his neck. Trevor Edge was standing behind him, accompanied by a taller man. The neon Neptuna sign behind them gave the taller man's hair a green tinge.

"I'm sorry to interrupt your evening, Mr Tarrant," Edge was saying, his eyes fixed on Robert. "I couldn't tell you this on the telephone and thought I had better bring Dieter with me." The tall man stepped forward and bowed.

"What is it? Have you found Leonie?" Excitement returning and all thoughts of Alita gone, Quinn rose from his seat. He turned, smiling and reaching out to shake hands with the man called Dieter.

The man looked awkward and turned towards Trevor Edge.

"This is Dieter Lange, Mr Tarrant, an associate of mine who has contacts throughout Florida. I'm afraid you had better sit back down."

"What? What?"

"Do you mind?" Edge asked Robert, sitting down at the end of the table without waiting for a reply. "I am Trevor Edge, pleased to meet you." He proffered his hand to Robert who took it hesitantly and said, "Robert Moncur," looking bemused. Quinn sat down, unable to resist a glance towards the café entrance to see if Leonie was joining them.

"Dieter, perhaps you could tell Mr Tarrant what you told me this evening."

Dieter Lange remained standing. He spoke with a strong accent Quinn thought might be European. "Mr Tarrant, I am here to tell you that your wife and daughter are dead. They were both killed by the PBC. Just after you last saw them outside Layton."

Quinn felt his lips numbing and his throat tightening. A fork clattered to the stone floor, tines ringing.

"No."

He couldn't look at Lange. His eyes fixed themselves on the little patent leather peak on Edge's Breton cap. He wondered if it was glued onto Edge's scalp and if his hair was false, like a clown's costume.

A muscular arm encircled his shoulders and gripped him. He looked blankly at Robert, who had moved round to sit beside him.

Chapter Twenty-Eight

Grief and guilt.

The lines cast onto the white wall by the slatted shutters were brighter than usual, slanting at a steeper angle. He played with them, opening and closing his eyes and watching the vivid yellow stripes glide and fade over the backs of his eyelids. His drowsy mind wandered. It was only a few weeks since he'd moved in to live with the Moncurs, but already jets roaring after take-off had become an unobtrusive part of the background to his sleep. In his three years in the Everglades he'd hardly seen a single plane.

He was drifting awake when it hit him. He was late for his fast-food job.

"Oh god! Man, how did this happen? Jeezuss!"

He'd missed the morning rush and would have to work late again. Quinn jumped off the bedroll and banged his head on the table by the shuttered window, reaching out for his ComerAquí uniform. But where he had left it on his chair, instead he found a folded white sleeveless shirt and a pair of dress shorts. There was a small food stain on the hem of the shorts.

He shouted "Robert! Alita! We're late!" over the noise of another jet. Swinging open the door to the narrow hallway he shouted again. He banged on Robert's room door, then pushed it inwards. The bed was neatly made, and the shutters cracked open.

"Alita?" he tried more gently outside her door.

Why had they let him sleep late? And where were his clothes? He looked back at the folded shirt and picked up the shorts. They felt heavy, and in the pocket he found a sleek cell phone with a bigger screen than he had ever seen. Whose was it? On the table was a note, written on Tres Reyes Transfers paper.

"Dear Sñr Tarrant,

> *I am sincerely sorry. I brought you here after what happened. Señor Edge is informing the BC. I will bring you almuerzo.*

> *Your true friend,*
> *Robert Moncur"*

He held the note in his hand, his eyes fixed on what followed Robert's formal words.

> *"Dear Quinn, Your poor wife and daughter. I am crying for your losses. I have pressed your shirt and shorts. Alita."*

Losses? Wife and daughter?

Disordered memories whirled. The BC, his apartment in town, and Trevor Edge arriving at La Neptuna. Reality speared him, air escaping in a deep moan as his legs melted, his weight buckling his knees.

His brush with grief didn't last long, though. Denial swept it away. When Robert came home with the promised lunch Quinn was sitting in his undershorts. He had come to lying on the floor with no memory of the previous night after arriving at the Neptuna. He'd had a nightmare, but was unable to work out why he had slept at the Moncurs' apartment. He wondered if he had been too drunk to go home alone.

Robert's condolences were meaningless. They bounced around his head as he stared into space, frowning in confusion.

He nibbled at the lunch, and any mention by Robert of Leonie and Riona was met by blank silence. Quinn talked only about the noise of the planes and how he would be in trouble for being off work. He'd tell them it was a migraine.

His mind had shut down like a failed business, boarded up and leaving no forwarding address for creditors.

Quinn returned to work after one day's absence. He expected to be fired, but the 7th floor manager took him aside.

"Your friend Monsieur Edge came to see me yesterday and told me what happened." She smiled at him and said she would keep his work light that day, a Friday. She went on, "But on Monday you will be all good, oui?"

Quinn smiled and promised he was already all good. He'd got away with it. They believed it was a migraine and not a hangover.

That Friday passed without him noticing. His mind returned to his work, and when colleagues approached with sympathy he swatted their concern away, wondering if they knew something he didn't.

It was Stringer who'd sewn the first doubts. "Sure you're alright, Mate? I heard what happened. Total shithouse." When Quinn had grinned at the Australian his mouth had been slow to cooperate. Until then the brief flashbacks to the nightmare he'd had two nights before had unsettled him only fleetingly. Now his colleagues' lack of engagement with his banter about hangovers and boozy nights made him wonder if the dream had been based on something real.

After work, he wandered along the busy sidewalks and through the narrow alleys with an uneasy feeling in his midriff. In his apartment, he sat looking at an empty picture frame on the wall. When the ComerAquí baker who had the apartment before Quinn had moved out, he'd left behind a black-and-white picture of a woman and little boy. Quinn had removed it from its frame, protecting it between sheets of paper. When Leonie and Riona joined him he would fill the frame with a picture of them, and trace the baker in Matanzas to return his photo.

Now, the empty frame seemed to look back at him. The emptiness in his stomach threatened to choke him, until a convulsive wave spread up through his chest and he heard himself emit a low wail.

He pictured Dieter Lange standing beside Trevor Edge. 'Mr Tarrant, I am here to tell you that your wife and daughter are dead.'

He would never fill the frame.

For what could have been minutes or hours he lay back on the bed and wept. He saw Edge's arrival in the café two nights ago and heard Lange's words over and over. Robert's kindness, Alita's note, and his colleagues' sympathy began to make sickening sense.

Trevor Edge called in on him sometime that evening, letting himself into the darkness of the apartment. Quinn was hostile at first, cursing Edge and telling him to leave. As if he had predicted Quinn's state of mind, Edge sat in silence with a neutral expression until Quinn was quiet.

"It's OK," he said.

Quinn slumped back on the bed. He knew it was irrational to blame Edge for giving him the information he'd asked for. Edge moved to sit close to him.

"I'm sorry I was the one to bring you such horrid news, Quinn."

For the next half hour Edge kindly but firmly steered Quinn towards acceptance. He repeated word for word what Lange had said. Your wife and daughter are dead. Hearing the words in another voice threatened to destabilise Quinn again and he had to force back sobs. He made himself ask for more details, and Edge was ready to supply them.

"They were both killed by the PBC. Just after you saw them being taken from the beach outside Layton." Edge expanded on what he said Lange had reported. He suspected the trafficker Quinn and Leonie had paid all their savings to had tipped off the PBC about the escape plan, in return for a cut of the money.

It was most likely, Edge said, that once they'd handed over their dollars, killing the occupants of the flimsy boats had always been the PBC's intention. They considered all escapees to be traitorous vermin.

Like a boxer with his opponent trapped against the ropes, Edge went on beating the cruel information into Quinn. "Regardless of any sex trade income the traffickers might be planning to make, the PBC would see fleeing refugees as fit only for extermination."

Quinn winced, picturing Riona's smile.

Even if the man Quinn paid had genuinely intended to help Leonie and Riona to reach Cuba, Edge believed they were never going to be spared. Dieter had heard of several similar massacres.

The PBC, Edge said, saw the money handed over to people smugglers as another income stream.

All the while Edge was giving his brutal assessment, Quinn was remembering Leonie and Riona being led away. He knew now they were dead. They died as collateral damage when the PBC took all the money the trafficker had collected. As far as Quinn knew, of all the hopeful refugees he was the only survivor.

His last memory of Leonie and Riona was the trafficker steering them towards his car, and now Quinn knew they had died soon after. Their fate in lawless Miami might have been worse. Perhaps their deaths were for the best.

He spent the whole of Saturday and Sunday in his apartment, his brooding interrupted by regular phone calls on his new cell phone. He knew Robert's fussing and offers to bring food were excuses to check on him.

He would have preferred to lie alone, staring at the black-and-white movie his mind projected onto the ceiling. He had fallen into a restless sleep the first time it played, waking in a shivering sweat, a scream locked in his mouth.

The film then ran on repeat. To look away was impossible, his head fixed and his eyelids pinned apart.

Set on the Florida Keys beach just outside Layton, it was filmed from a boat a little way offshore. Rocked by the waves, the action on the beach was jarring. A dark car drove along the highway above, shadowy figures dancing in front of its dull headlights, forcing it to stop. To a soundtrack of staccato gunfire, with dull explosions adding a rhythmless backing beat, Quinn saw a woman and child dragged out. As they were thrown to the ground, the car lights reflected from cartridge bandoliers slung over singleted shoulders. Men in pale bandanas surrounded the prostrate figures. Brilliant white muzzle flashes flooded the scene in terrible relief, until the picture faded into foggy grey.

His throat stifling a useless cry, the projector shuddered, the soundtrack now a jumping vinyl record, 'Quinn!–Dada!–Quinn!–Dada!–Qui...'

Then it started again. The whole weekend. Whether he was asleep or awake. If his phone rang or if Robert or Trevor Edge visited, like a rattling junkie Quinn could hardly wait until they left. He needed to get back to the compelling, punishing torment of his private movie show. He knew every muzzle flash, every scream.

His wife and daughter were dead, and he had let it happen. He deserved to die himself. In hell, he would watch their last moments over and over, forever.

Quinn acknowledged his mind had produced the film, and he was its target audience, the sole viewer. At the same time, though, he knew it was a documentary. News footage. Non-fiction. A true-life, true-death account of events that had played out on that beach at Layton, Fl, on a dark autumn night in 2034.

He'd seen the opening scenes for himself before he deserted his family. Now he'd seen the ending.

But when his wife and daughter had been taken away into the night by the man with the dark car, Quinn had been looking after his own interests, escaping, fleeing, deserting, abandoning. He hadn't resisted being pulled into the boat by desperate, panicking refugees. And his eyes had been shielded from the muzzle flashes. He'd been cowering, face down, arms over his head in the flimsy dinghy, saved from bullets by a doomed, defiant giant of a man he didn't know.

Since he left the Florida Keys, Quinn had played the part of a victim wrenched from his family by circumstances beyond his control. In his short time on Ragged Island, he had bathed in the Moncurs' sympathy, happy to play the brave, shipwrecked adventurer. In Cuba, he had flourished, improved himself, and become closer to the Moncurs than he should have. All the while, he'd made a pathetic pretence of searching and hoping for news of Leonie and Riona. Occasional cosy chats and banter with Felipe didn't equate to much of an effort, did they?

Chapter Twenty-Nine

At lunchtime on Monday, his second day back at work, Quinn went down as usual to the vending machine BC foyer. Unable to select anything he would eat, he turned to go back to his desk. A man was waving at him from outside on the sidewalk. It was Felipe. Quinn swallowed before scanning his ID to join the Cuban outside.

There was none of Felipe's feigned lewdness. Shaking Quinn's hand earnestly he said, "Sñr Tarrant, I am so sorry." His eyes were moist. In a breaking voice he continued, "I wanted to come to offer any help the Centro can give you."

Quinn was taken aback that Felipe could already know of his bereavement, and couldn't respond. Felipe filled the silence. "Sñr Edge told me what happened."

Quinn had forgotten Edge was linked to the Soporte by his work. He would rather have hidden away and spoken to no one, but Felipe had done a lot for him when he first arrived in Cuba. He spent the rest of his lunch break with the Cuban, whose frankness and sensitivity were easier to take than his colleagues' awkwardness.

To qualify for state subsidy of his hostel rent he had to continue his employment, and he had little choice other than to drudge red-eyed through long days at the BC. In the weeks that followed he was to find work would keep him alive.

The routine helped, and after a time he felt the need to watch his mental movie less often. When it played now there was a familiarity to it that could even leave him feeling a little dissatisfied. It didn't have the same shocking effect. Sometimes it would stop playing, interrupted by something that had happened at work, or if he remembered he'd forgotten to wash his socks.

At first his work colleagues had been sympathetic, muttering "sorry" as they looked at their screens or phones to avoid eye contact. Now, they seemed to have forgotten his loss and Quinn's days were more tolerable.

The only people he met outside work were Robert and Trevor Edge.

Robert visited two or three times every week. Quinn grew used to seeing the limo parked outside his apartment block when he returned from work. Sometimes, there was a bag of groceries with a note inside from Alita reminding him he must eat well.

When Trevor Edge arrived for a second time, the pain of his first visit was still raw. Quinn was reluctant to let him in, but Trevor's empathic expression disarmed him. He brought food and beers, and they chatted about nothing much for an hour. When Trevor had gone Quinn felt better somehow, and slept less fitfully.

For a while Trevor's visits were a regular part of Saturday afternoons. Weekend hours were slow and difficult without the distraction of work, but Edge helped him cope. With the prospect of a counselling session to break the weekend, Friday afternoons didn't fill him with such dense gloom.

Quinn came to trust and respect the Englishman. After two or three visits he could relate details of his life with Leonie and Riona without breaking down. Trevor was a good counsellor. Gently probing, he allowed Quinn the luxury of self-pity. He didn't seem to mind if Quinn drifted off the subject to talk of escaping from Ragged Island with the Moncurs.

Chapter Thirty

August 2035

As the weeks went by after the awful evening at La Neptuna, Quinn saw less of Robert. Often working late into the evening, when he returned home he sometimes found Robert had tried to visit. Quinn always seemed to be too busy to respond to notes, voicemails or texts.

Tonight, six weeks since they'd last met, Quinn approached the chosen café bar wishing he hadn't accepted his friend's latest invitation. He felt bad for shunning the Moncurs. He should have made more effort, respecting their kindness and what they'd been through with him.

His reluctance wasn't just down to grief. He'd been pathetic that April evening, jealous when he'd heard about Alita and Lance. At times he had to bat away the irrational notion that Edge bringing bad news had been some kind of divine punishment.

Soon after he arrived at the café bar, Robert's big smile and easy conversation allowed Quinn to enjoy a glass of local red wine while he looked forward to his fried pork ribs. Relaxing, he smiled and let his tongue loosen. After congratulating Robert on being promoted to supervisor in charge of seven Tres Reyes drivers, Quinn expounded on how much he was enjoying his work. He dominated the conversation, checking himself only when slight guilt reminded him not to neglect his grieving.

"To tell the truth, Robert, I think they're kind of – depending on me now. I mean, when I started it was a sort of try-out. To see if it worked. But now traders come to me when they want to take leave. I mean, to make sure I'm not scheduled already. It's like I'll never be able to get time off myself if I'm not careful. It's great, though, I like it."

When Quinn sipped his wine Robert took his chance to speak.

"You're really into it, man, I see that. You can't stop talking about it." He was still smiling, shaking his head. "But you've got to take some time for yourself. My old man used to say, 'If you don't ease off a gasket's gonna blow!'"

"I'm good, Robert. It's all copacetic. I–"

Robert spoke over him. "Q-T, can I call you that? Q-T you got to slow down. Since, you know, your wife 'n' all, you've hardly stopped. I mean–"

"How's Alita?"

"Stop changing the subject."

"No, I mean it, Robert. You never talk about Alita. And I've not even met Lance yet."

Quinn had used this tactic before. He didn't know why, but asking about Alita and her chauffeur boyfriend helped him somehow. He'd only seen Lance once, in the distance on his way home from work. Alita had been hand in hand with the tall black man as they'd turned to go into a restaurant.

Later, as they parted after their meal, Robert looked Quinn in the eye and pointed a finger at him.

"And don't cancel this time. Work's not that important, man!"

Robert planned to arrange a meal out with Alita and Lance, and had persuaded Quinn to join them. For reasons he couldn't explain, previously Quinn had always excused himself from meeting Lance, blaming extra work. And tonight, by the time he was turning the iron handle on the high door to his apartment building he had prepared a list of potential excuses.

He had another disturbed night. When he did sleep he was with Leonie and Riona, back in Rayville before the war. And his Dad was there again. In the morning, as he brushed his teeth in the flaky mirror he stopped, stared at his bleary self, and came to a decision. He had to move on with his life.

At lunchtime, he made a quick call on his cell phone. Then he sat back from his cafeteria table to compose an SMS.

Robert,
Esquina, Reservation for 4, 8 pm,
next Thursday, (20th),
I'm payin!
Q-T.

He smiled and pressed 'send'.

On his way to the restaurant, again Quinn had his disquiet about seeing Alita with Lance. He was still struggling to understand it when he sat down beside Robert. A short time later, Alita led Lance to the table. He appeared to tower over her, and Quinn felt a fleeting concern he couldn't explain.

Esquina de Cuba was even better than Quinn had heard. Alita, Robert, and Lance were all dressed up, but he'd gone in his usual casual clothes. He was paying, after all.

As the wine and conversation flowed, Quinn was able to relax, overcoming some initial awkwardness. The evening passed quickly. Lance's long limbs and short, straight hair contrasted with Robert's appearance, but even so with the same smiling eyes and confident, jovial manner they could have been father and son. Quinn liked Lance. He could see why Alita had fallen for him, and the couple appeared close and attentive to each other.

Lance talked a lot about cars, and boasted of the Mustang he'd once owned back home in Detroit. Alita smiled at Quinn, rolling her eyes with playful, fake boredom.

When Lance turned the topic to basketball that was something Quinn could relate to. He hadn't played since his ULM days, and when Lance said he shot hoops every Saturday morning with a group of friends, Quinn asked if there was a court where he might get back in practice.

"You should join us, man," Lance offered. "We're always looking for more players, even a shortass like you!"

"A beanpole like you won't be able to catch me." At 5 feet 7 inches tall, Quinn was proud of his skill and agility on the court, although since high school he had never played in a team. Lance smiled and wrote directions to the court so Quinn could join him and his friends.

The four agreed to meet again in a fortnight, and Quinn had to admit to himself he was looking forward to it. Walking home to his hostel room, he thought back over the evening, shaking his head and smiling to himself. He'd been putting off meeting Lance, using fake jealousy to mask the true reason. He'd associated Alita's boyfriend with the fateful evening at La Neptuna when he discovered his family was dead.

It wasn't Lance's fault. Having shaken hands with him and proved to himself that he could be pleased for Alita, he agreed with Robert. Lance was a good guy.

Grief is a normal process, he thought, and he needn't blame himself for having mixed-up emotions. But he was glad to be getting over his bereavement. At last.

September 2035

Saturday morning. Through a slight hangover Quinn could smell rubber and dirt. A sports shoe had smashed into his face. He was shaken from a momentary daze by strong arms pulling him up from the asphalt. There was laughter and a cheer as Lance, inevitably, scored more points. Lance was the enthusiast, the player, and a foot taller than some of the rest. Despite Quinn's enthusiasm and quick footwork, he was no match for the big man from Detroit.

"Sorry, bro! You OK?"

His rescuer, the player he'd collided with, was not much taller than Quinn. He was beaming and panting as he helped him up. Brushing some dirt from his cheek Quinn grinned back and readied himself to rejoin the melee. It would soon be coffee time.

He'd started to look forward to his Saturday mornings. The game was fun, a disordered rabble crowding around as Lance weaved and dribbled. But it was the company and banter that kept Quinn turning up at 9 am each week. The players were a loose grouping, mainly Cubans and many of them airport workers. He and Lance were the only Americans, and there was one Dutchman who Quinn thought he'd seen working at the BC.

Unless it was too hot, they usually played for an hour before moving on to a nearby café, some to nurse their bruises and others to soothe away the effects of the night before. Quinn had found coffee and raspadura could cure the worst hangover. The little cubes of raw brown sugar were the sweetest thing he had ever tasted.

Today was the fifth time he'd joined the group. In the café he walked to the same corner table as usual, still rubbing his cheek after the accident on the court. Squeezing past Lance and the Dutchman to reach a seat, he saw them eyeing a passing waitress.

"She's a honey! Ooh, baby! Come to me!" Lance rubbed his groin provocatively behind the girl's back.

"Don't be greedy, Beanpole. You're going steady, and with a very sexy woman. Is she good? You know – good?"

Quinn sat down. After yet again reassuring the apologetic guy who'd knocked him over, he caught up with the end of Lance's response to the Dutchman.

"…she's taught me things in bed I didn't know were possible! She's insatiable.

Chapter Thirty-One

"Trevor? Who's that?"

"Sñr Edge. Oh, I'm sorry, Q-T! I shouldn't have mentioned him." Robert was shaking his head, one hand on his heart and the other raised in apology. "I forgot it was him who told you about…"

"It's OK, Robert," said Quinn, noticing his friend's embarrassment. "I mean it, I'm fine. I know him quite well. He's been good to me. I just didn't know you two were in touch. Didn't cotton on it was that Trevor you meant, y'know." He took a bite of some flatbread. "Sorry, I'm starving, finished late again. So, d'you see much of him?"

"Not much. He came to see me at the office after – you know – to ask if he could help with anything. I thought he was touting for business, but it was more like he just wanted to ask questions. Still, he set me and Alita up with a better router. And he asks for me if he ever wants a limo." Quinn couldn't imagine Trevor Edge in a limo, somehow.

"And I know I've seen him somewhere," Robert continued. "I can't put my finger on just where."

Quinn took a mouthful of water and sat back in his chair. "You mean before we came to Cuba?"

"Yeah, I've seen him somewhere. Man, it bugs me every time I meet him."

They were having a drink before dinner while they waited for Alita and Lance to arrive. The music was loud, and the tables busy. It had been a struggle for Quinn to book a restaurant and he'd had to try three before he was successful. It seemed like every business was already booking Christmas functions, and it was only the end of November.

Uliana had explained to Quinn that when the BC was first established Christmas was barely marked in Cuba. Now the influx of workers from all over the globe meant commercialism was flourishing.

"You sure Alita and Lance are coming?" asked Quinn, looking at his watch. "He didn't mention it at basketball last week. Want another beer while we wait?"

Robert was picking at a splinter on the edge of the table. "Alita's been quiet. Not saying much, you know. I'm not sure what's going on." He looked up from the floor. "I worry she..."

He was suddenly jerked forward, spilling some beer. In the busy restaurant, neither of them had noticed Lance approaching until he slapped Robert between the shoulders. "Hey, man! How are ya? It's busy in here! Let's order. Alita, get some menus."

When Alita had collected four menus she sat down at the end of the table.

"Hi, Alita, I'm glad you made it this time. I missed you last month." Quinn's greeting appeared to be lost in the noisy chatter of the restaurant and Lance's gleeful account of his last few matches. He was playing regularly for the Havana Hornets, and Quinn was used to hearing about Lance's three-pointers and blocks.

"I'm gonna be in the first team by this time next year, you wait and see!"

The meal proceeded as Quinn expected, with Lance soon driving the conversation towards cars and sport. He liked Lance but sometimes missed the quiet chats he had shared with Robert and Alita in the early months after the three had arrived together in Cuba. Whenever Quinn tried to catch Alita's attention to ask how she was, she seemed to look the other way, laughing at Lance's latest joke.

After they'd eaten, they were having coffee and preparing to leave when Lance slapped the table and yelled over his shoulder to a passing waiter.

"Hey! Four margaritas." He turned back towards Robert and Quinn. "I've got an announcement. Me and Alita – we're getting married!"

To Quinn, the music stopped, and the bustling Christmas revelry froze for a moment as he digested what he had heard. He'd grown used to Alita being with Lance, and it surprised him how this news took the wind from him. He watched Robert move round the table to shake Lance's hand. As Alita smiled up at her fiancé, Quinn muttered his congratulations.

Chapter Thirty-Two

January 2036

Saturday morning basketball continued to provide an outlet for Quinn. Lance still dominated the play and revelled in running rings around everyone. Eyes were rolled behind him, but the fun was good-natured. They got their own back in the banter after the game.

Quinn enjoyed the endorphin boost the physical exercise gave him and would feel positive and energised for hours afterwards. Sundays were much harder though. Unless he was scheduled to work, the day would drag. After a few weeks of this, he started taking long and punishing runs, covering miles round the streets and the many large parks of Havana.

Gradually he adjusted to life alone. He still met Robert every week or two, and Trevor Edge sometimes joined them. He saw very little of Alita, and if he thought of her he wished her and Lance well. Robert said the couple were busy making preparations for their wedding.

One evening in January, though, Quinn was pleased to see Alita come into the restaurant with Robert. Trevor had been first to arrive, and he now rose briefly, bowing his head as he moved along to make space at the table.

"Hello, Alita. Lovely to see you," he said. "Where's Lance tonight?"

"He has to work, a conference." It was Robert who answered.

Alita smiled at Quinn and sat down beside him. She spoke little until Trevor coaxed her into talking about Ragged Island again.

"It must be over a year since you three arrived in Cuba, isn't it? Some story to tell, you have! Quite an escape."

"Fifteen months now," said Alita.

"Was it that bad there? A deserted island in the Caribbean? It sounds idyllic. Remind me who you were working for."

Trevor had set the subject for the evening. Alita found her voice, and she and Robert now did most of the talking about Ragged Island. Edge appeared intrigued when Quinn chipped in with snippets of what he'd heard the English men discuss. If they drifted onto another subject Trevor seemed to like to steer them back.

"So just who were these men? Tell me again, I always forget."

As on previous evenings with Edge, Robert gave an account of life on the island with 'those pigs'. This evening it occurred to Quinn that Edge seemed more interested in what details Alita could add. It was as if Edge was glad to hear about Ragged Island and its occupants from a new perspective.

"Just a morbid curiosity I have about my fellow Englishmen, I suppose," he said when Quinn asked why he was so fascinated. "How many huts were there? Three, I think you said, right?"

Later, when Trevor had excused himself for the night and they were having a last drink before departing, Robert shook his head. "It still gets to me every time. I know I saw Trevor somewhere before."

"Oh, Papa! Don't be silly. You and your imagination! You're always saying things like that." She laughed and hiccoughed. Trevor's coaxing and the wine had brought her out of her shell.

Quinn walked home thinking how nice it had been to see Alita. He'd forgotten to ask if they'd fixed on a date for the wedding.

Chapter Thirty-Three

July 2036 – Six Eventful Months Later

"My new wife Alita and I..."

Cheering broke out, allowing time for another glance at notes before the speech could continue. "Thank you, thank you. I am so proud. Alita and I thank you from the bottom of our hearts for coming here today."

Quinn was squirming inside as the awkward words stuttered across the room. He looked around him. Robert had been lucky to secure Esquina for the wedding. Quinn had gone with him to book the function room. Robert thought Quinn's position at the BC would impress the manager, and he was right. Other venues had declined such a small event, but La Esquina accepted their booking.

It had been in Esquina that Quinn had first met Lance. It looked different today. The ornate function hall had been decorated, though not for the wedding. It was decked out with national flags and bunting in preparation for the Revolution Day Celebrations due later that week.

The hesitant speech went on, and Quinn remembered how nervous he had been at his Cajun wedding years ago in peacetime. He pictured Leonie that day, and had to work hard to keep concentrating. Today's stilted words boomed and echoed between his ears.

"When I first met Alita and Robert, I never thought one day she would be my wife. My life is so different and better than I could ever have imagined."

One of the guests from the basketball group called out, "Just wait! It's the end of your freedom, man!"

There was laughter and hollering, and another voice added, "Will she still let you come to shoot hoops with us?"

Quinn looked at Alita who was smiling, the light from the tall windows reflecting off her eyes. The swell of her chest and her smooth brown neck gave him the same tingle as her first congratulatory kiss had, the day he'd told her about his new job. Beside her, he saw Robert glance up from his feet. There was a tear in the proud father's eye.

A lump formed in Quinn's throat. In his head a crescendo of staccato gunfire began to deaden the prepared words, and against the colourful flags and the flaking cornice he saw grainy flashes of Leonie and Riona on the Floridian beach. Then his bleeding, choking father.

At last, the torture ended. "A toast! To my beautiful Alita!"

The guests responded with applause, and as glasses clinked together a tear slid down Quinn's cheek.

Alita whispered in his ear, "That was lovely, Q-T. I love you so much!" She kissed him deeply, as raucous cheering filled the room.

One evening back in March, Robert had arrived for dinner with Alita. Quinn had been surprised and pleased to see her, but it soon became clear that something was wrong. Quinn wondered if they'd argued about something, to do with the wedding plans maybe. Trying to break the ice, he'd asked what time they thought Lance would be joining them.

"Will I just order a beer for Lance now? That's what he usually starts with."

Robert had spat his response.

"That bastard will never come near my daughter again!"

"Papa!"

The subject was closed. Quinn knew something bad must have happened. At one point when Alita was in the restroom Robert had looked at Quinn as if he was going to say something, but the evening continued in near silence.

A couple of evenings later Robert had knocked on Quinn's apartment door.

"I need to talk to someone," he said as he walked in. Two weeks earlier he'd spotted bruising on Alita's neck.

"She's never been able to lie to me," he'd said, wiping a tear away. "Who walks into a door with their neck?" He was shrugging, attempting a smile.

When she'd eventually admitted the cause of the handprint, Robert had gone straight to Lance's apartment, punched him once in the face, and left. The next day he sacked Lance from Tres Reyes and told him to leave Havana.

Though Lance was much younger and six inches taller than Robert, Quinn understood why he hadn't argued. Robert was fit, muscular and could be very imposing.

"He's gone," Robert had said.

Quinn realised why Lance hadn't showed up for the last two basketball sessions. The consensus of opinion amongst the other players was that he had been offered a manager's post in another Tres Reyes branch. Over the next couple of months, without Lance's enthusiasm the numbers turning up dwindled and the sessions ended.

###

Quinn lay on his back, looking around the big room with its dark wood furnishings and gilded mirror. Sunlight was penetrating the curtains and he'd heard the day's first few flights depart. Looking again at Alita, her snoozing face still smiling, he tasted last night's love on his lips. When he stroked her amber shoulder she roused and turned, and the white sheet slipped down. His passion rose to meet her searching hand as she pulled his body back into hers.

###

The apartment was in one of the older buildings near the airport, solid and comfortable though lacking the triple-glazing newer blocks around it had.

"This is the best wedding present possible," said Quinn as he lay back on the wide mattress. Robert had bought them a brand-new bed, and he'd insisted they move into his room in the apartment. He would now have Alita's smaller room across the hall.

Robert had stayed in a friend's apartment on the wedding night and taken his work uniform with him. Quinn had a day off work, and he and Alita had the whole of their first married day to themselves.

"Papa likes you so much, Q-T. He is so pleased."

"I didn't think he approved of me, being a widower and all. I mean, I'd been married."

They had discussed how they had come together many times before, but Quinn was still marvelling at his fortune.

She squeezed his hand. "I'm still sorry about Leonie, Quinn. And Riona. It's so sad."

They lay quiet for some minutes, and Quinn fixed his gaze on the white ceiling.

"I thought I'd die when I found out they were dead. I always thought they'd come to me. If only I hadn't left them on that beach."

"You've nothing to feel guilty about, Q-T."

"And then when I finally started getting over losing them, I started feeling sorry for myself. I thought I was the unluckiest man alive." Turning to look into Alita's eyes, he went on, "I was so jealous. Of Lance, because he had you. I wanted to kill him sometimes."

She held him tight, and he could feel her breath under his chin as she spoke. He knew what she would say next almost word for word, but he needed to hear it again. There was something else she hadn't told him yet.

"I wanted you Q-T, but you were married. I tried to make myself stop thinking of you. And then by the time you found out what happened to Leonie, it was already too late." She kissed his neck. "I was with Lance, and I thought I was stuck."

They were silent again, Quinn raging at Lance. He was jealous. And angry.

As if she sensed what he was thinking, at last this time Alita told him more. But not what he wanted to hear.

"I didn't let him – you know – I still kept thinking about you."

Quinn turned his eyes back to the ceiling. He had wanted her to be honest. He wanted to tell her what Lance had said at basketball. Then he could tell her that he didn't mind. That he understood.

He had to go on. "He told me, though. Well, I heard him bragging that you and he–"

She raised up on one elbow and put her finger over his mouth, shushing him and forcing him to look back at her. "He was all talk. I didn't let him. I know he said those things. Elena's boyfriend is one of the basketball guys. She told me what Lance was saying. After Papa sent Lance away."

Quinn was able to smile, tears in his eyes. Lance's lurid boasting had all been lies. He rolled towards Alita and pulled her tight against him. The tension trapped within him was escaping, and an enormous sigh of relief ended with a nervous chuckle. "You kept yourself pure for me."

Now he felt her tense in his arms. He cursed himself. They'd never spoken of the abuse she had suffered. All he had heard was what she had said that Sunday night on Ragged Island. He still had the RI7 card in his wallet. Domingo. 8.00 pm. Alita y Robert.

"I'm sorry. I shouldn't have…"

Deadpan, she murmured as if he wasn't there. "I have no tears left. I was worthless. Trash. I thought no man would ever want me."

Quinn was hating himself. "I'm sorry, I…"

But she continued, louder. She was shaking her head and her hair was tickling his shoulder. "It's not a secret. Why do I deserve privacy? Everyone can see I am a piece of shit, why should I try to pretend?"

"Alita, it doesn't–"

"Doesn't matter? Doesn't matter?" She pulled back and rolled to face away from him. He could see her shoulders twitching. She did still have tears.

When Alita's silent sobbing had ended and he knew she was dozing, Quinn rose and went to the toilet. He was brushing his teeth, staring with disgust at his reflection above the sink, when he felt her hands slide around his chest. She pulled him, and they padded back to the bedroom holding each other.

"When Papa told you about me, that night on the island, it was the first time he had told anyone. But I just felt – kind of numb. Like it didn't matter. It didn't matter people knew what I was."

Quinn now had the tears. Alita turned in the bed to face him and went on.

"But after we escaped, when we were in Cuba, I got angry at Papa. I was mad at him because he'd told you. I know I'd talked about it as well, that night on the island, but I was so mixed up then. Like a little girl. I blamed myself for being so worthless." She shook her head and sighed. "It was only later it mattered that you knew about me. You knew I was – dirty."

She paused and Quinn hoped she wouldn't break down again, but her body was relaxed against his. Though her eyes were fixed on him she spoke as if he wasn't there.

"Papa guessed I had feelings about you. He was worried about me, I see that now. But we had a big falling out. I didn't know what I thought. I knew you were married and I could never have you, but I was mixed up. I was shouting at Papa. Saying it was all his fault. You were the only one that mattered, and –"

Her words tailed off again, but Quinn didn't dare interrupt.

"Papa made me stop coming to the café on Thursdays. So I couldn't see you." She began caressing his shoulder.

Quinn recalled the night Robert had told him she was seeing Lance, and his warning to Quinn about being a married man. It had been later that night he'd learned that Leonie and Riona were dead.

"And then Lance started getting jealous. He thought he owned me. He was nice at first, good for me. I thought I was having fun. I didn't tell him about, you know–" She looked into Quinn's eyes and he was proud she trusted him with her past.

"But then he wanted to see me all the time, show me off. It was the day I told him I missed being able to see you sometimes – that was when he hit me for the first time. The night he made me agree to get married."

When they had made love again, Quinn rolled onto his back and said, "I'm starving. Have we got any rotis?"

She pinched his waist hard, able to giggle now. "I've told you all my terrible secrets, Sñr Tarrant. From now on I'll be your sex slave, and yours only. But I will never be your kitchen slave!"

Chapter Thirty-Four

October 2036

The café was growing quieter after the Friday lunchtime rush. Quinn still had 20 minutes before he needed to be back at his desk, and turned to Alita. "Y'know? I'm going to have another iced tea. D'you want one?"

"I've got all afternoon. I'm not in a hurry!" She smiled up at him.

Alita had the day off work and had joined him for lunch. As he made his way to the self-service, he caught sight of Trevor Edge at a table near the front window. He hadn't seen Edge since January, and he diverted on his way from the counter to say hello.

"Hi, Trevor. I haven't seen you for months. You been away on business?"

"Ah, hello, Quinn. I didn't see you there. I'm here waiting for a delivery. I've been meaning to call you, though. There're few things I need to ask you sometime. I hear congratulations are in order. You're married now, I understand. Would you care to join me?"

Quinn smiled. Trevor lectured rather than chatted. He hadn't been able to contact Trevor to invite him to the wedding. "I'll just bring Alita over. She'll be pleased to see you again."

Alita liked Trevor, even though she had told Quinn his English accent had reminded her of the men on Ragged Island and made her skin creep at first. Edge stood up when she approached the table.

"Mrs Tarrant, it's an absolute pleasure. Would you let me order you a drink?" He held a chair out for Alita. Quinn could tell she was stifling a laugh at Edge's formality.

"Don't you take deliveries at your office?" Quinn said, sitting down with his glass.

"A special delivery, by courier. Erm – urgent spare memory for a server I am building. It ought to be here by now. I've got to have it today." His eyes kept flicking towards the door. "How's married life, you two?"

When the delivery arrived Quinn had just made his way between the dozens of tables in the café to visit the restroom. He heard a motorbike engine through the open toilet window. When he came out the rider was facing away from him. He could see it was a woman, shapely even in grey leathers. On the back of her uniform, he saw the logo 'Havanaspeed.' It was reproduced in a smaller version on the back of her full-face helmet.

The delivery rider handed Trevor Edge a document envelope. Once he'd signed a docket she hurried back out of the café door.

As Quinn was making his way back to join Alita and Edge, he passed the café window and saw the rider climbing onto the motorcycle. Sitting astride it she paused, reaching into a pocket to draw out a cell phone. He could hear it ringing, muffled by the plate glass of the café window. With her other hand she pulled off her helmet to take the call, and Quinn gripped the edge of the bar, trying to stop his knees buckling. It was Leonie.

###

Quinn's afternoon went badly. His screens appeared blurred, and trades flashed by unnoticed. It can't have been Leonie. I know it was her. She's dead. Edge and Lange both said she was dead. Did she see me? Don't be stupid. You're imagining it. She's dead. It was her!

Round and round his mind went until it was time to leave for the day. It was Friday and he was off for the weekend, but Alita would be working both days. He was glad he was going to be alone. He spent the evening listening as intently as he could to her excited chatter about their plans. At one point Leonie's face superimposed itself on Alita's and he had to look away. They had the same olive skin, but Leonie's eyes were bright, pale blue. Alita's were larger and deep brown.

For their next weekend off together he and Alita had planned to rent a car from Tres Reyes and travel back to Camagüey for old time's sake. Alita was sure that if they had to pay anything at all she could get a preferential rate. When she asked why he didn't seem to be paying attention Quinn blamed tiredness. Work had been hectic. By ten o'clock she said, "Oh, just go to bed." He wasn't sure if she was annoyed with him or not.

Robert was also working that weekend, providing VIP transport for a conference. Quinn spent the time mooching around the apartment. He struggled to tear his mind away from the clear image of Leonie in the café, which seemed to be imprinted on his eyes. By the time Alita came home after work on Saturday he was desperate for a distraction. He needed Alita's company, but was worried she would sense his preoccupation. He made dinner before she came in, and fussed over her. She smiled beautifully at him, her head tilted slightly and her brow quizzical.

"What have you got to confess to, my lovely, cheeky little boy?" she said, reaching out and squeezing his cheeks together between her slender finger and thumb.

Quinn pulled her to him, embracing her to hide his guilty face. There was a lump in his throat and his eyes were moist. "I just love you."

He thought he maintained conversation well enough to get away with it, but at bedtime, Alita said, "I hope you feel better tomorrow, Q-T. You've looked so sad." She took his hands. "It's OK if you want to talk about Leonie and Riona. I don't mind. I know you still miss them."

All he could say was, "Sorry." After they put the lights out she kissed him sweetly, and he hugged her before turning away. He cried himself to sleep, biting his cheek to silence his sobs.

Alita's tenderness and sensitivity helped. On their way to Camagüey for the nostalgic visit, he wanted to say something to explain his distracted state. Camagüey reminded him of the time when he'd still had hopes of reuniting with Leonie and Riona, he told Alita. He felt guilty for making this up, but she squeezed his hand in sympathy. They'd gone on to discuss his grief for his father. She told him that he still cried out for his dad in his sleep, as well as Leonie and Riona.

Over the coming weeks, he decided that intense grief must have transposed Leonie's face onto the motorcycle courier's. He kept telling himself the girl had only had a passing resemblance to his dead wife. After all, he dreamt about Leonie and Riona almost every night, and their faces were never far from his mind.

Even with the joy he had found through being with Alita, it wasn't surprising his subconscious mind was still battling.

And as he lay at night looking at Alita sleeping, he remembered the dreadful experiences she was still trying to put behind her. What a pair of damaged souls they were.

Chapter Thirty-Five

As another Christmas season approached Quinn suggested that he and Alita buy Robert a special present. One November afternoon they were both off work and took a bus into central Havana, heading to a tailor's shop.

Alita had a picture of Robert in his favourite suit, on his wedding day. Quinn remembered Robert showing him the photo as they were preparing for their escape from Ragged Island. It had been difficult for Alita to borrow it from Robert's wallet that morning before he left for work.

"Oh, Q-T, I'm not sure about this. What if Papa notices the picture is missing?"

Quinn knew they both cherished the photo. Alita's mother had died when she was a young child but neither she nor her father had ever spoken to him about their life in The Bahamas.

"He'll be too busy at work to notice. There's another conference on, and he'll be buzzing about all day. We'll put the picture back when he takes his nap."

By the time they stepped off the bus, Alita had returned to her excited planning.

"I've made a note of all Papa's measurements from his work uniform." Quinn loved the lilt of his wife's voice.

They found the shaded street where Felipe had told him his uncle had his shop. "Sñr Tarrant, you must go to the best! The best tailor in Cuba, the whole Caribbean." The narrow street was bustling. Tall buildings with flaking coloured paint funnelled and amplified the noise of traffic and business.

The tailor assured them he would be able to make the suit in time for Christmas. As they stood in the tiny shop, whirring Singer sewing machines and reams of cloth on dusty shelves, Quinn noticed four motorbikes on their stands outside the building opposite. Two men, one short, one tall, and both skinny, stood smoking beside the bikes. They wore distinctive grey Havanaspeed leathers. Quinn recognised the logo, his stomach lurching as the vivid memory of Leonie removing her helmet filled his mind. He knew it had been her.

###

A week later the tailor rang to say the suit was ready. It was just after eight o'clock and they were preparing to leave for work.

"Can you collect it at lunchtime, Q-T?"

"Erm – no. I've got to meet with the new 7th floor manager."

"Oh, that means it'll be next week! If it doesn't look like it'll fit Papa there won't be time to have it altered before Christmas."

Every night since their visit to the tailor Quinn's sleep had been a roiling swirl of images. Motorbikes, a dark car in the night, Riona's eyes. Worst of all was Leonie in grey leather, beckoning to him from the pavement outside the Havanaspeed office opposite the tailor's workshop. He knew she hadn't been there, but simply seeing the logo again had been enough. He was no longer so certain he'd imagined seeing Leonie. Going near the Havanaspeed office was too risky. What if he saw her again? Or worse, she might see him. If she was alive.

Alita didn't know he thought he had seen Leonie delivering the package to Edge. He wondered about telling her now, hoping she would reassure him it was his imagination. He told himself it would be cruel to upset her, but he knew it was cowardice that stopped him.

Alita saved him from the dilemma. She smiled. "Oh, wait a minute. I've just remembered. I'm meeting Franca in town after work on Monday. I'll be able to go for it then." As she left for work she kissed him, saying, "I can't wait to see Papa's face when we give it to him!"

It was becoming clear to Quinn that he had to do something. He had to prove to himself he was not a bigamist, or he was going to go mad. If he could confirm that the courier in the café had not been Leonie, he could try to forget her and Riona. Again.

That lunchtime he used his cell phone to call Trevor Edge. "Hi, Trevor. Can I ask you something?"

"Yes Quinn, and I'm glad you called. I've been trying to reach Robert but his cell phone is off. Can you let him know I can't meet him later today after all? What can I do for you?"

"I need a quick favour. At work they've asked me to send an urgent package. I need a courier. Who do you use?"

There was an uncharacteristic pause before Edge responded, "I rarely need a courier, Quinn. It's months since I've used one."

"What about the woman who brought you that package that day? The one on the motorbike."

After another hesitation, "I didn't – I mean it wasn't me who arranged that, Quinn."

"Sorry, but can you find out? I've tried phoning a few places, but no one can help today." He found the lies surprisingly easy, and went on, "My boss is desperate, and I said I could arrange it. I don't want to lose my job."

He was worried he was going too far, but persisted.

"That courier you used did a special delivery. Urgent, you said it was. Where was it brought from?"

"Cienfuegos. Why?"

"That might be the best Havanaspeed office to try. Erm – 'cos they do urgent business. Thanks, Trevor." He cut the call before Edge could ask any of his questions.

His plan had worked. He already knew the Havanaspeed office near the tailor's workshop was one of many spread all over Cuba. He couldn't risk repeated furtive web searches using the BC system, and it would be impossible for him to visit all the courier's branches to look for someone who looked like Leonie. Now at least he knew where the woman he had seen had set out from. The woman he'd mistaken for Leonie must work at that branch.

Chapter Thirty-Six

December 2036

Using a different rental company was yet another deception. More guilt. He didn't dare use Tres Reyes again, preferential rate or not. Alita might see the booking.

"Will you be returning the car before 6 pm, Sñr? If not I will have to charge you the full day rate?" The man in the brown suit smiled at him.

"No, just a quick business trip. Cienfuegos."

"I'll make it a hybrid, Sñr, although the battery should easily take you there and back."

On the south coast, Cienfuegos took nearly three hours to reach. The black and white median strip zipping past him on the quiet, straight road was mesmerising. He could think of nothing but his task ahead.

He'd taken a day off work, lying to his manager that his wife was ill. He hadn't told Alita, and tried to justify the deceit as worth it to rid himself of the ridiculous notion that Leonie might be alive.

The navigation software in his work cell phone took him straight to his destination. Even without it, the grid system of numbered streets would have made it easy to find Avenida 45. He parked opposite a large modern clinic, next door to the Cienfuegos office of Havanaspeed. With a clear view of the front door and the row of motorcycles outside it, he sat watching the riders coming and going. If he was lucky he would see the woman who had delivered Trevor Edge's package.

He sat pretending to read a newspaper and trying not to be noticed. A delegation from Delhi and Beijing had arrived in San Francisco, he read. Hopes that they could broker yet another peace deal were not high.

His mind wandered back to a nagging feeling that bothered him. Something about Trevor Edge didn't quite add up. For some reason Edge had lied about the urgent delivery of "spare memory." Quinn had seen what the rider had handed over and it had been a paper file. And Edge asked too many questions, forever probing. Robert had noticed it as well. He had commented that Trevor always seemed to be contacting him, engaging him in conversation.

Still, that didn't matter today, he told himself, trying to concentrate on the Havanaspeed riders across the road.

After half an hour there had been no sign of the woman. Quinn became restless, cursing himself for thinking up his crazy mission. He still had to travel back to Havana in time to return the hire car and get home at the usual time. Coming to Cienfuegos had been too much of a gamble. The woman he'd seen in grey leather might work out of a different office. She might no longer even work for Havanaspeed. This was all a stupid waste of a day.

Climbing out of the car he strode towards the office. He would have one quick look inside. When she wasn't there, he would drive home and force himself to accept that the woman delivering Edge's envelope hadn't been his dead first wife.

Above the desk in the neat office was a board bearing bright, smiling pictures of the branch staff. Second from the left on the top row, a clear image looked out at him. 'Leonie Tarrant' was printed boldly below her beautiful face, as if to emphasise his guilt.

"You're late tonight."

"Yeah, sorry. I missed the usual bus. The floor manager kept going over some trades she thought someone had let through unchecked. There was no problem, though." Lying was becoming easier and easier, and Quinn was feeling worse and worse about it. At least one thing he had said was true – having to catch the later bus.

He couldn't remember driving back from Cienfuegos or dropping off the rental car. He had hidden near the back of the bus across town, wishing he didn't stand out in his coppery hair and pale complexion. At one point he had convinced himself Robert was at the wheel of a shiny limo in the queuing traffic ahead.

Quinn tried to behave as if everything was normal. For days he tried to deny what he had seen on the Havanaspeed office wall. But he couldn't. It was Leonie he'd seen delivering the package to Edge, and he was a bigamist.

It wasn't just Alita he was letting down. Robert had trusted him to care for his daughter. And Leonie and Riona, of course. Leonie was bound to be searching for him. It would be better if she thought he was dead. He hated himself when at his darkest times he wished the opposite – that Leonie and Riona really had been murdered.

He had questions for Trevor Edge, but had tried his phone several times with no success. Why had Edge lied to him? And Dieter Lange? How could they have got it so wrong?

Nights were pure hell. Leonie, and even worse Riona, haunted him as soon as he closed his eyes. Every morning Alita told him he'd been grinding his teeth and crying out their names. Her expressions of helplessness and sympathy almost made him disclose what he knew. He held back, though. Made excuses. He said he had no memory of his night terrors, no idea why they had started. Promising Alita he would get through it somehow, he tried to convince himself.

After two weeks, his exhaustion and mood swings were creating increasing tension. One morning as she was about to leave for work, Alita stopped at the apartment door.

"Tonight, Quinn, you sleep on the bedroll on the floor. I can't stand your thrashing any longer. And if you won't let me help you, you'll need to sort yourself out. I give up." She slammed the door on the way out. Robert was just leaving his room, pulling on his uniform jacket and hurrying to follow Alita. As he left he threw a determined look of concern back at his son-in-law.

Quinn knew he was going to have to confess.

Chapter Thirty-Seven

January 2037

Quinn might be facing awful trauma, but it was nothing compared to that his wives would endure. Revealing his bigamy would end both marriages, but he couldn't end them both at once. Eventually he decided the first to know should be Leonie.

It meant continuing to deceive Alita for a time, but he could see no other way. Leonie was unlikely to let him ever see Riona again, but if there was the slightest chance she would, Quinn wanted to explain himself to his daughter. Before she disappeared from his life forever.

Now he had a plan, Quinn relaxed. Alita noticed.

"I love you Q-T. I am so glad you're better. I was worried, Baby, when you were so sad." She stretched and rolled towards him, stroking his cheek. Unable to resist he turned to embrace her, feeling like a condemned man savouring his last meal.

Entering the narrow Havana street he remembered so well, Quinn passed a small plaza shaded from the late January sunshine by a few royal palms and banyans. The tailor's shop appeared to be closed, flaking green shutters drawn over the door.

Across the road Quinn could see the Havanaspeed office, its door propped open by a box of printer paper. Three motorcycles stood outside, each bearing the same logo he had seen on Leonie's leathers and helmet: a cartoon motorbike whizzing above the company name. The same adorned a garish sign above the office door. He swallowed, cleared his throat to make sure he could speak, and walked across the road.

"I have an envelope for one of your drivers," he said to a white-shirted man seated behind a corner desk. The oscillating grilles of an aircon unit creaked overhead.

"Leave it there," the man said, without looking away from his computer screen. "Did you book it online?"

"No. It's not for delivery, it belongs to one of your riders."

The man sighed. "What? Leave it there." He pointed to a clear space on his cluttered desk. "Which rider? They might be here today."

"Leonie Tarrant." The words felt strange in his mouth.

The man looked up at him for the first time. "You have it wrong, Señor. That's not one of our riders."

Quinn's throat dried. He had prepared his words a hundred times, but had to make two attempts to continue. The man shook his head in irritation until Quinn gushed out his lines.

"I think she might be based in Cienfuegos. It's just – you see – she delivered a package to me at work this week and a paper fell out of her pocket. I tried to catch her, but she was gone. I think she will want it back. It's personal. Private, if you know what I mean." He managed what he hoped was a knowing smile, man to man. To him his story sounded ridiculous.

The clerk shrugged, looking confused. Quinn felt he had to improvise. More lies flowed. "It's from a man. A lover, I think. I shouldn't have read it. Very personal. She will want it back." He tried to smile and wink.

The man tutted, shaking his head again but reaching out to take the envelope. Quinn had sealed it securely. Turning it over in his hands, the clerk said, "If you are sure she's one of our riders

I'll check the system. If I can, I will send it to her." The desk phone rang, and he waved Quinn away.

He hadn't lied when he'd told the Havanaspeed man the envelope contained a very personal note. He'd written it himself, after scrapping dozens of draft messages. His words had to be vague, but intriguing enough to entice Leonie to meet him.

> *'Hola, Señora Tarrant*
> *I know what happened to your husband Quinn Tarrant.*
> *I can show you proof.*
> *Meet me in Havana.*
> *You must know his fate and you must tell Riona.*
> *53-47-224893'*

He'd bought the cell phone at a street stall, the SIM card in a convenience store. Now he carried the phone with him whenever he was at work, checking it continually. Feeling like a spy, he hid them in a locker at the BC before going home.

One night while he and Alita made love, he wondered if Leonie had contacted him. He hated himself.

Over three weeks had passed when Leonie responded. Quinn silenced the phone in his pocket, mouthing "sorry" to Stringer who had looked up in surprise at the unusual ringtone. As soon as he felt able to leave without drawing attention to himself, he sat locked in a toilet cubicle looking at the phone in his hand.

He'd flicked the latch on the main restroom door as he entered, and checked each of the other cubicles was empty, but even so when he pressed the voicemail button he held the phone hard to his ear in case the message could be overheard.

Leonie's voice sent waves of love, sadness, and despair through him.

"I don't care who you are. I'm not giving you money. My husband is dead."

Quinn listened to the message several times. It was her Louisiana accent that affected him most. He sobbed as quietly as he could. When he returned to his desk Davy, a man from Glasgow who often sat opposite Quinn, said, "Y'awright there, pal? Yer lookin' a wee bit peely-wally." Quinn had once made the mistake of describing Davy as 'English'.

His next message to Leonie was a text. He spent two days looking at the phone before he could send it.

Reply to this message before you next make a delivery to Havana. I cannot visit your Cienfuegos office again. I will meet you with the proof.

He had started the hurt already. He knew Leonie would think someone was stalking her, but he had to let her know he was serious.

Chapter Thirty-Eight

March 2037

He'd chosen a quiet café near the Havanaspeed office. Her embrace was so tight it was hard for him to breathe. Smells of wet leather and Leonie's hair were intoxicating. Quinn wanted to stay like this forever. At last, she relaxed her grip on him and leant back in the booth wiping tears away. He knew he was going to remove the joy from her beautiful face. Older than when he'd last seen her, her cheeks had filled and she looked years younger. He realised for the first time how much weight she had lost in their years in the Everglades. Her eyes had regained their alluring blue sparkle. She embraced him again, her arms strong, not bony.

Their passion was drawing attention. It didn't matter. He loved Leonie as much as ever.

"Q-T! Q-T! I love you! Oh, Quinn, I thought – Riona thinks – oh, Quinn!" She held him again and he couldn't help himself. He squeezed her tight, kissing her neck and breathing in her fragrance and the smell of the road. The words he had prepared wouldn't come, a bitter taste caught in his throat.

"I thought you were dead," Leonie went on. "I saw the PBC firing at the boats. The bodies. Oh, Quinn!"

He had to tell her how he had reached Cuba, about the days on Ragged Island. She was like an excited child with question after gleeful question, smiling as she held his hand.

"But Soporte told me no one with your name had ever arrived in Cuba. I don't understand."

Quinn couldn't understand that either. Finding his voice at last he said, "I was told you were dead. And Riona. By officials."

For a moment Quinn was back in the Neptuna when Edge and Lange had told him his family had been slaughtered. How had they got that wrong? And how had he, Leonie and Riona all arrived in Cuba without Soporte knowing?

"It doesn't matter, Q-T. You are alive, and so am I. We can carry on. I *am* glad you've shaved off that beard, though." She winked an eye at him, and went on, excited. "Wait until you see Riona! She is so big. At school. Here, I have a pict–"

"Leonie. I have to tell you. It's because I thought you were dead I..."

"It doesn't matter, Quinn! You're here now! I love you, Quinn Tarrant. We are going to be togeth..."

"Leonie, I am married."

"We're married, yes, we are, we will be a family again. I..."

"I married someone else."

Chapter Thirty-Nine

Quinn didn't know how many bars he had been in, or how long ago he had given up searching the city for Trevor Edge. It was all Edge's fault.

He didn't know where the Edge IT office was and didn't dare ask at Soporte. If Felipe was there he would sense Quinn's distress, and he couldn't risk breaking down. He didn't deserve sympathy.

At first, in fury, he had rushed from bar to bar, café to café, scanning the customers for a man in a sailor's hat. He didn't know what else to do, but he had to do something. He had to find the man who had made him a bigamist.

Then in one bar, he'd sat down to cool off under the fans and ordered a rum. That was hours ago. Now he was maudlin, slumped and calling for more drink.

He should have expected Leonie's slap. He deserved it, but its suddenness and power had shocked him. There was a cruel look on her beautiful face. As he watched her race out of the café, his cheek was searing. Even now, through his stupor he could still hear the Suzuki's scream echoing between the tall buildings when she'd sped off out of his life.

"Have you no one to go home to, Señor?" A barman was shaking his shoulder.

"Fuck off!" He pushed the chair out behind him and heard it crash on the tiles. Outside, he bounced off smiling, babbling people as he searched for another bar.

###

He could see a tall glass of water and ice, just out of reach. Enticing condensation on its sides taunted his cardboard tongue. Reaching for it was out of the question. Any movement meant another blow from the mell hammer aimed at the back of his head. Next to the glass he could see several small cones of raspadura arranged on a folded paper bag.

Quinn worked out that he was at home, alone in the bed Robert had gifted him and Alita, but had no idea how he had got there. Some thoughts began to come into focus, but not the ones he needed. What might he have said to Alita? Had he told her?

The door cracked open, and he screwed his eyes tight against the light. If she thought he was asleep she might leave him alone.

"Q-T, try some water, please, Baby. And you need sugar." She was whispering.

He could hear her creeping around the bed. When she lightly brushed the edge of the mattress an earthquake rocked his world. His head swam and his throat fought against a rising tide of bile.

"Try it, Baby, please. For me." She had cooled her hand on the wet glass before she stroked his forehead.

Maybe it was an hour later when she tried again. For all he knew it was a whole day. This time he opened his eyes.

"That's better, Q-T, try to sit up. Let me help you."

Her tender touch and gentle support let him prop himself up on his elbow as she held a fresh glass to his lips. He tore his tongue from the roof of his mouth to swallow a few drops.

She was going to let him recover before she threw him out.

"I'm sorry." He didn't hear his words. They buffeted off the inside of his skull, echoing louder until they reached a painful crescendo.

"Ssshhh, Baby. Oh, Quinn, you poor man. Papa said this was coming. We've been so worried about you. Your ups and downs. You've been so depressed, Baby."

Over the day, Quinn found out that when he'd fallen asleep in another bar, the barman had taken Robert's business card from his wallet and called him. Alita said Robert retrieved him, and between them they cleaned him up and put him to bed. She had watched over him all night.

From her continuing kindness and concern, he guessed he couldn't have told her about Leonie. Yet. He worried that he might have said something to his father-in-law, but when Robert had called in on his lunch break he'd been almost jovial, unable to stop himself smiling as he admonished Quinn for his drunken foolishness.

The sugar in the raspadura seemed to help, and his screaming headache receded. But in its place gathered clouds of doom. He'd told Leonie, and now he had to tell Alita.

"It's just as well you didn't have work today, Q-T, you'd never have made it." Alita was grinning at him and shaking her head. "You'll be OK for tomorrow."

"Alita, I need to tell you something."

"Ssshhh, Baby. Have a sleep. I don't mind, I understand what you have been feeling. I hear you shouting in your dreams every night." She was stroking his forehead.

"I need to tell you what's been upsetting me. I have to. It's driving me mad."

"Go on. But it's OK. You can say anything you want. I will still love you."

It was painful, knowing how upset he was about to make her. But he had to tell her before Robert returned from work. Alita would throw him out straight away, and that meant he wouldn't have to face her father. He could remember the warning: 'I cannot let you hurt my daughter.' Leonie's slap would be as nothing compared with Robert's punishment.

"I have been dreaming about Leonie. And Riona."

"I know."

"Let me tell you, Alita. I have to." Her pitying smile made it hard for him to look at her, but he forced himself, speaking directly into her eyes. "I have seen her. She is alive. I went to find her. I'm sorry–"

"Oh, Baby! You poor Baby." She leaned in and hugged him to her, a finger over his mouth. "SShhh. SShhh. Don't upset yourself. It's OK if you think you have seen Leonie. She was your wife. You miss her, and Riona. I know, I know. Your mind plays tricks. But you will come to accept they are dead, Q-T, you lovely, lovely man." She was rocking him, crying herself now, and he dissolved into helplessness.

Alita's unbreachable trust in him was too hard to resist. He knew he was being a miserable coward, but he gave in, unable to bring himself to hurt Alita in the way he had Leonie. He made himself believe it was best for all if he carried on his life with Alita. Having to hide the truth from her and Robert for the rest of their lives would be his penance.

In the days that followed, Leonie's slap and hateful expression were fresh enough in his mind to continually remind Quinn of how badly he had betrayed her. Worse than that, Leonie now had to decide whether to tell Riona her father was still alive. If Riona knew, she would wonder why he wasn't coming back. Leonie might let her continue believing her Dada was dead. But then Leonie would be drawn into the deceit.

Deceit was his responsibility. It wasn't entirely his fault he was a bigamist, though. If anyone it was Edge or Lange who gave him false information.

But Leonie was blameless.

Quinn decided to try to contact her once more. Not to ask for forgiveness, the opposite. To offer to relieve her of deceiving their daughter. If she agreed, he would speak to Riona, confess to her himself. It would mean his beautiful daughter would also hate him forever, but it was something he could do for Leonie. And he wanted to see Riona again, one last time.

He wrote a pleading, apologetic letter to Leonie, posting it to the Havanaspeed office in Cienfuegos.

By mid-April, he had almost given up hope. For weeks he had pestered the new BC mailman every day. Then an envelope dropped on his desk. The postmark showed it had come from Paris, France. At first he thought it was another commercial mailshot, but it was addressed by hand. The handwriting was Leonie's.

He stared at the padded envelope for several minutes, before gingerly pulling back the adhesive sealing strip. He found a note inside, and a small parcel wrapped in tissue. It was written on a date-stamped page torn from a Havanaspeed memo pad.

No. You will never see me or Riona again. She believes you are dead. As you are dead to me.

He knew before he unwrapped it what the little parcel would contain. It was Leonie's wedding ring.

Chapter Forty

It was a week since Quinn had received Leonie's curt note. His nights were now dominated by Riona. Exhausted, he tried not to sleep, fearful of thrashing and calling out. Watching Alita sleep, her olive skin glistering in dim light, all he could see in front of him was Riona.

He was becoming angry. At himself for neglecting Alita, at the unfairness of his situation, and at something else he couldn't define.

An idea grew. He could confess to Riona in writing. He would plead with Leonie to keep his letter until Riona was old enough to understand how and why he had left her life. He would trust Leonie to do as he wished, appealing to what might remain of her respect for him. From there on he would concentrate on Alita, the one love he could hope to hold on to. Alita. Innocent, wronged, and endlessly trusting.

First, he had to find an address. All he knew was that Leonie had written to him from France. He tried phoning the Cienfuegos office one lunchtime, but each time he dialled and waited, gripping his cell phone and chewing his cheek, the number was busy. When the office was relatively quiet and no one was likely to pass his desk, he tried calling from a BC line later that afternoon. He was connected instantly and made his awkward, stuttering request.

"I cannot reveal confidential information about our staff."

"But can you just tell me the address? I have to know where my daughter is."

There was a pause. "Señor, I know nothing of your daughter, and I can tell you nothing about Señorita Tarrant. No matter who you say you are, Señor." Then a click, and the dial tone.

Hearing his wife referred to as 'Señorita' pierced Quinn like a dart. He put the phone down and sat back, deflating. For the first time, he began to accept defeat. Leonie had left Cuba, gone to France, and taken Riona with her.

"Are you OK, Quinn? You look like you've had bad news." Uliana was on her way from the water dispenser with a conical paper cup in her hand. Quinn wondered how she was going to put it down on her desk.

"Err, no, it's OK. Just something I had to check up on. It doesn't matter. It's fine."

Quinn tried to hide the unfocused, confused rage that grew in him, but the pity on Alita's face showed him he was failing. When the elusive source of his anger began to emerge like a shape in the mist, having a focus for it only brought more questions. They ate away at him like a fungus.

Had Trevor Edge deliberately deceived him? Why?

After his furious hunt on the night Leonie had slapped him and left his life, Quinn hadn't made any more attempts to contact Edge. He'd tried to convince himself that the Englishman and his German associate had been given false information. But niggling doubt about Edge grew and grew. If he didn't confront it he was going to drive Alita away.

He knew Robert also thought there was something not quite right about Edge, but Quinn couldn't discuss his suspicions with his father-in-law. That would mean revealing what Edge had got wrong, that Quinn had married Alita illegally. He'd seen what Robert had done to Lance to protect Alita. His fury at Quinn wouldn't stop at a punch on the nose.

###

One Sunday in late May when Robert and Alita were both working Quinn sat brooding in the apartment. The rainy season was well underway and a late afternoon thunderstorm had left puddles on the road outside. He watched steam rising into the humid air, and came to a decision. He was going to tell Edge that he knew Leonie was alive.

Quinn wanted to see how Edge reacted. His hunch was that Edge would be genuinely surprised to hear he had been wrong. Quinn could then finally conclude that his bigamy resulted from a misunderstanding. No fault to be laid.

But if Edge knew already, if the bastard lied to me, I'll kill him, he said out loud to the empty room.

Other than his phone call to ask about courier deliveries Quinn had had no contact with Edge for months. The last time they'd met in person was the previous October, the day he'd seen Leonie on the motorcycle. Before Alita and Robert returned from work he tried Edge's cell phone several times. Each time he received only a 'number unobtainable' message.

Despite his frustration, for the rest of the evening Quinn felt energised by the prospect of putting his anger to bed. He was able to make Robert laugh, and his good humour made Alita's eyes sparkle.

Over the next few days, he kept trying Edge's mobile, eventually coming to the conclusion Edge had changed his phone. He called Felipe and found out the office number and address for Edge IT Services, but the one time he had called it the phone rang out until Quinn hung up.

He began to wonder if Edge was avoiding him, but unless he had something to hide there was no reason for that. Maybe Trevor had left the country for good?

On his way home from work a few days later, though, he spotted Edge. Even through the misted bus window he was unmistakable in his Breton cap, coming out of a café. Quinn knew the Edge IT office was nearby. His limbs tense and his teeth clenched, he craned his neck to watch Edge until the bus turned a corner.

About to leave for work the next day, Quinn kissed Alita. "I'm gonna be home late tonight, Baby, a strategy meeting. And then it's Stringer's leaving party."

Stringer was leaving, but there was no party. One more deception. The last, he promised himself. Then he could really settle with Alita, even if it was to live a lie in an illegal marriage. He had to know if Trevor Edge and Dieter Lange had lied to him.

He told his floor manager he had a dental appointment, and was allowed to leave an hour early. After a day at work trying not to think of the confrontation to come, he stepped off a bus near the University with hollow nausea and an inner tremor.

Crossing a busy road, Quinn entered a tree-lined avenue between two modern glass blocks. Its paving was neat, traffic barred by huge, artfully-placed marble tubs planted with manicured evergreen shrubs. He found Edge IT Services listed on a directory board outside a building called 'Nuevitas House'. New life, he thought. Ironic.

When he pressed the button beside the engraved Edge IT plaque he heard no sound. Typical. An IT company with a busted doorbell. The main door was locked, and a sign told him a 6-digit code was required to permit entry. He stood for a moment wondering whether he should just wait at the door for Edge to come or go. Then his phone rang in his pocket. He pulled it out; 'Edge IT' was displayed as the caller. Coincidence?

"Hello, Quinn. Nice to see you. You're looking well. What can I do for you?" It was Edge's voice.

"How? Erm – where are you? I want to see you." Quinn was confused and off guard, his voice echoing.

"That would be nice, Quinn, but I'm out of town today. I'll be back in an hour, though. Wait in the café in the foyer." Edge ended the call before he could respond. The door buzzed and slid open, and he found himself walking in automatically. This was not what he had expected.

Inside the one-way glass that shrouded the building, he found a bright, welcoming atrium. A man in pressed linen smiled him towards a comfortable leather chair and set a glass of iced water on a low table.

"May I bring you a coffee, sir? Or some fresh fruit?"

"A coffee, thank you."

"I'll bring that right away, sir. Mr Edge asked me to tell you he will be down to see you just as soon as his meeting is over."

So, is he in his office or not?

While he waited, an armed security guard patrolled past twice. Quinn grew uncomfortable. He couldn't confront Edge here. His eyes swung back and forth between the front doors and a row of elevators as he wondered which direction Edge would appear from. In which direction to direct his rising anger?

"Here you are, sir, another espresso, and this time I have brought you some shortbread. I'm sure Mr Edge will not be much longer."

A voice from behind made Quinn jump, and he saw the concierge look up and smile as he set a tray down.

"It's OK, William, I'll look after Mr Tarrant from here, thank you. Quinn, I'm so sorry I have kept you. The traffic was heavier than I'd expected. Shall we go to my car?" Trevor Edge walked away towards a door Quinn hadn't noticed. He stood up and followed Edge like an obedient child.

Edge led him out to a car park and drove them into the traffic with a cheery wave to an attendant who lifted the barrier as the car approached. Quinn had a flashback to his job in Rayville before the civil war had tipped his life upside down, until Edge's easy chatter drew him back to the present, reminding him of the purpose of his mission.

"Where are we going?" he asked, cursing himself for being so passive. He had intended to tackle Trevor Edge full-on, but the older man's confidence and commanding manner had disarmed him.

"I thought we'd go for dinner. And a few drinks. How would that suit?" He glanced over at Quinn with a wide grin. "It's been a while after all. My treat. Anywhere you fancy?"

Trevor Edge had taken control. Soon they were seated in a busy café, Edge enquiring about Alita and Robert. "I'm sorry I have neglected you recently, all of you. But I have been meaning to get in touch. It's fortunate you came to visit me. Was there something in particular?"

Food was brought and Edge had poured generous glasses of red wine for them both. All evening he topped up Quinn's glass after every few sips.

"How did you know I was coming to see you? I mean, the concierge thought you were in the building."

"I don't always tell them where I am. And I do actually have *some* IT skills, you see." He winked. "I altered the building's security software a little. Reception now only see my video door alerts if I want them to. It lets me come and go as I please. And others, come to that." He winked again and tapped the side of his nose. "It's rather unofficial – you won't tell anyone, will you?"

An hour later Quinn was enjoying Trevor's company. His friend somehow always knew what to ask to keep him talking. As espressos arrived, each served on a small tray with a shot of aged rum, he realised he had almost forgotten his purpose. He'd drunk very little since his binge after meeting Leonie, and the wine had already affected him.

"Trevor, I wanted to ask you about my wife."

"The lovely Alita? What can I know that you don't?"

"No, Leonie."

"Oh, poor Leonie Dugas. Dreadful business! I'm so sorry for you, Quinn, losing her like that. And your little Riona. It must be awfully hard. Are you beginning to come to terms with it?"

"They're alive. Both of them. You were wrong. Why did you..?"

Quinn couldn't finish his accusation, his words tailing off. Edge appeared shocked and momentarily lost for words, but before Quinn could respond he knocked back his rum and continued.

"Come on, drink up. Let's go on somewhere quieter where we can really talk. You can tell me all about it." He was on his feet, holding Quinn's jacket out to him while he placed some banknotes on the table.

Chapter Forty-One

A taxi took them to a small bar. Once they'd passed the Museum of the Revolution, Quinn became lost in narrow backstreets. He thought he was somewhere near Havana's port area, but didn't care. Edge's reaction had reassured him. His friend Trevor had seemed just as surprised as he had that Leonie was alive.

But something Edge had said wasn't right, and as Quinn was taking his seat it hit him. 'Poor Leonie Dugas.' How did Trevor know Leonie's maiden name?

"Why did that German, Lange, say Leonie was dead? And why, how, I mean, what do you know about Leonie? You called her Leonie Dugas. Her name was – is Tarrant."

In the café and the taxi, Edge had been very much the convivial fellow. But now they were in a dimly lit bar booth he reasserted his authority over Quinn. "It's my job to know things. You don't think I'm *really* an IT consultant, do you?"

A waiter put a bottle of wine between them. Edge pointed at it and Quinn obeyed, pouring two glasses.

"Listen, I'm sorry. It was a calculated guess, I had to keep you on board. When I heard later that Leonie was in Cuba, I had to do some quick thinking. I still needed more from the Moncurs. At that stage you were my only link to them."

Quinn couldn't speak. He stared at Edge, more bewildered than angry. Edge must have sensed his confusion, and took him back to their first meeting.

"I couldn't believe my luck that time in Soporte when I overheard you tell dear old Felipe you'd been on Ragged Island. I'd been preparing my approach to Robert Moncur that very day.

I didn't even know you existed, Quinn. But by the time I came to meet you later that afternoon, at the BC, I knew all about you."

Edge was smiling, looking into his wine glass as he recounted what he had discovered.

"Your father's death in New Orleans, Quinn, well, I can tell you that gave me a few concerns until I confirmed he hadn't been targeted. 'Taken out' as you Yanks might say." Edge chuckled, before going on. "But it was random, Quinn. Poor Mannie was no threat."

Quinn was shaking his head, struggling to absorb what he was hearing. He shifted on the wooden bench of the booth as Edge continued. "And of course, it was easy to check out Ms Dugas." He looked up at Quinn, still smiling. "Sorry, I talk too much sometimes. Am I going too fast?"

Quinn found his voice. "You – you know all that? How? Why? My Dad! What the fuck?" He sat back staring, unblinking, his head against the cool stone wall.

"I work – used to work – for British intelligence services, Q-T. You might have heard of MI5. It's quite easy to find things out when you ask the right questions." Edge was tapping his nose and winking again. Quinn felt sick. Edge had raked through every small detail from his past like trash. He'd been violated. The smouldering anger deep inside him began to ignite.

Edge went on. "When I read the paper you had written at university – ULM I think, wasn't it? – I couldn't believe the coincidence."

Quinn lunged forward. "You bastard!" In a flash, Trevor Edge was round the table with his arm gripping Quinn's shoulders. He couldn't move, and felt himself sag. Tears of confusion and defeat welled in his eyes.

"Is everything OK, Señor?" The waiter had rushed over.

"Yes, thank you, my friend's just had some news. He'll be okay in a minute. Could we perhaps have some iced water?"

"Of course, Señor."

Edge relaxed his grip on Quinn. He took his arm from around him, but stayed close by his side. Quinn was trapped on the hard wooden seat with Edge between him and the world outside the booth. He had no choice but to listen as Edge began explaining his motives and intentions, checking now and then to make sure his subject was paying attention.

"So it was the actions of English money men like those you came across on Ragged Island that pushed over the first domino, so to speak. Purely to increase their own fortunes they set in motion the whole carefully staged drama that took England – the UK – out of Europe. The first disastrous link in a chain of events that led to the destruction of my country." He paused, turning to look straight at Quinn. "And yours, Quinn." Edge was smiling, but speaking through gritted teeth as if controlling rage. "The island you happened to be stranded upon, Ragged Island, was their retreat, their haven. And their hiding place. Are you following me?"

"I get what you're saying but why should I believe you? You're trying to tell me that just one country splitting from Europe caused the civil war in the US?"

"It's true, Quinn, I assure you. Well, with a little help from Russia and our Chinese friends. But really, I am sorry I deceived you about Leonie. That was very unfortunate. The truth was I had no way of finding out what happened to her. Traffickers deal in cash, don't keep proper records, you see," Edge said with a sardonic smile.

Edge took a long draught of the iced water.

"I only offered to help because it was a way of extracting more information from you. Or to be honest, more from the Moncurs." When you phoned and told me you were meeting with Robert and Alita that night, I just had to meet them. I took a calculated risk, told you your wife was dead. You have to admit it was most likely, given what you later told me happened on the beach at Layton."

Quinn was reminded of his smug professor at ULM, not only by the reference to financial misdealings causing world turmoil. Edge also appeared to enjoy the sound of his own voice.

"And my luck kept going. When you got together with Alita Moncur, I mean. Having you, Robert and Alita together couldn't have been more fortunate for me."

"You did that, told me lies, that my wife and daughter were dead – you told me that just to get to know my friends?" Quinn wanted to kill Edge, but felt powerless, overwhelmed, as if he was under the MI5 man's complete control. He tried to push aside the fleeting notion that Edge might even have steered him and Alita towards each other.

"Yes, Quinn. It's that important to me. Those useful idiots on Ragged Island are mere pawns in a much bigger game, but taking them out will not only be satisfying – revenge if you like – I might even get closer to the Table."

'The Table' again, thought Quinn. But none of that mattered. Still trapped in the booth and gripping the edge of the bench with both hands, he glared at his captor. "But Leonie is alive! And Riona. And she thought I was dead. Riona still does. Why couldn't she find me when she came to Cuba?"

"I was as surprised as you Quinn, when I was told she had turned up." He put on his sarcastic look again. "Well, perhaps not, but I honestly thought she would never have survived. But just in case she ever did make it to Cuba, I had altered your immigration records. I deleted you from Soporte files. If anyone searched to see if you had entered Cuba, your name wouldn't appear."

Quinn remembered Leonie saying that Soporte staff couldn't trace him when she'd enquired. A bolt of fury hit him.

"You were told when she arrived? Who told you?"

"That stupid fucker who brought her here!"

Quinn was surprised by Edge's sudden anger and didn't know who was its target. But he had a more important question.

"When?"

Edge went on as if he hadn't heard Quinn. "I remember having to think quickly." He raised his eyebrows and shook his head, smiling. "I altered her Soporte details pretty damn sharpish, in case Felipe or someone was still looking out for her. But it seems that somehow you have found out about her anyway."

Quinn's jaw was clenched hard as he tried again. "When? When did you hear she was alive?"

"I think it was October – no it was November. November '35."

"You bastard," Quinn hissed. He thought his fists were going to crush the wooden bench. "That was before I married Alita. Leonie was still alive."

Chapter Forty-Two

Quinn lay beside his sleeping wife, still trying to make some sense of the strange evening. He stared into the dark, anger focused on himself now.

Quinn's bigamy was a trifling inconvenience to Edge, it seemed, much less important than the geopolitical turmoil of the last few years. 'I took a calculated risk and told you your wife was dead,' he'd said, continuing before Quinn could object. Under Edge's compelling stare and against his flow of convincing rhetoric, Quinn had only been able to sit dumb, his fury dissipating.

Despite Edge's deception and manipulation, Quinn had meekly accepted the Englishman's generosity. After their shared taxi had dropped him off at the apartment, he had even thrown Trevor a friendly wave. Alita woke only briefly, relieved that Quinn was sober after Stringer's leaving night celebration.

With no choice but to listen as the Englishman went on outlining his version of recent history, Quinn had become intrigued. Much of what Edge had said went over the top of his head. The fantastical ideas about the origins of civil war in the Americas, and interference by China and Russia had made Quinn doubt anything Edge said.

And that Table nonsense. According to the former spy, this mysterious organisation he called The Table had arranged for US and UK assets like satellites and oil reserves to be sold off to billionaire financiers. Financiers that Edge maintained were themselves being controlled by Russia, China and even Brazil.

'When the dominoes began to fall,' Edge had said, 'the Table could manipulate competing interests into starting civil wars.'

Edge was a solid gold conspiracy theorist.

He had to admit, though, that Edge's ability to find out details of Quinn's past and his family had been impressive. He'd read Quinn's ULM thesis, and that was meant to be secure behind impenetrable online firewalls. Was it true that Edge had connections in the security services?

His next thought made Quinn sit up in bed, the sudden movement rousing Alita.

"Bad dream, Baby?" she mumbled. Before he could respond she was asleep again. He lay down, shaking his head slowly. He'd remembered Saul Dombey's fury on Ragged Island: 'And those stupid Yanks sold everything they had to the highest bidder! Refineries, pipelines, Christ, even the fucking satellites...'

Now Quinn knew why the name 'Saul Dombey' had seemed familiar when he heard it on the island. He had typed it several times in his thesis. Dombey had been a prominent commentator on the United Kingdom's economy, a spokesperson for the politicians in favour of the UK's exit from Europe.

As he traced more cracks in the plaster above, Quinn had realised that Dombey's claims about 'the stupid Yanks' lent weight to what Edge had said.

Since arriving in Cuba, he had seldom thought about Dombey, Witte and the rest. Like Cleeter, their crimes had been against Alita and Robert, and those poor youngsters who'd been flown in as sex toys for the RI7 and their guests to abuse. Though he was proud of helping Alita and Robert escape from slavery, those men on Ragged Island had done nothing directly to harm him. They hadn't even been aware Quinn had washed up on their island.

But Edge was trying to make out that the men had caused Quinn to lose his father, his livelihood, and his country. According to Edge, the UK's collapse into lawlessness had set the USA on its path to civil war. 'The first domino to fall,' he'd said.

He remembered Edge's bitterness towards the RI7 and his reference to 'taking them out'. Edge seemed to want some sort of 'revenge', and needed information from Quinn and Robert to help him plan for it. Quinn pictured Edge's face as he'd laid out his ideas. It had looked as if the Englishman was in a world of his own. An hour later Edge had told him it was time to leave.

By the time he got up to shower before work, Quinn had decided he was having nothing more to do with Edge. The Englishman was the only other person who knew Leonie was still alive, and he'd had no recent contact with Robert. As long as Alita and her father never found out about Leonie, Quinn had a chance of some happiness, even though he would never see Riona again.

"That bastard's had everything from me he's going to get. He's nothing more than a deluded fantasist," he said out loud.

Alita padded into the bathroom. "Were you talking to yourself in the shower?"

Chapter Forty-Three

June 2037

When the telephone on Quinn's desk buzzed, he jumped in surprise. He looked at it for a moment before reaching out and wiping a layer of dust from its answer button.

"Hello?" he said, looking around the office floor to see who might have called him on the BC internal phone rather than messaging his screen. Uliana was just going into the Floor Manager's office and all the other traders appeared to be as busy as ever, staring at screens and tapping into keyboards. It could only be Audit calling him. He panicked. He must have made some catastrophic error.

"A planning meeting, Quinn, tonight, 7 pm. Esquina."

At the sound of Trevor Edge's voice, Quinn's shoulders relaxed, before tightening again. He hissed, "What are you doing? Calling me here? This is an internal phone. How did you..?"

"Relax, Q-T. Remember my real occupation. This call will not appear on the BC's precious system, I assure you. Not even as an untraceable one. Just be at Esquina, 7 pm. You like it there, don't you?"

The commanding tone was hard to resist. Quinn had blocked Edge's number on his cell phone and hadn't heard from him since their evening out the previous week. Now the bastard wanted to meet him again.

"Trevor, listen, I don't think I want to. I mean I'm not getting involved with whatever you're planning. You could get help from your old MI5 pals if you want to hurt the RI7."

"This is unofficial, Q-T. My game. My rules."

Quinn put his hand over the mouthpiece and stretched up to let his eyes scan the room. No one appeared to have noticed he was on a call. He was angry at Edge and piqued that he'd been able to evade the BC's rigid security systems. And that he had tried to order Quinn to meet him. Despite it all, though, he felt himself sliding towards agreeing. "I can't. Alita..."

"I've just spoken with Alita. She's fine with it, Q-T. You have a lovely wife there. It'd be a shame for us to upset her. Wouldn't it?"

Hairs stood up on Quinn's neck and he gripped the receiver until he thought it might crack.

For the rest of the afternoon, Quinn struggled to focus as millions of Euros, Yuan, Rupees and Roubles whizzed down his screen. Normal world trading continued despite his or anyone's personal circumstances. His work had become as automatic as driving a familiar road – you arrive at your destination with no memory of the intersections and stop signs you have negotiated. Still, he thought, even if he slipped up and came to the attention of Audit it would be nothing compared to facing Alita if Trevor Edge told her Leonie was alive. Edge's implied threat had been unmistakable, and terrifying.

He stayed at his desk until after 6 pm. On the walk towards Esquina, he crossed busy streets and avoided oncoming pedestrians like a robot. Distracted after Edge's call, he'd forgotten to charge his phone and couldn't tell Alita himself that he would be out for the evening. At least Edge phoning her meant she wouldn't worry when he didn't come home. Another demonstration of Edge's power. It was only a week since he'd decided to have nothing to do with the Englishman or his crazy plans, but again, Edge had taken control of him.

As he dodged between hurrying bodies and bicycles, he drummed up determination. He was going to be firm. He wouldn't be helping Edge, whatever the mad fantasist was planning. Tell him he knew the crude threat to tell Alita had been nothing but a bluff. Despite his resolve, his mouth was dry and his heart beating up into his neck as he pushed open the door to the restaurant.

When he saw Robert Moncur in deep conversation with Edge all his courage melted away. They were at a corner table, a bottle of wine open between them, and Edge had a consoling arm on Robert's shoulder. Robert lifted his head with a doleful expression, seeming to look right through Quinn.

From behind him, Quinn could hear a waiter offering to take his jacket. His throat constricted and a weight like a medicine ball filled his stomach. Edge must have told Robert that Leonie was alive and his daughter's marriage was illegal.

"Ahh! Quinn, join us, sit down." Edge spoke like a compassionate clergyman. "Robert will be OK in a minute. He's dealing with something very painful for him."

"Robert, I'm sorry – I mean..."

Edge waved his hand at Quinn and said, "Robert, is it OK if I tell Quinn what we have been discussing? It always helps to share a problem."

Robert's silent stare at nothing continued, and Quinn started to turn. "I'd better go, I–"

"Sit down," Edge had his commanding voice back. "Robert has just been relating to me how his poor wife died all those years ago."

Quinn was sure there was a slight upturn at the left corner of Edge's mouth. The bastard was playing with him. He knew exactly what Quinn must have thought when he'd arrived to see Robert so upset.

Robert was wiping his eyes on a napkin. A wave of relief washed over Quinn as he sat down, followed by one of guilt. Robert's wife had died, unlike his own. Robert's loss was real. And Alita's.

Quinn listened in silence while Edge continued to counsel Robert. Alita's mother had died in a car smash when she was seven years old. Robert had told Quinn that much when they were still on Ragged Island. Now, as Edge gently encouraged Robert to open up about the accident, Quinn could understand why little Alita had been spared the details.

"They found her left foot thirty yards away. In a tree." Robert was choking sobs, and Edge's arm went back around his shoulders.

"I know, and the car ended up on its roof. Just terrible," said Edge. Robert appeared to stiffen in his seat and turned to look at Edge, who continued, "I was working in the Bahamas and saw the Fire Chief's report. Shocking business."

The same waiter who had tried to take Quinn's coat returned and asked if they were ready to order dinner. By the time food was being brought to the table, Robert appeared a little brighter. "It's good to be out with my son-in-law," he'd said looking at Quinn, "and to know he is so good for my Alita." Quinn squirmed, but it meant Robert didn't yet know about Leonie. He could relax a little, but he tried not to catch Edge's eye.

Quinn struggled to stay tuned in to everything Edge was saying, especially when he started rabbiting on to Robert about 'The Table.'

After they had eaten, Edge ordered more wine and said, "Let me get to the point: why I wanted you both here. I need your knowledge about Ragged Island, Robert. I want details of the layout of the cabins, and the access tunnel. And from you, Quinn, I want everything you can remember about the RI7. Even the most trivial detail might make the difference between success and failure. Planning for a mission like this must be meticulous."

"Mission?" Quinn said.

Is this madman planning to travel to Ragged Island? Until then Quinn had assumed Edge's intention to 'take out' the RI7 meant his revenge would be political or financial. And carried out remotely. Edge claimed he was an ex-secret agent, and had demonstrated how easy it was for him to hack through sophisticated IT security. It would be equally easy for him to disrupt his former countrymen's lives.

Robert was paying rapt attention, unblinking eyes focused on Edge.

"I am going to tell you things about myself you must never repeat," Edge continued. "When you suggested I seek the help of my 'MI5 pals', as you called them Q-T, it was a little ironic." He was smiling. "I am persona non grata with my former employers. Not at all welcome. I wouldn't be surprised if there were a price on my head."

Quinn remained silent. He'd been right about Edge being a fantasist, but he had to stay and make sure he hadn't told Alita about Leonie. Or even worse, told Robert.

"You know I've been away a lot over the last year or more." Edge had been uncontactable for much of 2036 and recently when Quinn had been trying to confront him about Leonie's survival. "That was because acquiring the necessary materials to equip our little team for the mission has been rather more difficult than it would have been before I took my leave of my British masters."

Edge was talking once more about a 'mission,' but the words 'our little team' worried Quinn more. He blurted, "Team? What are you saying..?"

"Yes, Quinn, the three of us. You're going back to Ragged Island with me. Won't that be nice?" Edge was grinning. "We're going to put an end to the RI7 and their little set-up."

"I'm not part of any fucking team!" Quinn surprised himself at the loudness of his voice. "There's no way in hell I'd ever..."

"Count me in." Robert's sudden interjection even seemed to surprise Edge.

Chapter Forty-Four

"Excellent, Robert! You won't regret it."

"Robert! You must be insane! You can't mean you're going to go along with this madman?"

"I'll do anything to stop Cleeter and those animals. I know what they did to Alita. And they are still doing it to more young girls."

And young boys thought Quinn. He saw a fleeting vision of the man called Isaac relishing an expected delivery of young male flesh. There was sick trade on Ragged Island, and who knew elsewhere, but how could Robert possibly think it could be stopped?

Quinn continued his protest. "But we can't do anything. I mean *you* can't do anything. I'm not going."

Edge appeared to be enjoying the interplay. There was a slight smile on his face as he flicked his eyes back and forth between Robert and Quinn.

Robert's voice had a firmer tone than Quinn had heard before. He was addressing Edge, but looking at Quinn. "We will both go with you, Trevor."

Edge reached out to shake Robert's hand. "Thank you, Robert. And Quinn, I promise you, the mission will not be dangerous for you. You will be our getaway driver, so to speak. You'll remain in the boat, ready to take us back to Cuba where Alita will be waiting to continue her happy new life with you." Edge turned to stare deep into Quinn's eyes. "Otherwise, you'll never be able to be altogether sure she won't suffer more trauma." The corner of his mouth turned up again.

Quinn sat back from the table, hating Edge. But it was useless trying to resist. Robert was going to avenge Alita, and he expected Quinn to help.

Robert appeared excited, with a rush of questions about the mission and how soon they could go. He leant forward pointing a questioning finger at Edge. "Quinn and I know why we hate those men on the island, and God knows Alita hates them, but what do you have against them? What makes you want to take them on? Money?"

Edge laughed. "Money? No. Anger, yes. And perhaps a bit of nostalgia for the way things were. Before they destroyed it all, I mean."

Robert was still staring at Edge. "Is it because you lost your job? With MI5, I mean? Is it revenge for that?"

That's exactly what it is, thought Quinn. He's no different from a disgruntled store worker who burns the shop down when he's passed over for promotion.

Edge paused before he spoke. He had both hands on his wine glass and was staring at it. "It's much bigger than that. Yes my, erm, profession has changed, but it's changed before. My first boss used to yearn for the good old days of the Cold War. But the focus moved on from the Russians. Chinese, Arabs, it didn't matter. We always found an enemy."

He took a sip of wine and shook his head slowly. "But 'we' always included the Europeans. That's why the CIA tolerated us."

Quinn thought Edge's voice was going to break. "Then ruthless, self-serving sociopath politicians took us out of Europe. They gambled away the family silver, didn't they? Everything went to hell. It started the rot. Then what happened?" He looked at each of them, palms upturned, eyes wide and jaw tight. "Same every-fucking-where. Bastards." Edge rarely swore, and Quinn had never heard him speak with such passion.

Robert leant forward. "Gambled? Someone lost a bet and that changed everything?"

"Yes. A gamble the people supposed to be in charge of the country didn't expect to fucking win."

At ULM Quinn had read accounts by others who believed the UK's departure from the European Union was the result of a game that had gone wrong. Despite himself, he felt some sympathy when Edge went on, now sounding more dejected than angry.

"All our businesses moved to Europe, Asia, any-fucking-where that wasn't the UK. The British people suffered. Prices rose, people went hungry." He looked at the floor. "The Far Right saw their opportunity. Stirred up race hate. Destabilised the whole system. Like the 1930s all over again." A tremor in Edge's left leg was catching the underside of the table, vibrating the wine glasses.

What he said next struck a chord with Quinn. Edge contended that similar right-wing groups then sought power in the US. At one time Quinn had been seduced by their promises of restoring the US to its rightful place at the pinnacle of world order. He'd gone on the march in New Orleans, expecting it to be the start of something glorious. Instead the States collapsed into chaos and civil war. Perhaps there was something in Edge's domino theory?

"Sorry, Trevor, I'm not sure I get it." Robert's brow was furrowed. "Are you saying Britain's exit from this 'EU' started the ball rolling for right-wingers in the US as well?"

Edge lifted his head. With a grim smile, he said. "Exactly, Robert. And fascists elsewhere. But it was financiers that encouraged it. The slimy, greedy fund managers. *They* didn't care. They were going to make their fucking fortunes whichever way the vote went." He now gestured over his shoulder with a thumb, in no particular direction. "And that lot – the fucking *RI7* – they were the worst of the lot of them. They bought Ragged Island with some of their spare cash, and the bastards even make money out of that." His anger was back. "When they're not on the island themselves – off at home pretending to be fucking family men – they rent their hideaway to Cleeter to entertain some other high-paying perverts."

Robert cleared his throat and said, "I don't care about any of that stuff you said about England and whatever. I still think you're just jealous of the RI7. It *is* their money you're interested in."

Edge flashed a smile and looked like he was going to agree. Then Quinn thought he appeared to check himself as if he'd dropped his guard.

"Erm – no. Simple revenge. I'm not interested in their millions. Billions." He fixed his eyes on Robert. "I've lost my country. That lot on Ragged Island robbed all of us of our dignity."

After taking a mouthful of wine Edge stared at his glass. When he went on Quinn had the impression his passion was forced, as if delivering a prepared speech.

"England's strength was built on working with our neighbours. At least we made them think we were working with them. Of course, we were manipulating them, making them work for us without their knowing it. But it was a sort of cooperation." He exhaled, theatrically. "England was never going to survive on its own."

Quinn thought he could see moisture in Edge's eyes. Even though he was a fantasist, a psychopath, he couldn't help suspecting the Englishman might also be an actor. It was hard to believe Edge's motivation for going to Ragged Island was simple revenge against those he blamed for destroying his beloved country. If he could remember correctly, the UK left Europe about twenty years ago. Perhaps it *was* just the money he wanted.

But Robert's enthusiasm to join Edge's mission was what worried Quinn most. He had to deflect him.

"He's crazy, Robert. Taking revenge for what he thinks some men lying on a beach did decades ago?" Robert turned to look at him, and Quinn went on, "And anyway, it's Cleeter who organises the abuse. Shouldn't we be going after him, not the men on the island? They're just Cleeter's clients." His words sounded feeble.

Robert turned back to Edge. "So, Trevor, when are we setting off?"

Edge looked pleased. Putting both hands on the table, he said, "Yes, back to business. I only managed one quick reconnaissance, that's why I need your knowledge."

Robert was all agog.

Chapter Forty-Five

The alarm clock showed 1.43 am. Quinn untangled himself from Alita's warm embrace and looked across at her satisfied smile. She sighed and slept on. A wave of pride and pleasure would have wafted him into a peaceful sleep, if his mind wasn't already back on the choice he faced.

He could go with Edge and Robert on the crazy trip to Ragged Island, or he could refuse and live with the threat that Edge would reveal the truth about Leonie and Riona. And live with Robert's disapproval. In the taxi home, Robert had made it clear that he expected Quinn to take part. Avenging the dishonouring of Alita by Cleeter and his clients was as much Quinn's responsibility as it was his, he'd said. It made no sense to Quinn, and he wondered if his father-in-law could have some other motive.

Edge had outlined his preparations so far. He had obtained arms and ammunition from old contacts. Enough ordnance to dispense with the RI7 ten times over, he'd said. He was working on acquiring a suitable craft to make the crossing to Ragged Island. Quinn worried that the former spy was so set on revenge he might take suicidal risks. Robert, though, had been hanging on the Englishman's every word. He'd answered probing questions about the precise layout of the cabins in the compound, the network of pathways, and where best to come ashore. It had seemed to Quinn that Edge already knew a lot of it.

Quinn had asked how to explain their absence to Alita. Edge and Robert were adamant that she was to be deceived yet again.

"You'll need a cover story," Edge had said, with a cruel smirk at Quinn, "she trusts you." Robert had smiled and nodded, unaware of Edge's backhanded compliment.

Edge's questions for Quinn were about the men on the island. He asked Quinn if he agreed with Robert that apart from perhaps Saul Dombey, none of the RI7 would present a physical challenge. Edge already seemed to know the men inside out, but Quinn had to tell him everything he could remember about each of them, the smallest details, and then Edge asked the same questions again in case he'd missed something.

Quinn had to admit it to himself: Edge's meticulous planning and focus on the minutiae were impressive. He couldn't say the same about the ex-spy's more outlandish theories. He now lay beside Alita, summarising them for himself.

Like a teacher addressing junior pupils Edge had claimed that a committee of super-powerful men and women controlled governments the world over. They manipulated world geopolitics to maximise their own wealth and power, paying no regard to the harm caused by the wars they started. According to Edge, governments of so-called superpowers were mere pawns of this syndicate. Edge had gone much further than Professor Carson at ULM had ever done. She had just been speculating.

It was a load of bullshit. Quinn had been surprised when Robert backed Edge up about some of it, until he remembered him suggesting something similar on Ragged Island. Quinn had heard the RI7 men discussing The Table himself, and Saul Dombey's ambitions for a seat at it. Bullshit?

Beside his sleeping wife, Quinn reflected on why Edge could want him in his team. He was to be the 'getaway driver' of their boat, but there was no need for one. Edge or Robert could steer the boat.

Robert, too, had insisted on Quinn's involvement. Quinn went to sleep planning to have one more attempt to persuade his father-in-law against the mission.

"¡No! ¡No! ¡Para!"

The three words, repeated over and over in Quinn's sleeping brain, roused him. The room was still in darkness.

"Oh, por favor, no, para." More plaintive now, a whimper.

He turned, stretching his arm over Alita, pulling her in close.

"Oh, Baby, it's OK. I'm here. Baby, I'm here."

He held her until her limbs became less stiff and her sleepy face replaced the grim rictus of terror. By then there was just enough light to let him count the cracks in the old ceiling plaster. At least she didn't go through it every night now, he thought.

Chapter Forty-Six

"I'll try not to wake you up when I get back." Alita kissed his lips lightly as they embraced at the apartment door.

"I'll never get to sleep without you there," said Quinn.

"You'll be snoring as usual!" Before leaving, she leaned forward and whispered close in his ear, "I'll wake you like you've never been woken before."

Her hot breath riffling in his ear made his face heat, but when he turned back after closing the door Robert was reading a magazine. His father-in-law was always tactful and reserved but Quinn was sure there was a slight smile on his lips. He knew Robert liked him and took pleasure from seeing his daughter so happy. Quinn was glad, though, that between Robert's bedroom and theirs were two thick stone walls. The heavy, wooden doors of both rooms were always discreetly closed for the night.

This evening it was Quinn's turn to cook. He brought two plates of his Cajun-style chilli, extra hot as Robert liked it. It was a week after they'd met with Trevor Edge, and they hadn't discussed Edge's plan since. Quinn hoped Robert would have reconsidered. This was the first time they'd been together without Alita.

He wanted to raise the subject, but for now Robert seemed happy to chat about Alita and Quinn, and how proud he was of his daughter.

"You are good for Alita, Quinn. I thought she'd never find happiness, but now I watch you two together and I know she loves you."

"I'm so glad she does, Robert. I never thought I would be happy again." He felt another stab of guilt. It was true he hadn't felt love and joy like this since before the war, but it was all based on deception. He hated what he had done to Leonie and Riona.

"I vowed I would always protect my Litl-A after her mother died." Robert was staring at himself in the tarnished mirror above the dark wood chest behind Quinn's seat. "But I failed. I tried, but I had to work. I thought she was safe in her school. But even in The Bahamas, that animal was selecting girls."

He looked back at Quinn but appeared to be staring right through him.

"Cleeter's recruiters toured schools and youth clubs, luring their bait. Even tonight, I know she is out with her friends, but still, I'm scared she is not safe from those bastards."

"Robert, it's OK if you don't want to talk about this." Quinn spoke as much to shield himself from hearing more as to protect Robert. But it was as if he wasn't there. Robert went on.

"When she had new clothes and make-up, she said it was some of the rich girls at school giving them away. She became a good liar. But I saw bruises. I made her tell me."

Quinn couldn't prevent tears from overflowing. He wasn't sure whether he was crying for Alita, Robert, or himself. Robert said, "I have no tears left, Quinn." He stretched over the table and placed a comforting hand on Quinn's. The skin of his thick fingers felt impossibly smooth.

"I know what it is like, Q-T, to lose a wife. But not a daughter as well."

Quinn flinched and looked up into Robert's earnest eyes.

"When Trevor told you that night, told you they were dead, I was no help to you. I am sorry. I was back in my own sadness."

Robert rubbed at the corner of his eye. "But I hope being with Alita will help you recover. From your grief." He pushed his chair back from the table and stood up, his face turned away. "I must use the toilet." Guilt and shame were crushing Quinn's insides.

They finished their meal and sat in silence. Quinn still hoped to raise the subject of Edge and Ragged Island but couldn't think how. A while later, Robert snapped his book shut.

"A fishing trip. That's what we'll say."

Quinn looked up from reading his tablet. He'd read the same few pages over and over, unable to concentrate on the story. "Fishing?"

"For Edge's mission. That's what we'll tell Alita."

Any remaining hopes that Robert had changed his mind about going with Edge seemed to drain away.

"Robert, I'm not sure–"

"We'll kill those bastard men on Ragged Island."

"But they didn't touch Alita. Those men, I mean."

"How do we know that? Some of them may have been customers of Cleeter before they came to Ragged Island. And Alita was too young to recognise any of them. If there's just a chance they touched her it will be worth it for some revenge. And we'll be hurting Cleeter."

Robert had stood up and was staring out of the window. Against the darkness, the bright airport lights shone through his tufted hair like a silver halo.

"Robert, are you sure Cleeter is the one who supplies the – erm..?" Quinn swallowed his words. Robert was turning back round. Quinn shrank from the fearsome look on his face as he spoke.

"I have seen him on the island. Ask Alita! And if he is there with the RI7 I will kill him, too. That would ice the cake!"

Robert's mind was made up. However Quinn tried to persuade him of the folly of Edge's mission, Robert had an answer. And he made it clear it was Quinn's duty to be part of the mission. "We've got to do this for Alita, Quinn!"

Robert's only doubts appeared to be about Trevor Edge.

"D'you remember I thought I'd seen Edge before somewhere? Last week at Esquina I remembered. I was wondering how Edge knew so much already about Ragged Island, and I was staring at him while he spoke. The red hair. He was the new fixer who delivered the girls. On the weekend we escaped the island."

"Edge? No. You mean he was working for Cleeter?"

"That's what I thought. But you remember he said he'd been on a 'reconnaissance'? To the island?"

Quinn nodded.

"He told me the next day he had used contacts to secure a job as Cleeter's fixer. Just to get access to Ragged Island."

Robert had been keeping in touch with Edge since the meeting in Esquina. All Quinn's hope was spent. He tried once more, though.

"Robert – are you sure? Do you believe him?"

"When I phoned him, he came to see me at the office. He showed me letters, a contract if you like, to prove it."

"But he could fake that. His profession, he was a spy. It's all about deception."

"It was real, Quinn. I saw him on the island, remember?"

Robert now wore a wide, grim smile of determination. He was going to avenge his daughter, no matter what the danger.

Quinn could now see no way out. He was going to have to take part in the mission. Otherwise, Edge would tell Alita and Robert that Leonie and Riona were alive. Even without that, Robert would never forgive him for not helping him to avenge Alita and salvage her honour. He tried to tell himself he might owe a similar duty of revenge to his other wife and his beautiful daughter. Who knew what abuses they might have suffered after that trafficker led them away into the night?

Quinn continued to weigh up the pros and cons. What tipped the balance was the last thing Robert had said before they each went to bed to listen out for Alita's return.

"Before I go to bed, Q-T, I will ask you only one more thing. Something very private. Does Alita still – does it come back to her? At night? Does she still cry out?"

PART THREE

RAGGED ISLAND

Chapter Forty-Seven

Morning, Wednesday 13th September 2037

"You'd better go, Q-T. I'll be here when you get back." Alita was smiling, wiping a tear from Quinn's eye as he forced himself to loosen his grip on her. He kissed her hard once more.

"You're sure you'll be OK? I mean…"

"Papa is waiting for you! Go, I'll be fine!" She laughed, her tears flowing now. "It's only a fishing trip, and I'll see you Sunday. Go on, I need to get ready for work."

Robert had booked an SUV for them and twenty minutes later they were in slow morning traffic on Via Monumental, still within Havana. Quinn now looked back at the cool boxes, six-packs, and rods they had packed the previous evening. There was a lump in his throat. Robert seemed to sense his thoughts.

"She'd agree if she knew, Quinn. Alita hates Cleeter and his clients as much as we do. But we couldn't tell her where we're going." Quinn didn't reply and stared at his hands. In the corner of his moistening eye he saw Robert glance across at him. "I'm as scared as you, Quinn, but we have a job to do."

A vast, shining building on the right caught Quinn's eye. A sign spelling out 'Global Data Center' was dwarfed by the familiar rainbow logo of *Cuubl:-)* with its hip, retro emoticon. The traffic began to thin out.

They were both quiet for a few miles, until Robert cleared his throat and said, "I just wish we were setting off from further East. It would be much less time at sea."

After some weeks of silence from Trevor Edge he let them know he had secured the fishing boat for their trip. The only

279

suitable vessel he could rent was in Matanzas. It meant just a 2-hour drive from Havana, but the sea crossing would take a full day and night.

"At a steady 15 knots it will be at least 20 hours," Robert moaned. "A fast boat from Nuevitas would have been better."

They had allowed five days for the trip. Two days of sailing each way, with a day in between to complete the mission. The action, as Edge had called it, was planned for Friday. He'd confirmed the date about ten days ago.

Rolling wooded countryside slid past as the car continued on the Via Blanca. Looking right, the intense blue sea and the pale, bright sky took Quinn back to another coastal drive, six years ago when he and his family had escaped to Florida. Now Riona was almost nine years old and at school. She hadn't even been six when he'd left her and her mother on the Layton beach. He hoped she still thought of him sometimes.

"Nearly there." Robert's words plucked Quinn back to the present. "It should be on the left – along here – there it is, Avenida del Muelle." He swung the SUV across the highway onto a road that appeared to lead away from central Matanzas. Five minutes later they drew up near a small harbour on the North side of a wide bay. Four fishing boats were moored against the harbour wall, and on the foredeck of the smallest one, Quinn could see Trevor Edge in his Breton cap.

Chapter Forty-Eight

Evening, Wednesday 13th September 2037

Havana

The apartment was quiet, empty. She'd been looking forward to having it to herself, but tonight Alita felt the absence of Quinn and her Papa like hunger. She checked her cell phone every few minutes, sighing every time. The end of five long days and nights was almost too distant to contemplate, and she dreaded another topsy-turvy day like the one she'd just had.

First to rock her morning was a horror in heels and stiff hair, who crashed through the office door demanding to see the manager 'right now'. Alita had barely started to explain that the manager would be out of the office for the rest of the week when the woman had slapped the counter. She was cancelling the contract and wanted a full refund. It was bad news for the business, and as Alita had listened to the scary events planner's screeching, she knew their branch of Tres Reyes would be in trouble.

At lunch, she picked at her food with growing distaste. She nodded hi to one of the Tres Reyes drivers who often used the same café, and when she stood up ready to return to the office it was lucky he was there. All of a sudden she felt woozy, a misty whiteness clouding her vision. Seconds later the driver had lowered her back into her chair, calling out for water. He sat with her until she felt able to walk, and insisted he would drive her back to work.

On the way to the office, he'd stopped the car outside the clinic. "Just to be safe," he said before stepping out of the car and opening the back door.

"Honestly, Miguel, I'll be fine." But she went in to see the clinic doctor.

Back at work half an hour later she had to deal with three bookings before she could take time to process what had happened. After listening, examining her and testing her urine the doctor had smiled. Her kind words confirmed Alita's suspicions. "That's what happened to me at the start of all of my pregnancies, Señora Tarrant."

Alita's evening dragged. Sporadic bursts of activity – reading, flicking TV channels, and wandering from room to room – hadn't tired her at all. In between times she'd kept checking her phone, hoping some contact from Quinn or her Papa would help her settle. She wouldn't be able to tell them her news; she couldn't do that over the phone. But it would help just to hear their voices.

Excited, frustrated and lonely Alita gave up and went to bed much earlier than usual. Now, lying down on the big, empty bed she let her tears out. She wanted her mother.

Chapter Forty-Nine

Wednesday 13th September

The Caribbean Sea

It was early evening. Stars were gathering as darkness intensified, and the sea was smooth obsidian, broken only by the churning wake to stern. Serene, Quinn thought, but for the rhythmic clatter of the diesel engine.

To keep up the pretence of an innocent leisure trip, they'd fished while they were still in shallower waters. Most of the vessels they passed were commercial fishing boats, with only a few leisure craft like the one Edge had rented. They motored northeast out of Matanzas on a heading that Robert said would have taken them straight to Andros Island in the Bahamas. After 25 nautical miles there were no other vessels in sight and Trevor changed course. Now on a bearing of 130 degrees, they were bound straight for Ragged Island.

Alita would be home after work now and Quinn needed to hear her voice. He knew they were too far away from land to make communication possible, but he made himself check his cell phone in case freak conditions might allow some signal. Disappointed yet again he switched it off. He climbed back below deck leaving Trevor in the cockpit.

Robert was preparing food in the small galley. The smell of fresh fish made Quinn's mouth water. He watched as rice was steamed and snapper grilled. It wasn't long before Edge descended the ladder to join them.

"I've set the navigation. Shouldn't be much chance of meeting any other boats this far out, but I'll keep an eye on the radar from time to time."

Quinn had grown used to satellite navigation systems and technology working on the fishing boats out of Destin. Robert wasn't so comfortable at sea.

"Shouldn't someone stay up and steer?" he said, carrying plates.

"Relax, Robert, we'll get you there, won't we Quinn?" Edge had a broad grin and appeared excited. "I've been preparing for this for years. I'm not going to mess it up now."

When they'd eaten and all had two or three glasses of rum, Robert was more relaxed. He sat back with his hands behind his head.

"So, Trevor, tell us again why you're so keen to destroy these Englishmen. The real reason this time." With a forefinger, he pointed to Quinn and then himself. "We want revenge, for Alita and all those other young girls and boys. But we can only hurt Cleeter by taking away some of his customers." He sipped at his rum, but Edge remained silent. "I mean, those men on Ragged Island have done nothing to you. Not directly, I mean, only your homeland." Edge looked into his glass and said nothing.

Quinn realised Robert shared his suspicions about Edge's motivation. The Englishman had spent years preparing for this, buying arms, putting together a team. He'd even gone undercover as a 'fixer', trying to become familiar with the layout of the Ragged Island compound. There had to be more to it than simple, foolish pride and nostalgia for the former United Kingdom. Edge reached for the rum bottle, but stayed silent.

"Trevor, this 'Table'. Could it exist? Really, I mean," Quinn asked.

Edge now sat forward, his eyes fixed on Quinn. "How much do you know about it?"

"I remember the RI7 discussing it, but apart from that I only know what you told me that night in Havana. When I came to your office to ask you about L..."

Quinn checked himself. Robert was listening, and he'd almost let slip Leonie was still alive.

"When I asked you about London, the UK, I mean." Robert was still looking back and forth between him and Edge, and Quinn felt panic rising. He rushed on, "And you said it was all down to this 'Table' lot. They'd been manipulating the US into selling off satellites to foreign agencies, you said, and some crap about oil refineries. But is it for real, this Table?" While Quinn prattled on trying to cover his tracks, he tried to look straight at Edge, but he could feel his cheek burning under Robert's fixed stare.

But Robert corrected him. "You're getting mixed up, Quinn, it was the night the three of us were in Esquina. I remember you telling us you'd heard the man called Saul say he was carrying out orders for The Table."

Quinn had got away with it.

But Edge had noticed too. He looked at Robert and spoke at last. "Ah, yes, the night I told you both about the downfall of my country." One corner of his mouth curled, and his eyes almost imperceptibly flashed in Quinn's direction. Relief, mixed with resignation, flowed through Quinn. It was another reminder that Edge could destroy his relationship with Alita and Robert, as he had with Leonie and Riona.

Chapter Fifty

The Table

For a few moments, the only sound was the steady thrum of the boat's engine. Edge clasped his hands and looked at each of his attentive crewmates.

"I suppose now that I have you here, both with no choice but to complete the mission, I owe it to you to explain a little more."

Quinn wondered if Edge also had something over Robert to force him to cooperate. But Robert didn't seem concerned and sat forward. "Go on," he said.

"Over the course of my years with MI5, I have become more and more convinced that there must be some explanation for the inexplicable, self-destructive decisions governments make. They all do it, and too bloody regularly."

"He's on about the UK leaving Europe again," said Quinn, rolling his eyes upward.

"Yes, Quinn, that is one of the stupidest examples. But think of all the others."

Quinn glanced across the square wooden shelf they had eaten their meal from. Robert was rapt, his eyes fixed on Edge.

"Think of the senselessness of Afghanistan. The Russians and then the Americans both going to war with the same raggle-taggle band of religious crazies. And both coming home with their tail between their legs!" Edge was counting the world events out on his fingers. "Iraq! Ukraine used as a proxy battleground! So-called superpowers inventing grievances to justify themselves."

"I think you're stretching things a bit far." Quinn was shaking his head, but Edge pressed on.

"Do you honestly think that fat clown they used to have running North Korea could have organised a nuclear program? Without outside help? And how did the US elect that crazy film star Finch as their president? Porn star more like!" Edge was laughing. "It would be funny if it wasn't so serious. Think about it, someone's got to be pulling the strings, driving them towards this madness."

Robert sat forward, his expression somewhere between intrigued and dismissive. "But that's nothing new. No one wins. Not overall, I mean. If one side makes a little progress the other side loses out." He turned to Quinn, as if for backup.

"Exactly, Robert!" Edge continued, nodding. "No one wins. But take that one stage further. Suppose some overarching power was directing all these disagreements, and conflicts. Wars. A worldwide power that always profits from conflict and suffering."

Quinn put his glass down, revolving its base and looking at it as he spoke. "That's what you mean by this 'Table' thing? You seriously believe in that? An all-powerful world government? Like the United Nations?"

Edge guffawed. "The UN? The useless talking shop? No, think for a minute, Quinn. Who holds the actual power in your country? In every country?"

"The President. The Government."

"Pah! Think again. You know all governments are corrupt."

"The church? I mean religion?" Robert took a turn to guess.

"Aah – the opiate of the masses? No. Religions control nothing. All the various creeds are both weapons and shields: tools used to whip up the troops on both sides, an excuse for the real people calling the shots!" He raised his eyebrows and chuckled. "Or who think they are."

"That's crazy," said Quinn, sitting back.

"Ha! Not crazy. The Table has existed for millennia. 'Religion' was just a tool they devised as a means of controlling the world population." He started counting off on his fingers, "Good, evil, God, the Devil, heaven and hell, all of them! Inventions of The Table intended to occupy the masses. An opiate, as our friend Marx so cleverly stated." He chuckled.

Quinn wasn't finding this so funny. Edge was animated, goading them, encouraging them to play his guessing game.

"Think! Who always profits from corruption and warfare?"

"Criminals?" Robert ventured.

"Bravo, Robert! But only smart criminals. What we call 'organised crime.'"

Quinn shook his head again. "The Mob? No, you've lifted this from some cheap novel. That's ridiculous."

"Look, we've known for decades that crime families buy up the politicians running the cities in the US. And that they all meet to divide the country between them to ensure they maximise their profits instead of fighting each other. Well, it's the same the world over. The Chinese, Indians, Brazilians, you name it, every country. Run by its criminals."

"Like the drug cartels?"

"Right again, Robert. And the Triads, Camorra, ISIS, Al-Qaeda, all of them. Some wear religious or ideological badges to fool their foot soldiers, but it's money that drives them. Profit is king!"

"Are you suggesting that this 'Table' has representatives from all these crime organisations?" Though still sceptic, Quinn had to admit the theory was intriguing.

"I am, Quinn. Well done, you're keeping up. It's an alliance with one aim: to maximise the wealth and power of each organisation, no matter what the cost. And in each country, the so-called 'upper classes' have latched on to the criminals' coattails to keep themselves at the trough!"

"But what has England got to do with that? Leaving Europe, I mean. I don't get it," said Quinn.

"Europe was beginning to take some decisions that would limit the criminals' profits. By really cooperating instead of pretending to, and by sharing their resources, the EU had started to become an economic superpower. I believe The Table decided to clip their wings." With a sardonic grin, Edge made a scissor gesture with his right hand.

"Go on." Quinn's mind flitted back to his ULM studies all those years ago, and Professor Carson's speculation.

"The unity of the European Union was its greatest strength," said Edge, "but the weak link was the UK. They were always the least committed of the wealthier members. The Table only had to work for a couple of years to exploit the UK's internal divisions." He slammed his empty glass down and reached for the bottle. "And that crew of degenerates on Ragged Island did what the money men always do. Made more money!"

"So, you mean the RI7 are this 'Table'?" asked Robert.

Edge was taking a gulp of rum and choked, laughing. "Christ, no, Robert! They just saw an opportunity. They played the markets, and used every trick they could to influence public opinion whichever way would make them more money. The real influencers were the social media moguls, of course – the Table owns them outright. The UK's so-called government had to be seen to be pulling the strings, and some of them believed they were. Incredible!" Edge was in full flow but paused for another sip at his drink and Quinn took the chance to speak.

"I heard one of them saying something about Saul Dombey getting a seat at the Table. He was supposed to be an adviser to the top politicians. Are you saying he was working for the Table?" Quinn stopped speaking, worried he might be starting to believe Edge.

"Dombey! Haha! Recruited at Oxford. He was one of ours for a while. Rather useful to us when we got him the SPAD post."

Quinn noticed Robert looking quizzical, and explained. "Special Adviser, Robert. We used to say spin doctor." Turning back to Edge he went on, "So that's what you mean about exploiting divisions? They got Dombey to change politicians' minds?"

"Politicians and the voting plebs. Herded like social media sheep, they were. Dombey set dark web specialists to work, Oxford Analytix he called them." Edge was slurring now. "But Dombey was too bloody good at it. They won their gamble. And then..."

Robert spoke over Edge. "It was Dombey that killed Myal."

"What did you say?" Edge sat forward, suddenly alert.

"I buried the body."

"Eliot Myal?" Robert nodded, and Edge went on, "The right-wing fuckwit? Are you saying Saul Dombey killed him? Christ. I heard it was cocaine."

It satisfied Quinn that for once he had known something before Trevor Edge. He stood up.

"I'm going on deck for some fresh air," he said, climbing the steep steps and out of the hatch. He moved carefully towards the little boat's bow, wary of slipping and glad his smooth rubber soles found grip on the ridged deck. In the darkness, he could hear the muffled conversation continue below his feet. He was glad of a break from Trevor Edge's conspiracy theories, and a little alarmed at Robert's apparent willingness to take him seriously.

He sat staring at the inky sky. The stars were dimmer and fewer than earlier and he guessed light cloud was gathering. Another futile check for a cell phone signal added to his growing despair at the situation. He was away from Alita, and trapped into participating in a dangerous venture led by a paranoid fantasist. If he refused, Robert would soon be told that his daughter's marriage was bogus, her husband a bigamist. Robert, who appeared intent on killing as many of the RI7 as possible to restore his daughter's honour, would almost certainly kill Quinn too.

Half a miserable hour later, after checking the radar screen showed no nearby vessels he reduced the boat's speed to 5 knots. Returning below deck, he climbed down the ladder, his back to Robert and Edge. He shook his head as he picked back up on their conversation.

"'My POTUS!' Fat Horace said it all the time," Robert spluttered. Trevor Edge was laughing, and Robert kept on, "Especially when he was drunk. 'Finch was my fucking President!'"

Quinn had also heard Witte saying it.

Edge was slurring when he went on. "Finch was put in place by the Table as well. And Witte paid for his campaign. Or Sevenquean Bank did. Witte's family founded Sevenquean."

"Seventeen what?" Robert had a red wine stain on his yellow tee shirt.

"Sevenquean, said Edge. Quinn thought Edge looked sad, or nostalgic. "A lovely word, that. I looked it up. Anglo-Saxon name, derived from heptaquine." He looked up at Quinn. "Oh, you're back. Heptaquine. The seventh queen."

"Fat Horace isn't a politician, then?" Robert said.

Edge laughed. "Good God, no. None of them are. Dombey did mix with politicians, bent the ear of ministers and MPs. The rest are money men, pure and simple. Financiers. Dombey brought them together, in fact he came up with the name. Radical Investments Sevenquean."

Quinn sat down. "Not the Ragged Island Seven?"

"No. Witte bought the island and I think they named their little club after his bank. To recognise his contribution." Edge furrowed his brow, hiccoughing. His words were beginning to slur. "Now you come to mention it, the R – I is a bit of a coincidence, isn't it? Hadn't thought of that. Oops." He laughed.

Quinn said, "Maybe they wanted to hide where they were going."

Edge had moved on, though.

"Eliot Myal murdered by Dombey. Who would have thought it?

"I'm going to get my head down," said Quinn.

Chapter Fifty-One

Thursday 14th September 2037

At 3 am Alita woke starving hungry. The tiles cooled her feet as she rooted through cupboards in the old kitchen, searching for something just right. After leftover ham croquetas with dill pickles, she burped with loud satisfaction. On her way back to bed a shiver interrupted her yawning. The nights are colder when you sleep alone, she thought, glancing into her Papa's bedroom as she passed. She tried not to notice the framed wedding picture above his single bed.

Moving on to the room Papa had given up to her and Quinn, she pulled a drawer open to find something warm to wear in bed. She paused, though, closed it and opened the one below. The smell of Quinn as she put on his old basketball shirt made her smile inside.

As she closed the drawer she saw an envelope. She must have dislodged it when she pulled the shirt from under a pile of Quinn's work clothes. Taking it closer to the lamp by the bed, under Quinn's name she read the address of the Bourse Cubaine. The handwriting contrasted with the circular stamped postmark. PARIS - FRANCE - POSTE - 3-Avril-37

Intrigued, and feeling a little naughty to be looking at Quinn's work things, she turned the padded envelope over. Something fell out onto the floor. A coin? It disappeared under the bed. Now guilty, Alita felt inside the envelope and extracted a piece of paper with a torn edge and a printed logo. 'Havanaspeed, Cienfuegos.' she read, with increasing confusion.

A date stamp said 03-22-2037. She read the handwriting below and one word made her feel sick. Riona.

Alita sat motionless, staring at the note. It made no sense. She read the words over and over. "No. You will never see me or Riona again." The 'me' could only be Quinn's wife. Leonie. But Leonie died three years ago. And Riona.

Alita looked at the date stamp and the postmark again. From the dates, it had been written and posted less than six months ago. Posted in France. Why France?

She slipped it back in the envelope and replaced it under Quinn's clothes. There must be some reason he had the note. Had he come across it at work? That was it, a letter about someone else called 'Riona,' not his daughter, and he'd felt compelled to keep it. She told herself he'd stuffed it in the nearest envelope and kept hold of it, even though it couldn't have had anything to do with his poor, dead daughter. If only she could see him, tell him it was OK. Poor Quinn.

It was another sleepless hour later that she remembered something had fallen out of the envelope. She jumped up out of bed. She had to put it back, or Quinn would know she'd found the letter. Lying on the floor she swept over the varnished boards with her outstretched hand. There was dust. She would clean that tomorrow night after work, she thought. Near the skirting board, her hand touched something small and flat. The coin that had fallen out of the envelope. Got it!

She pulled herself back up from the floor and sat on the edge of the bed, a little dizzy. Reaching for the drawer she took out the envelope to replace the coin in it.

It wasn't a coin. In her palm, catching the light from the lamp, was a gold band. A ring. Engraved round its inner surface she could see two overlapping hearts, and the words 'Quinn and Leonie Tarrant. Forever.'

Her husband's wife and daughter were alive. And he knew it.

Chapter Fifty-Two

Thursday 14th September 2037

Bright rays fanning out through a porthole above his head woke Quinn. There was snoring from the forward cabin. He lay on his bunk wondering if what he had got himself into could get much worse. Miles out at sea on a crazy journey to God-knows-what was bad enough, but now he had two hungover companions.

He still didn't know if Edge had any firm plans for how to take over the island and destroy the RI7. He was surprised and disappointed in his father-in-law. Last night Robert had joined in enthusiastically with the mad Englishman's ranting. It seemed he was as hell-bent on self-destruction as Edge.

His watch said 8.15 am when he climbed up on deck into dazzling sunshine.

"Good morning Sñr Tarrant." Robert's deep voice and Bahamian accent made Quinn jump.

"Robert! I didn't expect…" His words dried up when he turned round to the stern deck. What had shaken him most was not that Robert was bright-eyed, dressed and shaved. He was cleaning a machine pistol, with another lying at his feet.

"You look surprised to see me." Robert was grinning.

"I thought you might be a bit later. After last night, I mean." He couldn't take his eyes off the guns.

Robert laughed. "I finished only one glass of rum. Trevor, on the other hand – well, I managed to loosen his tongue, you must admit."

"You mean you got him drunk deliberately?"

"I wanted to find out a bit more. Have you noticed how he always controls the conversation? That thing he does when he always finishes by asking a question? Well, I wanted him to tell me what I wanted to know, not just what he wanted me to know." Robert kept his voice low, but Quinn could still hear Edge's snoring from down below.

"What did he tell you that you didn't already know? That he really is mad?"

Robert laughed again, but shook his head, "Not mad, Quinn, just determined. Like me. I'll take my revenge, don't you worry."

Quinn wasn't sure what Robert meant. "I don't like it, Robert. I couldn't believe it when you agreed to go back to the island. You're risking everything. What about Alita?"

"I'm doing it for Alita. Don't worry, I'll come back to the boat. We'll sail home to her."

There was noise from below. Footsteps and cursing. Robert smiled at Quinn and called out, "Have you got a headache like mine, Trevor? We both had a bit much last night. Quinn was a good boy, though. He kept us right on course."

Red-eyed and pasty, Trevor Edge poked his head out of the hatch, squinting against the sun. "How far away from Ragged Island are we?"

"While we were sleeping it off my clever son-in-law kept us on course. Just the right speed. At this rate we'll be near the island in about nine or ten hours, and if we hang back a bit we'll arrive in darkness. Perfect." Robert turned slightly and winked at Quinn. "Not so much rum tonight, though, Trevor! We need to row ashore before dawn tomorrow morning."

Robert appeared to be relishing the idea of what was ahead.

Chapter Fifty-Three

9.00 am, Thursday 14[th]September

Alita had rehearsed her lines.

"Ah, buenos días, Señor, I wonder if you can help me? I'm with Carter Mellon of Rayville, Louisiana. We are handling the estate of the late Mr Mannix Tarrant, and I am trying to pass on important family information to one of your employees, Ms Leonie Tarrant. I hope you can give me a forwarding address. I believe she transferred to France. Perhaps your Paris office? Paris, France, that is. I am sorry to trouble you with this matter, but it will be of great interest to Ms Tarrant."

"I have only been with Havanaspeed for three weeks, Señorita, and I know we have branches all over central America, but we have none in Europe."

Things would never be the same, and she didn't know what she thought any more, but something had told Alita she needed to confirm Quinn's wife was thousands of miles away. Cienfuegos was too near home.

All she had was the scrap Leonie Tarrant's note was written on. Trying the Cienfuegos office of Havanaspeed was a long shot, and now she was trying not to start crying again before she ended the call.

"I'm sorry to have troubled–"

"Uno momento, Señorita." Alita heard keyboard clicks. "I see that Ms Leonie Tarrant moved to the Manzanillo branch in March. I can find you the number, but it's 9 am now and I need to open the office door. Give me one moment, Señorita." She heard footsteps.

301

Before the man returned, Alita had put the phone down and rushed to the toilet to vomit. Leonie Tarrant was still in Cuba.

The night before last Alita had eaten with her husband and father. They had talked about their fishing trip, and she had enjoyed seeing her Papa so excited. Now, she sat at the same table nibbling at a spicy dry flatbread, trying to fight off nausea and burning flatulence. In just a day and a half, she had discovered that Leonie Tarrant was alive and that Quinn knew it. And now not only was his wife alive, she was still in Cuba. Her husband's other wife, she thought. His real wife.

Alita stared at the fine grain on the worn mahogany table, knowing she should be angry at Quinn. He should have told her Leonie was alive. What kept her anger at bay was the date on the note in his drawer. She turned the gold band on her ring finger. The note had been written in March, nine months after she and Quinn had exchanged wedding rings. It might have been an innocent mistake, and he didn't know his first wife was alive when he married his second. She couldn't imagine how awful he would have felt when he found out. Perhaps it explained some of his erratic moods.

But the note from Leonie was an answer to a question. 'No,' it read. Quinn must have contacted her before that. How long had he been in touch with her? Alita knew that if she found out Quinn knew all along that Leonie was alive she would never be able to forgive him. And he would never see their child.

Unable to tear her thoughts away from Leonie Tarrant, she flipped open the laptop computer she shared with her father. It booted up much faster since Señor Edge had updated the software and connected new superfibre broadband. Her Papa seemed to like Trevor, but though she couldn't explain it the Englishman with the strange hat made Alita feel uncomfortable.

The Havanaspeed website was up to date, and it did indeed list Leonie Tarrant as a motorcycle courier at the Manzanillo office. Alita stared at the head and shoulders picture above the name. Stylish short dark hair contrasting with an easy white smile. It was the impossibly blue eyes fixed on the camera that made Alita look away. She picked up her phone.

"Hello, is that you, Miguel? You were right to take me to the clinic. I have a terrible stomach upset. I think it was prawns. Can you please let the manager know I won't be in today?"

"Yes, Alita, are you OK? I'll–"

"No, I'll be OK. I'm keeping water down now. Oh, sorry, Miguel it's coming again I've got to go—"

She finished the call and stood looking at the phone.

Chapter Fifty-Four

Late afternoon

Alita passed the signs to Camagüey with a lurch of nostalgia and thought for a moment she might have to stop at the roadside again. Her nausea passed, though, and she drove on into the searing afternoon. She'd never driven such a distance and rarely drove alone. It was a relief to find that Papa had filled the hybrid's tank, as he always did. After driving for six hours, already the gauge showed less than half full.

###

She had taken a snap decision that morning to make the trip to see Leonie Tarrant. Now it was late afternoon and she had parked the car on a shaded street in Manzanillo. With her sunglasses on she sat watching the Havanaspeed office across the road. Tears kept gathering, blurring her view of the glass doors.

She'd never felt so alone and miserable. She sipped at her water bottle, wishing she had something to nibble at. As the clinic doctor had said it would, soaking up the bile helped the sickness a little. Her Mama would have told her that.

She had no plan. She didn't even know if she had the money for fuel to make it back to Havana. Seeing the face of the woman her husband had deceived her about was all she had set out to do. She knew from the Havanaspeed website there were two riders based at the Manzanillo office, and it had already occurred to her they might not always return to base. Leonie Tarrant might not even be on duty today.

The sound of a motorcycle approaching from behind prickled her nape. Without thinking she straightened up, smoothing her hair and removing the sunglasses to check her teary eyes in the car's vanity mirror, behind the blackened glass of the Mercedes. A figure in grey dismounted from the bike. A man. Deflating, Alita watched as he entered the office, pulling off his helmet and starting to peel off his leathers. End of the day, she thought. There are only two riders, and they won't both be working. She'd been stupid to come all this way on a whim.

Alita knew she had to go and find fuel, and was about to start the engine when a slim woman emerged from gloom at the back of the office. Wearing the same grey leather as her co-worker, she took a package from him and walked out towards one of the motorcycles. Slipping the package into a satchel, she climbed astride the bike and pulled a helmet down over short dark hair. With a wave to her office colleagues, she cranked the bike's kickstarter and rocked it forward off its stand. As the bike pulled out into the narrow street Alita pressed the ignition of the Mercedes, drawing out to follow Leonie Tarrant.

Chapter Fifty-Five

5.15 pm

Manzanillo

Leonie Tarrant's red helmet was easy to follow. Alita hung back as the traffic thinned. They were on a dusty road out of Manzanillo when Leonie swung off left into the narrow driveway of a single-storey house. A little car with garish 'Niños ... Seguro y Cuidado' detailing sat outside, and Alita steered past it and drove on.

She continued a couple of miles farther along a straight road between green and brown fields before pulling to a stop beside a deserted wooden shack with no roof. A long, pent-up sigh escaped. The sun was already low over the sea, and she still had to drive for all the way back to Havana. Alita hadn't thought about what she would feel when she saw Leonie Tarrant. She'd seen her now, and where she lived with Quinn's daughter, and she felt empty. She wished she was at home being miserable instead of hundreds of kilometres away.

On the way back to Manzanillo to search for fuel, she had to pass Leonie's house. Something made her stop a few yards past it. A rattling tin scooter screamed as it swung round the Mercedes, a small boy passenger hollering back angrily. As she reached for her water bottle, she saw that the fuel warning light had pinged on. Her water bottle was empty.

Looking over her shoulder she could see clumps of bamboo forming a rough hedge along the front of the house. The motorcycle was parked under a corrugated veranda to the side, and the child-care car had gone. It must have been waiting for Leonie to arrive home, she decided.

A horn blared behind, and she reached to put the Mercedes into drive. In the car's wing mirror, she saw the house door open and Leonie Tarrant emerge holding a little girl's hand. Alita turned for a better view and watched as the girl skipped over the road, pulling her mother with her. She was clutching a small case, and smiling children were waving to her from a yellow bus that had pulled up a short distance behind the Mercedes. Leonie was fussing over the little girl's auburn hair and smoothing her jacket as she pulled to join her friends.

Alita felt a lump in her throat. From behind the blackened windows, she watched her husband's wife stand at the roadside, waving until the bus was out of sight. She couldn't hate this woman. Or the little girl. Riona. Riona, who believed her father was dead. As Leonie closed the front door Alita stepped out of the car and crossed the road.

Chapter Fifty-Six

It was dark when she woke. She stretched, relaxing. She didn't need to get up for work yet. Turning over, she could see unfamiliar shapes on the bedroom wall. Elongated shadows of Minnie Mouse were cast by a weak, floor-level night light. Quinn must have bought it. Funny he didn't mention it. She felt for his body beside her, but her hand groped in the air. She was in a single bed. Lifting her head, alarmed, she called out, "Quinn! Papa!"

A door in the wrong corner of the room opened and a silhouette spoke. "Are you feeling better?"

"Who are – where am I? What?"

The person moved towards her, and Alita shrank back, pulling a patterned sheet around her.

"It's OK, it's OK. You're safe. You fainted, that's all. You're done in." It was a woman's voice. An American woman.

Memories flashed behind Alita's eyes like a slideshow: bamboo, a low house behind it, a yellow bus, and a little girl. The woman leant forward, "Let's see if you're ready to get upright. I'll steady you. Sit up a bit more. Here, have some more water."

Alita did as she was told, taking the cool glass. This was the woman she had driven all day to catch a glimpse of. Somehow she had ended up in Leonie Tarrant's home. She had to get out of there.

Before Alita could think or move, a cell phone buzzed and Leonie stepped back, reaching into her jeans pocket. "Sorry, I'll need to get that. Now, don't get up on your own. There's not much of you, girl, but I don't want to have to haul you up again."

Lifting the phone to her ear she waved Alita to stay where she was and backed out of the room.

"Michel, where have you been? You're late again. It's nearly nine o'clock, for god's sake. You missed Riona before she left."

The door remained partially open, and Alita could hear enough to tell there was an argument. She sat up on the bed and swung her legs out. Still dressed in her jeans and T-shirt, she saw her sneakers lying neatly by the door.

Drinking more iced water from the glass on the bedside cabinet, she tried to piece together what had happened. Her hand went to her jeans pocket – she must have left her phone in the car. Reaching out to switch on a lamp, she looked at her watch. 8.45 pm. So it wasn't morning.

If what Leonie Tarrant had said was true, she had passed out again. She had no memory after approaching the house door and guessed that Leonie must have found her outside and helped her inside to recover. This is awful, she thought. This must be the little girl's bed. Riona's.

Holding on to the back of a chair, she stood up and felt OK. As she crept across the room, a faint smell strengthened. Her mouth watered when she neared the door. Expecting nausea, instead she became deliciously hungry. She had to eat.

"No! I won't, and don't bother calling back! I'll see you on Sunday."

Leonie's angry voice and approaching footsteps made Alita scuttle back towards the bed, a naughty child.

"Men! Lord, I hope I never see another one! Are you ready to come through here yet, Honey?" Leonie said as she opened the door and flicked the light on. "I've got étouffée on the stove."

Chapter Fifty-Seven

Evening

"That was superb. I've tasted nothing like it." Alita had finished a small plateful. Her eyes strayed towards the pot on the stovetop.

"More? There's plenty. I can see you're hungry."

"No, thanks, I'd better go. I'm sorry I gave you trouble. I don't know why I wandered into your front yard. Sorry." Alita was rushing her words, trying to cover up the truth. Unable to resist some food, she'd agreed to stay until she was well enough to drive. Leonie hadn't asked her name, at least.

"I don't think you should go. My daughter's away for three nights with her school class. You can stay here tonight, leave in the morning."

"No, I couldn't. I mean, I have work tomorrow. In Camagüey." She was finding the lies easy, but she had to get away before Leonie Tarrant discovered who she was. She stood up. "I left my cell phone in the car. I'd better call home, let Papa know I'll be late."

But Leonie was holding out Alita's phone towards her. "I think it fell out of your pocket when I lifted you in."

Alita stopped and reached to take the cell phone, Thanks, I'll..."

"I know who you are, Alita."

Her mouth dried, and her palms were moistening. But she couldn't move or speak. Her eyes were locked on Leonie's.

"When I found you on the doorstep, I wondered who you were. I thought I was going to need an ambulance. Once I got you laid out on the bed I went to look and see if there was anyone else outside. That's when I found your phone. Your name and picture are on the lock screen."

"I – I need to go. I'm sorry, you've mixed me up with someone else. I don't know–"

"I know you're married to Quinn."

Leonie was talking in a matter-of-fact tone as if Alita wasn't there.

"When I saw the name Tarrant it was too much of a coincidence. I searched online – Quinn and Alita Tarrant, Havana. The first result was your marriage registration. 'Quinn Tarrant, Widower, USA.' it said." She looked at Alita. "I felt sorry for you then."

Alita sat down. "I don't know why I'm here. I'm sorry." She was weeping.

Leonie came round the table and sat beside her. "I knew it was always a risk we would meet sometime, by chance. But I didn't want to change my name, or Riona's." She was sobbing herself now.

Alita looked up. "I shouldn't be here. I'll go now. When I found out Quinn knew you were alive, I didn't know what to do. I found your note. I just kept reading it." She started to stand up. "I'm not sure why I'm acting like this. I'll go."

Leonie put her hand on her arm. "Don't go. You need rest."

That simple gesture, a kindly hand placed on her forearm, melted away the last of Alita's defences. She lowered herself back down and stared at the empty plate in front of her, unable to speak or move.

"He doesn't know, does he?" Leonie said. She stood up and went to the stove. "Quinn, I mean. He doesn't know you're here?

Or that you know about me?" She brought the pot over and served more étouffée with a steel ladle.

Alita looked straight ahead of her. "No. I didn't know what to do. I thought you were dead, but when I found your letter to him..." She exhaled, and went on with a brief shake of her head, "And the ring. I knew you were alive. I had to – I'm sorry – I still don't know what to do." She turned to face Leonie.

"Ssshh, eat."

Leonie stood up and left the table. She returned with a bottle of wine and two glasses. Alita was chewing slowly. She shook her head and put a hand over one glass. Swallowing, she said, "I have to drive tomorrow." She realised she was contemplating spending the night in her husband's wife's home. In his daughter's bed.

"He doesn't know you're pregnant either, does he?"

Alita could feel her face reddening when she looked up from her plate. Leonie was smiling.

"My Grandma used to say, 'When a young girl faints, look for a man, then look out your knitting pins.'" She poured Alita a glass of wine. "One drink will be OK."

Alita realised that Leonie didn't blame her for marrying Quinn. She began to relax. It was easy to talk to Quinn's wife, and before long they were chatting like close friends. There were tears in Leonie's eyes when she described meeting Quinn in Havana six months before. Alita had felt her throat constrict, but with pity rather than fury.

Leonie rushed on as if desperate to share the story. "I was so mad I thought I was going to explode. When I hit Quinn it hurt my hand and I could hardly steer the bike. I rode so fast I was back in Cienfuegos before I knew where I was. I was still real angry, and I didn't care that the visor was all steamed up with my crying."

She wiped her eyes and looked at Alita.

"Then I just got sorry. I cried every time I saw Riona. I got sorry for her, as well as me. And later even Quinn." Her tears kept flowing. "And I was sorry for you," she sobbed. "I didn't know your name or anything about you but – but I thought – I mean – I felt sorry for the situation you're in. We're in. Both of us married to the same man, I mean." She looked into Alita's eyes, a questioning, pleading look on her face. "I haven't told anyone any of this."

Alita couldn't speak. Leonie had gone through what she was trying to deal with now, and wanted to talk. She managed a slight nod, and Leonie continued.

"I stopped hating Quinn pretty soon. I know him. I had to believe him, when he said he thought I was dead, I mean. Jeez! I thought *he* was dead until he contacted me." Leonie was looking at the wall to her left as she spoke, where Alita had seen a picture of baby Riona in a crib. "He said he'd seen me by chance. In Havana."

Alita wanted to hold Leonie, embrace her and reassure her. But she couldn't. How could the three of them continue? She wished she had never come to find Leonie. She wished Quinn hadn't gone on his stupid fishing trip. Then she would never have found the note. Two days ago she thought Leonie was dead. Now her life, their lives, had turned upside down. She couldn't hate Leonie, or blame her. Or Quinn.

Leonie went on. "Cutting off all contact was all I could do. Riona already thought her father was dead. I spent days trying to decide whether to tell her he wasn't."

Alita was still thinking about Leonie's note. It was less than a day since she'd found it in Quinn's drawer. She could understand the cruelty of what was written.

"You were in Paris? When you posted the note," she asked.

"No, no. I didn't want to let him know I was still in Cuba."

Leonie explained she had posted the envelope to a contact in a European courier business. "I asked her to send it to Quinn from Paris." She laughed through her sobs. "I told her I was playing a silly trick on my husband." Wiping her eyes, she went on, "I hoped if Quinn thought we were in Europe he would accept that Riona was out of his life forever. If he thought we were thousands of miles away he might not be tempted to make contact."

Exhausted by 10.30, Alita had gone back to Riona's room. She would leave in the morning. She went to sleep feeling happier that Leonie was no threat. Leonie had moved on. Made the best of an awful situation, she'd said. Her partner Michel sounded nice. An events organiser, always travelling and going to swanky parties.

She knew her marriage to Quinn was false. Illegal. But it wasn't his fault. She had begun to understand the turmoil he must have been through when he'd found out. It explained why he'd been so distressed. Until now, she'd thought it was grief for the woman she'd just shared a meal with.

The moment the clinic doctor had told her she was pregnant Alita had been desperate to tell Quinn. Then she'd found

Leonie's letter, and vowed he would never see her child if he'd known Leonie was alive at the time of his second wedding.

Now, less than 24 impulsive, irrational hours later she was lying in his daughter's bed, friends with his wife, and wishing away the three days she had to wait until he returned from his fishing trip.

Chapter Fifty-Eight

6.30 am, Friday 15th September 2037

Ragged Island

Quinn used a foot pump to inflate the boat's tender while Robert and Trevor made their final preparations. He didn't want to know the details, but he'd seen them loading up their ordnance.

Once they were in the inflatable dinghy at the stern of the boat, he passed them down an oiled canvas bag. It was a relief when they took its weight between them after he'd strained to lift it over the guard rail. Inside were two Heckler and Koch MP5 machine pistols with silencers, two Glock 19 pistols for backup, and enough ammunition clips to massacre a baseball crowd. There were also four grenades – for a distraction, he'd heard Edge say – and two rescue flares taken from the boat. Both men wore camouflaged uniforms, and Edge had blackened his face.

As they pushed off from the side of the boat Robert waved a thumbs-up at Quinn. Edge still wore his Breton cap as he rowed them away towards the twinkling lights of the luxurious compound on Ragged Island. Above the outline of the low forested ridge that ran the length of the island the sky was still inky. He watched until he could no longer make out the vague shape of the dinghy against the dark sea, and wondered if he would ever see his father-in-law again. He knew the first hazard would be the electric fence. There was barely a breeze, but a current could push them towards it. A memory of burnt wild pig brushed his nostrils.

If they didn't return by the next sunrise, Quinn knew he would be sailing the boat back to Cuba alone. He started the engine and began to wind in the anchor. Before daylight, he needed to move the boat far enough South of the RI7 resort to be out of sight, before the waiting and listening could begin. Edge had said with a smile, "When it's done we'll send up a celebratory flare and you can come and collect us. You won't need to worry about them seeing the boat."

Chapter Fifty-Nine

6.30 am

Manzanillo

Someone was tapping on the door. The cartoon nightlight made it pink when it ought to be dark brown. A slash of light spilled under it. A creak from a floorboard scared her for a moment, but Minnie Mouse was smiling on the wall. The room she was in became more familiar, but the door was still pink.

The knocking continued.

"Alita, can I speak to you? Sorry to wake you so early." A slice of yellow appeared, wider as the door edged open.

"Hello. Yes," she said through a yawn. Last night emerged from the rosy dimness, shaking her from her sleep. "I'll get up and get away. What time is it?"

Leonie came into the room with a mug of coffee. It smelled wonderful, and Alita realised it was the first time in days she didn't feel nauseated.

"No Alita, you don't need to go. It's only about 6.30. Sorry. But quick, look at this," said Leonie, frowning. She set the coffee down and sat on the end of the bed as she opened a laptop. Alita had to shade her eyes from the bright screen.

"When you mentioned Quinn's fishing trip last night, you said one of his friends was called Trevor Edge, right?"

Alita nodded.

"I knew I'd heard that name before. I couldn't sleep, it was bugging me so much. Then it came to me. Michel had mentioned him."

"Your boyfriend?"

"Michel had a meeting with him in Havana last month. It's in his diary. Look." Leonie turned the screen towards Alita and pointed with her finger. A calendar entry read, '2.30 pm TE, Edge IT, Nuevitas House.'

Alita looked up at Leonie, puzzled.

"If you look up Edge IT Services, it's run by Trevor Edge."

"That is a coincidence." Alita smiled and reached for the coffee. "Thanks. She took a sip, and said, "That's good! I don't usually have sugar, but this is just great."

Leonie ignored her and took the laptop back. "But wait 'til you see this." A few more clicks and she turned the screen to face Alita. She'd opened up her partner's email inbox.

Alita put her hand over her eyes and turned away. "I shouldn't–"

"Look at the email headed 'Fishing Trip.'" Leonie spoke urgently, pointing at the screen.

Alita let her hand fall. Hesitantly and with lowered eyebrows, she clicked on the email. 'Trip arranged as agreed. Charter: Cacique-2, Matanzas 11 Sept. 5d. Please confirm picnic supplies ordered.' Underneath was a standard sign-off. 'T. Edge, Edge IT Services.'

"So? It means Michel also supplies provisions for boat charters." She was still wondering why Leonie had woken her.

"Look at the reply. There's a file attached." There was a paper-clip symbol beside the email heading.

Scrolling down Alita came to Michel's reply. 'As per. See receipt for picnic supplies. Sufficient? Michel Cochet, Events Planning.'

Leonie spoke again. "I've been up half the night trying to open the attachment. I found some encryption software on his laptop. Look!" she said, taking the laptop. Alita watched her drag the attachment file across the screen until it overlapped a programme icon on the desktop. The file opened, and Leonie turned the screen back round. It took Alita a moment to understand what she saw. A picture of guns. Pistols and bigger weapons. Laid out alongside them were neat rows of ammunition clips, and four grenades.

"I don't understand. Cacique-2 is the name of the boat Quinn is on. But–?"

"Look at Edge's reply, Alita."

Alita's nausea was returning. She went back to the email conversation. Trevor Edge had replied, 'That'll do nicely. RIP RI7!'

"It's not a fishing trip they are on," said Leonie. "Get dressed, there's more I need to show you, and we need to decide what to do. Hurry." She grabbed the computer and walked out of the room.

Alita took her time getting dressed. She was struggling to make sense of what she'd just learned. When she'd gone to sleep she had trusted Leonie. But now it turned out her boyfriend had provided guns for Trevor Edge. And he'd rented the boat for Edge. The boat her husband and father were on. She was wondering what else Leonie Tarrant had to show her. When she came out of the toilet and walked into the kitchen Leonie was on the phone.

"I'm sorry I was short with you last night, Michel. Come home. I want to see you." Leonie saw Alita enter, motioning her to stay quiet. "Oh, Michel, pleeease! Do you have to go straight to the airport?" She looked at Alita and waved a clenched fist at the phone's mouthpiece. She had gritted teeth, despite the tender pleading to her boyfriend. Alita felt in her pocket for her car key and edged towards the door.

"Oh, what time's your flight? Couldn't you just come here on your way from Havana? Just for a little while, so I can make up to you? Guantanamo is only an hour away from here."

Leonie was waving Alita to stay. Her urgent face made Alita pause, uncertain and scared.

"Oh, OK, Michel, I'll see you in a couple of days. Kisses, kisses! Bye!" When she hung up Leonie rushed to the sink and vomited.

Alita stood helpless, pity taking the edge off her fear. "Erm, what's wrong? Can I help?"

Leonie stood back up wiping her mouth. "Sorry. Bastard! I wanted to scream!" She had a cruel look on her face. "But I know what time his flight is."

"What in hell's going on?" Alita was shocked at how loud her words sounded. "If you don't tell me what's happening, I'm calling the Police. Is my husband in danger? And my Papa?" She had her cell phone in her hand.

Leonie's shoulders slumped and she sat down at the breakfast bar. There were tears in her eyes. She opened another file on the laptop and hundreds of pictures appeared. Alita sat on the stool next to her to see the screen. The pictures were all of a little girl. In some of them, she was in underclothes, others a swimsuit. In a few, she was naked. It was the eager little girl Alita had seen rushing away on her school trip the previous night.

Leonie wiped her eyes and spoke, her voice monotone. She outlined how she had met Michel Cochet. He'd just started a travel agent business in Miami when he came to the hotel Leonie was working in. She'd asked him if he could help her get to

Cuba. He'd made her laugh and relax, and they were soon living together. Six months later he had moved his office to Cuba, taking Leonie and Riona with him.

"It was wrong of me, to use Michel like that, but I had to get to Cuba. Michel knew nothing about my marriage. I was going to leave him as soon as I found Quinn. But he never made it to Cuba." She turned to Alita. "Or that's what I thought."

Alita couldn't keep eye contact. She turned away, then closed the laptop with a snap. But from the picture on the wall Riona smiled at her.

Leonie's voice was weakening. "After I found out Quinn was——I mean, I kinda stayed with Michel, sort of got used to it, y'know, the security, the money. And he adored Riona." She inhaled sharply, and Alita could see she was choking back sobs. She put her hand on Leonie's shoulder.

"That's Riona in the pictures?" She knew the answer.

Leonie let out a low wail, but gathered herself after a few seconds, sitting up and looking into nothing. "I Ie used to take her to the beach when I was working. She told me they had a special game. She had a hiding place in the dunes where he always made her go change into her swimsuit. He must have been watching her. With his fucking cameras. Bastard!"

Alita had to ask. "But I just heard you on the phone to him. 'Kisses, kisses'! And pleading to see him. What in the name of hell is going–?"

"I was trying to find out what time his flight was leaving. I'm going to kill him." Leonie's voice was stronger now.

Alita stood up. "I'm leaving. This is too mad. I need to..." She sat back down, her head shaking. "Kill him? What? How?"

Wiping her eyes Leonie reopened the laptop, quickly closing the photo folder. She spoke with more composure. "I want you to come with me. We haven't got long." Alita could hear her teeth grinding. The little arrow on the screen was sweeping all over as Leonie searched for something.

"Come with you? Where? I mean—"

"Remember I said he was an events organiser? Look where today's event is." Leonie turned the computer round. It showed Alita a list of events, the dates a few weeks apart, some at locations she had heard of and some she hadn't. Rio, Miami, Caracas, and London. Highlighted as today's date, she saw Ragged Island. She could feel herself shaking.

"No! No, it can't be." As realisation dawned, she put things together. The boat trip, the guns, Ragged Island. She looked at Leonie. "'RIP RI7'! That's what Trevor wrote in the email."

Leonie raised an eyebrow. "What is RI7?"

"Ragged Island. The Ragged Island Seven. It's the men Papa and I were made to work for. After Cleeter and the parties." She was staring into space.

Leonie looked shocked. "Not *the* Cleeter? All that stuff in the tabloids? Young girls? Parties for celebrities and princes?"

Alita spoke through a sneer of disgust. "The RI7, those men on the island, they were more of Cleeter's clients. He sent girls for them."

Leonie stood up. "Ragged Island is where Michel is going today, and it's got to be where the 'fishing trip' is headed. It must be Cleeter who Michel has been arranging events for. His flight leaves at half past eight. Let's go." She held a crash helmet out to Alita.

Alita sat down, shaking her head and holding on to the breakfast bar. "No, I mean – what can we do? It's madness."

Leonie put down the helmet and opened another file on the computer. She sat down beside Alita. "I wasn't sure whether to show you this."

An email conversation opened up.

MC-—RM and QT still up for it?

TE-—Y. Have agreed to targeting RI7 with me. Putty in my hands :-)

MC-—When RM has opened the security doors he's surplus, right?

TE-—Y. Only us in the dinghy back to the boat :-)

MC-—And QT?

TE-—Fish food

MC-—Understood

Alita held out the Mercedes key. "We'll take my Papa's car. You drive. Can we get fuel somewhere?"

Chapter Sixty

7.15 am

Leonie drove the Mercedes. She knew the roads and had said it would take about an hour to reach the airport.

Alita's mind was preoccupied, trying to make sense of the sudden turmoil in her life. It was Friday morning, and since Monday she had discovered she was pregnant, that she was married to a bigamist, and that Quinn and her father were about to commit mass murder before being killed themselves.

She glanced across at Leonie, who had her eyes fixed on the road ahead, her jaw clenched. Leonie was only a few years older than she was, but in the few hours since they'd met, she'd shown herself to be strong and smart. And determined above all to avenge the wrong done to her daughter. Alita wondered how her own mother would have acted if she'd been alive to know what all those men had done to her little girl.

Her Papa had done all he could to protect her from further harm. She didn't understand, though, why he had agreed to help Edge on his murderous mission. None of the men on Ragged Island had hurt Alita, and she'd told Papa that. She remembered every one of Cleeter's bastards, nightly in her dreams. And why had Quinn got involved? Did they know somehow that Cleeter would be there?

As if reading Alita's thoughts, Leonie spoke. "When you said, 'After Cleeter and the parties,' err – what did you mean...?"

Alita stared straight ahead, unblinking. "I was one of his girls. Taken to those parties and made to – old men – you know..."

They were both silent for a while. Then Leonie cleared her throat and spoke. "In Miami, in the 'hotel' I had to work in, I saw stuff like that," she said.

Alita looked up. Leonie's hands were crushing the steering wheel and tears trickled down her cheeks.

She went on, describing what had happened to her and Riona after they'd become separated from Quinn on the beach in Layton. Because she had a child with her, when they reached Miami the trafficker gave Leonie a job cleaning rooms in a former hotel, now a PBC barracks.

She'd kept Riona with her at all times and tried to hide the truth of their situation from her. "She was only six years old, and she'd just seen her Daddy die. Or that's what we thought."

Alita listened in horror. She thought about her own mother's death when she was seven, and her Papa's tears as he'd told her Mama had gone to join the angels. Last night she'd watched Riona skipping across to join her friends on the school bus. Leonie was still fighting for Riona. Alita vowed she would be just as fierce to protect Quinn's child inside her.

Leonie's bland account continued. There was a look of hatred on her face as she drove, occasional sobs breaking her flow. Alita knew not to interrupt.

"There were young girls from all over, herded from vans and distributed around the hotel rooms, bonuses for the brave soldiers." Leonie closed her eyes for a second, just before rounding a bend in the road.

"I hid from it. Pretended to myself it wasn't happening. But the noises I heard... And I had to clean up the rooms. Blood. Tufts of hair. I locked us in the storeroom at night. Our only daylight was when we went for stores and food. We stayed in that hotel for over six months."

Leonie paused and Alita saw her jaw tighten. "Riona knew what a crack-whore was when she was only six. I was scared for her. She'd soon be old enough to be put to work." She took a hand from the wheel to wipe more tears, before the monotone catharsis went on.

"Then one day in April, Michel just turned up at the hotel looking for customers for his new travel agency business. He was kind. He knew people and seemed able to go where he wanted. He said he liked me and gave me a job in his office. Not that there ever seemed to be any customers. It was better than the hotel though, and we didn't have to fight off coked-up men."

"Working for Michel was safer. I knew there was something not right about his travel business, but this morning I saw some more stuff on his computer. I know what he was really doing."

Alita wasn't sure what Leonie meant and said nothing. Leonie continued as if she was alone and thinking aloud. There was slight shaking of her head as she went on.

"I almost scrolled on by when I saw the name of the file." She let out a snort of hollow laughter, her face grim. "'Fresh Meat.' I thought it was a friggin' shopping list."

Alita listened with growing discomfort. The file's cruel, ironic name had hidden details of Max Cleeter's exclusive services, reserved for his highest-paying clients. Innocent youngsters, lured on a promise of modelling careers, delivered to exotic locations. Expecting a photo shoot, instead they were drugged and defiled.

"After their first time, like some sort of sick initiation, they were fed down the sex traffic chain. The girls I saw in Miami were on the last stop. Addicted, wasted, and only suitable for low-ranking soldiers to play with." Leonie was crying now. "One time I was in a McDonalds I saw a girl who'd been thrown out like trash. Just the day before. She was dead in the toilet with a needle in her arm."

Alita's horror at Leonie's account was dulled by her own memories. She'd never been taken anywhere as exotic as the Ragged Island compound before her Papa bought her freedom, but she'd been trapped in the same way. Gifts of make-up, shiny limousines, but no photographers or cameras. Parties of ugly businessmen in the penthouse suites of Nassau hotels.

They were both quiet now, as Leonie steered the car between fields and copses lining the road.

"I had to sleep with Michel, of course, but he was away on business a lot and I learned to put up with it. Then I sort of got to like him." Leonie was shaking her head again.

She had survived by learning to live with the control and abuse, Alita thought. She'd done the same herself when she'd been trapped in Cleeter's world.

Leonie now threw a glance towards Alita. "And Michel could get us to Cuba. If I stuck it out I could get back with Quinn," she said, rolling her eyes before turning away to face the road. Alita squirmed, but there was a sardonic smile on Leonie's face.

There was another silence. Alita looked to her right at the cane fields and trees whizzing by. She wondered if Quinn knew any of what his first wife had been through. Once again Leonie seemed to read her thoughts.

"I used to wonder if I would ever tell Quinn about Michel when I got to Cuba. But then I discovered he was dead. Or at least the Soporte told me he had never made it to Cuba. Until then I'd always held on to some hope there was a chance he'd survived the machine guns on that beach."

A mile or so further on a road sign told them they were nearing the airport. They soon took a right turn into the entrance. The modern terminal bore a big, shiny sign reading 'Mariana Grajales Cuello Guantanamo'.

Chapter Sixty-One

7.30 am

MV Cacique-2

An hour after Edge and Robert had disappeared into darkness in the dinghy Quinn was trying to settle himself for a long wait. He'd washed last night's plates, made more coffee, and checked his cell phone again in case they'd passed through an area of coverage. There were no missed calls from Alita.

Restless, he went into the cramped forward cabin. On the bunk to his right were a folded blanket and Robert's toilet bag. On the left was a jumble of discarded clothes, maps, and papers. Amongst them, he could see the laptop Edge had spent much of the journey poring over.

The day before, Quinn had looked over Edge's shoulder as he'd squeezed through the cramped lower deck. The mere glimpse of thinning white hair, angular features and radiant confidence was enough for Quinn to recognise the man in the head and shoulders picture. Below he read the legend 'Isaac Sprack to leave LucasBlue Investments to join new venture.' So that's his surname, he thought. Quinn had last seen Sprack walking with his cane on Ragged Island. He'd taken his time as he passed back behind Edge, and seen an array of folder icons. Headings included 'Early Financial Irregularities' and 'Recruitment: Potential Levers.'

Quinn couldn't resist it. Unplugging the laptop from its charger he took it up on deck, the silver case glistering at him in the early sunrise. He stared at it, guilty but intrigued. After a pointless, furtive glance around him, he opened it under the cover of the cockpit canopy.

An ornate logo filled the centre of the screen – a crown, a lion, and a unicorn, the British royal crest. Quinn recognised it from his research into the UK. Below the symbology a scrolled inscription read, 'DIEU ET MON DROIT'.

Two login boxes sat below the logo, the first pre-filled with 'TrevorEdge8654927', and the second blank. It was unlikely he would be able to guess Edge's password – the man was a spy after all. With a smile to himself, he tried 'Password' anyway, and the error message appeared as expected. It was the same with '123456789'. Quinn closed the laptop and looked at it. If he tried too many times it would be likely to lock permanently, and Edge would know he'd tried to access his files.

Accepting defeat, he was about to return the computer to Edge's cabin when he paused, stared at the screen for a moment, then gambled on one more guess. Edge wouldn't care once he'd completed his murderous mission, he reasoned.

The early sun was warming Quinn's back as he entered the second 'n' of 'Sevenquean'. The laptop screen flashed into action and a busy home screen appeared. Edge had been sentimental about the name of Horace Witte's private bank.

Whooping to himself at his minor victory, Quinn set about exploring the ex-spy's secret files.

Chapter Sixty-Two

7.50 am
MV Cacique-2

Dombey, Saul. Born 14/04/1980, York, England
Educ. Printfields School, Cambs.; Merton College, Oxford.
Notes: Special Adviser, Cabinet Office 2015-2019; Oxford Analytix; RI7;
*** Suspected as potential Table recruit since 2016. Tasked by Table with breaking up EU?

Edge had kept similar notes on each of the other RI7 members. Dombey was the only one who'd had any official political connections. Quinn was shocked by a financial web that linked Horace Witte, President Finch and various far-right organisations in the US and UK. Most of the other RI7 members were financiers and businessmen, whose social backgrounds were similar to Dombey's.

Eliot Myal stood out for being state-educated and from a modest background in East London. Quinn had been aware of him as a popular spokesman for right-wing factions in the US as well as Europe. Edge had noted Myal also had connections to extremist groups worldwide.

Myal's entry ended with:
'NB! Dead??? Murdered by SD?
(To be confirmed)
14/09/37.'

Quinn looked at his watch. '7.50 am FRI 15.' Trevor Edge had updated his RI7 files yesterday, adding what he had learned from Robert.

Quinn had found a kind of diary of Edge's work. More like the diary of a deluded fantasist, he thought, a 24-carat conspiracy theorist. More references to 'The Table.'

Quinn had to agree that some of the decisions taken by governments in the years leading up to the civil wars were hard to explain. Since working at the Bourse Cubaine, Quinn had become aware that the rest of the world was incredulous at the USA's choice of President. He hadn't admitted to his colleagues that before the strife had erupted, and before his father's death, Quinn had been a supporter. It was too much for him, though, to believe Edge's hyperbole about The Table. Professor Carson's theories had been mildly eccentric compared with the rot Edge spouted.

He was about to shut the computer when he caught sight of a folder called '*RI Research Contacts*.' With nothing else to do except wait he double-clicked it out of mild curiosity. It contained sub-folders: Miami, Keys, Cuba, London, and Interpol. Distractedly, he opened the Cuba folder. Among the files listed one jumped out at him: '*Q.Tarrant*.' The bastard Edge had kept a file on him!

Quinn's anger and resentment grew as he realised the level of detail in Edge's notes about him. There were facts about his dead mother even Quinn didn't know. He couldn't bear to follow a hyperlink to MannixTarrantAutopsyReport. Scanning the page he saw references to Rayville, ULM, and Joe Crannock who'd helped Quinn get his scholarship. There were even the names of his ULM classmates.

When he closed his own file on Edge's computer in disgust, he scanned some of the other names on the list of Edge's 'research contacts.' He skipped past files on Dieter Lange and Felipe from Soporte, and couldn't bear to think what secrets from the past might be recorded in Alita's.

He knew he shouldn't access confidential files on anyone other than himself, but Quinn was very tempted to look in Robert Moncur's file. He stared at the file's icon for a minute. Even knowing Edge was on Ragged Island and couldn't be watching, he caught himself looking over his shoulder. But it was Edge who should feel guilty, he reasoned. It was Edge who had made him deceive Alita, and betray Leonie and Riona.

The circumstances of the car smash that killed Robert's wife intrigued Quinn; in particular, why after discussing the accident Robert became much keener to volunteer for Edge's murderous mission. Curiosity got the better of him, but just as he was moving the cursor towards Robert's file another name caught his eye.

'L. Dugas/Tarrant'

Chapter Sixty-Three

8.10 am

Mariana Grajales Airport, Guantanamo, Cuba

Leonie parked the Mercedes in the shadow of the terminal building. The dashboard clock read 08:10, and across the tarmac they could see a large, sleek jet. A smaller plane was just coming in to land.

Two women in smart business suits and heels emerged from the terminal doors, accompanied by a tall man. The three walked across the tarmac, the women holding pashminas over their hair in the backdraft of the smaller jet as it taxied to a halt nearby. One of the women carried on up the steps to the open door of the big plane, while the other stayed outside with the man.

"That's Michel," said Leonie. Her voice was cold.

The first woman soon stepped back out of the plane and down the steps, followed by a line of slight figures. Alita counted nine of them, looking like kids on a school trip as the two escorts ushered them into a neat line. One was a boy. The man she now knew was Michel Cochet walked slowly along, appraising the young people like a general inspecting a guard of honour. The line was then dismissed back up the aircraft steps. The two escorts remained on the tarmac chatting with Michel Cochet, who was caressing the taller woman's scarf.

To Alita's horror, Leonie pulled a black handgun out of her shoulder bag and screwed a long silencer onto the end of the barrel. "I found this in his clothes drawer," she said, a grim look on her face as the window lowered and she rested the gun barrel on the frame, taking steady aim.

Michel Cochet was just thirty yards away, but before Leonie could fire he had turned, waved to the escorts and walked away out of sight towards the other plane. Seconds later the small jet taxied away.

"Shit! We're too late," said Leonie as she closed the tinted car window. Alita couldn't speak.

The two escorts marched back towards the terminal. Behind black glass, Alita shrank back as they passed within yards of the Mercedes, heels clicking on the tarmac.

Leonie opened the car door once the women were inside. "Come on, I know what we're going to do." Alita followed her to the terminal entrance. The smartly-dressed women were entering the restroom.

Chapter Sixty-Four

8.15 am

MV Cacique-2

What he had just learned from Edge's files made Quinn desperate to get onto Ragged Island. He had two people to kill.

The boat was anchored out of sight of the RI7 compound, more than half a mile South of the bay. With no dinghy to use he had to get closer to the shore if he was going to be able to swim. That meant moving the boat North as far as he dared, but staying out of sight of anyone on the island.

He had to risk starting the diesel engine, but at least its chugging would be muffled by the sea and the jungle. Using the anchor's auto winch was out of the question. The heavy iron chain links clanking through the mechanism would sound like a jackhammer and be heard for miles. He had to pause for breath after hauling the anchor by hand.

The RI7 men would still be in their cabins, but if he strayed too far into the bay the caretaker and Alita's replacement would be sure to spot the boat. When the electric fence on its pier was about 50 yards ahead of him he cut the engine. Drifting to a stop in the welcome silence, as quietly as he could he lowered the anchor into the sea. He had to uncoil seven loops of the chain before it went slack. About 20 feet deep, he thought, as he slipped into the water.

Minutes later Quinn stopped and trod water. He'd given the end of the pier a wide enough berth, and looking back through the fence grid the boat appeared sinister against the rising sun.

He noticed for the first time that instead of extending straight out into the sea, the ends of the fence curved inwards. Less than a hundred yards away he could see the end of the pier to the North of the bay. Access from the sea was much narrower than he'd realised. It had been a chance in a million that the storm had washed his little dinghy through that gap three years ago.

Reassured that the boat was still out of sight from the compound, he struck out towards the beach he had slept on until he'd escaped with Robert and Alita. When he had shaken himself off on the sloping sand, he shivered and dripped his way along the beach. His old palm-root cocoon was gone, its tree having fallen. It had kept him warm at night and cool by day. The memory brought the taste of Alita's rotis back to his mouth, and he wished he could have one now.

He followed footprints on the way along the beach. When he entered the edge of the bush the trail became less clear. Edge and Robert must have lowered to a crawl. Dried leaves covering the ground had been disturbed here and there by what must be knee and hand prints. Where the soft mud underneath was exposed, Quinn saw occasional imprints of stylised owls. He knew he was on track. He'd noticed Robert's distinctive boot soles the day before.

Creeping through vegetation, he approached the pool area. The smells and sounds took him back. Previous furtive searches here had been for food and water.

The dull thrum of the pool filter was almost hypnotic. A sudden screech jolted his senses and he threw himself down to hide in a manicured shrub border. A parrot fluttering and thwacking its wings through palm leaves in the high canopy brought him back to his purpose. Fear of what he was about to do chilled his back.

The hills were still shading the compound, but it was just light enough for him to see boxes on tables by the pool. He could make out the RI7 logo, and some were stamped CRISTALERÍA! FRÁGIL! Catering supplies had been delivered, confirming what he'd read an hour ago. He allowed himself a sly smile.

Quinn expected the trail to lead past the pool and straight to the cabins, but the footprints veered away into the deeper bush, towards the compound's perimeter. Until then, though he had no firm plan, he had been focused on attacking his targets at the cabins. Now that he didn't know where Edge and Robert had gone, his resolve slumped.

He had no idea how he was going to kill them. He was unarmed, unlike Edge and Robert who were each carrying a machine pistol and a handgun. For a moment he considered turning about and swimming back to the boat. He pictured the files on Edge's computer and began to crawl onwards to confront his prey.

Chapter Sixty-Five

8.30 am

Mariana Grajales Airport

They each carried one bulging tote bag up the aeroplane steps.

"Are you sure we are supposed to give them out now?" asked Leonie, adjusting the waistband of her suit skirt.

Alita turned back from the top step, and said, "Yes, I asked the taller one before I put her gag on. This suit is too big for me. Is it obvious?"

The pilot spoke over the PA system, and they had no time to prepare more thoroughly. Entering the passenger cabin, Alita took a deep breath and fixed a smile on her face, before speaking to the chattering group of young passengers. "Hola, niños y niñas."

She explained to them that one of two ladies who had brought them from Mexico had become ill and that her friend had stayed to care for her. They were fortunate, she said. Señor Cochet's careful planning meant replacement escorts were always available.

She and Leonie then proceeded to distribute packages to each of the fashionably-dressed teenagers. They took them like children visiting Santa Claus. Their excited chatter filled the cabin as they opened their bags of cosmetics and perfumes. Alita felt sick and wondered where she had found her courage.

The plane left the ground at 8.45 am. The slight delay was down to a refuelling problem, the pilot announced, but he would have them on Ragged Island at the scheduled time.

Chapter Sixty-Six

Robert's patience was wearing thin.

When they had landed on Ragged Island, Edge had insisted they both creep round the perimeter of the compound from one end of the electric fence to the other, and all the way back. Robert's questions about why they hadn't headed straight to the cabins where the men would still be sleeping were met with evasion.

"It's not time yet," or, "I want us to be prepared for all eventualities."

Robert had shrugged and followed on, with grudging admiration for Edge's attention to detail. When they then approached each cabin in turn, but crept back deeper into the jungle, Robert began to wonder if the Englishman was scared. It was nearly two hours since they had pulled the dinghy up the beach, hiding it where Robert, Alita and Quinn had set off from almost three years ago.

He tried again. "Why don't we just do it?"

Edge ignored him and continued creeping on through vegetation. Robert muttered a curse and crawled along behind. They had skirted the pool for the third time, crawling through the gardens he had tended until three years ago. Near the outdoor kitchen area he stopped moving. He wasn't going farther until Edge explained.

He waited in silence. Edge would have to return if he wanted the ammunition Robert was carrying. He kept looking forward, but by the time his watch showed several minutes had passed there was still no sound or movement from the bushes Edge had disappeared into. He was about to give up and follow when there was a rustle behind him. His nape prickled and his hand went to the holster on his belt. A moment later he jumped when a bush parted beside him and Edge's blackened face appeared. A shaft of sunlight made it through the leafy canopy above, highlighting his excited grin.

"OK," Edge whispered. "We're hidden enough here. I'll tell you a bit more before we keep going." Birds were calling from somewhere above, and for a second Robert was struck by absurdity and wanted to laugh. Edge brought him back to reality. "I want you to open the security doors at the tunnel."

Robert hissed back, "But the men never go in there! We don't need the tunnel. You can take them out in their beds. Like we said."

The teeth showed again as Edge allowed himself a soft chuckle. His eyes sparkled in the dappled shade, and sweat trails had begun to melt vertical stripes into the dye on his face. "The men are not the only prize. I need some time inside the tunnel."

The tunnel's further from the beach, thought Robert.

"Can't we just get on with it? Get away unnoticed."

Edge's left eyebrow rose, his mouth contorting in a sarcastic grin. "There won't be anyone to notice us, dear boy."

"Anyway, that's impossible," Robert tried. "Even with the security clearance, the computer will only let the doors open when there's a shipment scheduled to come in. And anyway, only the caretaker can open them. Triple security."

There was sarcasm in Edge's whispered voice as he went on. "On your first point, poor Robert, there is a shipment today.

Didn't you notice the pool area has been prepared for a party?" The flashing, sneering smile again. "And secondly, you were the caretaker here. Your fingerprints, retinal scan and facial recognition features haven't changed."

"What in hell have we been doing crawling around the jungle if the only reason you've got me here is to get you into the tunnel?"

Edge grinned. "We had time to waste, Robert. MC's delivering the package at 10 am. I thought we should spend the time having a bit of fun until then."

"You're mad!"

Edge ignored him and turned away, creeping on in the direction of the tunnel. Robert watched him disappear as if he had never been there. Edge has done this sort of thing before, he thought. He's reliving his youth as a spy. From behind him, Robert could now hear music. He glanced back in the direction of the pool. When they'd crept past, there had been boxes of crockery and glasses. Edge was right, he thought. There was to be a party. And Cleeter's arriving at ten o'clock. He shifted the weight of the pack on his back before crawling between bushes to follow Trevor Edge.

Edge had stopped at the top of a slight slope when Robert caught up with him. He was peering through field glasses, scanning the area below. Robert knew he was focused on the grey steel doors at the inner end of the tunnel.

"Cleeter's sending girls today?" Robert whispered.

"He is," Edge replied. He lowered the binoculars, and sneered, "Bringing boys too, remember, now that our friend Isaac's being more open about his preferences."

Robert shook his head. "But why do you want time in the tunnel?" he hissed. "And, anyway, I can't even open the doors. They'll have updated the security clearance. Only the new caretaker will have access."

Edge smiled back at him. "Don't you remember I work in IT? It wasn't difficult to hack in and re-activate your details." The sarcastic voice again.

"But why? I mean – why? You can just kill them all at the pool? Or in their cabins? I know the layout – I thought that's why you needed me here."

His smile gone, Edge spoke with quiet authority, his eyes fixed on Robert's. "Now listen to me. This is what's really going to happen."

Robert lay concealed in dank undergrowth, overlooking the tunnel's inner doors. What Trevor Edge had told him to do left him speechless. Until now, Robert had thought the only reason for the mission was to kill the RI7. Now he didn't know if the men even featured in Edge's plan. One thing was clear. However many people died, Edge didn't care. He would kill anyone in his way. And now there was a party of young people arriving.

Robert hadn't considered what would happen to the caretakers, the two unfortunates who had been recruited to replace Alita and himself. Edge had spoken coldly, seeming confident of Robert's blind obedience. He'd then slithered off into the undergrowth to carry out another 'recce,' ordering Robert to get ready for action.

Robert had opened the inner doors to the tunnel dozens of times when he was working for the RI7. The security arrangements meant only his eyes, facial features and fingerprints could unlock them. Only one entrance to the tunnel could be open at a time, and apart from when he and Alita had been brought to work on the island, he'd never seen what was beyond the outer doors.

Routine deliveries were left in the tunnel for him by a driver from the airstrip, who would then close the doors and depart.

If a consignment of girls was expected, it would be Cleeter's fixer whose features would unlock the outer doors to let them into the tunnel. Edge had been a fixer, and his own features must have been on the system, but they would only open the outer doors. It meant Robert's presence was essential if Edge was going to have access.

Robert had learned to tune out from the excited girls' chattering as they waited with their gifts and bribes. They always had one or two female escorts. When Robert opened the doors, the women would shepherd the unsuspecting victims into the hands of Cleeter's customers.

He took a deep breath, and was trying to process what Trevor Edge had ordered him to do when a hand grasped his ankle. He gripped his Glock.

Chapter Sixty-Seven

9.00 am

"Trevor..?"

His father-in-law's deep voice had a nervous Edge to it Quinn hadn't heard before.

"Ssshhh! Robert. It's me. Quinn. Quiet!"

He slid himself forward to lie beside his father-in-law. Robert's face was stiff with surprise and confusion.

"Put the gun down, Robert. I'm here to help you," he whispered. He'd been unable to settle on the boat knowing Robert might be in danger, he explained.

Robert lowered the pistol

"I want to help you and Trevor kill the RI7," he said, "Three's better than two, and I want to play my part." He couldn't tell Robert what he had discovered on Edge's computer, and hoped his words sounded convincing.

"How did you find me?"

"I followed your owl footprints. The freshest ones led this way."

Robert had looked so keen and focused when he rowed the tender away. Now there was a furtive, worried look about him.

"Why didn't you go straight to the cabins?" Quinn asked.

"Edge." Robert was looking into the bush, his eyes flicking side to side.

"Where is he?"

"Gone to scout around. He moves like a cat." Robert pointed over his shoulder. "I think he's more interested in something in

353

that tunnel," he whispered. "And now there's a group of young girls going to come through it. And Edge knew about them."

Quinn also knew there was another abuse party planned, but he couldn't tell Robert how. "I saw the boxes of glasses and things set out by the pool," he said. "Maybe Edge won't do the shooting in front of the kids? Wants to stop them at the tunnel?"

Robert shook his head and wiped sweat from his forehead.

"He doesn't care about them either way. I don't even know if he means to kill the RI7 after all." Robert continued as if he was thinking aloud. "I don't care about the RI7, either. Or this 'Table.' Fucking domino effects, who gives a fuck? There's only one target for me."

It chilled Quinn to hear his father-in-law's whispered cursing. This was a change in Robert. Quinn's mind whirled. Doesn't care about the RI7? Who did he mean by 'one target'? It's me. He's going to kill me. I'm his target. He knows about Leonie. Edge must have told him after they got to the island.

Robert looked up into Quinn's eyes as if he'd just remembered he was there. "But before I can kill him we've got to make those young kids safe. Now you're here you can help me."

'Kill him,' thought Quinn. 'You can help me.' I'm not his target. It's Edge. Robert knows something else about Edge. Something that makes him want to destroy him.

Quinn recognised a grim irony. If Robert was correct, Edge's primary reason for arranging the mission was not to kill the RI7 but to retrieve something in the tunnel. Now Quinn knew Robert was only here to kill Edge. That meant none of them was really on Ragged Island to kill its psychopathic English owners. All three had different motives.

He could feel himself shaking. He couldn't tell Robert the real reason he had left the boat. He had to keep up his pretence. "Couldn't we just get on with it now? Kill the Englishmen, I mean. Before the girls arrive."

Robert looked back at him. Quinn saw he still held his handgun, and his machine pistol was slung around his shoulders. "It's too late. Listen." He pointed upwards to a strip of clear sky above the path. The noise of a plane landing meant Quinn didn't have to look.

Robert turned towards the tunnel. "They're due to arrive at 10 am. It was always the same. A bus to bring them from the airstrip, with one or two glamorous whore-mistresses." He turned back to Quinn. "Alita had to serve them drinks and food. She hated the bitches for helping Cleeter, but they were just as trapped as we were." Robert's eyes were misting, and Quinn turned away, trying to muffle the terrified cries Alita let out nightly in her sleep.

They were still in shade, but the air was now hot and oppressive. Steam was rising from the tarmacked path leading to the tunnel, where a break in the jungle canopy had admitted some overnight rain.

Quinn wanted to focus on taking his own revenge. Both his targets were going to be in the tunnel. If Edge was desperate to have time in there that would be when to do it. But the girls. They had to save the girls. He checked his watch and looked back at Robert.

"We've got time. Can't we get in the tunnel now? Open it, try and stop the girls? Where the hell is Edge?"

"I told you. Gone on a 'recce.'" Robert spat. "Pretending he's back being a spy again."

"What's his plan? Why's he waiting?"

"He wants time in the tunnel before the girls arrive." Robert explained the security procedures in place and how Edge had exchanged the caretaker's ID profile for his own.

"So you could open the doors anytime? We don't have to wait until the girls are locked in the tunnel?"

Robert was shaking his head, but Quinn went on.

"Why isn't Edge already in there? It's nearly 9.30. He could be in there now."

"No," Robert said. "Edge doesn't want to be disturbed. The new caretaker will be coming at 9.45." With a look of disgust on his face, he went on, "I'm supposed to intercept him on his way here. Kill him and take his place."

Without saying any more Robert set off towards a bend in the path from the cabins. Quinn watched him crawl into the dense undergrowth, holding his silenced Glock in his right hand.

Chapter Sixty-Eight

Ragged Island Airport

At 9.25 the jet was landing again, this time on a much smaller airstrip. As they came in to land Alita saw it had been laid out in a clearing in the jungle. From the air Ragged Island looked beautiful, verdant against the cobalt sea.

Outside a modern building sat the smaller jet they'd seen Michel Cochet climb into. As their own plane taxied over towards it a shiny maroon coach approached across the tarmac.

Leonie and Alita had spent the flight whispering to each other, making plans for what they thought might happen next. Alita explained that the groups of young victims had always been accompanied by two female escorts when they had arrived at the compound for a party.

"I hated helping them, but what could I do?" Leonie had squeezed her hand. This time, Alita and Leonie would be escorting the innocent girls arriving as prey for the men on Ragged Island. There was also one boy, she remembered. Slight, blond and barely a youth.

Michel Cochet stepped down from the littler jet. He stood on the smooth, paved surface, chatting to the pilot through the open cockpit window. A heat haze shimmered above the silenced engines.

Alita felt Leonie tensing beside her. She put her hand on her arm, but Leonie made no move to reach into her shoulder bag. She had already agreed she couldn't shoot Michel here, in front of the coach driver and the plane staff. Both were intent on intervening to stop Edge and Cochet from murdering Robert and Quinn. They didn't know how, but they knew it had to happen at the Ragged Island complex.

Their most pressing concern was that Michel Cochet would recognise Leonie on their onward journey in the bus. With her pashmina tied high, and behind one of the escorts' sunglasses, Leonie led the party of youngsters quickly across to the bus. She nodded to the driver as she entered, making straight for the back seat and directing the boy and girls to sit in front of her. Alita followed them and stayed near the front. She would take the lead, and endure any contact with Cochet.

When Cochet sauntered over and boarded the coach he looked twice at Alita, then threw a glance towards the rear where Leonie sat. She stayed busy delving into the tote bag she carried, her face turned away.

"I was hoping the tall one would sit with me, the one who has two young daughters," he said to Alita. There was an expectant look on his face, and she felt deep nausea and a crawling sensation on her skin. Somehow she managed to smile and flutter her eyelids at Cochet, speaking in what she hoped was a light-hearted, flirty manner.

"My friend is often car sick, Señor, and prefers to sit at the back near the larger window. I was hoping I might please you." Alita was surprised by how easy she found lying to this man. He had, if not physically, abused little Riona.

It was clear, though, that Cochet hadn't realised that the escorts on the coach were not the two he had seen earlier. We all look the same to him, Alita thought. Bastard!

The coach set off on the smooth jungle road and Alita continued forcing herself to make small-talk with Cochet. She had to distract him from spotting Leonie. It was a struggle to keep the smile on her face. She was feeling sick at the thought she was helping to deliver these poor young victims into the hands of beasts. Men who had paid Cleeter to provide them with fresh meat.

Chapter Sixty-Nine

The Tunnel

At exactly a quarter to ten Quinn saw Robert walk along the path towards the inner steel doors. The pistol was back in its holster. As he approached, Trevor Edge emerged from perfect concealment in the vegetation on the other side of the path. Though Edge didn't glance once in his direction, Quinn still shrank back further into bushes.

With Edge at his shoulder, Robert moved towards a small panel to the right of the doors. He touched it with the index fingers of both hands. Quinn saw a small screen light up before Robert leant in close, his eye to a peephole in the panel. The doors slid apart, and lights came on inside the tunnel.

Edge hurried in through the gap and disappeared out of view, and Robert motioned Quinn out of his hiding place to join him at the tunnel entrance. He slipped down the sloping bank as silently as he could, the rustle of every leaf like crashing cymbals between his ears. He stood to the side of the tunnel entrance, trying to be invisible.

"The caretaker?" he heard Edge call from within.

"Dealt with as ordered," Robert replied. Quinn felt sick. The killing had started.

"Close the doors, Robert, and come to open this one," Edge continued.

"You want me to open the plant room door? It's just the boilers and water pumps." As he spoke Robert stood still at the entrance. With one hand behind him he pointed Quinn towards a recess built into the tunnel wall, just inside the doors. Quinn took the cue and squeezed in, his face close to hard concrete and his back against a grey metal cabinet. The doors began to move. He could hear and feel the motor whirring behind him, trapping him in the tunnel.

When the doors had fully closed there was a brief quiet. His breathing was now all Quinn could hear, and he tried to silence it as he watched Robert step forward and out of view.

"Why the plant room?" he heard Robert repeat, his voice echoing in the enclosed space. "What's so important in there?"

When Edge spoke, Quinn could imagine a smug smile on his face. "When you were working here, Robert, did you ever have to attend to the boilers? Switch them on and off?"

"No, it was all done by the computer, but–"

"And the electricity supply, the water supply, the waste pumps?"

Quinn thought he heard Robert sigh.

Edge went on, "No, you wouldn't have had to, Robert. That little computer in the plant room controlled them as well, didn't it?" Edge's sarcasm was never far away. "Come on, Robert, do some more of your magic on this entry panel."

Quinn heard Robert's footsteps, and a few seconds later another door motor.

"But we're going to kill them anyway." Robert's voice sounded urgent. Nervous. "Why d'you really get me here? Just to get in there? Cut off their power supply? Or water?"

Edge stayed silent, like a teacher waiting for a correct answer.

Quinn had guessed. The computer had to be the main server for the compound's network. And Edge's true objective. He had the skills to hack into any computer, but there must be something Edge wanted that was stored on the server alone.

Remote access to its files would have meant extracting login credentials from an RI7 member. The primary reason for Robert's return to Ragged Island had been Edge's need for his physical presence, his eyes and fingertips, to open the plant room door. It was all about direct access to the server. The RI7's files. Their money.

Chapter Seventy

The clock at the front of the coach read just before ten o'clock when the driver pulled up in a turning circle. The girls and boy became quiet, all watching Michel Cochet as he left the bus and walked purposefully down a few concrete steps. Alita had seen the aluminium security doors giving access to the tunnel once before, when she first arrived on Ragged Island four years before. They were a mirror image of the inner barrier.

"What time is it, Robert?" Edge's voice sounded distant, with a more pronounced echo. Quinn guessed Edge had moved into the side room off the tunnel and was already working at a computer terminal.

"9.59."

"Excellent. They should be arriving."

A light above the closed inner doors went out, leaving the tunnel lit only by a dim row of lights along the tunnel's crown, and light spilling from the plant room. The relative darkness was a relief. Ensuring he remained in shadow Quinn edged to his left until he could see some of the tunnel.

In the left wall, about 30 feet away, he could see the entry to the plant room. Facing into it stood the bulky figure of his father-in-law. Beads of sweat glistened on his black forehead. With both hands held straight out, he was aiming his handgun into the side room. Quinn's heart beat hard and loud in his neck. He was right. Robert intended to kill Edge.

A bright light appeared at the far end of the tunnel. Robert's arms dropped as he spun to face the outer doors. A white slit shone between them, throwing an angled stripe onto the floor, growing wider as they separated. Sunshine soon flooded the far end of the tunnel.

Emerging from the glare and framed by the tunnel opening was the silhouette of a tall figure. Quinn could just see part of a maroon bus behind, sunshine reflecting from a polished wheel arch. The man walked towards Robert, his hand outstretched in greeting.

Quinn realised it was Dieter Lange. Both of the men he was going to kill were within the tunnel.

Time seemed to slow. Hatred and rage filled him. Early that morning he had discovered that Lange had been trafficking women and children to supply PBC brothels in Florida, as well as for Cleeter.

Quinn didn't know if Lange was connected with the trafficker who had taken Leonie and Riona, but it was clear he had known they were alive and in Miami. And Edge had ordered Lange to travel there to kill them. He didn't know why Lange had disobeyed Edge, but at Neptuna they had both lied to him, told him they were dead. He wanted to kill Edge and Lange, but he was unarmed. He came to a quick decision. Robert intended to dispatch Edge; somehow, he would deal with Lange himself.

"Aah, you made it, Dieter!" Edge's voice boomed from the plant room. "I'm in. Their *security* is so twentieth-century. I'm almost ready to make the transfers."

Robert was looking back and forth between Dieter Lange and the plant room, his brow furrowed in confusion. "You're the man – the restaurant – Quinn's wife. What–?"

"Dieter and I will be very rich in a moment, Robert! It's the reason we're here. We've been working towards this moment for years. We deserve it. The real prize!" Edge's gloating voice continued. "Just one – more – click. That's it – we've got their billions!"

Lange was approaching the plant room door. Robert appeared to be stuck in time, his gun behind him. Quinn heard footsteps from the plant room and a second later Edge's beaming face appeared. He was walking towards Lange in triumph when a new voice spoke.

"Michel Cochet."

Quinn recognised the voice. His heart flipped, and he leaned out of his nook as far as he dared, trying to see the other end of the tunnel. Without fully revealing his presence he could only see one half of the open outer doorway. There, looking terrified and lit by a shaft of sunlight, stood Alita. It couldn't be! He blinked and shook his head. She had gone.

There was a look of shock on Robert's face.

Dieter Lange turned towards the voice, staring in apparent disbelief.

"This is for Riona!"

Stupefied by the words, Quinn's ears savoured the voice. How?

Lange stiffened, and the back of his head erupted. Quinn heard splattering on the steel door beside him. Lange crumpled to the floor of the tunnel convulsing, a round hole in the centre of his forehead.

Edge ran behind the safety shield of Robert's bulk and lifted his Glock 19. Robert was like a statue, staring towards the spot where Quinn thought he had seen Alita.

Quinn had to see more. He stepped out from his hiding place just as a silenced shot from Edge's pistol tore his wife's throat away. Leonie Tarrant slumped gurgling to the floor. The heavy clatter of her pistol on the concrete beat Quinn's ears as he watched her die.

Chapter Seventy-One

Quinn shrank back into cover, his wife's dead body now out of sight but clear in his mind. He could still see Robert and Edge outside the plant room door. A rhythmic thudding slowed to a stop and he knew Lange's convulsing right leg had died. Silence.

Edge's voice echoed.

"Change of plan, Robert. Open the inner doors."

Robert didn't move. He was still staring away from Quinn, over the bodies and towards the light at the outer end of the tunnel.

"Now!" Edge's voice boomed, demanding attention. He stepped away from Robert. With a wave of his pistol, he directed him away from the light, in Quinn's direction.

Robert turned his body to obey the order, then hesitated. "I – can't," he stuttered. "Only one end at a time..." He pointed back towards the open outer doors.

Quinn saw a sarcastic sneer on Edge's face. "IT, remember? Christ, I can't do everything!" Pointing back into the plant room he said, "I've just changed the door settings, but I can't disable them or they'll both close automatically. And I can't hack into your fucking fingerprints!"

Edge had taken command, seemingly unfazed by the sudden deaths of Dieter Lange and Leonie Tarrant.

Robert turned and trudged to the steel doors, his Heckler and Koch slung on his back. From his hiding place a yard away Quinn watched his father-in-law put his hands and face to work. He looked old. Ashen. The motor soon vibrated against Quinn's back, and he saw the doors begin to part.

Edge came to stand beside Robert, right in front of Quinn. Pointing back towards the other end of the tunnel he said, "Right. Now go back out that way and shoot everyone in that coach. Then toss a grenade in for good measure."

Robert stared at him, motionless.

"Go on! We can't take them with us. Worthless pieces of trash."

Robert's face darkened, but Edge took him by the shoulders and turned him round to face the outer doors, where Quinn had seen the bus. And where he had imagined he'd seen Alita.

"Get on with it! Then follow me this way, to the pool." Edge had his pistol against Robert's neck.

Robert disappeared back along the tunnel and out of Quinn's eye line, swinging the machine pistol round from his back.

Quinn's chest burned with rage, his senses sharp and limbs primed. He processed in intense detail every word spoken and every frame of the violent horror film that had just played. Witnessing his wife's murder had poured even more adrenaline into his blood. He had no fear.

As Edge walked into light outside the tunnel Quinn lunged forward. He barged into Edge, grasping his trunk and pinning his arms to his side. The machine gun hanging on Edge's back dug into Quinn's midriff.

They overbalanced and fell into some shrubbery bordering the path. Edge was grunting and kicking out, his Breton cap askew and his face squashed into damp mulch. Quinn tried to pin him down, but a flailing boot smashed into his kneecap. Pain paralysed him, loosening his grip.

Edge slithered forwards, up the sloping bank. When Quinn righted himself Edge was sitting up, aiming his pistol at him.

"Where did you come from?" he sneered. Beige mud and rotting leaves coated the left side of his smudged black face, like a ghoulish phantom mask.

"You killed..." Quinn paused, looking back into the tunnel.

Edge smirked, and sneered, "It's OK, Mr Tarrant, I won't tell your father-in-law who she was. Not that it will matter."

Edge seemed to think aloud. Still pointing the gun at Quinn, he spoke as if to himself. "It would have been OK if Dieter had taken out Leonie Dugas in Miami. Like I told him to," he said, looking into Quinn's eyes. "But the dirty fucker liked her little girl too much! Serves him right! Now she's turned up here and killed him."

Quinn was struggling to understand. Riona?

Edge continued talking, a smug look on his face. "You're only here, Quinn, as part of the cover story. Three friends on a fishing trip. Oh, and the boat is rented in your name, so when they discover what's happened I'll have disappeared and no one will even know I was here. You really are surplus to requirements."

Quinn's eyes were fixed on the handgun in front of Edge's grimace. The the silencer was about three feet away from Quinn's face, and he could see a plug of black mud blocking its end. Edge's finger flexed against the trigger. A crack of thunder speared Quinn's ears. Sizzling pain seared into his right side.

The world then played in silent freeze-frame: a puff of smoke; black shapes spraying out from where the handgun had been; blood spattered on Edge's shocked face; a bleeding thumb on a banana leaf; his own hand grabbing his loin.

With his left hand, Edge was trying to swing his machine gun round from his back. His mouth seemed to be trying to speak, but Quinn was deaf to all sound. There was a crazy smile on Edge's face as he dug his heels into the banking, pushing himself backwards up the slope.

Quinn shook his head to try to clear his ears. The movement drove a spear of pain into his side, but let him detect a deep bass rumble. More of his hearing returned, until some of Edge's words became distinct. "Basta ... money transf– ... fucking mine! ... all mine now ... my billions ... fucking RI7... pah! ... who cares? ... Oh, my fucking hand! ... aargh!"

Edge kept kicking his way up the mulchy banking, looking down on Quinn. With pain in his side pinning him to the damp earth, Quinn could only watch helplessly. Chilled and beginning to shiver he waited and watched as Edge worked the Heckler and Koch round into a one-handed firing position.

Crazed and bloodied, Edge struggled to his feet and raised the weapon, looming enormous over Quinn. Laughing like a maniac, he tilted his head back, preparing to fire.

Lightning struck, and blue and yellow flames filled Quinn's vision for an instant and a smell of burnt hair reached his nose. Sparks flew from Edge's head, his face contorted in agony as flames spread down to engulf him, clothes on fire and flesh melting.

As Quinn lost consciousness, he thought he could smell a hog roast.

Chapter Seventy-Two

He was floating feet first in a turbulent stream, escorted through a dark tunnel, towards a bright light. A velvet voice spoke to him. A god?

"Quinn. Quinn. Stay with us, man."

The angels escorting him into the light weren't making his passage onwards easy. The one behind was gripping Quinn's upper arms, strong hands keeping him afloat. A pain burned in his side, every movement stabbing him with a jagged blade. His legs were weightless.

Quinn's eyes began to clear. Ahead of him, the angel holding his ankles wore maroon. He rolled his eyes to look behind and above. Robert Moncur's large, round face smiled back at him, upside down.

"That's it, man, you're with us again."

Quinn saw the roof of the tunnel passing by overhead. Some of what had happened came back to him.

"Edge?" He felt his mouth move but wasn't sure if he made any sound.

"Dead. Fried himself on the electric fence. His head caught fire."

Quinn could feel the smell in his nostrils. Charred meat and singed hair. Fleeting memories of Edge's blackened face.

Robert was breathing heavily, and spoke in short bursts as he carried Quinn. "And when he went down his machine gun must have touched the fence. It exploded – blew him in half," he said. "Serves the bastard right – wanted me to kill those youngsters."

Quinn remembered the glossy bus. "Are they – ?"

"They're fine. Out here with their escort." Robert indicated ahead of him with his eyes. There was a wide, upside-down smile on his face. "Wait 'til you see who it is."

They were moving into daylight outside the tunnel. As the top rail of the sliding doors passed by overhead, Quinn remembered them sliding apart, a tall man silhouetted in between. Had there been someone else there? Near the maroon bus?

"That was some crazy stuff happened back there, man." Robert said. "And who was that woman?"

Woman? Quinn's eyes closed and he felt his brow crease. A vision of Alita zipped across his mind, gone before he could process it. He remembered a voice, echoing. A voice he'd recognised. Dieter Lange dying on the floor of the tunnel. A woman. Crumpling, blood gushing from her neck. Not Alita. Leonie. A bad dream. She's in France. He screwed his eyes tighter, but he could still see her.

"Quinn? You goin' again, man? Stay with us."

Robert and whoever was holding his feet were speeding up. The jolting forced Quinn to focus on pain.

"Youch!"

"He's still with us," Robert called. "C'mon, by the bus there. Set him down."

Movement stopped. He could feel hard ground underneath him, bright sun on his face. He opened his eyes, lifting a hand to shield them. They had laid him down beside the coach he'd seen. Above its glinting metallic side he could see shaded windows. Indistinct faces looked down at him.

The man who'd helped carry him climbed aboard. His maroon suit matched the paintwork. Robert was crouching beside him, his gentle hands placing a cushion under his head.

"There you go, man. Lie there, 'til your nurse comes."

Nurse?

There was a sad smile on Robert's face, his eyes misting as he turned towards the coach door. "It's safe, now," he called. "Come out. He needs you."

When Quinn saw Alita stepping down from the bus he tried to sit up. Pain punched him unconscious.

Something wasn't right. Alita was sitting beside the bed, the rest of the room out of focus. Their mattress was harder than it should be, and Quinn shifted to make himself comfortable.

"Youch!" He reached down to his right loin.

"Quiet. Lie still. Drink this." Alita was holding a water bottle to his lips, her other hand supporting his head.

"Thanks, Baby," he said, trying to smile. Some water dribbled down his chin. She didn't smile. His vision cleared and the sky appeared overhead. His real situation began to seep back in. He was still lying in the shade of that maroon bus.

"Was I shot? My side..?"

"No. Just a burn."

Alita was pale, expressionless. Her pupils were huge black holes looking through him as if he wasn't there.

"What are you doing here?" he asked.

The blank, silent stare continued.

"How did you get to the island?" he tried.

"We flew." She looked away, biting her lip.

"We?"

Something was different about Alita. She looked quickly over her shoulder towards the bus door. Quinn could just see the outline of Robert's head and shoulders through the dark window glass.

"I'm sorry she's dead, Q-T." Alita's voice was toneless.

"Who?"

A dying woman flashed before his eyes. The one he'd seen on the floor of the tunnel. Blood spurting from the neck. He looked at Alita's stony, cold face. 'I'm sorry she's dead, Q-T.'

Leonie. Not in France. Dead. Reality hit home.

Quinn wept freely, letting out a long, mewling wail as the blue of the sky roiled with tears. Minutes later when his choking sobs subsided, he saw that Alita's shocked, frozen face had melted. She was crying too.

Out of the melee in his mind questions began to form. Why was Alita here? Did Robert know she was coming? How did she know Leonie? And did Robert know who..?

He fixed his wet eyes on Alita's. With a brief sideways nod he pointed to the bus. Robert was looking down at them.

Alita read the question on his face. With a slight shake of her head, she whispered. "Doesn't know it was her."

Quinn closed his eyes for a moment, then quickly opened them.

"Riona," he said, tears overflowing again.

Chapter Seventy-Three

The Coach

With support from Robert and Alita, Quinn managed to stand. He needed more help to climb into the coach. Each step up seemed to force the jagged knife deeper into his loin. Alita didn't let go of his hand, squeezing it tight until he lowered himself into a double seat at the front. Robert had sent the coach driver outside. Through the windscreen, Quinn could see him, Latin features pale grey above the maroon suit.

Robert was standing by the bus door. "I've got a couple of things to do before we go," he said, looking back and forth between Quinn and Alita. "Then I want to know what the hell's going on." He pointed his thick finger at Alita. "You still haven't told me how you got here, girl, or who that woman was." He turned and stepped out of the bus, heading off towards the tunnel. Alita rushed out to follow him. Quinn heard her call, "Papa. I need you to..." She moved out of his earshot, and he saw her talking earnestly to Robert, who looked confused.

When Alita climbed back into the bus she stood beside Quinn with a grave expression. He looked into her eyes. Neither of them spoke, but there was a slight nod of Alita's head and he understood what she asked her papa to do.

The youngsters had all moved as near the back of the coach as they could. Some were in tears, others talking in hushed tones. Even if the silenced gunshots in the tunnel hadn't been audible in the coach they would have seen Robert's machine gun, Quinn thought, and heard Edge's guns explode.

Alita stood up at the front of the bus and spoke to them. She told them they'd had a lucky escape. Quinn listened, impressed by her composure as she told them what would have happened instead of the glamorous experience they had been told to expect. They would have been plied with champagne, then drugged and used in whatever way the men on Ragged Island wished. Alita silenced their gasps and hesitant questions with two palms held up. "Trust me. I know."

Cushioned in the soft leather of the coach seat Quinn was sitting half upright. Alita crouched down, fussing over him and inspecting the wound on his side. Quinn had never felt pain like it, but it hadn't been a bullet. Instead of the hole he had been expecting he saw an oblong blackened area of skin. Red blisters had formed around it, and there was a burnt smell. Alita told him while he'd been unconscious she'd found a piece of Edge's shattered Glock stuck to his singed shirt.

"You'll be sore for a few days, but it'll heal," she said, smoothing his hair.

Quinn lowered his voice to a whisper. "Alita, I need to tell you something. I don't know how Leonie found you, or how she made you come here, but I need to tell you something." Alita put her finger over his lips to stop him.

"Quinn, it was me who found Leonie. I went to her home."

His mind went blank for a second. "Her home? France–"

"She wasn't in France. She made you think that, so you would stop looking for her."

Quinn stared, his mouth open. Alita took his hand, and explained about finding the ring and Leonie's note, her fury at him and her need to see Leonie for herself. As Quinn listened he bowed his head. Leonie and Riona had been living hours away from him in Manzanillo while he had blanked them from his life. On the other side of the world he could forget them, and his guilt. He'd been able to deceive himself they were as well as dead, no longer a threat. But they had still been in Cuba.

Alita interrupted his self confession.

"I know you knew, Quinn. That she was alive. And I know you didn't know it when we were married. It wasn't your fault."

He looked at his hands, cradled in hers. Two new wedding rings. "I'm sorry I didn't tell you. I tried."

"Leonie told me how it happened. And that you met."

Quinn tensed. He'd hidden so much from Alita.

"She hit me." It was all he could think of to say.

"She says she hates herself for that." Alita dropped his hand, saying, "Oh god. Leonie." She was crying.

Quinn looked up at her. She had overcome her shock, but there was an edge to her voice he didn't recognise. Or was he imagining it, in his fragile state?

He'd just witnessed his wife shoot a man dead, before being murdered herself. He had faint memories of tackling Edge, a severed thumb on a green leaf, and the smell of burning hair. But much of what had happened was a murky mess of uncertainty.

An emptiness was gathering around him, inviting him to dive in. He was held back from the brink by two questions he knew he had to ask.

Alita's brown saucer eyes were misted, red in the corners. So innocent, knowing. So perfect, broken. So wronged.

He forced himself to speak.

"Why did Leonie kill Dieter Lange?"

"Who?"

"In the tunnel. She shot him."

"You mean Michel?"

Michel? Leonie's words in the tunnel echoed between his ears. 'Michel Cochet.' And just before Dieter Lange's head erupted she'd said, 'This is for Riona.'

Something Quinn had read on Edge's laptop came back to him. Lange and Cochet must be the same person.

Before he could say more Alita went on. "Michel was Leonie's boyfriend. French. It was him she came to kill." It was Alita's face that looked puzzled now. "Lange? Wasn't that the man who told you Leonie was dead?"

Quinn was quiet for a moment, then nodded. "Lange was Cochet."

As he watched understanding dawn on his remaining wife's face, Quinn pictured Leonie. He heard again 'This is for Riona,' and fought to stop the vacuum within swallowing him.

"Why did Leonie want to kill Cochet?" he asked, dreading the answer.

Taking a tight grasp of his hand, Alita said, "Something she found on his computer."

Alita paused, and Quinn's flesh began to creep. He knew what she was going to say. As she told him Leonie had found the images of Riona, the searing pain in his side melted away and fury strengthened him.

"The bastard! That's what Edge meant! Riona!" He had raised his voice and Alita reminded him with her eyes that the young people at the back would hear him. "Are you sure Lange is dead?" he murmured through his teeth, pushing himself up further to turn and look back towards the tunnel entrance.

"He's dead, Quinn. I saw what happened." Alita was looking over Quinn's head, speaking quickly. He watched her face change to reflect her words as she relived what she'd seen. "Leonie was determined to kill Michel. I was supposed to stay on the bus. Keep the girls quiet. But I told the driver to wait with them. I had to get to you..." Her words tailed off and she now looked into his eyes. "I saw them both die."

Quinn was trying to process what he had heard. Leonie had come here for revenge, for Riona. He had to know why Alita had come. That meant asking his other question, the one he dreaded most.

Alita went on before he could speak. "When Papa came out with a big gun I thought it was him who'd killed Leonie." She was looking into space again. "I couldn't move. I just stood outside the tunnel and he walked towards me like he hadn't seen me. He took my hand and led me into the bus. He didn't speak. Then we heard the blast and he seemed to wake up. He ran back into the tunnel, but then I heard another explosion." She was shaking her head, her eyes wide, glazed.

Quinn remembered Robert saying Edge's machine gun had exploded. Just after his handgun, he thought.

Alita was quiet at last. Quinn opened his mouth to speak, dreading asking her more.

Chapter Seventy-Four

He'd never known Leonie to wish harm on anyone, but she had come to Ragged Island with a gun, intent on avenging their daughter. And she had done it. Alita now knew the truth about him and how much he had wronged her. She'd said 'I had to get to you...'

"Alita, did you also come for – revenge?"

She just looked at him, her head tilted and her brow furrowed.

"I mean, you said you wanted –" His voice sounded strangled, his next words a choked whisper, "to get to me."

There were drying tear trails on her cheeks. Realisation appeared to dawn on her and he thought he saw the beginnings of an ironic smile flash over her face. She took a sharp intake of breath before she spoke.

"Edge and Michel Cochet were going to kill you. And Papa. That's why I came."

It was Quinn's turn to look shocked.

"We read their emails, Quinn. It's true." She told him he was to have been 'fish food'.

Quinn's thoughts were coming thick and fast, and he spoke them aloud.

"So which was his real name? Cochet or Lange? French or German? And the plan was to kill us all? Edge didn't care about those Englishmen. He just wanted their money." Things were beginning to make sense.

He took Alita's hand in both of his. "But how did you get on Cleeter's plane?"

"We took the place of the two women who were escorting the girls. And a boy. The escorts are still tied up in a storeroom back in Cuba. But I gave them water before putting the gags on." She put her hand to her chin. "Oh!" she said, standing up and looking out of the bus window. "We can't leave them too long. Where's Papa? We've got to go." Her voice was louder and the murmuring from the back seats stopped.

Sitting back down, Alita kept going. Quieter again, her words gushed. "Leonie had to keep a veil over her face, in case Michel saw her. But he sat up front on the bus, and I sat near him, distracting him in case he looked back. It was horrible, sitting near him. Knowing what Leonie had said about..."

Quinn shook his head and stared at the beige vinyl roof, trying to keep up. Whispering and sobbing had restarted in the back seats.

A crash of thunder rocked the bus on its springs. Girls screamed and a handbag fell from the luggage rack. Quinn strained to look behind him. Smoke billowed from the end of the tunnel.

"Papa!" Alita shouted. She was rushing towards the bus door when there was another blast.

Chapter Seventy-Five

Towards Ragged Island Airport

"Oh! Papa! Thank god you're OK."

The pain in his side meant Quinn was slow to rise to see over the back of the seat. Alita had stopped on the bottom step of the bus door and he could only see the top of her head. Out of the smoke emerged Robert with a man and a woman. They wore tan shorts and polo shirts and the man was helping Robert pull a low cargo trolley. Whatever lay on it was wrapped in towels that bore the RI7 logo.

As they approached, the driver directed them round the bus and out of Quinn's sight. He heard the hinges of the luggage compartment squeak open and closed. Sitting upright was painful, but it allowed Alita to come and sit with him. She held him while he tried to pretend Leonie's dead body wasn't stowed just beneath him.

When Robert climbed up the steps the man and woman followed him. The driver was already in the driving seat, and there was smooth swish and a solid clunk as the coach door closed. Then a few seconds of enclosed, air-conditioned silence.

Alita looked quizzically at Robert, who turned and said with a gesture of introduction, "Señor and Señorita Pineda. Rogelio and Silvia took over from us when we escaped, Alita."

"Gracias, gracias," said the man called Rogelio, placing a case on the rack overhead. Silvia nodded and looked back towards the tunnel, a horrified look on her face. They took seats towards the back of the bus.

Robert stood in the aisle near Quinn and Alita. She looked up at him. "Why were there more explosions, Papa?"

Robert's grim face relaxed into a wicked smile. "Two grenades in the plant room. It was a shame not to use them." He looked pleased with himself.

Quinn realised the RI7 men had not only lost their servants. They were trapped on the island with no power, water, or communications. As if he had read Quinn's mind, Robert said, "And the back-up batteries will keep the fence electrified for weeks." With a sarcastic shrug, he said, "They don't know there's a boat hidden outside the bay. I s'pose they could always swim straight out to Cuba..." He was chuckling.

Robert now moved forward to speak to the driver, who started up and guided the coach onto the smooth asphalt road back the way it had come.

The caretaker and his wife were talking quietly in Spanish. Quinn could see the vague imprint of a gag on Rogelio's cheek. Instead of killing him as Edge had ordered, Robert must have overpowered him but left him unharmed.

As the coach wound its way up a twisty incline there was a gap in the trees. Looking serene in bright sunlight Quinn caught sight of Cacique-2, the boat he had moored just a few hours ago, well out of sight of the RI7 compound.

He now had another huge problem: what to do about Leonie. He didn't know if Alita had told Robert whose body he and Señor Pineda had loaded into the bus, but if not he was going to have to be told. Quinn owed it to Leonie to arrange a decent burial and that meant getting her back to Cuba. He couldn't do that without facing the wrath of his father-in-law. He didn't have long to wait.

Robert came back and stood in the aisle.

"Alita, could you move, please? I need to speak to Quinn."

With a worried look on her face she did as she was told, and Robert sat down beside him.

"Tell me what's really going on, Quinn." It was a command, though his voice was little more than a whisper. "Why did you suddenly decide to swim ashore? I don't believe your 'three's better than two' crap. It was something on that boat."

While Robert waited for his answer Quinn squirmed, trying not to look at him.

Robert hadn't finished. "And who was that woman?" he said, turning to look across the aisle at Alita. "And why the hell were you with her?"

Quinn couldn't put off the inevitable any longer.

"It was something I read on Edge's computer," he said. "He had files on all of us." Robert turned to look at him. "And there was a file on my wife. My first wife. Leonie."

Robert's dark brown eyes were aimed at Quinn like gun barrels. When he couldn't hold the silent stare any longer he turned to Alita. She was nodding him to go on.

"Leonie is alive. Well – she..."

Above the hum of the coach engine all Quinn could hear was the girls behind whispering and consoling the sobbing boy.

Robert blinked at last, his head bowed as if in prayer. When it lifted he leaned in close to Quinn. He flicked his eyes to his right with the slightest movement of his head. "Alita," he mouthed. "She knows?" His jaw was clenched.

From behind Robert's head Quinn heard Alita's voice. "Yes Papa, I know about Leonie." Robert sat back slowly and turned to face her, his mouth open. She went on, "It was her, in the tunnel. With the gun."

"Edge told us she was dead," Robert mumbled, sitting back, his shoulders dropping.

"She wasn't, Papa. She killed the man in the tunnel, Papa. She was a good woman. But now she's dead and Riona is..." A tear rolled down her cheek.

Alita had boosted Quinn's courage.

"I really thought they were dead, Robert. Edge and Dieter Lange lied to me that night when they came to the Neptuna." He wanted to reach past Robert to take Alita's hand. "I didn't find out until after the wedding."

Robert was staring blankly at him.

"Edge threatened to tell you and Alita if I didn't join in his mission. I was only supposed to look after the boat. But I got into his computer."

Still Robert said nothing.

"I read Leonie's file. Edge sent Lange to Miami to murder her. And Riona. Just to make sure nothing upset their plans." He looked at Alita, then Robert. "I knew Lange had lied to me that they were dead, and when I read another email saying they were both going to Ragged Island today I decided to swim ashore. I was going to kill them both."

"And Papa, I knew Edge and Michel were going to kill you both. Leonie showed me their plans on Michel's computer. It's why we came."

Robert turned to face Alita, his eyebrows lowered. "Leonie? You met her? Quinn's..?" He paused, shaking his head slowly and his voice weakening. They could see realisation in real time, as he put things together for himself. "That's why you asked me to collect the body from the tunnel. It was her."

None of them spoke for a mile or so. Quinn watched the smooth road surface below the window. At times he was transfixed, the mesmerising whizz a welcome distraction from Leonie's body under his seat. And the question of how he was going to get her back to Cuba.

Quinn was startled when Robert's decisive voice broke the silence. "Right. We're going to take her body back to Cuba with us."

Alita also looked up when he spoke, smiling across at Quinn. Robert had recovered some of his engaging, assured demeanour.

"This is what we'll do when we get to the airport."

.

Chapter Seventy-Six

Ragged Island Airport

It was just before midday as they approached the airstrip. Both planes had been put under cover, visible through the open doors of the single hangar.

Men could be seen lounging in deck chairs outside a corrugated lean-to at the far end of the huge building, beyond the shiny jets. The coach driver had said the two pilots and one cabin crewman from the larger jet would be staying overnight at the airport. There was also one airport technician, who he would later be taking home, a few kilometres to Duncan Town.

Robert told the driver to stop outside the hangar's huge metal doors. He had swapped shirts with Rogelio Pineda, and now walked towards the four men, holding a mobile phone to his ear. They all put out cigarettes.

A few minutes later Quinn saw Robert walking back towards the coach. Alita told everyone else to stay in their seats, while she helped Quinn out of his. They met Robert outside, Quinn clutching his side but pleased to find he could move more freely.

"We've got about an hour. It'll take them that long to tow this one out and make it ready," Robert said, pointing at the bigger of the two jets. "The pilots will be occupied, and the two flight crew."

"They didn't ask questions?" Quinn asked.

"They seem used to changing plans. They get paid either way, and they're pleased they don't have to spend the night here."

As agreed, Robert had told them four of the RI7 men had food poisoning. They weren't well enough to party, and Cochet was staying with them.

"And they just believed you?" said Alita. Like Quinn, she had been concerned the pilots would want to call Cleeter's offices.

Robert winked, and waved his mobile phone. "I was just finishing a call when I reached them. 'Yes, of course, Mr Cleeter, sir, I'll do that right away, sir.'" He acted out what he had said, hamming it up, and looked very pleased with himself. "They're filing updated flight plans, now. As soon as they're all occupied with the jets we'll get on with it."

The transfer went more easily than any of them expected. Robert had told the pilots that to save time they would handle their own luggage. As soon as the tractor had towed the plane out of the hangar, Robert told everyone but him and Rogelio Pineda to leave the coach and wait outside. The driver manoeuvred into the hangar, parking next to the rear of the smaller jet. The swing door of the baggage compartment was just below the port side engine. The airport technician had opened it for them, and with a wheeled step already in place it was a simple job for Robert and Rogelio Pineda to place Leonie's body inside.

Quinn didn't watch. He stayed outside with Alita, bright sunshine on their faces. Minutes later Robert was back. He nodded as he approached, then stood in silence. Rogelio and the driver joined Silvia Pineda who was talking with the huddled teenagers.

Before they left to board their plane, the Pinedas spoke to Quinn and Alita. They had experienced Ragged Island parties, they said, and as soon as they had escorted the children to safety they were going straight to the police in Monterrey to report the abuse.

The innocent victims had told the Pinedas they were from Mexico. Their plane had brought them that morning from Monterrey, rendezvousing with the smaller jet at Guantanamo.

Earlier, on the coach, Cochet had told Alita that only when he had inspected the 'cargo' for suitability, he revealed the onward destination to the pilots. He had boasted to her that on the flight to Ragged Island he had been the Gulfstream G700's only passenger. This time no politicians or princes had been invited to the party.

The new instruction, Robert had told the pilots, was for the larger plane to fly straight back to Monterrey. Air Traffic Control in Miami sanctioned 'Cleeter's' updated flight plans without question.

Fifty minutes later the larger plane took off. On board with the trafficked youngsters were the Pinedas, the coach driver and the Mexican cabin crewman.

Once the quiet returned after the big jet's departure, Quinn, Robert and Alita waited for their plane in the crew's deck chairs. Quinn spoke first.

"What the hell went on back there?" he said, exhaling and shaking his head. He looked at Alita, then back at Robert. "Edge was going to kill anyone in his way? Even the girls and boys?"

Robert said, "The bastard was capable of anything, believe me." Again Quinn wondered if Robert knew something else about Edge. Something that made him want to kill him. It had to be why Robert had agreed to the mission so willingly.

Alita was frowning, her deep brown eyebrows almost meeting. "And the man who told you Leonie and Riona were dead was actually Michel Cochet, not the German man?"

Robert said, "I think I've worked it out."

He outlined his theory. "It was always about the money but they had to get into the plant room computer to steal it. Lange and Edge were in it together, but I wonder if they trusted each other."

Quinn looked at Alita who appeared to be as confused as he was.

"Lange – or Cochet – would have insisted on being there to make sure Edge didn't steal it for himself," Robert went on. "But that meant the mission had to coincide with a party," he explained. "It was the only time Cochet was authorised to open the outer tunnel doors."

Robert believed that Cochet had inveigled himself into Max Cleeter's organisation solely to be in the tunnel with Edge when they did the money transfer. "And Edge needed me to open the inner doors."

It sounded far-fetched to Quinn. "But why did you want Edge dead, Robert? And couldn't you kill him on the boat, or as soon as you got to the island?" he asked.

Alita gasped. "Kill Sñr Edge, Papa? You! Why?"

Robert looked at Quinn, ignoring Alita's question.

"I was going to, Quinn – well, not on the boat, too dangerous. I was waiting for the opportunity to shoot him and get away without being caught. But when he said 'MC's delivering the package' I thought he meant Cleeter was coming to the party. The chance of killing him as well as Edge made me hesitate."

"But 'MC' stood for Michel Cochet," said Quinn, nodding slowly.

Alita spoke. "And Edge and Cochet were going to kill everyone? When they'd taken the money. All those girls."

"Everyone who had seen them," Robert said.

"You, Papa," said Alita shaking her head. She turned to Quinn. "And they said, 'fish food!'"

They were quiet for a moment, then she went on, "I still don't know why you agreed to go." She looked at each of them in turn.

Quinn said, "The RI7, erm...well...Edge said they caused the US–" He knew it didn't sound convincing.

Robert spoke over him. "I told Quinn it was his duty, Alita. To help me get justice for you." He looked at the floor. "But I'm sorry. I wasn't being completely honest."

He looked at Quinn now. "I needed you there. When I had killed Edge I was going to send up a flare, so you would come and collect me. Otherwise I had no way of getting off the island."

Quinn had misread Robert, but thought there was still something else his father-in-law wasn't saying. Before he could think further, Robert went on.

"Edge's main objective was to get away with the money and be untraceable. Anyone who knew he'd been to the island was a danger. And that meant us, QT."

Quinn had a flashback. While holding him at gunpoint, Edge had said, 'Oh, and the boat is rented in your name.' The Englishman had planned his exit meticulously.

With a furrowed brow and a slight shake of her head Alita asked, "The RI7 knew Edge had been on the island. So, was he going to kill them or not? "

"I doubt if the RI7 ever knew Edge existed," Robert said. "When he was Cleeter's fixer he used an alias. He showed me the contract, and his fake passport. Those fools had no idea he was having a '*recce*'." He rolled his eyes. "Anyway, the RI7 would be dead if Edge needed them dead. I know how ruthless he was."

There has to be something else Robert isn't saying, Quinn thought. And he appears excited, somehow.

Quinn sat back in the deck chair, looking up at the hangar's corrugated roof. Edge had claimed his mission to Ragged Island was all for revenge on the RI7 for causing England's downfall. But the ex-spy's eyes had been on 'the real prize.' Quinn's nagging feeling about Edge's sincerity was confirmed. He had been acting, simply a scheming thief.

A few hours before, when he'd been alone on Cacique-2, Quinn had pictured bloodied corpses of the RI7 floating in the pool. He would have sailed back to Cuba with Robert and Edge. Now it seemed Robert was never going to return, and Quinn would have been 'fish food'.

Chapter Seventy-Seven

Leaving Ragged Island

The new flight plan for the Gulfstream included a stop at Guantanamo to drop Alita, Robert, and Quinn. It would then follow the other jet to Monterrey, having picked up two more passengers. Once Alita had freed them from their bindings and given them water, the two escorts would fly back to Mexico in luxury.

It took the pilot less time than expected to ready the aircraft, and it was 12.20 pm when Alita helped Quinn up the aircraft steps. She insisted he lie on a sofa upholstered in the most luxuriant leather he had ever touched. They moved to armchairs with seatbelts a few minutes later when the pilot made the pre-flight announcement. He tried to hide the pain of moving again, but his face didn't cooperate and she fussed over him.

Robert stayed on the tarmac until he had finished his cigarette, and was last to board, taking the seat opposite. Quinn hadn't seen him smoke since they first arrived in Cuba.

###

When the pilot told them they could release their seatbelts, Robert finally lifted his head. Until then he had sat looking at the floor between his feet, and Quinn felt like he was facing a firing squad. Robert would banish him for deceiving his daughter, even though Leonie was now dead. He was holding Alita's hand across the space between their chairs, watching her as she stared into space. She had started sobbing.

397

When Robert lifted his head there were tears in his eyes. He unclipped the seatbelt and stood up slowly. He stepped across to kiss the top of Alita's head, then began pacing the thick-pile carpet of the passenger cabin, with a pained expression. Quinn felt Alita's hand tighten round his, and she dropped it when Robert stopped beside her.

Standing between them Robert laid a hand on Quinn's shoulder, and he tried not to flinch. His pulsed quickened as he waited for Robert's ire. The grip on the ball of his shoulder was firm, but not aggressive. If he hadn't been so scared Quinn might have taken it as a gesture of comfort.

Robert had to clear his throat to speak. "Alita, I have to tell you something. Something I have kept from you since you were a child." He paused, the only sound the muted engine thrum. Chilled air was blowing on Quinn's neck.

When Alita turned to look up at her father Quinn saw her hand tighten on the seat arm.

"Trevor Edge killed your Mama."

Alita's mouth dropped open.

"That's why I went to Ragged Island to kill Edge." Robert's voice almost broke.

"What? The accident?" Alita was shaking her head.

Robert swallowed. "It wasn't an accident, Litl-A. It was a bomb."

The word 'bomb' was shocking, but it was the pet name that brought a lump to Quinn's throat. It was incongruous and perfect. He was embarrassed and honoured to witness Robert's revelation to his baby daughter. She was quaking, staring at her tear-stained father.

"I couldn't tell you." Robert shook his head as he spoke, his eyes streaming and his nose running. "I was to pick up a Saudi sheikh from the airport and drive him around Nassau. Your Mama was helping me that day. She picked the car up for me after it was valeted." A tear dripped from his chin, a dark spot on the tan nubuck of Alita's seat arm. "The bomb went off just as she drove away." Robert dabbed his face with a hairy forearm. "She was bringing the car to me so I could go and collect the Arab."

"Oh, Papa."

Robert crouched down and now wrapped his muscled arms round Alita. "I've got to tell you this, Alita." Her shuddering continued.

"Edge told me he'd read in the Fire Chief's report that the car ended up on its roof, but men from the valeters came out to the street and turned it upright. They tried to help your Mama. And there was no 'Fire Chief's report'."

Sobbing was rocking Alita's head, but her body had stilled.

This is what Robert had been keeping to himself, Quinn thought.

Robert went on, still holding his daughter, his voice strained. "Only someone who saw the explosion could have known the car was on its roof. Edge watched the bomb go off." He sniffed, and shook his head. "He told me he had worked in Nassau for the British secret service. It had to be Edge. He planted the bomb."

Alita pulled herself free of Robert's embrace. "But why? Why kill Mama?"

"He must have been trying to kill the sheikh, planted the bomb in the car when it was being valeted. But he didn't do it right, did he?"

Robert stood up and resumed his pacing, spitting angry words. "The bastard must have followed the car, seen her get behind the wheel. He knew your Mama was in the car. And when his fucking bomb went off he didn't try to help."

"Oh, Papa!"

Stopping now, Robert stared into space between Alita and Quinn. "And as soon as his bomb went off he escaped like a coward. Gone before the valeters turned the car over."

He looked at the floor. "That's why I agreed to go on Edge's mission. To kill him."

Quinn moved across beside Alita's chair. As he took his turn to hold her she said, "Papa. If Edge had got it right, his bomb would have killed you with the Saudi."

They were all quiet for a moment and Robert sat down in the seat Quinn had vacated.

Quinn felt secure enough to speak. "You never did intend to harm the RI7, did you, Robert?"

"No. If they had to die I wouldn't have been sorry. But my only target was Edge. If Cleeter had been there that would have been different, but I didn't care about the RI7."

Robert's body loosened, his face softening. With a grim smile he said, "It will be good for those fancy-pants perverts to be trapped on Ragged Island with no food or water." Alita smiled too, wiping tears away.

Quinn thought of the strange, privileged Englishmen helpless on a deserted island. Lords of the Flies.

"And Edge and Lange stole all their money," he said. "Before they died. We'll never know where all the money went."

Robert tilted his head, his eyebrows raised. He was fingering something in his pocket. His face broke into a knowing smile, but he said nothing. There was that glint in his father-in-law's eye again. Quinn wondered if he had even more to reveal.

They were quiet for a few minutes. Quinn held Alita's hand, watching the sea below them and the approaching coastline. She spoke first.

"How are we going to explain Leonie's body?"

That was exactly what Quinn had been thinking.

Robert turned towards them. Just before the pilot announced the plane was about to land, he said, "We're going to call the police."

Chapter Seventy-Eight

Guantanamo, Cuba

Quinn squeezed Alita's hand when the jet touched down on the runway at Mariana Grajales Guantanamo. A decade ago Cuba was a land he would never have dreamt of visiting. Now it felt like his home. But a home that was bound to be taken away from him.

Robert appeared buoyed. "All three of us need to be consistent."

They had agreed the police had to be informed, and would say Trevor Edge had threatened to kill Alita if Robert and Quinn refused to go with him to Ragged Island to help them steal from the RI7.

Cochet had disturbed Alita and Leonie while they read details of his sex trafficking work on his laptop. He forced them to accompany him to Guantanamo airport or he would harm Riona. He then bound and gagged Clecter's escorts and made Alita and Leonie replace them. When they got to Ragged Island, it became clear Cochet was going to kill them.

"That explains why we were there, but the police will go to the island. They're going to arrest us." Quinn had said.

"I'm sure they will," Robert said, "but we have to explain why we have Leonie's body with us."

Some of their prepared story was true: Edge had blackmailed Quinn, and Cochet had threatened Riona's safety. To explain Leonie's death, they would explain that for some reason Edge and Cochet had fallen out. There had been a gun battle near the electric fence, Edge and Cochet dying and Leonie caught in crossfire.

Quinn saw no choice but to agree to the plan. Even after the violent and murderous events he'd been part of on Ragged Island, his greatest fear was still exposure of his first crime. When the police uncovered Quinn's bigamy, even though Leonie was dead he would be separated from Alita. And he'd never see Riona again.

When the jet taxied to a halt the clock above the cockpit door read 13:04. Robert went forward, knocked and went in to speak to the pilot. Coming back he nodded to Quinn and Alita, stopping at the exit door. Once ground staff put steps in place he opened the door himself.

Before he could step out Alita called, "The escorts first, Papa." She and Quinn watched him walk smartly to the terminal building, their hands locked together.

Minutes later Robert reappeared, accompanied by a man in a suit. Behind were two overalled staff pushing a trolley. Quinn was glad he couldn't see Leonie's body being lifted out. It wasn't until the trolley rounded the front of the plane to head back across the tarmac that he saw a blanket had been laid over her, covering the bloodstained RI7 towels.

Quinn was numb as he followed Alita from the plane. Before they set off towards the terminal the suited man whose badge read 'Airport Manager', handed Alita folded overalls and bottles of water. With a worried look, he mouthed something Quinn guessed was 'for those women.' Though idling, the jet's engines prevented speech and made the air acrid.

The two escorts had been detained for over four hours, and Alita wanted to free them as soon as possible. Quinn followed her to a small storeroom at the side of the terminal building. She'd told him she hadn't thought she and Leonie would be able to overpower them, but Leonie had Michel Cochet's pistol and the two Mexican women put up little resistance.

The storeroom adjoined the terminal's restrooms, separated by a locking door and with its own access to the outside. Quinn stayed outside while Alita went in. He knew the women were tied to a steel shelf unit, wearing only their underwear. Through the door he heard Alita's voice, and seconds later the women speaking. She had removed their gags.

He was unable to follow all of Alita's rapid Spanish, but worked out that as she untied their wrists and ankles she explained what had happened on Ragged Island. When they came out of the storeroom wearing overalls and gulping water, there was horror in their eyes.

"They're glad to be going back to Mexico," Alita told Quinn while the women were on a toilet break. "They didn't know they were trafficking girls for sex."

"They must have."

"No, Cochet had just recruited them."

"Really?"

"Their first trip, like the kids they were looking after. A modelling shoot as usual." Her face twisted in disgust.

Quinn pictured the teenagers as they'd been on their way back in the bus, shocked expressions and tear-streaked make-up.

"As usual?"

With cold detachment, Alita told him what Leonie had said about Max Cleeter's exclusive services. "His highest-paying clients were always promised fresh meat."

Quinn knew she hadn't learned it all from Leonie.

They walked the escorts to the plane, stepping back to watch minutes later as the Gulfstream taxied to the runway. When the noise lessened, Alita said without looking at Quinn, "One of the escorts had two little girls. Cochet wanted to sit with her in the coach."

Quinn's rage threatened to rise again. He was glad Cochet was dead, but wished he could have done it himself. For Riona.

Alita took his hand. "It's over, Q-T." She led him back towards the airport terminal building.

Quinn stopped outside the automatic doors. "Alita. I want to––Riona..."

"I know," she said, looking into the foyer. On the far side was the airport medical room where Leonie's body was being stored. "We need to help her. I grew up without my Mama, and now Riona's Mama is dead. She will need us."

They sat down near the Airport Manager's office. It overlooked the terminal concourse from behind a glass wall, and between vertical blinds Quinn could see Robert inside. Holding a desk phone, his eyebrows were rising and lowering as he listened, his head nodding as he spoke. With the receiver still to his ear he smiled when he caught sight of Quinn and Alita. Quinn hoped it was meant to be encouraging, but still expected to be detained very soon.

When Robert joined them in the airport lounge he was beaming.

"What's happening?" Quinn asked, standing up.

"They'll be here in half an hour. They want to talk to us as soon as possible."

Quinn felt as if the floor was moving under him and his legs were going to buckle. He was going to jail. He was going to be sent back to the US.

"It's going to be OK, man," Robert said. He whistled as he sat down beside Alita. "Wait 'til you hear this."

Robert had outlined to the Airport Manager some of what happened, stressing the need to help the escorts. While Alita and Quinn had been freeing them, Robert had related the prepared story to the duty officer at Manzanillo, the closest police office to Guantanamo. The policeman had stopped him suddenly.

"It was when I mentioned Cochet. It was like an alarm had gone off, I tell you," Robert said, animated. "I was put on hold, spoke to a Captain, next thing I knew there was some big shot in Havana on the line." He chuckled.

When Quinn interrupted to ask what they said about Leonie, Robert shook his head as if he couldn't believe what he was saying.

"They swallowed it all, didn't question a thing. All they wanted to know about was Cochet."

Security services in Cuba and beyond had been tailing Cochet for months. They knew he was working for Max Cleeter, and when Robert mentioned Ragged Island and the sex parties he was put on hold again, told to wait at Guantanamo until agents arrived to take statements from them in person.

"What about Edge? Were they watching him too?" asked Alita.

"They didn't seem to have heard of him," Robert said. "It was Cleeter they were interested in. It was like they'd been waiting for a chance to get him, and this was their big break."

Two Interpol agents soon arrived at Guantanamo. One was Danish and the other Iraqi, and both were respectful in the interviews, sensitive to the ordeal they had endured. As Robert had said, the circumstances leading up to the events in the tunnel were of secondary importance. Cleeter was the main focus.

Until now, Interpol had been unable to connect Cleeter directly to the trafficking operations. Now they had his employee Cochet at the scene, and the testimony of Robert and Alita who had witnessed the sex parties on Ragged Island.

Cleeter's jets were being intercepted at Monterrey. The pilots, bus driver and the escorts would be interviewed, but the abused youngsters would be spared.

The men trapped on Ragged Island would be left to fend for themselves for now. The agents made careful notes when Robert told them about Eliot Myal's murder. A separate investigation would be launched, and it might be a few days before a team was put together to arrest and process the RI7 for their crimes. They wouldn't be going anywhere, the Dane said with a wry smile.

Having been watching Cochet's comings and goings, and doing background checks on his associates, Interpol knew about Leonie and Riona. As soon as Robert had told the local police Leonie was dead the Soporte was alerted to make plans to care for Riona.

Chapter Seventy-Nine

When their statements had been taken, Quinn, Alita and Robert were told they were free to go but they would be contacted again. Robert and Quinn hadn't eaten since before dawn, and Alita the previous evening. There was a small café, and Quinn went to buy pastries and coffee using Alita's credit card.

Robert sat beside Alita. With an ironic smile he asked, "Is that my Tres Reyes car parked behind the hangar?"

"I'm sorry. I was in a panic, Papa, I–"

"That'll be why I found this in Leonie's jacket, then," he said, lifting the key out of his breast pocket, with a flourish. "I'm going to find fuel for it when I've had something to eat," Robert said.

As soon as they had wolfed down their snacks, Robert went to the car. Alita stood up.

"Come on," she said, pulling Quinn's hand. "We need to phone Soporte. Papa said they've been told about Riona. They'll have to agree to let her come to live with us, Quinn. You are her Papa."

Quinn had left his cell phone on the boat, and Alita's was in the Mercedes. He knew he could use a payphone to make a free call to Soporte, and without thinking he dialled the number from memory. It was answered in Havana, a familiar voice saying, "Centro de Soporte, Havana North. How can I help you?"

"Felipe?" Quinn said, looking at the phone in his hand. Then, shaking his head, "Sorry, I rang the wrong–"

"Sñr Tarrant? I know your voice, and man, it's been too long since I heard it!"

When Quinn tried to explain his error Felipe insisted on helping connect him to the Manzanillo office. He asked for brief details of the reason for the call and Quinn hesitated for a second.

"Something is wrong Sñr." Felipe's empathic voice helped. Soon, Quinn had told his old friend that his family had been alive and living in Cuba after all. When he knew Leonie had just died and that Riona was motherless, Felipe took control.

"He's going to call back in a few minutes," Quinn told Alita. Exhaling, he slumped down beside her.

Alita put a hand on his arm. He was staring at the payphone on the wall.

A short time later he mumbled, "Riona thinks I'm dead. How can I tell her about Leonie?"

"We'll get through it, Q-T."

He looked at Alita now. "I have to tell her myself. But how can I?" He let his head drop. Facing the floor, he said, "She'll blame me."

Neither spoke again until the phone rang. Quinn jumped up.

"Hello? Hello?"

They were to make their way to the Manzanillo Soporte, where Felipe would be available by video call to confirm Quinn's identity until he could provide documents.

"He said there'll be specialist counsellors to help with Riona," Quinn said, uncertainly.

Alita put a hand on his shoulder. "I'll help you. And they'll help us, Quinn. The Soporte are good people."

"I have to use the restroom," he said, standing up. When he returned a few minutes later he looked around him. Outside the terminal building Quinn could see the Mercedes.

"Where's your dad, now?"

"He came back in and said he was going to ask to use the manager's computer. Check his emails, he said."

"Emails?"

Alita shrugged. "I don't know what he's up to. He looked excited about something."

"What's he going to say about Riona?" said Quinn, looking towards the manager's office. Robert was already studying a computer screen.

"He'll want her to be cared for, Q-T. I was about the same age when I lost my mum. And when he knows..." Her words tailed off. There was a sparkle in her eyes, and Quinn wondered briefly if she had been going to say something else, but she looked away.

When Robert emerged from the office Quinn was girding himself, wondering what to say.

Robert, though, had a purposeful look about him. "Thank you," he called over his shoulder as he left the office. "I found the email I was looking for. Bye."

There was a wide grin on his face as he walked across towards Alita and Quinn. He was waving something small and metallic with his right hand.

"Sorry about that," he said, standing in front of them.

"What email, Papa?"

"I'll tell you in the car." Robert nodded towards the doors. "This way, Mr and Mrs Tarrant, I'll escort you to your limo."

411

They followed him, exchanging confused glances. Quinn paused at the terminal door, looking back one more time at the medical room door. Alita squeezed his hand and drew him onwards.

Robert insisted they sit together in the back. "I am your personal chauffeur," he said, miming a flourish of the cap he wore at work.

Driving along the same road Leonie and Alita had used earlier, Robert spoke. "I've been thinking. Your daughter needs you, Quinn. She can come to live with us."

Alita took Quinn's hand. She had an excited smile and was nodding, mouthing "Yes" to him.

"Are you sure, Robert. After–"

"Man, she needs a family. If you'll let me be her abuelo." Robert glanced over his shoulder to flash his wide smile at them both.

Quinn's mind flipped through images of his dead father and his Cajun wedding in Monroe. Riona would never see Mannie, and he had no way of knowing if Leonie's parents in Monroe had survived the wars.

Robert went on. "We might need to move to a bigger apartment. We'll need another bedroom."

Quinn looked into Alita's eyes. They were fixed on his, a coy, beguiling smile lighting her face when she spoke.

"Papa, we'll soon need two more bedrooms." She drew Quinn's hand to her, resting it on her tummy.

###

After meetings with counsellors and Soporte officials in Manzanilla, they waited in a small lounge. Alita's news meant Quinn's concentration had been patchy.

For the rest of the car journey he had held Alita, weeping with joy and grief. Robert had been crying too, elated at the prospect of being abuelo twice over. Alita had said she couldn't wait any longer to tell them.

There was a TV on the wall in the lounge, the sound muted. A Spanish news channel showed interviews with politicians, weather reports about an expected hurricane, and sports news.

"Look at that," said Robert, pointing to a scrolling banner along the bottom of the screen.

Max Cleeter arrested in Panama –– Reports coming in about possible Sex Trafficking charges –– Max Cleeter arrested...

"They moved fast," Robert said, shaking his head. He leant back against the wall, looking at the ceiling from under a furrowed brow. "And we need to move quickly too."

From the look on her face Quinn could see Alita was as mystified as him.

Robert drew the small metallic lozenge he had waved when he came out of the airport manager's office. It was a memory stick. "I pulled this from the computer in the plant room before I rolled the grenades in. Edge's initials are scratched on it." He waved the storage device, grinning. "Once he'd transferred the RI7's money to his own account he must have been so excited he forgot to take it out."

"You weren't checking your emails back at the airport, were you?" Quinn said.

"I couldn't wait to have a look on here," Robert said, waving the device. It looked tiny between his finger and thumb. "There's a big folder on it called 'The Table.'"

"I don't want to know," said Quinn.

Robert's white smile had never been wider. Or more wicked.

"Better than that," he said, "it's got Edge's bank details. Zurich. And no one knows it exists. Except us."

END

I hope you enjoyed Ragged Island. Even if you think it could be improved, ***please leave a review*** on Amazon, Goodreads, or your favourite platform. Or let me know directly on njedmunds.com

I depend on feedback.

Thank you.

Nick Edmunds
May 2025

Acknowledgements

Over more than four years as I wrote Ragged Island I have had help, advice and encouragement from more people than I can reliably remember. I have listed many below, and apologise to anyone I may have omitted.

All of following people read, commented on, and suggested improvements to the many iterations of Ragged Island as it progressed from the kernel of an idea to a full length novel: **Sue Leckie, Gillian Ainsworth, Darren Houston, John Bell, Sue Partridge, John Patton, Emily Macdonald, Philip Healey, John Petrie, Andrew Jackman, Robin Tones, John Harkin, Bridget Scrannage, Ellie Ness, Elizabeth Coby, Joe Durham**.

Sandy Paterson told me about guns. After a long career as a Firearms & Explosives Officer with the National Crime Agency there cannot be anything Sandy doesn't know about armaments. Thanks, pal, I'll buy the next pint.

Ken McDonald of iScot Magazine is always supportive and encouraging. He gave generously of his design and publishing skills.

My daughters. Laura checked and corrected my use of Spanish, and **Rachel** helped with cover design and more.

And of course my wife **Helen.**

Thank you all.

Nick Edmunds, May 2025

Also by N J Edmunds

MILES AWAY
Memories Can Kill

Miles Away is book one in the *Flint and Masson* series. A twisty crime thriller set in Scotland in the 1970s, it was first published in 2022.

Flint's phobias are interfering with student life. Hypnotherapy helps, but with disturbing side effects. Deep in his subconscious, Flint finds deadly secrets that connect him to a number of murders.

These grisly crimes remain unsolved and unconnected, until Flint joins up with PC Craig Masson. They race around Fife trying to unmask the killer, but will they succeed before the next victim is slain?

MILES AWAY
Memories Can Kill
by N J Edmunds
is available in Paperback and eBook
**Book two in the *Flint and Masson* series
will be published in 2025**

Don't miss out!

Visit the website below and you can sign up to receive emails whenever N J Edmunds publishes a new book. There's no charge and no obligation.

https://books2read.com/r/B-A-FLPKD-EESCG

BOOKS 2 READ

Connecting independent readers to independent writers.

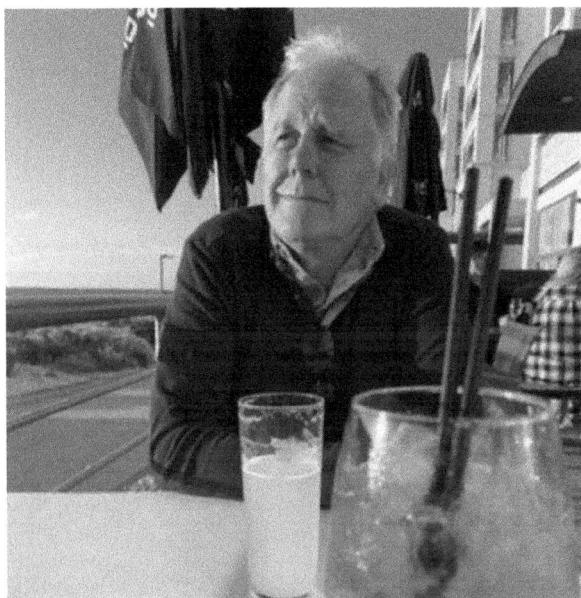

About the Author

Nick Edmunds enjoyed decades as a doctor in Scotland. He now lives in Stirling with his wife and spaniel.

Read more at www.njedmunds.com.